CARNIVAL OF THE ANIMALS

LORETTA CLINE

Waylon Fitzgerald Press

Cover and typeset by Matthew Revert.
ISBN: 979-8-218-75330-6
eBook ISBN: 979-8-218-89275-3

First Edition 2025
Printed in the USA.

Table of Contents

Chapter 1
The Fatted Calf

The calf was found mutilated on the same day that the girl went missing from the small town of Verde, Texas. The events unfolded separately. Tilly Hutto was involved in only the former.

It was Tilly's fourth month back in her hometown of Verde after more than a decade away. She had only recently gotten her veterinary practice up and running and had not yet unpacked her last moving box. She got the call about the calf not long after sunrise. It was November. The morning air gave its first hint of a coming chill.

The ranch where the calf was killed was about twenty minutes out of town. The sun brightened as Tilly drove and the morning endured, and the south-central Texas landscape met the sun's light with a re-splendence of greens—it had rained lately—and shades of yellow and orange. The leaves were beginning to turn for autumn.

Tilly arrived at the same time that the county sheriff did. Tilly was surprised to see him. She wondered why he was there. All she had been told on the phone was that there was some situation in-volving a dead calf. She had suspected that the ranch owner wanted her to perform a postmortem diagnostic, to make sure the cause of death was nothing contagious—some diseases survived in the body after death and persisted to plague the herd even in the host's afterlife. In those cases, the carcass had to be burned to kill the disease that immunity couldn't. Tilly had imagined she was there to advise on the burning. But in light of this likely purpose, the sheriff's presence was curious.

Sheriff Valdez waved her through the entrance gate ahead of him, and they drove in single file to the pasture that the rancher had directed them to. Their destination was a grim scene.

Several people stood in a rough circle in the center of a hay field. They surrounded a largeish something on the ground. It was the calf.

Tilly got out of her truck and said her hellos. The sheriff did too.

"Good morning, Tilly," Sheriff Valdez said. "You remember me? It's been a while."

"I sure do," Tilly said. Paul Valdez had been the sheriff of the county for some thirty years. He lived in Tilly's memory of a high school party, fifteen years ago at least, when he had busted Tilly and her friends drinking stolen booze in a field behind a classmate's house. He said he wouldn't call their parents if they all just went home. And he kept his word, as far as Tilly knew. Tilly shook his hand.

"Good to see you again," Tilly said, then paused, regretting her too-jovial tone. "If only it was under better circumstances."

Tilly looked down at the corpse of what had only recently been an otherwise healthy-looking Charolais steer-calf. The calf was not peaceful in death. Its previously white hide was stained shades of red and pink with blood. A dark pool of drying blood surrounded the carcass, in hues of maroon and black. And suddenly the sheriff's presence made sense. A black ache crept into Tilly's stomach.

"Thanks for coming out, Sheriff Valdez, Dr. Hutto," the ranch owner—one of the people standing around the body of the calf—said. His name was Tom Wills. One of his sons had been in the same grade as Tilly in school. In fact, she was pretty sure he had been at the aforementioned busted party. Tilly briefly wondered where he had ended up. Then her mind turned back to the grisly scene at hand.

"I wasn't sure who to call," Wills said. "But I figured one of you might be able to figure out what happened."

"What time did you find it?" Sheriff Valdez asked, as he walked in a circle around the carcass, examining it. Two buzzards perched on fence posts about a hundred yards away from the gathering. Watching. Waiting.

"About seven this morning," Wills said. "When I came out to check the water troughs."

"Hell of a way to start the day," Tilly said. The sentiment went for her own day, too—this was a most unusual beginning to a workday.

"And has anyone touched it?" Sheriff Valdez produced some latex gloves from his pocket and snapped them onto his hands. Tilly, who had been staring at the corpse in a sort of gruesome trance, came to her senses and decided she better do the same.

"No, no one," Wills said. The sheriff said that was good. He continued to ask the sort of questions to be expected in such a situation.

Tilly, staring again at the calf, tuned the questions out, and she began to examine the injuries.

By far the most jarring—and most obvious—injury was that the calf's skull had been cleaved open right down the middle into two distinct halves. Each half had an eye—or, rather, a bloody hole where an eye should be—like some monster of Greek mythology. Despite years of veterinary practice and countless animal dissections in vet school, Tilly had never seen such a macabre display of anatomy.

"Something gouged its eyes out," Wills narrated.

Tilly knelt at the calf's head and took a closer look at the animal. It was not a sight for the squeamish. "No, not gouged," she said. "'Pulled out' is more like it. The eyeballs are completely gone."

Tilly lowered herself to the calf's would-be eye level. She looked him right in the eye sockets, and she saw daylight looking back. Tilly's brow furrowed. "That's . . . *odd.*"

After the sheriff assured her that it was okay for her to touch the carcass, Tilly gingerly wedged her gloved thumbs into the gouged skull.

She pulled the two halves apart in a sickening stretch of skin and bone. Tilly peered into the cavern of the skull. She gasped.

It wasn't what was inside the skull that shocked her. It was what *wasn't*. Inside the skull, where the brain should be—there was no brain. The insides had been scooped out, leaving an empty sphere of a brain cavity.

"What is it?" Sheriff Valdez asked her. "What's wrong?"

"His brain is gone, too," said Tilly. The black ache took a stronger hold on Tilly's stomach.

"What'd'ya mean, 'gone'?"

"There's nothing in here." Tilly angled the opening of the skull so that the sheriff could see inside. "Even the optical nerve—gone."

"Well, I'll be damned," the sheriff said, looking into the opening. "Is that something an animal would do, Doctor? A predator of some kind?"

"None that I know of," Tilly said. She had never seen anything like this. "Unless we're counting animals of the human variety." She let go of the skull and had the sudden urge to wash her hands, even though they were gloved, and despite the fact that she routinely saw blood and guts in her practice to little disturbance. "I think this is more in your wheelhouse than mine, Sheriff."

"That's what I'm thinking," he said. He, too, knelt beside the animal. "What do you think we have going on here?"

He ran a finger along the calf's spine. Tilly followed the finger down a bone-deep incision running the length of the animal's back. The calf's spine stuck all the way out in places, with vertebrae spiking out of the skin in an unworldly ripple. By the looks of things, the spine injury was the source of most of the blood.

Tilly pulled the incision open to get a better look at the spinal antics. The sight of the undulating, ripped-away spine made her skin crawl, though she usually was not squeamish. As she examined the calf's insides, she identified what bothered her to nausea.

"It's upside-down," Tilly said.

"What's that?" asked the sheriff.

"The spine is twisted upside down," Tilly said. "It took me a second to even realize. This just isn't something you see. Look here." She ran an index finger along the arc of a vertebrae, which should have been curving downward to protect the spinal cord, but instead was curving upward, with the ends pointing to the sky. Then she noticed.

"The spinal cord is missing. They took the spinal cord." It had been ripped right out of the spinal column, leaving an empty shell of ragged bone. Tilly wondered what sort of person—because it had to be a person—could rip the very essence of a living thing from its body in this way. She hoped that she never had to find out.

The sheriff took a moment, looking and thinking. Then he asked, "Is there some kind of black market for animal organs that I don't know about?"

Tilly shook her head. "Not that I know of."

"Maybe it's some kind of cult thing," Wills said. "Or aliens." He couched the suggestion with an insincere I'm-only-joking-I'm-not-crazy chuckle.

"I have no idea," Tilly said softly. She couldn't look away from the calf. "Poor thing," she muttered to no one in particular.

"Notice anything about the incisions? Anything noteworthy, from a doctor perspective?" the sheriff asked.

Tilly took another look. The cuts to the skin and tissue looked relatively clean, if not precise. "It looks like they were made using the right kind of instruments, or something pretty close. But whoever did this didn't have a medical background. This is pretty rough." She eyed the jagged incision at the spine. "They knew what they were looking for, though. Like where to find the spinal cord."

The sheriff nodded. "So someone familiar with anatomy."

Tilly nodded.

Tom Wills spoke up. "Hell, that could be anyone around here, though. Hunters, cattlemen, anyone involved in agriculture, really."

"That's true, it don't narrow it down much," the sheriff said. "Look here." He nudged a boot into the calf's shoulder. "See that? Bullet wound." There was a small hole right in the middle of the calf's shoulder that Tilly hadn't noticed before, for the other blood and gore.

"Right through the heart," Tilly said.

"Goddamn, I missed that before," Wills said.

"Hard to see with all the blood," Tilly said. "At least we know it was a quick death."

"Yeah," the sheriff agreed.

They stood around the thing in a leering circle, all transfixed by the little hole in the calf's should-be-white shoulder. The pose and positioning of them all felt, to Tilly, like a ritual. An initiation into something unknown, something dark.

The sheriff cleared his throat. "That must be our cause of death, then. And that settles the question—definitely 'people' work. Tom, you hear a gunshot or anything?"

"No sir, not a thing."

"Alright. I'll have some of my guys come out to look for prints and tire marks. We'll bring the dogs out to see if they can pick up a trail. Leave things as they are, for now."

Just then the sheriff's phone rang. At almost the same moment, Tilly's phone began to ring too. They shared a glance. "We're popular this morning," the sheriff said.

"Weird," Tilly said, shaking her head, and at the same time trying to shake off the solemnity of the situation. She answered her phone, and the sheriff answered his.

Tilly's call was about an injured whitetail breeder buck at one of the commercial hunting ranches in the county. Tilly said she'd be there soon and, after hanging up, began saying her goodbyes to the rancher and other onlookers.

"Thanks for coming out, Dr. Hutto," the rancher Wills said. "It's good to see ya. And hey, listen, I'm sorry about your daddy. He was a good man."

Tilly looked down at her boots, unable to bear eye contact at the mention of her recently deceased father. She couldn't trust her emotions in the face of sympathy—or worse, pity. Instead, she said to the ground, "Thanks, Mr. Wills."

Sheriff Valdez finished his call. "I gotta go, folks," he said. His face had paled.

Tilly was curious about the call but decided it was none of her business. "Are you done with me here?" she asked him.

He told Tilly that he was, and reassured the others that he would send deputies out to investigate further and keep everyone updated with any developments. Then he left, and Tilly did too. The image of the no-eyed calf skull followed her.

Chapter 2
The Sacrificial Deer

There is a season for hunting whitetail deer. It's about eight weeks from November to January. The season was about to begin, and Tilly had been busy for that reason.

Tilly had been called out to the 999 Ranch, which was the largest and most profitable hunting ranch in the county. The ranch cultivated whitetail deer, which it sold to wealthy people who came to the ranch to hunt their purchases in simulated sport. The hunters, if they could be called that, left the ranch and returned to the city—they were almost always from a city—with a trophy rack of antlers and a sense of adventure. The whole production was terribly morbid and terrific for the local economy. It was also good for Tilly's veterinary business, because the economics of the enterprise required the deer to remain healthy until their eventual slaughters.

"Morning, Tilly," Royce Wilson greeted her when she arrived at the deer pens.

Royce managed the deer breeding operation on the 999. He was also an old friend of Tilly's from childhood. Royce had tried to leave Verde upon freedom from primary education—and he did, for a while—but, like a planet reaching the apex of its outer orbit, he could never break fully free from the sheer force of Verde's gravity, and it eventually brought him right back to the place of his beginning. Tilly realized that Verde's gravitational pull had finally caught up to her, too. She, at least, had returned to Verde with her veterinary career; Royce abandoned an accounting career in the city where he started it.

"Good morning," Tilly said. They stood near an enclosure that held twenty or so four-month-old fawns that milled about in the shade of a great live oak tree. The fawns still had the ghosts of the white spots with which they had been born. But they were quickly fading.

"Where's my patient?" Tilly asked.

Royce said, "Follow me."

Tilly did. Royce led Tilly to a pen not far from the one that held the young fawns. Their boots crunched on the gravel path. Royce carried a bucket of dried corn.

As they walked, Royce asked, "Any interesting adventures in medicine lately?"

"As a matter of fact, yes," Tilly said. And she briefly told him about the mutilated calf of the morning.

"Shit, that's not something you see every day."

"And not something I ever want to see again," Tilly said. She shuddered at the memory.

"So what's the diagnosis? Aliens? Some kind of animal sacrifice?"

"Beats me," Tilly said. "Maybe Sheriff Valdez will come up with something."

Tilly and Royce reached the pen into which the patient, a buck named Remington, had been enclosed when he was brought up from the pasture. The pen was a little bigger than the one that held the fawns. Remington stood near the gate, head down, picking at the overgrazed grass, his impressive crown of antlers curling and spiking over his head. Because of his massive antlers, Remington had been allowed to live past the typical hunting age so that he could breed. His offspring had proved valuable.

Now, Remington had reached the ripe old age of ten years old, and Tilly had seen him several times recently for the health problems of age. Royce whistled, and the buck raised his head to look at them, his neck muscles permanently bulging under the weight of his antlers.

Royce gave the bucket of dry corn a little shake—the kernels rattled. Remington heard, and he strode expectantly toward Tilly and Royce. Or he tried to, at least. A limp in his left front leg hobbled his stride into a stagger. Tilly winced on his behalf; the deer was clearly in pain. Remington reached them eventually and was rewarded with handfuls of dried corn strewn out onto the ground before him.

Tilly went into the pen with the buck and knelt beside him.

"Careful, Til," Royce said. "Do you want me to get the dart gun? He almost gored one of the hands last week."

"No, it's okay. I'm pretty sure I can outrun him in this condition. Let him eat a minute, poor guy." Tilly visually examined the buck's leg. It was swollen below the knee, the culprit a nasty gash of blood and flesh.

"Looks like he got his leg hung up in the fence," Tilly said. "I don't think it's broken, but we should probably x-ray it just in case."

"Sure thing," said Royce. "Let me go get the tranquilizer gun to dart 'im."

"Hold on, I've got a syringe of ketamine in my bag there." She pointed to the medical bag she had left outside of the pen. "In the outside pocket. Hand it here."

"You sure?"

"Yeah. Give it to me."

"I don't think that's a good idea, Til."

"Royce, he's in pain. Just hand me the syringe." Tilly's voice was calm and low, so as not to frighten the animal, but stern. Years of working on frightened animals, large and small, had steeled her nerves in these situations.

Royce pressed his lips together in a thin line and shook his head. Tilly met his gaze with a glare that Royce knew he could not refuse. Resigned, he retrieved the syringe of tranquilizer and passed it through the fence to Tilly.

"Thank you," Tilly punctuated the transaction. Remington still had his head down, nibbling at the corn despite the conversation.

Tilly reached a slow hand toward his shoulder. The deer—prey by instinct—watched Tilly's hand out of the corner of his eye, even as he continued to eat the dried corn on the ground. Tilly watched him watching her, and observed his demeanor, waiting for his muscles to tense. If the slack went from his muscles, Tilly would try to step away. Quickly.

Tilly made gentle contact with Remington's shoulder. The buck flinched but did not move away.

"There you go, it's okay," Tilly soothed in a quiet voice. She slowly brought the syringe to her mouth and pulled the cap off with her teeth. "Here we go," she said, talking around the syringe cap in her mouth like a cigarette.

She ran her hand toward the deer's neck, stopping just past his shoulder blade. Then in a quick, fluid motion, Tilly pierced his skin with the needle of the syringe and pumped its contents into the muscle of his neck. Remington started and went to move away from the needle, but the effects of the tranquilizer hit him almost instantly. He seemed to forget about running away as his legs wobbled and he swayed back and forth. His injured leg gave way first and he collapsed toward Tilly. She reached her arms out to catch his fall, straining to ease his 180 pounds to rest on the ground.

"See? Easy." Tilly smiled at Royce.

Royce breathed out a stunted laugh and shook his head. "You're insane," he said, but he couldn't stop the corners of his lips from curling up.

"You get him blindfolded. I'll go get my portable x-ray machine," Tilly said.

"Yes ma'am," Royce barked, mock saluting Tilly with a two-finger salute from his forehead. The twinkle in his eye gave away the joke.

When Tilly brought the x-ray machine back from her truck, Royce had Remington blindfolded. This was so he wouldn't be so frightened when he came to his senses.

"Are y'all ready for opening weekend?" Tilly asked as she set to work with the x-ray machine.

"Oh yeah, we're all set. Ten hunters are coming in for the weekend. Five of 'em are on a corporate retreat from some fancy Dallas law firm. Then two from Houston, I think, and three buddies coming in all the way from Miami."

"How much are y'all charging this year?" Tilly asked as she aimed the x-ray machine at the buck's injured leg.

"It depends on the deer. We price them based on the size of their antlers, you know—five, fifteen grand. Somewhere in there. We have four bucks at fifteen in this year's crop, and they've all been reserved for opening weekend."

"What a racket," Tilly said. She huffed a single, wry laugh. "I remember when you could kill a deer for the low, low price of a hunting license and a bullet."

"Yeah, well, inflation's a bitch, ain't it."

"I guess y'all can charge just about anything to these city people, though," Tilly said. She had finished with the x-ray machine and was examining the images it produced on an app on her cell phone.

"Hey, I was a city guy for a little while, and I think at one point I would've probably paid five thousand dollars for some fresh air. And what's the point of a wilderness adventure if you can't prove to your friends back in Houston you had one? Gotta bring back a dead animal to prove it."

"Dead deer or it didn't happen, I guess," Tilly said. She looked up from the x-ray images on her phone. "Speaking of dead deer—"

"Oh no, don't tell me." Royce's expression darkened. Tilly smiled.

"He's fine," Tilly said. "No breaks."

"Goddamn it, Tilly, you scared the shit out of me." Royce laughed with relief. "I got the insurer halfway dialed."

Tilly grimaced at the reminder of the financial nature of the animal's life. "I'll get him cleaned up and he ought to be good as new in a week or so. I'll give him some penicillin to ward off infection."

"Sounds like a plan," Royce said. "I can handle reporting that news to the boss man."

Tilly rummaged through her bag for the appropriate supplies. She gave Remington a shot of penicillin in the same manner as the tranquilizer, then cleaned the gash with antiseptic. She sealed the wound with an aerosol bandage—a fine silver mist that coalesced on the wound to form a shiny barrier that would keep the world out.

"There we go, all set." Tilly patted the deer on his shoulder. "Just keep an eye on him as he comes to. You know the drill."

"Got it. Hey, before you go, wanna see our new breeder buck?"

"Oh, Bubba decided to hold on to one this year? Which one?"

"Number 147," Royce said, referring to the deer's ear tag number, which was the method of differentiation between the animals. "Here, let me show you. Follow me. Huge rack this year, couldn't hardly let him go with Remington getting so old. We'll need a new head sire pretty soon."

The pair walked a few pens down the line to one that held several young-looking bucks, probably all three years old, the age at which they are usually sold for hunts. Tilly knew right away which deer was Number 147, the one that would live past age three to breed. His rack spanned at least two feet across at its widest point and his tines—sixteen of them, Tilly counted at first glance—towered into the air above his head. A long drop-tine plunged down from the left side of his massive antlers.

"Woah—big boy," Tilly said. The animal was somewhere between beautiful and monstrous, his antlers overgrown in a way that would never—could never—happen in nature. The antlers were twisted, gnarled, *disfigured* with human intervention. The grotesque result of generations of selective breeding. But still, the buck had a certain majesty that Tilly couldn't ignore.

"Yeah," Royce said. "He's bigger than Remington ever was."

"Is he one of Remington's sons?"

"Yep. We must've gotten the mix of genetics just right with the doe."

"He's beautiful," Tilly said, unsure whether she meant it. "What're you going to name him? The ones that get to stick around to breed get names, right?

"That's right. Bubba was leaning toward 'Wesson,' I think."

"Well, that tracks," Tilly said. Number-147-soon-to-be-Wesson-probably looked over at them as they talked. He started to walk toward them, leading several of the other bucks over to the fence, probably on a quest for dried corn handouts. One of the smaller bucks walked right up to the fence and stuck his nose through, sniffing. He likely smelled the remnants of corn in Royce's bucket.

Tilly reached out and touched the buck's nose. It was wet.

"That's Number 86," Royce said, "One of the Miami guys has him opening weekend."

Royce produced a few kernels of dried corn from the bucket and fed them to the buck. Number 86 eagerly lipped the kernels from his palm. Tilly met the buck's big, round eyes. She turned away.

"I'll see you later, Royce," she said, and she left him there, communing with the sacrificial deer.

Chapter 3
Introduction and
Royal March of the Lion

As Tilly walked back to her truck, the owner of the 999 Ranch, Francis Skinner, approached her. Francis—or Bubba, as he insisted everyone call him because he hated his given name (*Francis is a goddam Yankee name,* he'd say)—was a local high roller and a known scoundrel. He was respected in the community only because he was rich, which, for whatever reason, often rises to the greatest virtue when measuring a man.

Bubba's money came from indeterminant sources. A little oil money here, a little inheritance there, a piece of land bought for a penny and sold for a mint now and then. And of course, the 999's hunting operation was very profitable. Rumors of sordid business practices—shirking debts, cheating business partners—had always swirled around Bubba, but never quite managed to dim his shining reputation. *He's good at making money,* people would say, as if that settled any question about the man. The mystery surrounding Bubba's success only seemed to add to his mythos, so that he had achieved a sort of reverence from many in the community. The mystery that drove some to awe made Tilly suspicious.

"Tilly!" Bubba called. "Wait up!" He mock-jogged toward her, his beer gut jiggling under his button-down fishing shirt.

Tilly reluctantly stopped. She turned and, thinking of her monthly invoice to the 999, forced a smile. "Hey there, Bubba. What's up?"

"Nothin' but my taxes, baby," he said with his winningest grin. Tilly fought an eyeroll and managed to force a polite laugh.

"I actually want to discuss a new business opportunity with you." Bubba dropped his smile, all business. *Here we go*, thought Tilly.

"With me?" Tilly clarified. "What could that possibly be?" Whatever it was, Tilly had already decided that she probably wasn't interested.

"Indeed," Bubba said. "And I cain't tell you what it is just yet."

"So you want to tell me about a business opportunity, but you can't tell me about the business opportunity?" Tilly raised an eyebrow.

"Right. Well, not yet, anyway."

"Okay, well, call me when you're ready to talk about it." Tilly turned to leave.

"Woah, hold your horses, darlin'. It's just kind of a secret. And we have to make some arrangements before I can tell you the secret."

Tilly stopped, intrigue creeping in on her annoyance. She turned back around. Bubba had another grin waiting for her.

"Let me just get your autograph on this form here, and then I can tell ya." He pulled a folded piece of paper out of the back pocket of his jeans and held it out to Tilly.

The form was titled, in bold letters:

NONDISCLOSURE AGREEMENT

Tilly looked at the form, then at Bubba. "You've got to be kidding me," she said. Tilly took the formality as a symptom of Bubba's inflated sense of self-importance.

"It's just saying you promise not to tell anyone what I talk to you about," Bubba said. "Or show you," he added. The last statement, no more than an afterthought, stirred Tilly's curiosity. She took the paper from him.

"Yeah, I gathered as much based on my ability to read English," she said as she scanned the document.

Bubba laughed. "I forget that most people aren't as slow as me," he said good-naturedly. "I only know as much as the lawyers tell me."

"And this 'business opportunity,' it's for a veterinary job?" Tilly asked as she reached the end of the text, which threatened her with a lawsuit if she revealed what Bubba told her after signing.

"Of sorts." Bubba winked. Tilly was not comforted by Bubba's efforts to sell the idea.

Tilly's gut told her to hand the unsigned agreement back to Bubba, get in her truck, and drive home. But something stopped her. It had been a morning of curiosities, and her curiosity about the mutilated calf went unsated. The nondisclosure agreement sang a siren song. It offered an answer to something, some satisfaction.

Curiosity killed the cat, Tilly thought, thinking of the cats she often saw in her clinic that had come out on the wrong side of inquisitiveness.

She took a deep breath. "Alright, you got me, Bubba. Do you have a pen?"

Ten minutes later, Tilly was in the passenger seat of Bubba's ATV, still none the wiser about the secret job she was now contractually bound not to disclose. They left the main office, where Tilly had been parked, and drove past all of the deer pens, beyond the brush-cleared fields where the hunts took place, deep into the unmanicured, overgrown pasture of the 999.

Oak and cedar trees crowded together, their branches intertwining in places to form impenetrable walls of vegetation. Where the trees gave each other some space and allowed sunlight to reach the ground, prickly pear cacti abounded. The only sign of human intervention in the landscape was the ghost of a road, which was less a road, and more a path beaten into the grass over time. The ATV swerved around trees and bumped over rocks. A few times, they had to squeeze through spaces so tight that cedar tree branches reached into the ATV and scraped Tilly's arms, leaving bright red scratches.

"I'd love to know where we're going," Tilly shouted over the drone of the ATV engine after they had gone deeper into the pasture than she thought possible.

"The Back Forty," Bubba said with a grin that made Tilly want to hit him.

"Helpful," Tilly yelled.

They drove in silence again, the noise of the engine and the mystery of the destination filling up all of the space between them, leaving no room for words. The road seemed to narrow even further as they went along, and it seemed to Tilly that the pasture itself, with its tree and shrub and cactus appendages, was closing in even tighter around them as they drove. As if trying to capture them in a trap she couldn't yet see, which would only reveal itself once it sprung. By then it would be too late.

And then there it was. Tilly didn't know what she had been expecting, but she knew they had reached their destination when she saw it.

Ahead of them, at first barely visible through the trees, then all Tilly could see, rose a massive metal fence, unlike the typical fences one would see on a deer ranch. It was tall—at least twelve feet, much taller than practical for any ranching operation—and solid. It was almost more of a wall than a fence, and it was adorned with an equally massive gate, which was the target of the ATV.

Bubba removed a small remote from his front pocket. With the press of a button, the gate slowly began to open, the whole time protesting its own weight with creaks and groans.

"Bubba, what is this?" Tilly asked, her voice taking an uneasy tone. The sight of the industrial fence in pasture setting was jarring.

"I told you, the Back Forty."

They proceeded through the gate. A road stretched out ahead of them, cleared of brush on either side. Tilly had the feeling of emerging from a tunnel into lightness, and she took a deep breath of the cedar-scented air.

Another iteration of the massive fence ran along one side of the road. Tilly contemplated it as they went along. Fences on deer ranches were usually tall, so as to prevent deer from jumping over them to escape. But this fence was much taller than that. Excessively so. Tilly wondered what sort of animal this fence was meant to contain.

She searched the dense brush on the other side of the ATV, looking for the creature that required these fences, and apparently required her veterinary services. She saw nothing.

Then, like a mirage shimmering into being in the desert, a building materialized before them. Elegant, all straight lines and glass, the structure was hugged so tightly by trees on all sides that it was hard to tell where the woods ended, and the building began. The building was so overwhelmed by glass in places that the eye could see straight through several layers of structure to the building's other side. The pasture beyond the building traveled in refractions and reflections to the front, so that the building itself was just a blur of the scenery, a rift in the visible dimension. A window to somewhere similar, but not same. The mind could almost write the whole thing off as a trick of the light.

"Alright, Bubba, what is going on? You have to tell me what this is." Things were starting to feel mysterious beyond the scope of the intrigue that Tilly had signed up for, and the events of the day had worn her.

"Due time, Tilly, due time," Bubba said.

They drove into a small clearing beyond the mystery building, and up to the gate into another enclosure formed by another tall fence, this one made of the usual posts and wire. A man waited for them there. Bubba brought the ATV to a jarring stop next to the smiling stranger. He jumped out of the ATV and shook the stranger's hand.

"Abner, this is the lady vet I was telling you about, Tilly. Tilly, this is Abner. He's been working on this new little project for me, too."

"Hi," Tilly said, reaching a hand toward him for a handshake. "I'm really just a plain old vet. No special lady tricks." She softened the barb with a smile.

"Nice to meet you," Abner said. He smiled back. After a moment, an odd jerk of the corner of his mouth disrupted the friendly smile. His mouth cascaded into a series of erratic movement, his lips parting and closing again, as if mouthing speech. Tilly felt for a moment like she was watching a movie on mute.

"Sorry, I didn't catch that," she said.

"I said 'nice to meet you,'" Abner said, taking control of his mouth for the sentence. Then he smiled again, and the movement began again. Abner did not acknowledge—and almost didn't seem to notice—the acrobatics.

He was dressed in jeans, boots, and a button-down shirt, like just about every man who worked on the 999. But small aspects of his dress were inconsistent with the usual style. His jeans were not starched, and perhaps a bit too slim cut. His boots were round-toed and looked freshly polished. His shirt was more a dress shirt than a work shirt and would have been more at home under a blazer than on a ranch. The little anomalies added up to an outfit that looked like a guess at what one who worked on a game ranch might wear—a costume.

"Are you a vet too?" Tilly asked Abner. His outfit told her he wasn't, but she couldn't think of any other reason he might be here.

"Of sorts," he said. "At least, in this context. But I am actually a—"

Bubba interrupted. "Abner, why don't we show Tilly what you've been workin' on." He opened the gate to the high-fenced pen.

"Yes sir." Abner gestured for Tilly to step through the gate first, then followed her in. The enclosure boasted the native landscape that graced the rest of the ranch: oak and cedar trees, prickly pear cacti, huisache, whitebrush, and guajillo shrubs.

Tilly didn't see anything unusual.

"Anyone care to fill me in on what I'm looking for?" Tilly asked. She knew that only an animal would make her presence necessary, but she saw none. It was getting late, and her initial curiosity was wearing off. She was growing impatient.

"Just give it a minute," Bubba chided in his slow drawl.

As they stood and waited for the mystery to solve itself, waiting for the landscape to give up whatever it was hiding, the insects that filled the pasture with noise suddenly went quiet.

The sudden silence raised an army of goose bumps on Tilly's arms and sent them marching up to the nape of her neck. Then a low noise disrupted the quiet, beginning almost imperceptibly, then growing louder, louder. It was the guttural rumble of a growl. A growl from what sounded like something very, very big.

"Should we be inside the pen?" Tilly asked in her loudest whisper. She began to walk backward toward the gate, eager to get on the other side of it, away from the source of the growl somewhere in the brush. The growl lent a thickness to the air, a tension, which seemed to make movement and speech, and even thought, difficult. It grew louder, pervading Tilly's mind, the sound taking shape in her mind's eye into something solid, an unidentifiable thing with legs and teeth and claws.

Before Tilly got an answer, a flash of movement behind a prickly pear bush caught her eye. The growl exploded into a roar. Something large emerged from the brush in a blur of orange and black. The anonymous growling beast in Tilly's mind took its true form.

A tiger.

Electric, primal fear shot through every nerve of Tilly's body.

And then the tiger was charging toward her all at once, a horror of rippling muscle. It opened its jaw and screamed another roar, its teeth catching the sunlight in a terrifying spectacle.

Tilly stumbled back, back, trying to get to the gate and out of the enclosure. Her foot caught on something unseen, and the force of her momentum sent her flying backward to the ground. And then the tiger was ten feet away, then five. Tilly, realized, helplessly, that her final moments were upon her. She screamed.

The tiger leapt toward her, claws outstretched. Tilly closed her eyes.

Chapter 4
The Tiger

A sudden thud. Then silence. A moment passed, and then another, and Tilly was still not mauled or dead or maimed. Confused, she opened her eyes, struggling for shaky breaths.

The tiger lay inches away from her. It had collapsed upon itself, legs askew in unnatural directions.

Up close, something looked *off* about the tiger. Tilly couldn't immediately put her finger on what was wrong with it. But somewhere deep in the recesses of her mind, in a place not consciously accessible, the sight of the thing called up a profound revulsion.

Tilly realized she was crying when she felt cool air on her face in the tracks left by hot tears. She wiped her face with a trembling hand and tried to take a deep breath, but her lungs would only accept small, shallow ones. She looked over to Bubba and Abner, expecting them to be in similar states of shock.

They weren't. Bubba was laughing. He was doubled over to the extent his large stomach would allow, almost in tears of an entirely different sort to Tilly's. Abner wasn't laughing, but his expression was irritatingly indifferent.

It took a moment longer than Tilly would have liked for her to realize that she'd been the butt of some kind of joke. Heat rose in her chest, her swelling anger dissipating the tight coil of fear that had seized her.

"What the *fuck* is going on?" Tilly demanded. She stood, still a little shaky, and dusted off her jeans. Bubba was still laughing too hard to answer.

Tilly looked again at the lifeless tiger on the ground, trying to connect the dots as to what happened. Her first thought was that one of the men must have shot it, but she didn't see any blood, and neither had a gun visible. She nudged the tiger with the toe of her boot. It was impossibly stiff for an animal that had been alive and pouncing moments ago.

She turned to Bubba, who still couldn't contain his amusement.

"I'm glad this is so funny to you, Bubba. I thought I was about to die, jackass."

Bubba regained his composure just enough to wheeze between breaths, "Now don't get yer britches in a wad. It ain't real!" Then he broke back down into hysterics.

"I'm sorry, what?" It had sure *felt* real. Tilly looked to Abner for clarity.

He cleared his throat. "I suppose I can fill you in now. This is one of my creations." He gestured toward the tiger. "We have been building a line of animatronic animals." The word "creations" stuck in Tilly's ear, sending an uneasy echo through her mind, though she wasn't sure why.

"Um, they—the animals—they can be controlled by remotes." Abner waved the small remote in his hand as a way of explaining the tiger's sudden collapse. "I would not have let it actually attack you. Its software actually does not currently have a protocol for attacking, if that makes you feel better. It has not learned that yet."

Tilly looked again at the tiger on the ground, which now looked much more like a robot than it had before she knew it was a robot. The proportions of the animal's body—its length compared to its height, the size of its head compared to the mass of its body—were not quite right. And the coat—the skin—crinkled and rippled over the body in a way that was divorced from the mechanical muscles beneath it. In retrospect, its movement had been too jerky and a bit stilted—ungraceful. Still, the near accuracy impressed Tilly.

"But—well, I don't understand. Why?" Tilly couldn't piece together everything that was happening into any sort of cohesive scheme.

Certainly not one that would require the skills of a veterinarian. Her curiosity cooled some of her anger.

"Hunting. People like to kill things they ain't 'sposed to. You cain't hunt tigers in the wild, see. So, voila." Bubba gestured to the tiger. "If I cain't get real tigers for hunting, the next best thing is to make 'em myself."

"So people pay—actual money—to hunt a fake tiger?"

"Not yet, but they will. You're looking at about a hundred-and-fifty-thousand-dollar hunt right there." He knelt down next to the mechanical beast and ran a hand over its fur—almost petting it.

"It's the perfect setup. We don't get in trouble with the law and our hunters get an unforgettable experience."

"Plus, no animals are harmed," Abner chimed in.

"That's right, no animals were harmed in the making of this hunt." Bubba beamed. "It's vegan hunting! PETA approved!"

Tilly shook her head in disbelief at Bubba's apparently newfound stance against animal cruelty. How convenient that it coincided with a way to make money.

"And the best part," Bubba went on as he reached for the tiger's neck, "is this."

As he said it, he squeezed in at the base of the tiger's neck with both hands. There was a click, like the release of a latch. Then the tiger's head came away from its body in Bubba's hands.

"Ready to mount!" Bubba held the head up triumphantly. The mouth was stuck open in a snarl. "Einstein over there worked out a way for us to reuse the robot bodies. We just have to add new heads every time. It's downright economical!"

"And make minor repairs from the bullet holes," Abner added.

"Oh that reminds me—wait'll you see this. Abner, turn this bad boy back on."

Abner pointed the remote at the now-headless tiger and pressed a button. The body sprung to life, gathering its legs under itself and standing.

Tilly took a step back. The tiger's teeth may have been in Bubba's hands, but the decapitated body still had claws.

Bubba pulled a pistol from his belt and leveled it at the tiger's shoulder. He fired, and the tiger again collapsed to the ground. Red liquid gushed from the bullet wound and began to spread, seeping through the tiger's fur.

"Blood's a nice touch, huh?" Bubba looked up from admiring his handiwork and looked to Tilly for approval.

The sight recalled the violence of the calf discovery that morning and made Tilly's stomach churn. Tilly could tell by Bubba's reaction to her face that she hadn't done a good job of hiding her revulsion.

"What exactly is my role in all of this?" Tilly asked. "Seems like another benefit of animatronics is that you don't need veterinarians." The tiger's wound was still oozing fake blood. Tilly had an illogical urge to reach down and put pressure on it to stop the bleeding.

"We have a few, um, bugs to work out before we can roll out this little program," Bubba said. "I want you to work with Abner and his team to get the animals to be more lifelike. Look like tiger, act like a tiger. The hunters are paying big bucks for these hunts, and I want 'em to feel like they're baggin' a Bengal in the jungles of India."

Tilly looked around at the Texas brush country and wondered if Bubba was going to do anything about the obvious lack of jungle flora that would pierce a hole or two in his desired illusion. "I see. So I'd be a consultant? As an animal expert?"

"Exactly." He drew out the word's syllables. "You're the expertest animal expert I know. And I trust you." He punctuated the sentence with a knowing look at Tilly. She wasn't sure what he meant by it.

"Why don't we go back to the office to hammer out the details—assumin' you're interested yet," he said.

Tilly looked again at the tiger, then at Bubba and the gun in his hand. Her anger flared anew. The whole enterprise sat wrong with Tilly. She couldn't quite put her finger on why, but thought it might be the sheer *unnaturalness* of it all—the placement of something so *artificial* in the vivid wilds of the Texas countryside. *It just didn't belong.*

Still, something about the project tempted her. The art of creation, she supposed. Even if it was creation for the sole purpose of destruction.

Bubba heard Tilly's hesitation in her silence. "Just come back and talk it over with us," he said. "We need to talk figures and such. That might bring you around."

Bubba held the tiger head tucked beneath one arm. It was looking right at Tilly. She met its gaze. And in the space between her eyes and the tiger's, Tilly found her answer. She started to shake her head.

"No," Tilly said. "No, I can't."

"What do you mean you 'can't'?"

"It's just not right."

"'Not right?' You're a good negotiator, Tilly." Bubba laughed. "How much I gotta pay you to make it 'right'?"

He laughed again, and the laugh struck the angriest part of Tilly's brain—the part that held on to anger over the tiger attack, and a million other little things like the horror of a mutilated calf—like the hammer of a gun. *Bang.*

"You know what, Bubba? You can go fuck yourself."

Chapter 5
Fossils

Tilly commandeered Bubba's ATV and drove herself back to her truck, then drove herself straight into town. Deer-hunting season was quickly approaching, and the town buzzed with activity in preparation. A banner strung across main street said "Welcome Hunters!" Shops had all of their camouflage wares on display, and the butcher advertised a special deer-processing deal (*Butcher a Buck, Have a Doe Butchered Half Off!*). Every business with a cash register, from the feed store to the grocery store to the auto body shop, had fifty-pound bags of dried corn stacked outside their doors for sale.

Tilly pulled into the parking lot of the Resthaven Nursing Home. She was still fuming from her Bubba encounter. And the thought that she had signed away her right to even tell anyone about it only stoked her anger.

Tilly went inside. The familiar scent of lemon cleaning solution—trying its best to mask another, unsavory and unmentionable odor—hit Tilly's nose when she walked into Resthaven. The nursing home had the depressing atmosphere common to all places visited frequently by death. The air itself felt thick and old.

The design of the place was a collage of yellowing linoleum and round-edged furniture. The front room of the facility was a communal area, strewn with card tables and rocking chairs. In one corner of the room stood a tall glass-sided cabinet that held a fake, leafless tree. Live birds flitted from bare branch to bare branch inside.

Tilly stopped at the nurse's station. Her favorite nurse, Rosa, was working. Rosa's whole being radiated warmth. She made all of this just a little easier. Just the sight of her loosened the coils of tension in Tilly's shoulders. They exchanged hellos.

"How is she?" Tilly asked.

Rosa's perma-smile faltered for a moment. "She's been having a rough day, mija."

"Not a lucid one today?" Tilly asked the question as if she was asking about the weather, hiding her disappointment with an almost-too-casual tone.

"No, she's living on the moon. She told me the Mennonites were trying to kidnap her last night." Rosa's smile returned.

Tilly couldn't stop an escaping laugh. She shook her head. "God, sometimes I feel terrible for laughing at stuff like that."

"You either laugh or you cry," Rosa said. "It's just a little thing we can do for ourselves—give ourselves permission to see the humor. I mean, the Mennonites—ay chingoa!"

"I guess you're right." Her smile stayed with Rosa's permission.

"I double-checked that she took her morning meds when I got here. You never know with the night crew."

"Thanks. I'm going to go check on her. I'm glad you're here, Rosa."

Rosa's face darkened. "Tilly, wait. I'm sorry, but I have a note from the administrator to tell you—" She looked down at the desk.

"Tell me what?"

"Well, I don't think the payment for this month went through." Rosa looked up again, meeting Tilly's eyes with sympathy.

"What do you mean? It's a direct draw from her savings account."

"I only know what they told me, mija. It didn't go through. I'm sorry." She sounded like she really was.

Tilly's brow knitted. "Okay. I will check on that. Thank you for telling me."

Rosa went back to sorting through papers on her desk. Tilly made her way to the end of the hall. She passed by the open doors of several rooms. Residents in different states of health looked out at her. One old man whistled an old-timey catcall. Another woman called out to her: "Helen! Helen!" Tilly waved and walked on.

Tilly went into the last room on the hallway. The room was generally drab, as such rooms always are. Standard-issue hospital-type bed; tan tile floor for easy cleaning; furniture that was outdated by about twenty years, but had never been stylish, even when new. The muted television was tuned into the Food Network, and some celebrity chef or another was silently miming how to prepare a Thanksgiving turkey.

There was an old woman there. She sat in an upholstered recliner, staring into space.

"Hi, Mom," Tilly greeted her.

Tilly's mother's eyes lit up when Tilly entered the room.

"Oh hi, Jet," she said, smiling. Jet—Bridget, for long—was her mother's long-dead sister. The woman's Alzheimer's-addled mind frequently summoned ghosts. Tilly had been her Aunt Jet, her mom's college roommate Janice, and Mrs. Thompson, her mother's Sunday school teacher. As disease ripped her mother's mind away, it took Tilly away, too—hollowed her out, erased her. Each failure to recognize Tilly—and the failures were more frequent all the time—made her feel a bit more translucent, impermanent. Like she might fade away at any moment, and there was nothing she could do about it.

"How are you today, Mom? They treating you okay?" Tilly sat down on the edge of her mother's bed.

"Oh, yes," she said, her voice shaky with age. She was in her mid-seventies, but her illness had added years to her. The weight of time had pressed deep wrinkles into her skin. Still, she looked more youthful, somehow, when she was impersonating her younger self.

She went on, "Last night, Betty Hendricks came into my room and spilled her bag of chicken feed all over the place. It was just everywhere.

Those chickens kept me up half the night, their damn pecking. I don't know why someone didn't come and get them out of here."

"Well, hopefully you get better sleep tonight," Tilly said gently. "How are you feeling?"

"Never been better," her mother answered. "Oh, look at me, I'm being rude. I haven't even offered you coffee. Let me put on a fresh pot." She moved to rise from the chair.

"Oh no, Mom, it's okay. I've had enough coffee today," Tilly said. The old woman lowered herself back into the chair, to Tilly's relief. She had almost fallen last time Tilly had visited, when she got up to make coffee in her nonexistent kitchen. The last thing Tilly needed today (what a *day*) was a fall. Her mother's mental decline was almost too much for Tilly to bear—she couldn't face her physical decline as well.

The old woman settled back into her chair and into silence. Tilly, who often didn't know what to say to her mother these days, joined her in silence.

Tilly looked around the room. She had tried to make the room feel like home for the old woman—she'd brought the very end table, lamp, and rug that had been in her mother's old living room and arranged them just as they had been arranged there. She'd brought photos from her mother's home for the dresser and nightstand, and a little portrait of an Angus cow-and-calf pair in a tranquil green pasture that had always hung in her mother's kitchen. Tilly didn't know where the painting came from—it looked old, but she didn't know if it was an heirloom, and now it was too late to ask—but she had always liked it and thought it looked good hanging above the drab nursing home bed.

But despite Tilly's efforts, the room was depressing. The circumstances and the setting did not give it much choice.

All at once, Tilly's mother reanimated with a renewed energy for socialization.

"Oh, Jet," she said, "Did I tell you that Momma and Daddy came to visit me yesterday?"

"No, you didn't. How were they?" Tilly asked. *Besides dead for twenty years*, she thought to herself. Her mother's time travel had increased in frequency as her illness progressed.

"Good, good. Daddy went huntin' but he didn't get anything."

"That's too bad," Tilly said. Then she had an idea. Her mother's non-sense ramblings had led her to a loophole.

"Mom, you won't believe what Bubba Skinner is up to." Tilly sat up straight on the bed, suddenly enthusiastic.

And Tilly told her mother the story of the tiger attack. It was as if Tilly had opened a pressure valve in her body, every word of her story escaping steam, and slowly she came down from the adrenaline and anger that had filled her to the bursting.

Tilly's mother seemed to dutifully listen to the tale. And when Tilly finished, the old woman asked, "Jet, are you still going with that Augie Wilson?"

Tilly looked down at her lap. She had hoped—ridiculously—for a bit more of a reaction. That perhaps her mother—her *real* mother, who really knew *her*—was somewhere in there, and would emerge to be her knowing confidant. It was a silly notion, and she shook it off. At least she got to tell her secret and keep it too.

Tilly forged ahead. "Yes," she said, answering her mother's question. She had learned that the kindest way to treat a mind afflicted with Alzheimer's was to play the part it assigned.

"Good, he's a nice boy."

"He is," Tilly agreed. *He's eighty-four*, she thought to herself.

"That reminds me. Jet, will you get a chicken out of the icebox? The Johnsons are coming over for supper."

"Will do, Mom," Tilly said. Her voice cracked.

She felt tears well in her eyes. *Goddam it*. Her mother had been in the home for a few months and dealing with Alzheimer's for longer, but sometimes the pain of the situation still snuck up on Tilly. She felt like she had already lost the woman who sat before her. Tilly decided to leave before the welling tears could escape her eyes.

"Well, I better get going," she said. "It's been a long day. And you should get some rest, too."

Tilly went to her mother and kissed her on the forehead. "I love you, Mom."

Tilly turned to leave. She was almost out the door when her mother said, "Oh, Tilly, before you go—"

"Yes?" Tilly's heart jumped when she heard her mother say her name. Tilly was another of her mother's ghosts, rarely summoned. She turned to the old woman.

"Be careful. Daddy says he's not a nice man."

"Who?" Tilly asked. Her mother answered with silence, staring blankly at her. "Who's not a nice man, Mom?"

The old woman smiled at her, a veil falling over her eyes. "Are you leaving already, Jet? Give Augie my best, will you?"

Tilly stood in the doorway for a moment, searching her mother's face for any sign of lucidity. Then she said, "Of course. I will." And she left.

Chapter 6
The Coyote

Tilly drove straight home and found the stack of mail that sat, previously forgotten, at one end of her kitchen counter. She frantically rifled through it.

She found the most recent bank statement for her mother's savings account. Unopened. Tilly knew that the statements from the last several months were the same way. She had been busy with her move back to Verde and setting up her veterinary practice—time and chores had slipped right by her.

She opened the statement. Her eyes went immediately to the balance at the bottom. It was well into the four figures—but enclosed by parentheses. The negative balance had been lowered even further by overdraft fees when the nursing home payments bounced.

"Fuck," Tilly said aloud. Her border collie, Ranger, looked over at her from his perch on the couch. "Fuck, fuck, fuck."

Tilly's vet clinic didn't yet make enough money to cover even her own expenses—and even when it was fully developed, Tilly couldn't see her small-town, rural veterinary clinic being all that profitable. That monthly nursing home bill was a whole lot of neutering, vaccinating, and Coggins testing.

Tilly didn't like the place where her mind went when she thought about how she might make more money. She felt the air tightening around her, the potential energy of a trap about to spring. She tried to escape it by leaving her house and going to the town diner for a late lunch.

The diner was the sort common to most little towns. It was a general eatery, and it had booths with vinyl cushions, and a counter with barstools, and a glass-enclosed display of different pies for sale. The floor was checkered linoleum tile. It did not have the contrived charm of period-themed diners, with their consistent 1950s flare. Instead, things were brown and yellowed. The decor was more defined by an economic, utilitarian style than by any particular time period, and Tilly had always thought that the diner was neutral in both time and place. The diner did not have a name—the sign outside said only "Diner."

Tilly walked into the diner to an unexpected clamor. A crowd was gathered inside, and their chatter filled the air with electricity. Conversations jumped from table to table. People stood in the aisles. It was unusual.

As Tilly made her way through the crowd, aiming for the counter, where she hoped to grab a stool, a hand reached out to stop her. It was the town's treasured eccentric, Harold Schmidt. Tilly had recently performed a cesarian section on one of the kangaroos he kept at his ranch—two healthy joeys and a healthy mom. He was sitting by himself—unusual for him, he usually presided over a gaggle of old men at the diner—and had an evaporating, long-cooled cup of coffee in front of him. He did not come to the diner for sustenance of the physical variety.

"Good afternoon, Dr. Hutto," Mr. Schmidt said.

"Not very good for me so far. It's been quite the day," Tilly said. "And—for God's sake, Mr. Schmidt, how many more times do I have to tell you—call me Tilly."

"At least one more time, it looks like," Mr. Schmidt said. He smiled at Tilly, then his brow furrowed. "I guess you've heard?" He asked. He gestured around the room at the crowd.

Tilly searched her mind for things she had heard that day. Her thoughts immediately went to the tiger, but then she remembered that it was a secret. Then she thought of her mother's negative bank account, which surely hadn't gotten around town. He must mean— "You mean the calf? Yeah, I was there. It was awful."

Mr. Schmidt's face scrunched in confusion. "No—no, what calf?"

Tilly started to answer, but Mr. Schmidt went on, "No, I'm talking about that Gonzales girl."

Tilly frowned. This was new. "What about her?"

Mr. Schmidt's face darkened. "She done disappeared." He widened his eyes and made a *poof* gesture with his hands.

"Disappeared?"

"Yep, just gone into the night. Her daddy went to wake her up for school this morning, and she just wadn't in her bed. No signs of breakin' and enterin', nothing."

"We're talking Rachael Gonzales, with the black lab?" Tilly tended to identify people by their animals. "Isn't she in high school?"

"I don't know what kind of dog she got, but yep, she's a sophomore."

"So do they think she ran away or something? With a boyfriend or . . . ?"

"Nope, they done ruled that out. Her car's still here, and her boyfriend is too."

"Damn." Tilly shook her head. "Poor girl." She thought of Rachael's family, and her heart twinged in the same way it did when she had to tell a patient's family their pet wasn't going to make it.

"That's what everyone is all wound up about," Mr. Schmidt said, gesturing around the clamoring diner. "They's talking about getting a search party together."

"Jesus. What a weird fucking day."

"I'll say. Things like this just don't happen in Verde." Mr. Schmidt looked mournfully at his nearly full cup of coffee.

"Until they do," said Tilly. Silence welled between the two, and the waitress took the opportunity to take Tilly's lunch order—grilled cheese, side of chips. It had been Tilly's go-to order at the diner since she was a kid. It surprised her how quickly she had reverted to childhood tastes when back in her childhood environment.

When the waitress left them, Mr. Schmidt said, "Wait a minute—what's this about a calf that you were talking about?"

The mutilated calf incident seemed like it happened days ago, though it had been only hours. And it was somehow shaping up to be one of the least-bad parts of Tilly's day. She told Mr. Schmidt what had happened.

When she finished describing the empty eyes, and the missing brain, and the snake of a spine, Mr. Schmidt shivered theatrically. "Did it have any blood left?"

"Not inside, hardly. It bled out everywhere," Tilly said. The waitress, shuffling behind the counter, briefly paused her work and looked up at them, no doubt on edge from the more human goings-on.

"But there *was* blood." Mr. Schmidt raised an eyebrow.

Tilly lowered her voice. "Yeah, pooled outside the body." She became acutely aware of the ketchup bottle on the diner counter. Red.

"Hmm. Wasn't the aliens, then. They always drain the blood." He said this with a straight face but a twinkle in his eye, and Tilly couldn't tell if he was joking.

"Hmm," Tilly echoed, humoring him. "At least we can rule one thing out."

"You know something," he said to her. "This morning I saw a coyote on my way into town. It crossed right in front of me, and it was headed north." He drew the coyote's path in the air with a hand. "You know what that means."

"I don't think a coyote could have done this, Mr. Schmidt. It was . . . precise. Plus, the calf was pretty big. I don't think a coyote could have taken it." The waitress sat Tilly's grilled cheese down on the beige Formica counter in front of her.

"No, that ain't what it means. Coyote crossin' your path means trouble's coming."

Tilly sighed and took a bite of her sandwich. "I think it's already here," she said around a mouthful of white bread and American cheese.

"Seems so." Mr. Schmidt turned on his stool to give Tilly the up-and-down. "Is that what's bothering you then? You seem a little blue today."

Tilly laughed at the underwhelming description and put her sandwich down. "'Blue' is one way to put it."

"What's funny?" Mr. Schmidt asked.

"God, my entire life feels like a joke right now, actually." Tilly sunk her forehead into her hands on the counter.

"What's the punch line?"

Tilly looked up at Mr. Schmidt. His eyes shown with kindness. She almost started in about the tiger, but the thought of the NDA stopped her. She didn't presently have any money to spare for a lawsuit.

Mr. Schmidt held her gaze until she cracked. She told him what she could. "It's my mom. I'm just having a hard time taking care of her." Tilly purposefully didn't mention finances. She didn't want Mr. Schmidt to think she was fishing for charity.

"It's hard, when a parent gets older." Mr. Schmidt nodded. "You just have to do what you can. You're doing a good thing, taking care of your mama, what with your daddy gone and all." Mr. Schmidt placed his hand over Tilly's on the table. It was warm. And admittedly nice.

Tilly sat with what he said for a moment, and let herself be comforted. And then, without thinking, she asked, "But what if what I can do—something that will make it easier for me to take care of her—what if it's . . . what if it's *wrong*?"

"Wrong," Mr. Schmidt repeated, weighing the word. "Well, all things are relative, at least that's what I think. Is the 'wrong' thing worse than not being able to take care of your mama?"

For a moment, Tilly sat quietly while she thought about it. And then the trap finally sprang around her. She had come to a moment of karmic intersection, and her choice was made clear to her. It was as if the fact had always been. The only thing left was acceptance.

She sighed. "I think I need to talk to Bubba Skinner."

"Well, that sounds like a bad idea, if I've ever heard one," Mr. Schmidt said.

"Yeah, yeah," Tilly said. "Mr. Schmidt, I have to go. I'm glad I got to see you."

"I'm glad you got to see me too," he said. "Better to be seen than viewed, at my age." He winked. Then he looked around, sheepish. "Oops, maybe not the time for that kind of joke."

Tilly laughed anyway, and left Mr. Schmidt sitting at the diner to drive back to the 999.

* * *

She found Bubba in his office, where he sat at a mahogany desk surrounded by wild game mounts on the walls. The menagerie of dead and taxidermied decor ranged from domestic animals to the exotic. Several whitetail bucks, like the ones he sold on the 999. A blackbuck antelope. An axis deer. Then the more exotic animals that that Tilly had to mentally page through a veterinary textbook to even name. A gemsbok. A bongo. A dama gazelle. Worse than those—Tilly's heart twinged—a zebra. Tilly wondered if Bubba had traveled to Africa to hunt the zebra, or if he had killed it on an exotics ranch here in Texas. Hunting exotics was big business, and ranches would import all kinds of obscure—and some very familiar—creatures for contrived, expensive hunting adventures. Tilly hadn't encountered any to-be-hunted zebras in her veterinary work around Verde yet, and she hoped she never did.

Perhaps worst of all, towering behind Bubba's desk, was the entire six-foot-tall head and neck of a giraffe. The base of its neck was mounted to the wall close to the floor, to accommodate its height. Its head nearly touched the ceiling, looking down on Tilly and Bubba and the rest of the animals in the room like a disappointed god. The office of animal specimens, safari that it was, would make an interesting scientific study if it didn't all make Tilly so sad. What wasted life, all crammed together in Bubba's office.

Bubba looked up from his work when Tilly walked in, looking surprised to be interrupted, and even more surprised that the interrupter was Tilly. He rose from his chair to greet her.

"Tilly, what can I do you for?" Bubba asked, ever the salesman. He sat back in his chair with a thud.

"How much are we talking?" Tilly asked. She planted both hands on his desk, hoping to look authoritative. A negotiator.

"What?" Bubba looked at Tilly like she was speaking an alien tongue.

Tilly deflated a bit. "If I do it—if I agree to work for you. How much are you going to pay me?" Bubba's face went from confused to gleeful.

"Let's see," Bubba said. He wrote something down on a piece of paper and slid it across the desk to Tilly. A number.

"What is that, for the whole project?"

"That's per week," Bubba said. His chair creaked as he leaned back into it, crossing his arms.

"Oh," Tilly said. She sat down herself in one of the overstuffed leather chairs opposite Bubba's desk. It was an impressive figure.

"That's what I thought," Bubba said. Smug.

Tilly had never known Bubba to be generous in pay. In the few short months she had been back in Verde, he had called her three times to negotiate the 999's vet bill down. "Where's this money coming from, Bubba?"

Bubba spread out his arms around him. "We do pretty well around here, Tilly, in case you hadn't noticed."

Tilly raised a suspicious eyebrow but decided not to question it further. That much money hitting her bank account every week would solve her nursing home problem by a mile, so she decided to file any questions about the provenance of the funds into the "none of my business" category. And that was probably the point.

"And on that note," Bubba said, "you'll have to sign another nondisclosure agreement."

This, Tilly couldn't square. She asked about it. "That's another thing I don't understand—why the secrecy? Don't you want people to know about this, so they come out and pay to hunt these—these things?"

"Don't want no one stealing my idea. Plus, word will get around anyway, and the secret makes it more fun—rich folks love exclusivity."

Tilly rolled her eyes. Bubba either didn't notice or didn't care. Tilly looked over the NDA, which, as far as she could tell, was more of the same as the first one, except this one was geared toward not revealing anything she worked on, not just what she saw. The list of things she couldn't reveal to anyone included *Devices*; *Drawings*; *Computer codes and programs*; *the identity of hunters*.

"You don't need to be talkin' to no one about this, okay?" Bubba summed up the document as she read through it. "Especially not Royce, I know you two are tight."

"Roger that," said Tilly. She gave him a mock two-finger salute. "What happens if I slip up? Like if I mention something on accident?"

"Clause Twenty-Two." Bubba's tone was stern, like a lecturing father.

Tilly flipped through the few pages of the document and found the twenty-second clause. It was titled *Liquidated Damages*.

"Holy shit," Tilly said when she saw the figure in the paragraph.

"Yep, you're agreeing that's how much you pay me if you, as you said, 'slip up.'"

"I don't have that kind of money."

"So you ain't gonna slip up, right?"

"Yeah," Tilly said. "Right." She was already wary of her decision to do this.

"So are we good?"

Tilly nodded. She felt the glass eyes of the taxidermied animals watching her, judging her. She took a pen and signed the NDA. Her hand trembled just enough to wobble her signature. They squared away an employment contract in the same way.

A heavy feeling followed Tilly home from the 999.

* * *

Sleep did not come easily to Tilly that evening. She lay in bed looking up at the ceiling of her childhood bedroom. She hadn't been able to bear moving into the master bedroom when she moved back home into her parents' house.

Tilly closed her eyes and fought for her mind to leave her head, to go to where the dreams are, so that her body could rest. She pictured it leaving through the middle of her forehead. She turned off her eyes, trying not to see the reddish darkness of the inside of her eyelids, willing the sense of sight away, and hoping her waking mind went with it, into oblivion. She tried to be very still. Nothing. But not the kind of nothing she wanted. She opened her eyes. Ranger was lightly snoring from his bed on the floor.

Even the darkness of the room itself seemed to fight away the night, refusing to surrender into complete blackness. Moonlight seeped in through the curtains; the alarm clock sent out a warm red glow; the tiger's eyes in the corner of the room shone bright yellow, like two mirrors.

Tilly gasped. She opened her eyes. The world rushed back into her head. She wasn't in bed. And she hadn't been awake. Instead, she sat at her kitchen table. She had a pen in her hand. Tilly pushed back from the table, heart pounding, and flipped on her kitchen light.

Strewn across the table and the floor were dozens of slips of paper—checks. Her checkbook lay open on the table, mutilated by rip after rip of check away from spine, in all manner of jagged edges. She picked up one of the checks from the floor.

It was made out to 'Resthaven Nursing Home' for the exact amount of her mother's overdue balance, and the memo line said "Ottalie Hutto." The check was finished with Tilly's signature.

She picked up another check. The same. And another. The same again. And so were all of the rest.

Tilly sat down, head spinning. She hadn't sleepwalked since high school. Her head sank into her hands on the kitchen table.

And that's when she saw the rest. Peering through her hands to the table, she read:

Resthaven Nursing Home $8,967.13
Eight-thousand nine-hundred sixty-seven & 13/100

Memo: Ottalie Hutto   *Tilly Hutto*

It was written in blue ink on the table, scratched into the wooden tabletop again and again, gouging a quarter-inch-deep scar into the wood.

Chapter 7
Aquarium

The next afternoon saw Tilly once again driving to the 999. She took a back road to the far entrance of the ranch, as directed by Bubba, so that her truck would not be seen going into the usual entrance. It was raining.

Tilly had brought Ranger along, as she often did when making ranch calls. Today, especially, she felt she needed the backup. He rode shotgun.

The blurriness of the rain on the windshield—the wipers had a hard time keeping up—made Tilly question whether she knew the way. But soon enough she was traveling down the road to the workshop, or laboratory, or factory, or whatever one might call the building where the animatrons were made.

The rain picked up its pace to welcome Tilly and Ranger to the workshop. They sprinted from the truck to the front doors, managing to get fairly soaked in the process.

A woman with purple hair waited inside the building's front door. She held out her hand to Tilly, and Tilly took it. "I'm Anna," she said.

Tilly introduced herself. "I didn't know there were any other people in Bubba's secret little club," she said, unable to keep a cynical note out of her voice. The air-conditioning of the building chilled Tilly's wet skin to the bone.

"There are a few of us," Anna explained. "Myself and—I think you met Abner—we are in charge. Well, mostly Abner is in charge, I guess. And we have a few helpers that come in to help with labor now and then. Need-to-know basis, and all that." She smiled warmly in a show of welcome.

"And now *you're* in the club, and"—Anna turned to Ranger, squatting down to his level—"who do we have here?"

Ranger happily wagged his whole body, flinging droplets of water from his wet fur all over the foyer. It was then that Tilly decided she liked Anna, because she knew Ranger to be a good judge of character.

Tilly introduced Anna and the dog. And as she did so, she realized that they had brought their own little rainstorm inside with them. Rivulets of water streamed from her clothes and Ranger's fur and puddled on the floor.

"Sorry—god—we're soaked. Let me get something to clean this up—"

"Don't worry, I've got it," Anna said, and she got towels for Tilly and Ranger and the floor.

Tilly took off her jacket, managing to excavate a dry layer of clothing underneath.

"Let me show you to Abner's workshop," Anna said. "We're starting there today."

Tilly walked beside Anna down the main hallway of the medium-sized building, with Ranger padding not far behind. Tilly's boot heels clip-clopped on the tile floor as she walked, like the steady stride of a horse, the echoes of her steps making the building sound and feel bigger than it was. Still damp in places, Tilly was captured by a shiver. Ranger did not seem to be as bothered by his wet circumstances.

"I'm so glad you've joined us," Anna said as they walked. "It was my idea, you know. To get you—a veterinarian. I just know that you'll be able to help all of this along." Anna swirled her hand in the air in a global gesture at the building.

"I'm not sure how helpful I'll be," Tilly said. "But I'll do my best."

The place gave Tilly an odd feeling, an unsettledness. Though she could not pinpoint a reason—the building was ordinary enough.

It seemed Ranger caught the odd sense too. He interrupted his dutiful trailing of Tilly to growl at a passing door. Tilly stopped when Ranger did. Anna stopped when Tilly did.

The door at which Ranger was growling was unremarkable. It was closed, and wooden in the classic, utilitarian style. Ranger crept toward the door, a low rumble maintained in his chest. He carefully pressed his nose into the darkness of the crack under the door. He sniffed. His hackles rose. His tail tucked. He spun around and took a step behind Tilly. He watched the door from his hiding spot between her legs.

"Woah there, buddy," Tilly said. "It's all right." She patted his head and felt the vibration of his growl under her palm. It traveled up her arm and into her chest, into her heart. Tilly had only seen Ranger like this once before, when they were walking in a park at night, when Tilly still lived in the city. A man had stepped from behind a tree in their path, approaching them. Ranger erupted in a snarl, like thunder. Like he had never seen a monster before. A warning. Tilly never found out if Ranger was right about the man. He passed them without saying a word.

Tilly looked at Anna. "Isn't it?" she asked. "All right?"

Anna was looking between the dog and the door. "Yes," she said. "Yes, it should be. That room is just storage."

Ranger continued to growl. Anna looked bemused. "Here," she said to the dog. "Look."

She grasped the door handle and twisted. It did not move. She looked confused. Anna again gave the handle a hearty jiggle, this time leaning against the door with all her weight. Nothing.

Tilly reached past Anna and knocked on the door. Anna huffed a laugh. "There's no one *in there*," she said. Though her voice was tinted with uncertainty.

Tilly waited in silence for an answer to the knock, though she doubted the object of Ranger's ire would open the door; she had no way of knowing if the thing was a person capable of door-opening, or an animal with no means of so doing, or something not alive at all. Perhaps it was nothing. Anna fell into silence as well, almost as if she, too, was waiting. Ranger's growl continued.

No one—and nothing—answered.

Tilly shook her head. "Must be nothing," she said. Anna nodded. She continued to lead Tilly down the hallway to Abner's workshop.

Abner was there. He had a smile for Tilly, but then he noticed Ranger. His smile dissolved. "What is this?" he asked.

"This is my assistant, Ranger," Tilly said. "Don't worry, he'll stay out of the way."

"Your . . . assistant." The statement dripped with skepticism.

"Yes. He's nonnegotiable," Tilly said. She was on edge from whatever had just happened at the door in the hall, and that feeling of unease manifested as defensiveness. "I talked it over with Bubba," she added, lying. She could hear the events of the past few minutes in her voice—shrill, self-justifying. She felt like a child trying to explain away a bad grade.

Abner looked skeptical, and the room was silent while he gave Ranger the up-and-down.

"C'mon, Abner," Anna chimed in, "look at that little face. He's harmless."

For his part, Ranger looked at the three of them with his best puppy-dog eyes.

Abner forced his mouth back into a smile. "Right. Of course. As long as it stays out of the way. Fine." He nodded in emphasis. His smile tumbled into twisting and jerking, and his lips formed phantom, silent words. Both Anna and Tilly politely ignored it.

"That's settled then," Tilly said.

She looked around the lab. The atmosphere of the room did a fair impression of a high school science lab, except the usual suspects of scientific equipment—microscope, beaker, eye-wash station—were replaced by more grown-up characters. Welding equipment, a large boxy contraption with a robotic arm, and an industrial-looking sewing machine. Every tool that Tilly could imagine—and many more she couldn't—hung upon a massive pegboard that covered one wall. At the middle of the room was a table with something large and lumpy and tarp-covered on it.

The scene was altogether curious, but curiosity of another subject got the best of Tilly first. "Hey, Abner, what's in the third room down the hall? With the locked door?" Tilly asked.

Abner and Anna exchanged a glance. "I think that one is storage," he said.

Anna nodded in agreement. "Like I told you," she said with a reassuring smile.

"Well, there—there's something in there that Ranger doesn't like," Tilly said. "Anna saw, he was growling at something behind the door. He doesn't usually do that—growl at things. Ever, really." Tilly patted Ranger, who sat dutifully beside her, on the head.

"Well, there is nothing scary in there," Abner said. Then, looking down to address Ranger, he said, "Only some old science equipment." Abner's mouth opened and parted and twisted as if it was trying to add something of its own accord.

"And," he said. "It is locked. So we know it has to be that. No boogeyman."

"I don't blame him for being scared of science equipment," Anna said, "I have been since freshman chemistry in high school." She smiled and fake-shuddered. Then she looked at Ranger, too, and added, "The worst, right?"

Tilly shook her head. "Must be nothing then."

"Right," Abner said. Then after a beat he clapped his hands together. "So, let us begin."

Abner walked over to the table in the center of the room. He ceremoniously placed his hands on the tarp-covered-lump at the center of the table.

"Tilly, you have joined us at a momentous time," he said.

Tilly once again raised her eyebrows, skeptical of the whole affair. "How's that?" she asked.

"As you have already witnessed in our prototype—"

"Is that what we're calling the thing that attacked me?" She was residually combative.

Abner ignored her and continued, "As you have seen, we are on the precipice of something truly great."

Tilly resisted the urge to roll her eyes, but just barely. She looked at Anna, who was rapt.

"Between Anna and myself, and now you, we will make something that the world has never seen before. A man-made miracle."

In one quick jerk of his hand, Abner pulled the tarp away from the mass on the table, revealing an orange and black and metal and wire monstrosity. The tiger, undone.

"Creation," Abner announced with more than a little drama in his voice. He gave Tilly a moment to soak in the sight of the tiger.

"It's your old friend," he said when she didn't react immediately. "I call him Abraham."

For the second time that day, Ranger began to growl.

Abner heard. "Never fear—soon you two will be good friends." He reached for Ranger's head to give him a pat. Ranger ducked away from his hand.

"I see," Abner said to him. "Well, maybe you will change your mind about us when I program him to play with you." Anna laughed. Tilly did not.

The tiger looked a lot different than the last time Tilly had seen it. It was now mid-metamorphosis; it had shed its skin. The tiger-striped pelt hung half-attached and drooping from a four-legged metal frame. Its exposed insides were a tangle of silvery pieces, sharp metal joints, and wires.

The thing looked almost nothing like a tiger with its pelt askew, exposing the machinery beneath. The only giveaway—besides the four legs—were the eyes, which were in their proper place in the tiger's metal and silicone skull.

Ranger backed away from the group and found a spot under a low table at the back of the room. He kept a wary eye on the tiger.

"So what exactly is my job here?" Tilly asked.

"To help us bring him to life," Abner said. "We need to work out the finer points of how Abraham looks and behaves and thinks. You will work with Anna on his appearance and with me on his behavior."

"What do you mean *thinks*?" Tilly asked. "Isn't it remote-controlled?"

Abner laughed. "No, he is not remote-controlled. This," he said as he pulled the remote from his pocket that Tilly remembered from the first day, "This turns him on and off, essentially. The rest of the time, Abraham here thinks for himself."

Tilly's brow furrowed. The knot in her stomach twisted.

Abner explained. "I have created something—if I may say—truly marvelous. Are you familiar with the concept of artificial intelligence—AI?"

Tilly nodded. "I'm familiar with the concept, but not much more than that."

"That is okay. Abraham has an artificial brain. It is made only of computer chips and circuitry, of course—but it is the software on that computer, the *mind*, that is truly groundbreaking. I have mimicked the neural network of a thinking being, and put that programming into this computer." Abner patted the tiger's head. "And the result? Abraham is artificially intelligent."

"You've mimicked the neural networks? What does that mean?" Tilly asked. She was picturing a diagram of a neuron from one of her biology textbooks in vet school. A cell with a web of filaments reaching out from it in all directions. She did not see how such a thing could be man-made in any way.

"I assume, because of your trade, you have at least a basic understanding of how a brain works."

Tilly's scientific curiosity overwhelmed her, so she ignored Abner's condescension and nodded.

"Right, so you know that our brains, and the brains of all living things that have one, conduct thought by sending electrical signals through webs of cells called neurons. Neurons have filaments called 'dendrites' extending out from them, and those dendrites are covered in synapses that receive electrical signals from other neurons. When the electrical signals—the stimulus inputs—reach a certain threshold, the neuron 'fires.' And another neuron receives that electrical signal in the same way as the first, and the process starts anew, and the signal moves in this way from the brain and down the spinal cord and out through the body through the nervous system, all working toward some ultimate end of moving a muscle, et cetera. It is like a game of telephone, or the firemen bucket brigades of old. One to the next." He gestured with his hands to illustrate.

Tilly nodded, mildly impressed with Abner's ability to sound so pedantic in discussing freshman-level biology.

"So, in the quest to make computers think like humans—or, in this case, tigers—we have attempted to re-create this neural scheme of communication through layers of artificial neurons that send signals to each other in much the same way as biological neurons. These artificial neurons are, of course, not neurons at all—they and their relationships are all represented by algorithms. If the input-driven signals pass a certain threshold, our artificial neuron will 'fire.' And then it is on to the next one and the next one until the computer reaches a solution regarding an action it should take. Do you follow?"

"I think so," Tilly said.

Abner continued, "So an initial input—say, one of Abraham's sensors detects an object in front of his left paw while he is walking—starts a chain reaction in Abraham's artificial neural network that should result in his algorithm-mind triggering the correct motor that will trigger the right mechanism to cause Abraham to lift his left paw over the object."

"Okay," Tilly said, "but how does the computer-brain figure out which, um, 'neurons' should fire to cause a given result?"

Abner's mouth spread wide into a grin. "It *learns*. It learns the correct result given a certain input—like an object in front of a paw, for example."

"It learns? How does it learn?"

"Yes. Right now, Abraham has what we call 'narrow' or 'weak' artificial intelligence. He is essentially trained to do one task: walk around without running into or getting stuck on anything. He has a few other functions that trigger a certain reaction. Like this. Here, look."

Abner pressed a button on the remote, and the half-clad robot started to life. Switched on, a gentle expanding and contracting motion took hold of the tiger, its head bobbing slightly with the movement. It was breathing. Or doing a good impression of it.

From his lookout under the table, Ranger barked at the thing.

"Ranger," Tilly said, without taking her eyes off the animatron. He stopped barking. The rhythmic in and out, in and out of the tiger's chest and ribs—it was hypnotic. She couldn't look away. Tilly walked to the animatron and took a hard look at its exposed insides, searching for where the machine ended, and the life began. She came up empty.

"Now watch this," Abner said. He reached his hand toward the head of the tiger, right for its eyes. When his hand was only a few inches away, in one swift movement the tiger pulled its head back and let forth a snarl. Then, in an instant, it opened its jaw and clamped down on Abner's hand.

Tilly involuntarily screamed. Abner didn't make a sound. And the blood Tilly expected didn't come, and when she looked from what should have been Abner's maimed hand to his face, he was laughing.

"What the fuck?" Tilly said.

Abner pulled his hand out from the tiger's mouth like a magician pulling a rabbit from a hat. "Ta-da!" he said. He turned his uninjured hand backward and forward for Tilly to see.

"Biting an object close to his mouth is one of Abraham's learned behaviors," Abner explained. Then he turned the tiger off and pried its mouth open, revealing its teeth. He took one of the tiger's inch-long canine teeth between his fingers and pulled it forward. It bent in half under the pressure. He released the tooth and it sprung back into place.

"Silicone," Abner explained. "We have Anna to thank for how real they look."

Anna did a little curtsy. Abner was beaming now. Mid-grin, his mouth jerked to the left several times, as if impersonating a skipping movie reel.

"So, how did Abraham learn to bite an object that gets close to his mouth?" Abner asked, rhetorically. "Well, the bite itself is programmed directly. So are other actions, like putting one foot in front of the other, raising a paw to step over something, leaping to clear an object in his path. But I only program the parameters. Then the intelligence comes in to take Abraham the rest of the way. Abraham has had to teach himself *when* to do each of those things as he interacts with his environment."

Abner paused for reaction, but Tilly didn't have an expressible one, only the dark feeling in the pit of her stomach.

"Well," Abner continued, undeterred by Tilly's silence, "that is where the magic happens. I put Abraham's artificial neural network of algorithms—his *mind*, if you will—into a simulation program. I modeled the program with stimuli inputs to mimic those Abraham might encounter out there." Abner pointed out of one of the workshop's windows into the pasture.

"And then Abraham guesses a reaction given his current relationship to his environment. Say he is ten steps away from a log. What does he do? Abraham does not know what to do. So, his algorithm guesses one of his pre-programmed actions at random. And he does this millions of times—remember, this is all happening in a computer simulation—until he happens to take ten forward-moving steps toward the log in front of him, and steps over it. And then, when he accomplishes that task, the simulation is programmed to 'reward' him, by giving more numerical weight to the algorithms that triggered the actions leading up to Abraham stepping over the log. So then, next time he encounters a log, he is more likely to choose to step over it than to, say, roar at it, or try to bite it."

"I see," Tilly said. And she did. Kind of.

"It is much like training a dog, I imagine," Abner said. He looked at Ranger, under the table. "All about positive reinforcement. And time."

"Isn't it fantastic?" Anna asked.

"It's . . . really something," Tilly said.

"Naturally," Abner went on, "we have some finer points to tune. And that is where you come in. I need to know how a tiger might behave in certain situations, given certain inputs, so that I can program the rewards in the simulation accordingly."

Tilly nodded, lost for words. She thought of her mother in the nursing home. "Alright," she said. "Where do we start?"

The trio decided that Tilly would work with Abner on behavior today and with Anna on appearance and function the next. Anna left them then, and went to her own workshop.

For the next several hours, Tilly answered Abner's questions while he feverishly scribbled notes.

When Abner had exhausted his questions, he went immediately to a computer at a standing desk in the workshop and started typing. After a few minutes of this, Tilly asked, "Um—Abner. Are we done for the day?"

"Oh," Abner jumped when she spoke, like someone who thought he was alone. "Yes. Dismissed. Come back tomorrow." The last sentence was not a question. He gave his attention back to his task, barely missing a keystroke as he bid Tilly farewell.

Tilly left, a sense of imposition not lost on her. She speed-walked down the hallway to the exit, suddenly eager to leave. Ranger seemed to share her sentiment and followed close behind.

The feeling of unease that had come over Tilly when she arrived at the workshop now visited her again. Suddenly the whole place seemed hostile to her, like it was eager to spit her out. She decided to let it.

Chapter 8
Cocks and Hens

Bubba had instructed Tilly to pick up her first payment for her new work at his office. His office was near the front of the ranch—the part familiar to Tilly, where the deer pens were. She parked in front of the nondescript building. The building was dark.

Tilly peered through the glass front door. The lights were off, and it appeared that no one was there. She tried the door handle. Locked.

"Fuck," Tilly muttered. She needed that check.

She got back into her truck, the frustration of the moment building at the corners of her eyes. She angrily dried them with the collar of her shirt. Ranger looked at her from the passenger seat. "What do we do, pal?" she asked him. He didn't know.

She thought about driving to Bubba's house on the eastern side of the ranch to hunt him down. But before she landed on a plan of action, she noticed that there was an abnormal amount of activity around one of the common buildings in the lodge area where visiting hunters stayed. She drove there. A truck that looked like Bubba's was parked outside. "Wait here," she told Ranger. He did. Tilly let herself into the building.

Tilly was greeted by a cloud of cigar smoke. An assault on her nostrils, it held the whole room in a hazy feeling of a time long past. The smoke came from a round table in the corner, around which sat several men. One of them was Bubba. The men were playing poker. Tilly rolled her eyes. *Of course they were.*

"Fellas," Tilly greeted them as she approached. They looked up at her. In addition to Bubba, Royce was there, and Sheriff Valdez. There were a few other men whom Tilly did not recognize, and for that reason she assumed them to be hunters visiting from out of town. Wads of cash were piled in the middle of the table.

"Fancy seeing you here, Tilly," Bubba said. He barely looked up from his hand of cards. Royce gave her a sheepish wave. He looked the worse for wear—tired-eyed and disheveled, with the glassy eyes of someone who is very drunk.

"How can I help you, Tilly?" Bubba asked. He was sorting the cards in his hand.

Aware of the others in the room and her vow of secrecy regarding the tiger project, Tilly didn't know how to answer. She began, "Well . . . "

In response to the ensuing silence, Bubba finally looked up at her. She meaningfully raised an eyebrow at him.

"What?" he asked. "Spit it out."

"Can I have a quick word?" Tilly asked. "Outside maybe?"

"I'd oblige you, but I don't trust these sonsabitches not to cheat while I'm away." Bubba chuckled. "C'mon, there's nothin' you have to say that my closest friends here cain't hear."

We both know that's not true, Tilly thought to herself. *Fine.* If Bubba wanted to play that way, Tilly could too.

"Well, I wanted to speak to you in private about this, but alright," Tilly said. "You owe me money. You're overdue on your last invoice, and I need you to pay me."

The talk of debt draped the room in an uncomfortable stillness. Several of the men exchanged glances. Bubba, seeming to realize at last why Tilly was there, pressed his lips together.

"Tha' ain' true," Royce slurred, whiskey dripping from his speech. "I sen' last mon's check myself, I know I did." With his accounting background, Royce kept the ranch books in addition to managing the deer operation. He would have been responsible for paying Tilly's regular veterinary invoice for her work on the deer. Royce turned to Bubba.

"I did," he insisted, afraid that he had messed up, or that Bubba would think as much.

"Shut up, Royce," Bubba said.

Feeling empowered, Tilly doubled down. "You told me to come pick up my check, remember? I figured you were being cheap about postage."

A couple of the hunters chuckled at the barb.

"Alright, alright, that's enough," Bubba said. He rose from his chair. "Wait here," he told Tilly.

"Sheriff, you keep an eye on these cheating bastards while I'm gone," Bubba called over his shoulder as he went for the door.

"On my badge, I swear I will," Sheriff Valdez said in an exaggerated serious tone. He winked at Tilly.

The door closed behind Bubba. After a beat, Sheriff Valdez grabbed Bubba's face-down hand of cards from the table.

"Let's see here," he said, examining the cards. "An eight, a two, and three jacks. Three of a kind."

"Goddamn it," one of the hunters said, throwing his cards down. Another surreptitiously snuck a wad of bills from the cash pile in the middle of the table back into his pocket. Royce stared straight ahead through the whole scene, looking faraway.

"You alright, Royce?" Tilly asked.

Royce was startled back to the present time and place. "Tilly," he said, as if noticing her for the first time. "Wha're you doin' 'ere?"

"Oh, I just thought I might join this little illegal gambling ring," Tilly said, with a pointed look at the sheriff.

The sheriff raised his hands in mock surrender. "You got me."

"Oh," Royce said, and then he lapsed back into his own mind.

"Hey, Sheriff," Tilly said, "any update on the calf from the Wills ranch?"

The sheriff shook his head. "Nothing," he said. "'Course, our efforts have been focused elsewhere. You heard about Rachael Gonzales going missing, I guess."

Tilly nodded. "Any news there?"

The sheriff pursed his lips and shook his head. "I'm afraid not," he said. "We have volunteers searching the county on foot, going ranch to ranch, you know."

"So bad," Royce chimed in. "Just terrible. How could—" He interrupted himself with a shake of his head, and almost looked like he was about to cry.

Tilly ignored him. "Fingers crossed you find something," she said.

Then Bubba came back inside with an envelope in his hands.

"Here," he said, with little ceremony. He handed her the envelope.

"Thanks," Tilly said. "Does it feel good not to be in arrears anymore?" she joked.

"Ha, ha," Bubba deadpanned. "Funny." He was clearly annoyed.

Tilly smiled. "I'll leave y'all to it," she said. "Thanks, Bubba."

Tilly left to Bubba picking up his cards, which Sheriff Valdez had carefully laid back where he left them, and Bubba telling the men, "It's a wonder you boys didn't try to cheat. Sheriff here might make honest men of you yet."

Outside in the cool air, at the end of the long porch that wrapped around the building, a silhouette in the porchlight caught Tilly's attention. It was a woman—tall and thin and, most noticeably, a stranger. Verde didn't get many of those. The woman raised a cigarette to her lips and inhaled; the glow of the tip lit up her face, her hair. A narrow lock of snow-white strands streaked through her otherwise dark hair. It faded to black with the dimming of the cigarette—the same, then, as the rest.

Tilly caught herself staring and moved along to her truck. The stranger noticed the movement.

"Jesus," she said. A hand shot to her chest.

"Sorry," Tilly said. "I didn't mean to scare you."

"It's alright," the woman said. "I get the creeps out here in the middle of nowhere. They almost done in there?" She gestured to the lounge where the men played poker.

"I'm not sure," Tilly said. "Are you waiting for someone?"

"Sort of," the woman said. She took another drag on her cigarette, and Tilly was once again mesmerized by the streak of white illuminated in her hair.

The woman blew smoke, but didn't say anything more. With nothing else to say herself, Tilly got in her truck and drove home.

Chapter 9
The Garden

Tilly's new job at the 999 didn't mean she could neglect her old one; she still saw patients at her clinic two days a week, and made ranch calls the rest of the time that she wasn't at the 999. Today was a clinic day. Tilly had an unexpected visitor.

Sheriff Valdez darkened her office doorway shortly before noon, looking much more grim than he had at the poker game the night before. "Mornin', Tilly," he said. His voice was heavy.

Tilly sat at the cluttered desk in her small office. She was in between patients and catching up on paperwork in the meantime. Tilly invited the sheriff to sit down, and he did.

"We've been seeing a lot of each other lately," Tilly said. "How can I help you, Sheriff?"

Lips pursed, the sheriff pulled a plastic evidence bag from his front shirt pocket. It held something small. The sheriff slid it across the desk to Tilly.

"Royce Wilson found this on his Uncle Augie's place this morning. We have a search party goin' for Rachael Gonzales, you know, walkin' the ranches around town. Today, they were out to Augie's. Royce joined in, of course."

Tilly had a passing vision of a hungover Royce trudging through his uncle's pasture. Then she looked at the thing in the bag. Small, silver, sharp. Covered in dried blood. It was a familiar thing—a scalpel. Not unlike the ones Tilly used regularly in her practice.

Tilly looked at the sheriff, waiting for him to say more. He didn't.

"Okay," Tilly said, sensing he expected her to speak. "So, I am sure you know it's a scalpel," she offered.

"Right. Well, it has a brand name on the handle there, see." The sheriff tapped the scalpel through the bag.

Tilly looked, and she saw. Small script on the handle of the scalpel read *Prairie Veterinary Supply*.

The name made Tilly's stomach drop. "That's where I order my vet supplies," she said.

"I had a hunch," Sheriff Valdez, said. "Know anything about why a scalpel might have been found out on Augie Wilson's ranch?"

"No," Tilly said. "I haven't been out there since I got back to Verde. God, I haven't been out there since high school. I think he sold all of his cattle?" With no animals to treat, Tilly would have no reason to visit Augie Wilson's ranch.

"He did, about a year ago," the sheriff said. "Getting old, you know. But that makes the presence of veterinary supplies out there all the more curious, don't it?"

"I mean, it could be old, I guess," Tilly said. A dog barked in the waiting room of the clinic—her next patient. Tilly fought an urge to usher Sheriff Valdez out of her office.

"Well, no, that's the thing—" The sheriff paused, took a deep breath, then continued, "You sure you don't know anything about this?"

Tilly shook her head, her chest tightening. "Not a thing. You're making me nervous, Mr. Valdez. Should I be worried about something?" Somehow a ballpoint pen had found its way from Tilly's desk into her hand. She caught herself clicking it, protracting and retracting the ballpoint over and over. She forced her hand to put the pen back on the desk.

"We—well, Royce—found this scalpel out in the pasture at Augie's, right near a big bloody mess in the pasture."

Tilly's own blood drained from her face. "A bloody mess?" The image of the bloody calf crept its way back into her mind's eye.

"Yep, blood everywhere. Like something real big bled out."

"What kind of something?" Tilly asked. A cold sweat had sprung on her forehead. A guilty feeling crept up on her, purely by her association with medical supplies.

"Yet to be determined. We sent the blood off for testing."

"And it's just blood, no dead animal or anything?" Tilly caught herself clicking the ballpoint pen again. *Click. Click. Click.* She again forced herself to set the pen down.

"Just blood. And we don't know if it's from an animal." Sheriff Valdez's expression darkened.

Tilly nodded, her mind in a cloud. "I'm confused," she said.

"You and me both," the sheriff said. "Obviously, the scalpel and the blood are related. See the dried blood on it there?" He tapped a finger on the blade of the scalpel.

"Right."

"Well, with that much blood, and a scalpel, and no corpse or nothing—well, all signs point to this being people work, not animal work."

"Like the calf," Tilly said. *Click. Click. Click.*

"Well, sure, maybe. I'm more worried about Rachael Gonzales." The statement ballooned into the room, taking up all available space. Compressing Tilly's chest.

"Oh god," Tilly said, realizing. "Jesus Christ."

"Yeah," said the sheriff. A pregnant pause filled the space between them. "Tilly, I am afraid I have to ask to take your fingerprints."

"*My* fingerprints? Why?" She felt like running out of her office, out of the clinic, to her truck, and driving home.

"I am very sorry about this, Tilly, but procedure dictates that I rule you out as a suspect. Knowin' you have access to this sort of scalpel and all. And you're the only vet in town."

Tilly closed her eyes. "Jesus, you don't think I had anything to do with this, do you?" She scrunched her eyes closed, willing away reality. It lingered anyway. "Anyone can order from Prairie Vet, you know."

"I don't think you had anything to do with it," the sheriff said. "But we just have to be sure. You know how it goes. We'll have to 'print the rest of your staff, too. Anyone with access to your vet supplies."

Tilly did not know how it goes, but she nodded anyway, eyes on the scalpel. "Yeah, okay. Of course."

"Do you have a minute now to come with me? Down to the station? The fingerprinting stuff is there. It's all high-tech now, you know. Computers and scanners and stuff, no ink." He was rambling. Awkward.

"Now? Oh, god—um, yeah, sure," Tilly said. "If it will help."

Sheriff Valdez walked her out. Tilly told her receptionist to hold her afternoon appointments.

"For how long?" the receptionist asked.

Tilly looked at the sheriff. "Thirty minutes?"

He nodded.

"Thirty minutes," Tilly told the receptionist. A cat meowed in the waiting room. Tilly gave a feeble, embarrassed wave to its owner and mouthed, '*Sorry.*'

She followed Sheriff Valdez outside. He opened the passenger door of his squad car for her. Tilly shook her head. "Can I drive separately?" she asked.

He said she could, and she did.

They did the whole fingerprinting business at the sheriff's office. Tilly's face and chest were flushed the whole time. She felt mortified. Ashamed. Guilty?

"We'll have the analysis back in a day or two," Sheriff Valdez told her when they were done.

Tilly was disappointed; she thought she'd be ruled out right away.

"You're free to go," the sheriff added. It hadn't occurred to Tilly that she wouldn't be. She left in a hurry. She was thirty-seven minutes behind schedule for her afternoon appointments.

* * *

Later, in the immutable safety of sleep, Tilly dreamed that she was in a garden, planting flowers made of scalpels. Blade-side-up in the dirt, each scalpel dripped with a different shade of crimson. Tilly kept planting until the garden was filled with rows of pretty red flowers. She wore gloves the whole time.

Chapter 10
The Shadow Man

Tilly returned to the workshop at the 999 the following day. Ranger once again came with her. She went to the workshop the same way as before, but today, instead of the rain, the air held only an unseen repulsive force that warned her away from the place. She felt like the positive pole of a magnet approaching a negative one. The closer she got to the workshop, the greater her sense of foreboding, and the harder it got to keep going. Just when the repulsive pressure became so immense that she didn't think she could continue, the workshop came into sight. Something within her released, or surrendered, or broke; she arrived at the workshop and went inside.

Alone with just Ranger this time, Tilly took her time walking back to the same room they had worked in before, where she assumed she was to meet Abner and/or Anna. Sunlight, through the glass windows and walls and skylights, suspended the whole place in a tincture of light. And this time, the quietness and emptiness of the place struck Tilly not only as disconcerting, but also as deeply lonely.

Tilly passed the door that housed whatever had driven Ranger to growl. And to Tilly's surprise, the door was open. Just a crack. But not locked. Not like before.

Tilly stopped at the door, and when she did, Ranger once again struck up a guttural growl.

Wary, Tilly looked around herself. No one was there. She leaned toward the door and peered through the crack between door and wall. On the other side was darkness. Unlike the rest of the building, there did not seem to be any windows in the room at all. The room was large, enough so that the walls perpendicular to the door faded completely into darkness before reaching the back corners that put a stop to them. Without the benefit of a visible back wall to stop her line of sight, the room seemed to go on forever, stretching infinitely into darkness.

The only light in the room came through the cracked door from the hallway. Tilly pushed it open further to let in more light. She looked up and down the hallway again to ensure she was still alone. She was.

It was the darkness, Tilly thought, that kept her from walking inside. Instead, she stood frozen in the doorway, peering in. With the aid of the additional light and her adjusting eyes, Tilly was able to look further into the room, probing the darkness. She saw tables stacked against the wall, boxes piled neatly in groups. There were shelves lining one wall, holding things of amorphous shape—scientific equipment not readily identifiable to Tilly. Metal and glass and plastic things. Just as Abner and Anna said, the room did appear to be for storage.

Still, Ranger's continued growl underscored Tilly's curiosity. She squinted, scanning the darkest corners of the room, the places on the outskirts of the dim light of the hallway. And at the edge of its reach, the glow suspended a form in the darkness. Amorphous at first, when Tilly focused on it, the form began to take shape. An oval atop a rectangle. The unmistakable head and torso of a man. Tilly's heart jumped to her throat.

Ranger's growl increased in volume, as if he sensed Tilly's sudden fear.

"Tilly!" A voice called. Tilly jumped. The voice came not from the room, but from down the hall. Tilly stepped away from the doorway and looked in the direction of the voice, toward the workshop, to see Abner rushing toward her. She was still holding the door open.

She took a quick glance back into the room, but her eyes had adjusted back to the light of the hallway. Once again, the entire far end of the room was shrouded in uniform darkness.

"I did not know you were here already," Abner said. He forced a smile to mask the displeasure in his voice. He walked to Tilly and reached past her for the knob of the storage room door. He firmly closed it. He made eye contact with Tilly as he did so, and something in his scolding expression made Tilly say "Sorry." Though she did not feel all that sorry.

Tilly tried to think of a reasonable explanation for her snooping, but none came to mind. So, instead she asked, "It there someone else here? Besides Anna?"

"No, it's just us," Abner said. He had forced his voice into a cheerful tone, but Tilly noticed the corner of his mouth jerk down.

"Come this way," Abner said. He led Tilly and Ranger past the workshop where he and Tilly had worked together the first day, with its harsh metal and computer screens. They came to another room down the way.

It was smaller and warmer. Unlike the reflective and cold workshop, this room seemed to capture the light from outside and hold it. It did not have the dark feeling that the rest of the building was bound up in. This was Anna's workshop. Anna was there.

"And now I will leave you in the capable hands of Anna," Abner said. Tilly felt like a child being deposited at the sitter. Abner left.

"Come in," Anna called over her shoulder. She sat facing away from the doorway, her back to Tilly, her attention captivated by something on the table in front of her. Tilly couldn't see what it was from her angle of sight.

Tilly could see the rest of the room, though. And it was full of curiosities. A bookcase against one wall hosted several clay models of various animals, most identifiable to the natural world, but some creatures of myth, like a phoenix. On a table in the corner was a life-style clay sculpture of a tiger's head. *The* tiger's head.

Lying on that same table was an orange tabby cat. Ranger went to him and gently touched the cat with his nose. The cat flicked his tail a few times, but otherwise ignored the dog. Ranger got the message and found a spot to lie down.

On another table was a glass case containing a realistic-looking human heart. Tilly went to it.

Up close, every smooth-muscled artery, aorta, and vein was visible in perfect detail. On close inspection, the heart looked like it was made of some kind of rubber. It was painted or dyed in various shades of red, in such artistry that the whole thing appeared wet and shining. Tilly had seen plenty of hearts—both living and dead—in her practice. This one looked as real as any she had ever seen.

Anna saw what she was looking at. She rolled her chair back from her desk and turned toward Tilly. "You've found my heart," Anna said. "What do you think?"

Tilly didn't answer.

Anna said, "Press the button on the side of the box."

Tilly found the button and pressed it, not knowing what to expect. As soon as she did so, the heart came alive. *Thump-thump, thump-thump.* The heart expanded and contracted in perfect beats of two. It looked so realistic in this movement that seeing the thing outside of a chest cavity made Tilly uneasy. She felt the medical instinct to *do something*, to *act*, even though there was nothing to act upon. It was unsettling.

"What do you say, Doctor?" Anna asked. "Give it to me straight, I can handle it."

Tilly tore her eyes from the heart—they didn't want to leave—and looked at Anna. Anna's expression was genuinely hopeful.

"It's . . ." Tilly said. "It's fantastic. Like magic." She looked back at the beating heart. "I want to—to hold it, for some reason." Tilly laughed at her own absurdity.

"Technology often disguises itself as magic," Anna said. "Or is it the other way around? I can never remember."

"What's it for?" Tilly asked.

"The heart? It's not for anything. I just wanted to make something beautiful, I guess." Anna gazed at the heart lovingly, like a mother looks at her child.

"You *made* it?"

"I did. This is what I do for a living, as you've witnessed with the tiger." Anna swept an arm around the room, gesturing to the models and other artistic curios that dotted the tables and shelves of the workshop. "I specialize in mechatronics."

"Mechatronics?" Tilly had never heard the word.

"It's sort of a crossover between robotics and electronic engineering." Anna looked back down at the heart and ran her finger along the side of its box. "I like to say there's an artistic element as well."

"I'd say so," Tilly said.

Anna's fingers found the button on the box. She pressed it. "Be still my heart," she said, with a wry smile. The heart stopped.

"So you are the one responsible for the tiger's, um—well, the whole thing, pretty much?"

"I built the animatron, yes. But I just make the vessel—Abner programs the, well, the spirit, if you will. Without his programming, the tiger would just be a moving art piece, like the heart."

The word "spirit" grated against an ancient part of Tilly's mind. She pushed it away. Tilly had more questions now than ever—ones she hadn't even thought to think about before.

She started asking. Anna patiently answered. Anna unpacked the process of building an animatron for Tilly. First, she would sculpt the figure out of clay or—for larger sculptures—dense polystyrene foam. Then she would brush fiberglass over the sculpture to form a mold that she could use to cast the silicone skin of her creation.

The body, as Tilly had seen in the workshop yesterday, was made mostly of plastic and metal, and had a lot in common with a real skeleton. Large, flat plastic ribs to support the skin and protect the machinery within; a precisely replicated skull and mandible; appendages with joints in all the right places. Anna used a computer program to aid her in designing the inner mechanics of the things. The animatrons were animated by several motors, large and small, spread throughout the body like organs. The organs communicated through a nervous system of wires with muscles made of hydraulic pumps. The muscles brought moving parts called actuators to life, which could be created in any form to effect any movement imaginable. Anna had both a plastics and a metal 3-D printer to render into existence any piece or part or tangible thing she could dream up.

The artistry came at the end, and there was no common process; every animatron called for different finishing touches. Airbrushing, sewing, pouring resin eyeballs and claws and teeth.

"The truth is in the details," Anna explained. "The animatron is story. You have to get the details right for people to believe the story—to believe the animatron."

Tilly asked a question that had been burning her up since Bubba and Abner had introduced her to the tiger on that first day.

"How do you make them bleed?" She thought of the bright red blood oozing through the tiger's coat.

"That's actually one of the simplest designs of the whole thing. I build in, essentially, a second skin beneath the outer one. And then I put the fake blood in the pocket between the two layers of silicone skin. There's a small tank of blood inside the body. In the tiger, it's near the tail. It's connected to a pump that's activated when the outer skin is pierced. That's how we get the actual 'flow' of the blood."

"Like a heart," Tilly said, looking at the one in the glass box. The similarity of the mechanical systems that Anna described to the biological systems familiar to Tilly both fascinated Tilly and carved out a hollow feeling in her chest. There was a wrongness to the replication, though Tilly couldn't quite pinpoint why. The word *bastardization* sprang to mind.

"Yeah," Anna said, "sort of. So. Is the magic fairly ruined for you now?"

Tilly wasn't sure if Anna meant the magic of the animatrons or the magic of biological life, but she realized that the answer either way was, "Yes. A little."

"It's a bit like the movies," Anna said. "Not so spectacular when you get to peek behind the curtain."

Tilly agreed. There was something she had yet to reconcile about all of this, and she asked Anna about it.

"So how—and I mean this in the nicest way possible, because you're obviously very talented—how did you end up here? In Verde—at the Triple Nine?"

"I ask myself that just about every day," Anna laughed. "Sometimes I think I must have done something wrong in a past life. Or maybe I did something right, I don't know." Anna looked to the table in the corner of the room, where the cat was curled up in a sunbeam by the clay sculpture of the tiger's head. "Maybe the whole thing has been a conspiracy of the universe to bring Tiger and me together."

"The cat's name is 'Tiger'?" Tilly asked, a little smile sneaking onto her face.

Anna nodded. "A coincidence," she said. As if on cue, Tiger jumped down from the table and wandered over to Anna; he rubbed up against her leg. Anna absently reached down to scratch behind his ear.

"But anyway, I understand what you're asking, about how I ended up here," she continued. "You suspect some sort of fall from grace, I bet."

"No—no, I—"

Anna waved her hand good-naturedly, dispelling Tilly's attempt to backtrack. "It's a logical assumption," Anna said. "And, as it happens—it's correct.

"I'll take the liberty of starting the story from the beginning, so you have some sympathy for the main character when we get to the sordid climax." Anna's eyes crinkled with a warmth Tilly found comforting.

Both women moved away from the heart art piece and sat down around a table scattered with sculpting tools and paintbrushes, and freckled with a rainbow of paint smudges.

Anna went on. "My whole life, I always wanted to be a mechatronics engineer. When I was a little kid, my parents took me to a theme park, and they had this exhibit with talking animatron versions of all the former U.S. presidents."

Tilly nodded. She had been to the same theme park.

"The android Abe Lincoln—he was just magical. It felt like he was really in the room, giving a history lesson—like traveling through time." Anna closed her eyes, remembering.

She continued. "I'll never forget how I felt the first time I saw him—it—just so—so *alive*. And I decided then, at that moment, I wanted to make other people feel how I felt, you know?"

Tiger jumped up on the table between Anna and Tilly. He situated himself on a dried splatter of red paint.

"So that's my origin story," Anna said. "From that day on, I knew what I wanted to be when I grew up, what I wanted to do. And I did it. I worked on movies, building mechanical special effects—just like what we're doing here." She gestured around the room.

Then Anna looked down at her hands, suddenly interested in the webbing of veins across the backs of them.

She paused long enough for Tilly to feel awkward. So Tilly encouraged in a soft voice, the one she used in her practice when she had to break bad news: "What happened?"

Without saying a word, Anna rolled up the sleeve of her shirt and turned the crook of her elbow toward Tilly. And Tilly saw what happened. Like a spider's web, the raised whitish scar tissue traced the veins on Anna's forearm from the crook of her elbow to her wrist. Nestled in the crook of her elbow was a cluster of angry red-pink bumps of scarring. Some of the larger bumps had visible divots in the center. Track marks.

"Heroin," Anna said in explanation. "Don't do drugs, kids." She laughed a short and dry laugh and rolled her sleeve down.

"I like to blame the onset of CGI, but I'm the real agent of my downfall, of course," Anna said. "I used to joke that I started using when I saw the movie *Avatar*."

Tilly laughed, and immediately felt bad for it. She stopped herself, and her discomfort must have been evident, because Anna said, "It was a joke, you can laugh. Recovering heroin addicts are allowed to be funny, you know."

"Sorry," Tilly said. "It was a good joke."

"I know," Anna said. "I've worked on this material for a long time.

"Anyway, yeah, my career took a few setbacks when CGI got cheaper and easier and better-looking. And I was going through some personal shit around the same time, and—yeah, well, you know the story. Downward spiral." Anna twirled her finger in the air like a twister to illustrate her point.

"Shit, I'm sorry," Tilly said. She didn't know what else to say.

"Don't be," Anna said. "I've been clean for about a year now, and I'm here." She spread her arms wide. "And I live in this cute little town, and I adopted Tiger, and I've met good people like Abner and you. It's all going how it's supposed to. It always does."

Anna stopped talking, and it was Tilly's turn to say something. "Well, um," Tilly didn't know what to say. She landed on, "thank you for your candor." She had never been artful in these sorts of conversations.

"Yeah, yeah. It's off-putting, I know. And you don't know what to say." Anna smiled at Tilly. "It's part of my recovery—honesty to self and others. It's the only way to be accountable."

Tilly nodded. She thought of the lies she had gotten so good at telling since she had gotten involved with all of this.

"And how did *you* get here, to Verde?" Anna asked Tilly. And then, when Tilly hesitated, she added, "C'mon, I showed you mine—you show me yours."

"It's not that," Tilly said. "I'm just thinking of how to answer. There's two parts, I guess. The first part of the answer is that I am from here. Born here, raised here. But I left for school, of course. Never to return, I thought at the time." Tilly looked down at the paint-splatted tabletop and traced an arc of blue paint with her finger.

"And the second part is how you came back?"

"The second part is how I came back. My mom," Tilly's voice got hooked on the word, and broke right in half. She tried again. "My mom has Alzheimer's. She's in a home here in Verde. My dad died about a year ago, so she was all alone. I came back to take care of her."

"Let the circle be unbroken," Anna said.

Tilly nodded, a faraway look in her eye.

"Do you have other family here, or . . . ?" Anna asked.

Tilly shook her head, suddenly unsure of how the conversation had gotten to this point between two people who had just met. The newness of Anna took shape into a chasm in Tilly's mind. And she was on the opposite side of it from the woman who sat a few feet from her.

Tilly looked around the room, and when her eyes found what she was looking for, Tilly called to him: "Ranger."

The dog dutifully trotted to her. "There you are," Tilly said. She cupped his face in her hands and stroked his ears.

After what felt like length of silence long enough to close the door on the prior subject, Tilly asked Anna, "So—what are we working on today?"

Then they got down to business. Anna had been struggling with the mechanism that would enable the tiger to realistically leap over obstacles. She couldn't get the back legs to spring in the way that a real tiger's legs would spring. When she mimicked the movement of a tiger's back legs, the animatron did not get very far or very high off the ground. She could only mimic a tiger's leap with a much more acute, unnatural bend to the legs.

"Does that matter?" Tilly asked. "The average eye isn't going to know the angle a tiger's leg is supposed to bend at when it jumps."

"Devil's in the details, remember? They might not know what angle the leg is supposed to bend at, but they'll know the tiger looks weird when it's jumping, even if they can't put their finger on why."

Tilly wasn't sold, but she didn't argue. The problem seemed to be one of physics, which Tilly felt was out of her wheelhouse. She said as much to Anna.

"But cat legs are in your wheelhouse," Anna said.

Tilly looked at her, not understanding. "I'm not sure—"

"How does a cat's leg work?" Anna interrupted. "What are the muscles, or the ligaments or whatever, that make a cat able to jump?"

Tilly nodded—slowly, and then more quickly as the understanding dawned on her. In a rush of sudden enthusiasm, Tilly explained the parts and the mechanics in the best way she could. Anna sketched in a notebook as Tilly spoke.

"Like this?" Anna held up her drawing to Tilly for inspection. It was a cat leg—but also, not a cat leg. The shape and form and angles were right, and the parts where there, but the parts were pieces of machine. Ball bearings for joints. Steel rods for bones. Metal cables for tendons.

"Yeah, that looks good." Tilly nodded, even though she found the mechanical replication of the natural body jarring and somehow . . . *blasphemous*. The living body had become sacred to her, in a way, over her years of practice as a veterinarian. Something she could understand to a point, in the functions of all of its organ systems, but that would always hold a mystery that was beyond her—the sum would always be more than the parts, which shouldn't work together to build a living creature to begin with. But somehow, muscles and veins and bones and skin made a thing that could think, and feel, and love. The mystery of the final step—of how it all came together to make something *alive*—was what filled Tilly with reverence for the living body. It shouldn't all work together—shouldn't be so. But it was.

Tilly looked again at the sketch of the mechanical cat leg and thought, *I've created a monster*.

Anna went to her computer. She had design software that let her digitally build out mechanical systems and test them through simulation. With Tilly looking over her shoulder to add a constructive comment here or there, Anna modeled the robotic leg in the digital realm, adding a hydraulic pump here and a motor there. And when she ran the simulation, the leg performed as it should.

Anna shook her head in disbelief. "Now that I see it this way, I don't know why I ever designed it any other way. This is obviously how it should be." Her eyes were trained on the simulated spring of the leaping leg, which ran on a loop on the computer screen.

"Nature knows best, I guess," Tilly said quietly, as if trying to convince herself of the statement, which she wouldn't have questioned only a few weeks before.

And then when she got a sudden sick feeling in her stomach, Tilly said, "I have to go."

"Oh, okay—" Anna started, but before she could turn around from her computer screen, Tilly was out the door. Anna saw only the puff of Ranger's black tail trailing around the corner.

Chapter 11
Beasts According to Their Kinds

The next day, Tilly woke up with the dark feeling still hanging about her. She couldn't stop thinking about the silhouette of the man in the storage room. And because it was Sunday, and her clinic was closed, and she didn't have any ranch calls scheduled, the only way she could think of to run away from herself was to go visit her mother. So she did.

When she arrived at Resthaven, there was a commotion in the common area. Not one of the residents' creation, or even human creation. It was the birds in the glass cabinet. They were mid brawl when Tilly walked in the door, feathers flying in some primal battle over food or a mate or shelter. Tilly walked to the cabinet and watched them.

Distracted by the greater threat of a giant looming next to their enclosure, the birds stopped fighting and flitted off to their respective branches on either side of the cabinet. The aftermath did not reveal to Tilly what the birds had been fighting about. She wondered if the birds had already forgotten, too, what the issue was.

She watched them for a while. They seemed to have made up almost instantly and were all friends again within minutes. Then Tilly made her way down the hall to her mother's room. Other residents called out to her from their rooms, some in words, and others—the unlucky ones from whom time had robbed language entirely—just in primal, animalistic noises. Tilly passed a woman in a wheelchair slowly making her way down the hallway. When Tilly came within range, the woman grabbed her by the wrist.

Too stunned by the sudden contact to do anything, Tilly just looked at the woman. Her eyes were blue, and wide, and had a lens over their light that Tilly recognized as the same there-but-not-there obfuscation in her own mother's eyes. The fog that had come with the Alzheimer's.

"Have you seen my daughter?" the woman asked. "I don't know where she went."

Tilly's heart broke for the woman, lost and wandering in her own mind. She gently took the woman's hand from her wrist and squeezed it. "No, ma'am, I haven't seen your daughter," Tilly said. "But I will keep an eye out and let you know, okay?"

The woman seemed satisfied enough by that answer to let Tilly go. Tilly continued down the hallway to her mother's room. As she neared, she heard a man's voice coming from inside.

Tilly stopped in the doorway, leaning against the frame as she listened to him.

"And there was evening and there was morning, the fifth day. And God said, 'Let the earth bring forth living creatures according to their kinds—livestock and creeping things and beasts of the earth according to their kinds.' And it was so."

The man's voice was captivating.

Tilly watched the back of his head as he continued. "And God made the beasts of the earth according to their kinds and the livestock according to their kinds, and everything that creeps on the ground according to its kind. And God saw that it was good."

Tilly's mind went away with the sound of the man's voice, and for a few minutes she drifted back in time, and she relived scenes of mother-mandated Sunday school and church and Easter dresses. The man had not noticed that Tilly stood behind him, and her mother's eyes were closed. Like the child Tilly conjured in her mind's eye, Tilly was a ghost in the room, unseen.

The man's voice ran through her like a memory, as he continued, "Then the Lord God formed the man of dust from the ground and breathed into his nostrils the breath of life, and the man became a living creature."

After a few more moments in reverie, Tilly came back to herself again, a little embarrassed, if only to herself, of the hold this man and his voice and his words had taken over her. She cleared her throat.

The man stopped speaking and turned, and it was who she had guessed it was. She didn't know him personally but had seen him around town, and his white collar gave him away.

"Father Francisco," Tilly said to the priest of the Catholic Church of Verde. "Hello."

Tilly introduced herself and oriented Father Francisco to her relationship with the old woman leaning back with her eyes closed in her chair.

"Ah," Father Francisco said, "you're the vet. I should have recognized you from the photos." He pointed to several family photos on her mother's dresser. Tilly forgave him for not recognizing the twenty-years-younger teenager in the pictures.

"That's me," Tilly said. She felt her small talk running out of steam already. So she went straight for the hard stuff. "So what's going on here?"

Father Francisco laughed and held up his Bible as a demonstrative. "It's my week to give communion. We—me and the protestant preachers in town—we take turns bringing communion to the folks at Resthaven on Sundays. I'm always the first Sunday of the month. I like to read a little scripture before the ceremony."

"I see," Tilly said. "You know, she's not Catholic. She's Methodist."

"I know, I think that's on her chart." Father Francisco gestured to the clipboard on the wall where the nurses kept notes for each other about her mother's condition.

The joke caught Tilly off guard, and she laughed. "I'm sorry, I don't mean anything by it," she said, "I just thought that non-Catholics weren't allowed to take communion from a Catholic priest. I didn't want you to get in trouble with the big guy." Tilly pointed to the ceiling.

"Oh, that's absolutely right," Father Francisco said. "The trick is . . ." Father Francisco looked at Tilly's mother, who still leaned back in her chair with her eyes closed, then lowered his voice and leaned conspiratorially to Tilly. "The trick is, when they get old and feeble-minded, I convert them to Catholicism when it's too late for them to know any better."

He winked. "Everyone in this place is a Catholic now, including your mom."

Tilly laughed again, and she felt the dark thing in her chest lighten to a shade of gray. "As Catholic secrets go, that one's pretty mild," Tilly said.

And then it was Father Francisco's turn to chuckle. And then he said, "You got here just in time, Tilly." He held up a little chalice. "Who wants wine?"

"Oh, I'm not—" Tilly started, but before she could explain that she hadn't been to church since she left home for college, Father Francisco began the communion ceremony.

He said the usual recitations and gave her mother a communion wafer, which he tried to wedge between the woman's closed lips—she seemed to be sleeping now—to little success. Coming away from her mouth with the wafer, he said, "It's okay, it still counts."

And then he went through the same with the wine, adding his own scriptural flair: "For the life of the flesh is in the blood, and I have given it for you on the altar to make atonement for your souls, for it is the blood that makes atonement by the life."

He looked at Tilly, a little sheepishly, as if she would know any better. "When it's just me and them, sometimes I like to freestyle."

When he reached the point where her mother was supposed to take the Blood, and drink it, Father Francisco, noting that the woman now appeared to be asleep, said, "Maybe next week. That's okay, more for us." He held up the little chalice of wine to Tilly.

"No thanks," Tilly said. "Not for me." And when Father Francisco raised his eyebrows, she said, "I'm not Catholic. You haven't converted me, remember? I don't want to burst into flames and burn the nursing home down."

"Well, okay, good thinking. At least not before I finish giving my converts communion," he said. Then he winked at her again and said, "Give me time, maybe next month."

"I'll mark my calendar to stay away from this place on the first Sundays." Tilly smiled at the priest.

"Fair enough." The priest laughed as he rose to pack his communion paraphernalia. "But all joking aside, it was very good to meet you. I hope to see you again."

Tilly didn't know what to say, so she just nodded. And then he left.

Tilly sat with her mother, who slept the whole time she was there.

* * *

Upon her return home after visiting her mother, something shining caught Tilly's eye on her porch. Tilly came and went through her attached garage, so she rarely had the occasion to traverse her front porch, and she certainly didn't take it in on a daily basis. But the late-morning sun caught something on the porch just right. She stopped her truck in the driveway and went to investigate.

The porch had window boxes for flowers beneath the windows on either side of the front door. Tilly's mother used to keep the planters brimming with flowers for every season; Tilly had let them go. But they were still filled with dirt and the dried brown corpses of the flowers that had lived there last. And now something else.

Among the skeletons of flowers of seasons past, shining silver scalpels stuck upright in neat rows. Tilly's heart pounded.

She ran to the garage, not realizing until she was halfway there what she was looking for. On a shelf was a cardboard box of relics from vet school that Tilly hadn't yet unpacked, mostly because she didn't know what to do with them. She pulled the box down from the shelf with a rattle and a hard *thud* to the floor.

She rummaged in the box until she found what she was looking for: a smaller box of forgotten disposable scalpels. The picture on the front looked like the ones in the flower planters. The box was empty.

Tilly went back to the porch and took in the sight once more. She wondered who had done it, and when. She thought about calling the sheriff and reporting that someone had been in her garage and on her porch. And how long had they been there? She looked around at her neighbors and the street, trying to gauge how easily one of them or a passing car could have seen the scalpels.

She looked back at the scalpels and suddenly a memory returned to her, or a dream, and in her mind's eye the silver blades shone red, and looked like petals, and then, heart pounding, Tilly plucked them from the planter one by one and returned them to the box as quickly as she could.

Chapter 12
The Cuckoo in the Depths of the Woods

Tilly returned to the 999 the following day. The day was cold and clear. She went the usual way to the workshop in the pasture and found Abner outside. The tiger was with him. It stood still, eyes open, and not moving a motor. Turned off, it was an inanimate object—out of place in the living, breathing pasture around it.

When Tilly parked her truck and got out, Ranger did not get out with her.

"Ranger," Tilly said, slapping her hand on her thigh. "Come here."

Ranger didn't come here. Instead, he sank onto his belly on the seat of the truck, and looked warily out of the truck's open door. He could be stubborn sometimes, and he seemed to be having a stubborn day.

"Fine," Tilly said. She tried to respect his autonomy when she could. "Don't come here." She rolled the window down for him.

Tilly went to Abner and the tiger and greeted them both, Abner with a "hello," and the tiger with a pat on its head. Its pelt felt close enough to real fur to fool Tilly—she briefly wondered what Anna's secret for a perfect pelt was, and if it was of a sinister origin—and the head beneath the fur was rock hard. The skin did not have the normal flex and stretch and squish of biological skin. And the tiger was the same temperature as outside—cold. Tilly withdrew her hand almost as soon as she made contact with the thing.

Abner started in on the day's task. He asked, "Do you remember what I told you about how Abraham's AI learns?"

Tilly told him that she did.

He continued, "I have been running simulations for about a week now. And I think Abraham has learned a great deal about what is expected of him. Today, I want to test him in the wild, so to speak." Abner swept his arm around to indicate the surrounding pasture, with its cedar and oak and mesquite trees.

"Okay," Tilly said. "And what exactly am I supposed to help with?"

"Just another set of eyes, I suppose. I am sure you want to see your creation take its first steps."

"I guess," Tilly said, not actually feeling so keen.

Abner had arranged a sort of obstacle course in the clearing, with logs and rocks strategically placed around the prickly pear bushes and small shrubs that always called the clearing home.

"These obstacles replicate the obstacles that Abraham should have learned to navigate in the simulation program."

"Isn't that backwards?" Tilly asked.

"What do you mean?"

"Don't the so-called obstacles in the simulation replicate the ones out here?"

"Yes. Is that not what I said?"

"No, you—never mind." Tilly stuffed her hands in her pockets as the day's chill started to get to her.

Abner held the small remote that Tilly had seen before. He pressed a button. The tiger came to life. Again, Tilly noted the gentle breathing motion that moved its whole body. The tiger blinked.

From his lookout post in the truck, Ranger began to growl.

Abner heard, and turned to the dog and said, "I take it you have not missed your friend?"

Tilly frowned at Abner but did not say anything.

"Alright," Abner said, with some ceremony in his voice. "Here we go."

He pressed another button on the remote. The tiger began to walk forward. Its movements were not quite natural, with brief halting pauses interrupting the fluidity of movement that one would expect from a biological creature that had the benefit of cartilage and ligaments, so that, in movement, the robot looked less like a real animal and more like a stop-motion animation flickering across a vintage silver screen. The sound of it, too, was wrong—it stomped through the grass, every footfall a thud, infinitely louder than the quiet sneaking of a flesh-and-blood predator. Tilly wondered how she had been so easily fooled on the first day, when Bubba had made introductions.

The close-but-not-quite approximation of a tiger was not creepy on its own, exactly, but something about the way it fit into the nature scene around it—disjointed, its imitation of life juxtaposed with the vivid heartbeat of the pasture—made Tilly uneasy. Maybe it was the silhouette of the man in the darkness in the workshop that lingered in the back of her mind, but Tilly couldn't shake a chill.

"Anna is working on giving him more natural movement," Abner said as she watched the tiger trudge forward.

"So, what, it just walks forward in a straight line?" Tilly asked. She had expected more based on all of Abner's ceremony.

"Until he encounters something that he needs to avoid. Then he should step or leap over low obstacles and turn when he encounters larger obstacles, like a tree."

The tiger was approaching the first obstacle it would encounter: a log lying horizontally on the ground, about one foot high.

"Come on, Abraham," Abner said softly, as if giving himself a pep talk, when the tiger was only a few steps away from the log.

Tilly found herself holding her breath, waiting for the tiger to lift one paw, then the others, to step over the log. But it didn't.

Instead, the tiger kept walking in the ordinary way, with steps of ordinary height. When it got too close to the log, the log caught a paw and stopped the tiger in its tracks. The tiger's other three legs kept trying to take steps in their ordinary manner. When the other front paw hit the log, the whole tiger pitched forward, teetering on its stuck front legs while its back legs tried to keep walking. After a few precarious moments, the tiger fell forward and to the side, settling at an angle on the log. Its legs kept trying to move it forward.

"Oh," Abner said. He pressed a button on the remote to still the tiger.

A silence welled as they contemplated the stilled tiger, filled only by the pasture noises of chirping birds and rustling trees. Tilly broke the silence. "Well. What happened?"

"I guess—he must not have recognized the log as something to step over." Abner went to the tiger and tried to right it. He tried to pull it upright by its shoulder but was unsuccessful.

"Can you lend me a hand?" he asked Tilly. She went to the tiger's other side and pushed while Abner pulled. Together, they righted it, but not without some effort—the animatron had to weigh several hundred pounds.

Abner pulled the log out of the tiger's way. "Never mind," he said. "Just a one-off, I am sure. And a learning opportunity." He took a deep breath. "Let us try again."

Abner once again pressed the appropriate buttons to bring the tiger to life and set it to walking. It trudged ahead in the same way as before.

The next obstacle in its path was a prickly pear bush, its paddles reaching about three feet high.

"Let us see what he does here," said Abner. "He will either leap over it or go around it. I cannot be sure."

Abner bounced up and down on the balls of his feet. His mouth took a spin around the lower half of his face. The tiger lumbered closer to the cactus.

"What do you mean, you can't be sure?" It seemed to Tilly that Abner should have a pretty good expectation of what the tiger would do based on its programming.

"Shh," Abner shushed Tilly, waving his hand to silence her.

Tilly rolled her eyes. They watched the tiger. When it was about ten feet from the cactus, it stopped walking and, in a fluid motion, sat back on its haunches for a moments before springing forward. The tiger's powerful motor sent it flying off the ground. Its massive body arced through the air, front paws outstretched. When it hit the apex of its leap and began to arc downward, the flaw in the leap became clear.

"Oh no," Abner said again.

The tiger seemed to accelerate with the assistance of gravity—right into the cactus. Hitting a solid object that wasn't the ground confused its systems, and it arranged itself in a landed position even as it continued to fall, crushing the cactus beneath its immense weight. The failure caused it to hit the ground at an unnatural—even for the robot—angle. It crumpled.

Tilly gasped, feeling like she was watching the crash of the Hindenburg. Abner was silent. The tiger did not move after it came to its final resting place atop the flattened cactus.

Tilly and Abner stood there for a few moments in silence. "That did not happen like it was supposed to," said Abner. The left corner of his mouth twitched up and down.

Tilly nodded, not sure exactly what should have happened, but knowing it wasn't *that*. The tiger had jumped several feet too soon, evidently miscalculating its distance from the cactus, or perhaps overestimating the distance it could leap.

"Can't you just program it to jump when it gets closer to the obstacle?" she asked. It seemed simple enough.

Abner took a deep breath and then let it out in a sigh. "No, I cannot."

"Why not?"

"He has to learn on his own. The algorithm—" Abner paused and took another deep breath, as if trying to find some patience. It rattled its way into his chest. "The machine learning algorithm—it is not something that I can fix by simply adding a few lines of code. I—you see, I do not know how Abraham arrived at this—at this—this thinking that he should jump when he jumped. It is not knowable to me."

"I don't understand," Tilly said. She was staring at the tiger, hoping, she guessed, that she could see some outward manifestation of what Abner was talking about.

"Of course you—" Abner interrupted himself with another deep breath. When he spoke again, his tone was calm.

"The algorithm that is Abraham's mind teaches itself how to act based on a system of rewards that I have devised. It has millions of layers of algorithmic 'neurons,' so to speak, that communicate with each other to recognize patterns in the environment and select actions in response to stimuli.

"The communications within that neural network are just numbers that signal something to each next layer of the network. The numbers mean something the algorithm but mean nothing to me. The artificial mind has assigned meaning to numbers and figures and patterns that I could not understand even if I looked at entire chains of communication between each 'neuron,' layer after layer. The algorithm has devised its own language for communicating within itself." Abner shook his head. "It is a black box to me. It would be nonsense. Just numbers."

Tilly nodded, though she wasn't sure she actually understood. She could tell by Abner's expression that he was also doubtful that she understood.

"Let us try this again," Abner said. "Perhaps he has at least learned to go around objects too big for him to leap over. Then I can triage the issues. Here, help me." Abner went to the tiger, and waited for Tilly, and then together they pushed and pulled and strained the animatron into an upright position. Tilly balanced it in place while Abner turned the thing back on. When it started to life, it assumed its resting position—so it reordered its legs beneath itself, once again supporting its own weight.

From there, via remote control, Abner oriented the tiger to face a large pile of logs that he had stacked as an obstacle. He started the tiger to walking, and it walked forward, toward the pile.

Tilly and Abner watched the tiger approach the pile of logs with bated breath, its every footfall pulling the air around them tighter, until the tension was almost unbearable and pressed in upon the both of them in a vise so constrictive as to not allow even for the slightest exhalation.

When the tiger was just a few feet away from the log pile, and when Tilly was just beginning to see darkness on the edges of her vision, the tiger made a sudden movement to the left. It turned ninety degrees and avoided the pile of logs. Tilly exhaled. So did Abner.

"Oh, thank god," Abner said.

When it turned to avoid the log pile, the tiger turned to face Tilly and Abner nearly directly. It lumbered straight toward them.

Right about the time that Tilly thought of moving out of the tiger's way, and just about when Abner grabbed for Tilly's arm to force her to do so, the tiger stopped in its tracks. It cocked its head toward Tilly and Abner.

And then it cocked it again in the other direction. And again. And soon its head was turning back and forth in an endless ticking motion, steadily like a clock. Abner let go of Tilly's arm as they both watched the tiger's movements. Tilly was mesmerized by the rhythmic motion. It was so unexpected, so divorced from any natural movement of a real animal—the whole scene was surreal. Tilly thought of the head-spinning scene from *The Exorcist* as the tiger's head rotated back and forth, back and forth.

Its head continued to rotate from one side to the other in a steady beat. Then the tiger picked up its front paws in a stand-still march. One, two, one, two. Tilly thought of dancing. It was as if the tiger was trying to hypnotize them. It looked ridiculous; Tilly couldn't look away. Ranger, from his perch in the truck, growled.

Tilly watched in fascination and Abner watched in horror as the tiger's meltdown came to a climax when the tiger began to lift its back paws in a march as well. It did not get past beginning. It raised its back left paw at the same time as its front left paw, and the vacation of support on its left side sent it careening in that direction. It continued to attempt a lopsided march as it fell to the ground.

A beat of silence. Then the noise. It started low, somewhere between a growl and a moan. Then it rose in decibel and tone in a primal crescendo. It was animal. And it came from Abner. What started as an amorphous shout, a pure expression of emotion unbound by the usual structures of diction and phonics, took shape into words as Abner ran to the tiger.

"Goddamn, goddamn it!" He kicked the tiger in the head as if targeting a soccer ball. The tiger's legs were still moving in its horizontal march. Abner drew back for another kick, and another one, and let loose a frenzy of kicking and stomping and shouting and damning. Tilly watched in horror, unsure of what to do. *Daddy says he's not a nice man.*

When the assault finally stilled the tiger, its legs stopping mid-march, Abner turned his anger to himself. He slammed his open palms into his forehead again and again, and he let forth a wail, and threw his head back. He grabbed his hair in clinched fists and began to pull.

After the initial shock at the spectacle, Tilly finally snapped to her senses when the hair-pulling started. She grabbed Abner's wrists and forced his hands down to his sides. She pulled Abner into a vise that was almost like a hug, but for the circumstances. Abner strained against her grip.

With Abner struggling in her forceful embrace, Tilly started to hum. First quietly, then louder. She hadn't planned on humming anything in particular, or humming anything at all, really, but soon enough she was midway into the refrain of "La Vie en Rose." And soon it was the humming, and not Abner's wailing, that predominated the aural field of the clearing.

Abner stopped trying to free himself and suddenly went limp in Tilly's arms. She had no choice, under his weight, but to lower him to the ground. She sat him there and let go of him and stood.

Abner folded in on himself, bringing his knees to his chest and burying his head in them. His screaming had dwindled into quiet sobs.

Tilly backed away from the crying man. Her heel caught on something behind her. The tiger's tail.

Tilly's eyes followed the tail to the body and the mangled and bent appendages. Sometime during the incident, the tiger's silicon skin must have broken, because dark red blood oozed from somewhere and pooled beneath it.

Tilly bent down and started to straighten out its legs. She tried to arrange them in a natural position, but two of them were bent so badly that she couldn't.

"What on earth is going on here?" someone asked from behind them. Tilly stopped trying to reckon with the tiger's damaged head and turned to face the speaker. It was Anna.

"I—I'm not sure, honestly," Tilly answered. Abner still sat on the ground with his face buried in his knees. Every few seconds his whole body was wracked with a sob.

After a stunned second or two watching Abner, Anna noticed the tiger.

"My god," she said. "What happened?" She dropped down to touch one of the tiger's leg joints, which was twisted in a terrible contortion.

"The tiger sort of had a meltdown," Tilly said. "And then—" Tilly glanced at Abner, then said in a low tone, "And then there was another meltdown."

"He does not work," Abner said, raising his head from his knees. His eyes were rimmed in red and puffy. Tears were drying on his cheeks.

His voice was tight, as if the very sound of it was squeezed in a vise. "He is a failure."

Anna squatted down next to Abner and rubbed her hand over his shoulder blades. "I'm sure you can get it into shape in no time, Abner," she said softly.

He shook his head, first slowly, then furiously. "No," he said. "By Saturday? It is impossible." He dropped his head into his hands.

"Abraham does not know how to do anything," he continued, his voice muffled by his hands. "It was when he saw people—when he saw us, his systems failed completely. The simulation did not account for people. I—I . . ." Abner took a big, shaky breath. "I have to start over."

"Maybe we can get Bubba to delay the first hunt," Anna said. "We'll figure it out." Then, more to herself, she added, "I could use extra time to fix this mess too." She looked at the mangled physical body of the animatron.

Abner nodded absently. There was a vacant look in his tear-shined eyes, and Tilly almost felt bad for him. For her part, Anna began to pick up the pieces, now in the literal sense of gathering parts that had broken off the tiger.

"So the first hunt is supposed to be this Saturday?" Tilly asked.

Anna said that it was. "But I am going to ask Bubba if we can push it back a week," she said. "Maybe the weekend after Thanksgiving. How does that sound, Abner?"

He didn't respond. Instead, Abner was staring at Ranger in the truck. Ranger, in turn, was staring loyally at Tilly.

Tilly made eye contact with her dog. Then all at once, the events caught up with her, and the air itself took on such a tension, a pressure, that Tilly suddenly felt like she was underwater. As her chest tightened, she realized that she had to get out of there.

Tilly pulled her phone out of her pocket and thought quickly of a lie. She said, "I need to go. I just got a text about a colicking horse."

The other two accepted this explanation without question, and Tilly found herself speeding away from the workshop in the woods. Then, with Ranger in the passenger seat, she found herself driving the same old way into town.

On the county road leading away from the ranch, Tilly spotted a familiar green truck driving toward her. It was Royce Wilson.

He must have seen her too, because he slowed down. He stuck his arm out of the window and waved for her to stop. She pulled alongside him and they stopped in the middle of the road, driver-side window facing driver-side window.

"Hey, Til," Royce said, beaming his big grin. "You coming from the Triple Nine? Something happen while I was gone? I didn't think we had you scheduled today."

There was a second when Tilly almost told the truth, before she remembered that she had signed not one, but *two* NDAs agreeing to tell no one—Royce especially—about Bubba's special project.

"Oh, um, no, I've been at the Fischer Ranch up the road," Tilly said, thankful that she remembered another ranch on the same rural road as the 999. "One of Mrs. Fischer's mares was colicking." *Liar*, Tilly thought to herself.

"Poor thing. She okay?"

"Yeah." Tilly nodded. "She's good."

"Good," Royce said sincerely. "Listen, I'm glad I caught you. I was wondering what you are doing this Friday—do you want to come hunting with me opening day?" His tone was hopeful.

"Oh," Tilly said, taken off guard. "Well, you know how I feel about hunting, Royce. It's kind of the opposite of what I do for a living, you know?"

"I'm not gonna make you kill anything. I'll do the shooting, if it comes to it. C'mon, it'll be nice to get out in the pasture, watch the deer. Plus, the deer have a fighting chance with me—I'm a pretty bad shot." He winked.

"Royce, I haven't been hunting since I was a little girl. I don't even remember how it goes."

"You don't have to remember anything. Just come and sit in the deer stand with me. It'll be peaceful. We can be one with nature, and all that."

Tilly thought for a minute. And then she resolved that it would indeed be nice to spend the evening outdoors.

"Okay, sure, I guess I'm in," she relented. Royce's grin came back, wider than ever.

"Alright, alright. Well then, I will pick you up Friday afternoon," Royce said.

They parted ways, and Tilly continued on her path into town, the twisting head of the tiger haunting her mind's eye as she drove. She found herself studying the wooded areas on either side of the country road leading into town, searching for a flash of orange.

And before she knew it, she was in a familiar parking lot.

Chapter 13
Tortoises

The sun had just set, and the cold fluorescent glow of the Resthaven Nursing Home's lights was already beginning to seep into the parking lot. Tilly went inside. Rosa sat at the nurse's station. "Hello, Tilly," Rosa said when she spotted Tilly approaching from down the hall. And then, "Oh, you don't look so good," when Tilly got closer.

"It's been a long day."

"You look like it. Everything okay?"

Tilly took a moment before she answered. Then she said, "Yeah, just had a tricky animal situation today."

"At the Triple Nine? You work out there for Mr. Skinner, right?" Rosa asked. Tilly's mind, still occupied with the hypnotic head-tilt of the tiger, immediately went to her work with Abner and the animatrons, and her stomach dropped. Did Rosa know about the animatronics operation? Had she overheard Tilly talking to her mother, somehow? Tilly certainly hadn't said anything. Had her mom? No, surely not—she didn't think the old woman could possibly have retained anything she had said about the animatron project. The price tag of disclosure from her nondisclosure agreement flashed through her mind. She took a beat too long to respond and Rosa noticed.

"Don't look at me like I caught you with your hand in the cookie jar. I was just guessing. I know you work on the deer out there, mija."

"Oh." Tilly laughed off her awkwardness. Of course Rosa was talking about the deer. "For a second, I thought you had been following me or something, Rosa."

"No, are you kidding? I see enough of you here!" Rosa laughed her hearty laugh. "I hope you got the animal problem worked out."

"We'll see," Tilly said, thinking of the bloodied animatron, mangled on the ground, and Abner in shambles. Not very "worked out."

"I bet you did. You're the best vet in town."

"I'm the only vet in town."

"I know—so I coulda said you were the worst vet in town, but I didn't!"

"To be determined, I guess," said Tilly. She changed the subject, eager to stop thinking about the 999. "Anyway, how's Mom today?"

"Not so good, in her mind. She ate good and everything, but she's having a cuckoo day."

Tilly sighed. "Seems like we've been having more of those lately."

"Yeah, it must be the weather, mija. Change of the season."

"Maybe that explains all the other crazy stuff that's been happening around here, too," Tilly said. Her mouth pressed into a thin line. "Well, I'll let you get back to work. I'm gonna go say hi."

"Okay, you be careful out there with those crazy animals, Tilly."

"I will, Rosa," Tilly said. As she walked to her mother's room at the end of the hall, she wondered if Rosa was talking about the actual animals she worked with, or the people. Could be either; could be both.

The fluorescent lights of the nursing home hallway pulsed and buzzed, and the lemon-smell of cleaning solution overwhelmed Tilly's nostrils. She wished she could turn her senses off.

Tilly found her mom in her throne of a recliner, rocking slowly backward and forward. She looked up when Tilly walked in, but her eyes gazed right through Tilly into another time.

"Hi, Mom," Tilly said.

"Ruth!" the old woman greeted her. "You have some nerve coming here, missy." Tilly wasn't positive who Ruth was, but the year-crossed wires of her mother's mind often projected Ruth's image onto Tilly.

"Why, what did I do this time?" Tilly asked, dutifully playing along, as she always did.

"Oh, don't you play dumb with me. You know exactly what you did." The old woman's voice boiled with sincere anger.

"I'm sorry, I don't. Remind me?"

Her mother sat in silence a moment, thinking. Then confusion clouded her face, her brows knitted, and the corners of her mouth tugged downward into a frown. The anger seeped from her eyes, leaving behind a lost look. "I don't remember," she said.

"Oh, well, whatever it was, I'm sorry." Tilly placed her hand over her mother's, trying to anchor her drifting mind. Her mother's hand was cold, the tissue-thin skin a topography of raised blue veins and bumpy scabs.

"How are you feeling today, Mom?" Tilly tried to redirect her mother's attention from her forgetfulness. Her mother didn't always realize when she couldn't remember things—she often lived blissfully on another plane of existence. But when she did notice her own confusion—that she was a stranger to the world around her, an alien visiting from the world she knew in her mind—the realization broke her spirits. It also broke Tilly's heart.

"Oh, just fine, I guess." The old woman looked down at Tilly's hand on hers, as if wondering where it came from. Tilly patted her mother's hand, then took her own hand back, to minimize her mother's confusion.

"Has the food been okay?" Tilly asked. She watched as the soft confusion in her mother's face hardened into conviction, setting again in the certainty of her own reality. In an instant she passed through the veil between this world, where her daughter sat before her, and the personal universe of her mind, where time and place were unstable fluids.

"Not bad for jail food, I guess. But the sheriff makes me eat peas." She wrinkled her nose and stuck out her tongue.

Tilly couldn't help but smile. "Are you in jail?" she asked.

"Yes."

"What for?"

"Stealin' that goat from Mrs. Turner's field."

"Well, if that's all, I bet your sentence isn't that long, just for stealing a goat. You ought to be outta here in no time."

"I don't think I'm ever getting out of here."

The inadvertent truth of her mother's words gut-punched Tilly into silence. *You're probably right*, she thought. Aloud, she said nothing. She couldn't.

Instead, she changed the subject again. "I've had quite the day." She looked over her shoulder to peer out into the hallway, double-checking there was no one there—no one to hear her. The coast was clear. She leaned forward toward the old woman, who appeared to be blissfully absent, her eyes closed now. Tilly said, quietly, "We live-tested the robot tiger for the first time today, out at the Triple Nine."

"Is that right?" her mother said, a socially appropriate note of curiosity in her voice—she had picked up on Tilly's conspiratorial, almost gossipy tone. Old social instincts die hard. Tilly was almost fooled into thinking that her mom was really there, really listening to her story. But she knew better.

"Yeah. It didn't go very well. The tiger—well, it just melted down. It didn't really work at all."

Tilly launched into the whole story and told her mother about the tiger's malfunctioning and Abner's subsequent breakdown. The old woman listened in silence, dutifully nodding when she thought she was supposed to.

When Tilly told her how Abner had kicked the animatron, her mother said, "What a rascal." Her eyes were closed, and she rocked back and forth in her recliner, a peaceful expression on her face.

"Yeah," Tilly concluded. It felt good to get the day off of her chest, even to someone who probably already forgot what she said. Or, perhaps, *especially* to someone who already forgot what she said.

In the few moments of ensuing silence, Tilly's thoughts welled up in her mind again, ballooning, pressurized, into the sides of her skull. In a continued effort to get them out of there, she said quietly, "I haven't been sleeping well lately."

Her mother didn't say anything. "I think I'm sleepwalking again," she said. Quietly, confessing. "Like I used to in high school."

"Uh-oh," her mother said absentmindedly.

"Yeah," Tilly said. It felt good to say it out loud. "I had this dream about scalpels the other night, and then—" Tilly took a deep breath. She wasn't sure how to explain the scalpels in the flowerboxes, and so she didn't.

Tilly and her mother shared silence for a few minutes. Tilly heard the beep-beep-beep of another resident's activated call button down the hall, summoning a nurse.

Then, Tilly's mother spoke to fill the silence. "Those damn Mennonites came to get me again."

Tilly couldn't help but let out a laugh. It grew from a chuckle to an all-out howl, as the tension of the day lifted out of Tilly with every increase in decibel. Her mother laughed too, thinking that she was supposed to.

Tilly sat with her mother for a while longer, both contently absorbing each other's presences, without really speaking each other's languages. Tilly left the old woman with a hug and a kiss on the cheek and a promise to come back soon.

Chapter 14
Deer God

Friday morning came, and Opening Weekend was upon Verde all at once. The town was busy with hunters that had streamed into the town over the prior few days.

A cold front had blown in overnight, bringing with it an unseasonably early freeze and striking up a sense of atmosphere for those who would huddle in frigid deer blinds all weekend.

Tilly had tried to forget about the workshop and the tiger and the shadow man and the scalpels and her fingerprints as she had finished her week focused on her veterinary work. And she was almost able to.

Royce arrived right on schedule Friday afternoon. After saying hello and standing outside for a few freezing moments too long, Tilly loaded herself into the passenger seat of his truck. Royce's rifle, in its case, took up most of the back seat. The accompanying box of bullets glared at Tilly from next to a pair of binoculars.

"Is it weird?" Royce asked as Tilly slid into the passenger seat. Tilly looked at him, images of scalpels in flowerpots floating to the front of her mind.

Royce must have noticed her confused look. "Weird to be back, I mean." He pointed at her house.

Tilly looked at the house, as if checking to make sure she knew what he was talking about. "Um, yeah. Yeah, it is, honestly."

"I can't imagine moving back into my parents' house," Royce said. "I mean—no offense. I just mean, it must be hard."

It *had* been weird. The house had not changed much since Tilly moved out to go to college, but it felt so different now. Alien, almost, like she hadn't spent the first eighteen years of her life there. It struck Tilly, just then, that the hollow feeling of the house was the absence of its heartbeat—her parents.

"Well, the rent is cheap, and I don't have any roommates, so . . ." Tilly let the topic die with the sentence.

Royce started to drive. Johnny Rodriguez's "Ridin' My Thumb to Mexico" played softly from the truck radio. Tilly looked out the window, watching the cactus and cedar trees zoom past.

"Where are we going, anyway?" Tilly asked after a while.

"My Uncle Augie's place," Royce said, "up north of the old cemetery on County Road 2676. He always lets me get a doe on opening weekend to fill up my freezer for the year."

"That's nice of him," Tilly said. She blew air into her hands, trying to warm up. The truck's heater, it seemed, couldn't muster the energy to do much good against the cold afternoon.

"How is Augie?" Tilly asked. She had fond memories of drunken high school parties at the hunting cabin on his property, hosted by Royce. Beer pong, bonfires, first kisses. As blurry as those memories were, they were good ones.

"He's old."

Tilly surprised herself by laughing. "God, time just doesn't stop, does it? I know how that one goes." She looked over at Royce. Time hadn't spared him either—fine lines spanned his forehead and gathered at the corners of his eyes. Tilly knew her own face had the same wear.

"It sure don't," Royce said. He looked at Tilly, met her gaze briefly, then quickly trained his eyes back on the road ahead. "But he's doing okay, all things considered. You know my Aunt Sharon died about two years ago."

Tilly looked at her lap. "Yeah, I heard about that when it happened. I'm sorry. Sorry to miss the funeral, too." Tilly had felt even more guilty about missing Royce's aunt's funeral when Royce dutifully attended Tilly's father's.

Royce waved his hand in the air to dismiss Tilly's concern. "Cain't go to every funeral," he said. "But since then, ol' Augie's had a bit of a downhill health slide. You know how that goes."

"Yeah," Tilly agreed. She did. Her mother's Alzheimer's hadn't fully shown its face until after her father died, as if her mother had been depending on him for her own vitality; maybe she had.

"I been helping him out more around here, you know, mending fence, that kind of thing. He's alright."

"He's lucky to have you," Tilly said.

"Well, he basically raised me. With Dad . . . how he is, and all." Royce cleared his throat.

"Yeah. Yeah, I know."

Silence filled the truck cab again. Tilly's mind swirled with memories of old times—younger times—and thoughts about aging, and how time really isn't fair, is it?

"You alright, Til?" Royce asked after a while. "You seem . . . I don't know. Not quite yourself."

Tilly's throat tightened without warning. "Yeah," she croaked.

She felt Royce's eyes turn upon her, boring into the side of her head. Tilly looked out the passenger-side window. The county road twisted its way around trees and ranch property lines. The cold air outside seemed almost visible in its crispness, bringing everything it touched— the prickly pears and the bur oaks, the cedar trees and the bluestem grass—into sharp clarity. Until Tilly's eyes welled to blur it all.

"Til," Royce said.

Tilly was suddenly overwhelmed with the weight of it all. She wished she could go back in time, and wished in that past life she was driving out to the ranch with Royce, and a healthy, young Uncle Augie would be there—the Augie she remembered—and she would not know a thing about animatronic wildlife or have ever set foot in Resthaven Nursing Home. But time's burden could not be undone.

Tilly took a deep breath that was unexpectedly shaky. "I'm just—I'm so *tired*," she said. It was all she could think of, but it seemed right—it was true.

Royce gave her a hard look. "It's a stressful time, with your parents—your mama. I think losing a little sleep is a pretty natural response."

Tilly nodded and sniffled. Her nose had started to run. "Yeah," she said. But the tired she felt wasn't the sort that sleep could fix, she was afraid.

"I'm sorry, though," Royce said. Tilly nodded again, wiped a tear that snuck over the rim of her bottom eyelid, and sunk back into silence.

Tilly knew they had arrived by the sign on the ranch gate:

MEMBER

Texas & Southwestern

Cattle Raisers Assoc.

August J. Wilson

Tilly got out of the truck to open the gate so Royce could drive through it. The chain that held the gate closed felt like shards of ice in Tilly's hand. She danced from foot to foot as she held the gate open, then ran back to the warmth of the truck as soon as she closed the gate behind it.

They drove some distance through the pasture, following barely cleared paths—they could hardly be called roads—that were marked only by the continuous parallel strips of bare rock and dirt where truck tires had stripped the earth of its grass through years of tread over the same route. They wove through the nondescript landscape—every twist a prickly pear bush, every turn a cedar tree—until they arrived at a clearing. On the edge of the clearing, there was a hunting blind. In the middle of the clearing, there was a deer feeder.

Royce parked the truck behind a clump of thick cedar trees. He freed the rifle from its case and shoved a handful of bullets in his pocket. He handed Tilly the binoculars. "I only have one pair, so we'll have to share," he explained.

When they left the truck to sneak over to the deer blind, Tilly glanced back at it, surprised at how well the green truck blended into the stand of cedars. She could barely see it through the trees' sprays. The deer wouldn't be able to see it either.

The hunting blind was old and clearly hand-built. It was made from plywood scraps, odd and misshapen pieces hewn together against all odds to form a cohesive little structure. One wall of the blind included a reflective orange highway sign that read "ROAD WORK AHEAD."

Royce noticed Tilly noticing the sign. "You know ol' Augie used to work for the highway department," he explained. "He purloined some materials from the State to build that one." His voice was hushed; to avoid spooking the deer, they wouldn't speak at normal volume again until the hunt was either ended by a kill or the sun's evening retirement.

The blind was barely big enough for two people, the space made tighter by the hilariously unexpected presence of a large, upholstered recliner.

"What an elegant touch," Tilly whispered to Royce.

"Augie values comfort, nothin' wrong with that. You can take the recliner. I'll sit here." Royce produced a folding chair from behind the recliner and squeezed it between the recliner and the opposite wall. Tilly looked at the musty recliner—it looked like it might have been blue, once upon a time—and saw several places where something had chewed right through the upholstery fabric to the cushioning beneath.

"Oh no, you're the hunter, you should have the recliner," she whispered. "I'll take the chair." She shuffled past Royce and into the clean-by-comparison folding chair before he could argue.

"Suit yourself," he said, settling into the old recliner. He loaded the rifle, flipped the safety switch on, and propped the gun in the corner of the blind. "Feeder goes off at five o'clock."

They sat in silence, both watching the landscape out of the blind's narrow window, waiting for something to happen. The deer feeder, a metal vessel supported by a tripod, held court in the center of the clearing. The scene was tranquil, and the strong scent of cedar trees was nostalgic to Tilly and calmed her racing thoughts, even though she was so cold that she thought her nose might fall off. The tension in her shoulders eased. Her jaw relaxed—she hadn't realized she'd been clenching it.

After a few minutes sitting in the cold, Royce produced a flask from his jacket and passed it to Tilly. She looked at the flask, then looked at Royce. His eyes twinkled like he had just let her in on a secret. Tilly's mouth crept into a smile. She took a swig from the flask—whiskey—and passed it back. The liquor set her chest on fire for a few blissful, warm seconds. Tilly had a flash of déjà vu, or something like it. How many shots had she taken on Augie Wilson's property over the years? Several liquor bottles' worth, she guessed.

Tilly raised the binoculars to her eyes, searching for any sign of life in the pasture around them. A family of squirrels waited at the edge of the brush, patiently watching the deer feeder, waiting for it to give up its contents. Several turkeys, all hens, sat perched in one of the oak trees that surrounded the clearing. These non-deer animals also enjoyed the delicacy of dried corn. A few minutes before 5:00, a first-year whitetail spike—a buck with the undesirable feature of antlers that don't branch or fork—crept out of the brush to wait by the feeder. A doe soon joined him.

All of the creatures—including Tilly—jumped when the feeder sprang into action at 5:00 sharp. It released its contents from a spinning wheel on its underbelly, flinging dried corn in all directions. The sound of it was jarring. Like a dinner bell, the noise of the feeder summoned deer from the brush. Some ran. The ones that walked seemed to materialize out of nothingness, their brown bodies almost invisible, camouflaged, in the brush and its shadows, until suddenly they were there in the clearing. Their fluid movement, their grace, made Tilly think of the simulated tiger's leg, jumping again and again on Anna's computer screen. She shook the memory away.

There were probably ten or twelve deer around the feeder, picking corn from the ground. The few bucks that arrived had relatively small racks of antlers, especially compared to the massive horns of the selectively bred bucks at the 999.

Tilly elbowed Royce and handed him the binoculars. "Lots of options," she whispered in her quietest voice.

Royce slowly raised the binoculars to his eyes, cautious against any sudden movement that might startle his prey. He looked through the binoculars for a few moments, then he lowered them and handed them back to Tilly.

"Pick one?" Tilly whispered.

He nodded. But he didn't reach for his rifle. Instead, he sat there and watched the deer. Tilly didn't ask what he was waiting for, and instead joined him in quiet observation.

A social opera unfolded before her, rich in its complexity. Two does fought over something not entirely clear to Tilly—they reared onto their hind legs, each swinging their front legs wildly at the other, in a slapping fight that looked almost human. Their hooves hit each other in *click, click* noises. Two more does arrived in the clearing, one large and one smaller. After the two new arrivals ate for a while, the smaller one ducked under the larger one and began to nurse. And then it looked much smaller to Tilly, and she saw it for what it was—a fawn, mostly grown.

Yet another doe, who had arrived at the feeder alone, kept a wary eye on the deer blind where Tilly and Royce sat. At one point, Tilly couldn't contain a sniffle—it was so cold, and her nose was running—and the doe alerted at the noise, looking right at the blind, with ears pricked forward, eyes wide. *Caught us.* The doe stomped the ground in warning to the others. Her stare at the deer blind felt accusatory, and Tilly couldn't help but think she was right to accuse.

For a brief moment, Tilly thought about coughing, or clapping, or drumming her hand on the inside of the deer blind wall—anything to make noise, to scare the deer away. But she felt Royce beside her, and she stopped herself. She lowered the binoculars, half hoping the wary doe would spot the movement through the window of the blind and run for cover. But she didn't.

And then after a few more moments of waiting, when Tilly couldn't bear to watch the deer any longer, knowing that one of them was in its final moments—they were so *alive*, so oblivious—Royce reached for his rifle. He slowly inched it out of the open window of the blind, resting the barrel on the sill and the butt against his shoulder.

"Cover your ears," he whispered, as he turned the safety switch of the rifle off. Tilly did. She closed her eyes too, for good measure. She preemptively winced, bracing for the loud sound of gunfire. She could think of few noises that she hated more.

A few long, silent seconds stretched out while Tilly sat there in her self-imposed darkness. Then, *CRACK.*

The sound of the gunshot ripped through the air and into Tilly's mind; her hands over her ears didn't do much good to stop it. Tilly opened her eyes just in time to see a large doe stagger a few steps, then drop to the ground. She wondered which one it had been—one of the fighters, the watcher, the mother? But Tilly couldn't tell and no longer had the context of the rest of the herd to make a determination—the other deer had already disappeared back into the brush.

"Got her," Royce said at normal volume. He shucked the shell casing that had formerly held the now-used bullet from the barrel of the rifle.

"Let's go get her," he said.

They climbed out of the blind and walked over to the lifeless deer on the ground. The outside air felt somehow even colder now. Tilly shivered.

When they got close to the doe, the deer moved. Though collapsed on her side, she jerked her head and moved her legs as if trying to gallop away. To Tilly, she looked like the fallen tiger, marching on its side.

"Goddamn it," Royce said. "Still alive."

"Jesus," Tilly said.

The deer continued to struggle on the ground as blood spread from the wound on her shoulder. She had an illogical urge to help, to try to fix it, even though the only thing that could help the doe now was to end her suffering.

Royce pulled a pocketknife from his back pocket and snapped the blade open. He lowered his knee onto the deer's shoulder, holding her down with his weight. Tilly watched in silence. She wanted to turn away, but something in her made her keep watching—to bear witness. Royce grabbed the doe's head to steady it, placed the knife at her neck, and pulled it across her throat in one fluid slash. The doe went still.

"There you go, ol' girl," Royce said softly, "Out of your misery." He laid her head back on the ground and rose.

Royce looked at Tilly and must have seen the sadness on her face. "You don't approve, huh?" he asked gently.

Tilly shook her head. "It just makes me so sad for them."

Royce nodded. "I know." After a moment or two, he brightened and said, "I know what will make you feel better. Something Augie used to do when I would hunt with him."

Royce removed his beanie and took Tilly's hand. His hand was warm. "Let's bow our heads," he said in an exaggerated pontifical voice.

"Dear God," he began. "That's d-e-e-r god," turning to Tilly, in an aside, he said, "I don't want them to get our wires crossed." He pointed upward. Tilly smiled.

"Great Spirit, Universe, or whoever else may be listening, we thank you and this deer for your sacrifice so that we may eat. Amen."

"Amen," Tilly repeated, forcefully.

"Feel better?" Royce asked.

"A little," Tilly said, though she wasn't so sure.

"Good," Royce said, and he got to work in the aftermath of his kill. He dragged the deer away from the feeder, into the brush and field-dressed it—gutting the deer to remove its organs—leaving the innards in the brush for the buzzards to find.

They drove back into town. The sun sank below the horizon as they hit the county road, and by the time they reached Royce's house the only thing illuminating the sky was a smattering of stars.

Royce hung up the deer carcass in his garage to let the blood drain from it, to prepare it for butchering. The cold night air would keep the carcass fresh until the morning.

Royce left Tilly alone in the garage for a moment while he went inside to clean up so that he could drive her home.

Tilly stared at the dead deer, hanging upside down from its back legs. She was absorbed by the form of it. She looked at the angles of the body, the juncture of the joints, the lines of the muscle, through a re-newed lens. She saw these things, for a moment, as machine. And in the empty chest cavity, Tilly saw a beating, rubber, human heart in a glass box. And the *drip, drip, drip* of the deer's blood into the bucket situated beneath it was propelled by a hidden pump near the tail. Anna's voice in her head. *Is the magic fairly ruined for you now?*

Tilly didn't know how long she stood there. She was pulled from her reverie when Royce gently said, "Ready to go?"

Tilly jumped. She had thought she'd been alone. Alone with the deer. And the *drip*, *drip*, *drip*.

Chapter 15
The Elephant

The next morning was supposed to be the first tiger hunt. Tilly called Bubba to ask if he'd decided to postpone the hunt given the difficulties they'd had with the tiger on the test run.

Bubba answered the phone with a gruff "Yeah?"

"Good morning to you, too," Tilly said. "We still on for today?"

"Why wouldn't we be?"

Tilly paused, processing his question. She could think of a million reasons why they wouldn't be. The glitching tiger. The glitching Abner. "Did you talk to Anna? Did she tell you what happened?"

Bubba audibly huffed. "That damn hippie? She sure as hell did," he said. "Commies just never want to work. We're doin' it."

Tilly rolled her eyes. She said, "It was pretty bad the other day, Bubba."

"It'll be fine," he said. "Be here at ten." And that was the final word on the matter.

Tilly went to the diner for breakfast before the hunt. A flier of Rachael Gonzales, the missing girl, greeted her on the diner's bulletin board—her hair curled, eyes shining forever with the light of the camera's flashbulb, the word "MISSING" typed across the top of the flier.

The usual suspects were there—Mr. Schmidt presided over a table of older men and Royce. Mr. Schmidt waved Tilly down to sit with them. She did.

The men spoke of the usual things. Theories on the missing girl. The price of cattle. How many hunters had come in for opening weekend of deer season. Who had killed the biggest buck in the county so far (the pen-raised deer didn't count). Mr. DeLeon thought he saw a bobcat last Wednesday. Mr. Nunley's grandkids were in town. The Parsons were getting a divorce. It might rain next week. They sure needed it.

Tilly sipped her coffee as she took in the town gossip. She contributed what she could about her encounters with the mutilated calf. They all had theories on that.

"Gotta be aliens," said one of the old men. Several agreed with him.

"That's what I've been saying," Royce said. He told them about the scalpel he had found, and the pool of blood. Tilly had been trying not to think of it.

"Do you think aliens would use a scalpel?"

"Probably not one from Prairie Vet Supply, that's for sure," Royce said. The men all looked at Tilly.

She raised her hands in a show of surrender. "Hey, don't look at me. I don't know anything about that."

But the men did look at her, for a beat too long, and the heat rose in Tilly's cheeks. Then Mr. Schmidt broke the silence. "It's well established that the aliens use lasers to do their cattle mutilations," he said in redirection. "And there wouldn't be blood."

"Maybe it's a cult or something, doing animal sacrifices. Like Satanists."

"Or maybe it's just kids?"

"What's the difference?"

The old men all laughed. Just then Sheriff Valdez walked in. Mr. Schmidt waved him to the table as well. It's not an invitation to be refused, so the sheriff obliged.

"Any updates on the girl?" Mr. Schmidt asked.

Sheriff Valdez shook his head. His eyes drooped. And—though he wasn't a young man—Tilly thought he looked even older now than when she had seen him just a few days before.

"Search parties haven't turned up anything. Nobody has heard from her. She's just gone," he said. Defeated. "Her poor parents." His voice was stretched out with the tension of the ordeal, and he looked down at the Formica tabletop.

"A crying shame, sure enough," Mr. Schmidt said softly.

After a few seconds of silence, Royce asked, "Sheriff, you get any good out of that scalpel I found?"

Tilly's stomach dropped.

The sheriff sighed. "Well, your fingerprints were on it because you picked it up at the scene, like a dumbass."

Royce turned red. "I said I was sorry about that. Wasn't thinking."

Instead of elaborating, the sheriff turned to Tilly. "Tilly, can I have a word outside?"

Now Tilly's stomach did a somersault. "Of course," she said. She followed him outside.

He led her to his squad car, which was actually a truck with a blue-and-red stripe down the side and police lights on the roof. Tilly had a brief fear that he was going to put her into the back of it. He didn't. Sheriff Valdez leaned against the truck and took a deep breath. "Tilly, someone else's fingerprints were on the scalpel."

Tilly raised an eyebrow. "Whose?" she asked, though she already sensed the answer.

"Yours."

The ground wobbled beneath Tilly. She put a hand on the truck to steady herself.

"Any idea what that's about?" Sheriff Valdez asked her. He looked at her kindly, with a furrowed brow.

Tilly shook her head. "No," she said. "None at all." She thought for a minute, pondering how it could have happened, and thinking of the scalpels in the window boxes. Sheriff Valdez pulled a can of snuff out of his back pocket and tucked a wad of it between his teeth and lower lip.

"Maybe it was a used scalpel?" she offered. "One that I had already used at the clinic. We use secure sharps boxes to dispose of things like needles and scalpels and syringes, but maybe one slipped through the cracks, and someone got it out of the trash."

"I was thinkin' something like that. Do you have cameras at the clinic?"

Tilly told him that she didn't. He asked her some more questions, and she did her best to answer them. Tilly could feel the group of old men watching the pair of them talk through the diner window. Tilly pulled her coat tighter around herself and wished she could disappear into it altogether.

"So what does this mean?" Tilly asked. "Am I a suspect?"

"Suspect?" The sheriff looked surprised. "Should you be?"

"You said you were taking my fingerprints to rule me out. And now my fingerprints were on the scalpel. So it sounds like I am not ruled out."

"Ah, right—"

He was interrupted by a truck driving past the diner, which gave a friendly honk, and a man yelled out its window, "Hey, Sheriff!" Valdez waved, a reflexive smile temporarily overtaking his grim expression. Then it fell away, and he was back with Tilly.

"Right," he continued. "We got the test results back on that blood where the scalpel was. Deer blood. Not human. So no crime, we don't think. Other than killing a deer out of season, maybe, or trespassing on Augie Wilson's land."

Tilly was overwhelmed with relief. "Thank god."

"But it might be related to that whole thing with the Wills calf, which was definitely a crime, so we still need to get to the bottom of it if we can. Weird shit going on in this town lately." He spit brown tobacco juice onto the ground.

"You're telling me," Tilly said. "Let me know what I can do to help." The sheriff said he would.

As Tilly went back inside to pay her tab, Royce was walking out of the diner. He spotted the sheriff getting into his truck.

"See ya, Sheriff," Royce called to him across the parking lot. "We'll call you if we see any little green men wandering around."

"They aren't green," Mr. Schmidt called through the open diner door, at the same time Sheriff Valdez said, "Please don't."

* * *

Tilly left the diner and went to the 999, with Ranger in tow. Abner was waiting outside the workshop. Next to him sat the tiger, reclining on its haunches. It sat stock-still—it was powered off. Besides its disconcerting lack of movement, the animatron looked more or less like a living thing, one that was the victim of someone pressing the pause button on time, freezing the beast mid-frame.

Abner was alone there, with the tiger. "Where's Anna?" Tilly asked.

"She is working on something, I suppose," Abner said. He waved his hand in the direction of the workshop. Tilly wondered what that could be—with the tiger out here, she didn't know what Anna could be working on inside. She didn't ask.

For his part, Abner looked worse for wear. He had somehow lost a shade or two of skin tone since Tilly saw him last, and now sported skin so pale Tilly thought she could almost see right through it. Red veins shot through the whites of his eyes, and he looked like he had missed the morning's shave. His hair went in all directions, none of them good.

"Long week?" Tilly asked. Neither Abner nor Anna had called on Tilly's services that week, so she hadn't seen Abner since his meltdown.

"Indeed," he said. "I had to start over completely." He rested his hand on the tiger's head.

"Did you make any progress?" Tilly appraised the tiger, looking for clues. It had been put back together physically, that was clear. That was

Anna's work. Abner's internal work on the tiger's programming was not outwardly visible.

"I think so," Abner said. "The simulation seems sound. I accounted for people this time."

"How so?" Tilly asked. Ranger was leaning up against her leg, and she felt his whole body vibrating with a growl of too low of a decibel to be audible. Tilly looked around the clearing to see if there was perhaps an animal in the brush—a deer or hog or turkey—that had drawn his ire. Nothing. Just the tiger.

"I taught him what to do if he sees a person," Abner explained.

"What's that?"

Abner grinned. "Want to see?" he asked.

Before Tilly could answer, Bubba arrived in an ATV. Tilly and Abner stopped talking, and even Ranger stood at attention, as Bubba extricated his large belly from behind the steering wheel.

"Here's the plan," said Bubba when he had finally removed himself. "We are going to set the tiger loose in the north pasture here." He gestured to the expansive wooded area on the other side of the fence that surrounded the workshop.

"He's gonna get a good head start. After we get him going, I'm gonna go back to the main office to pick up our hunter. I'll bring him back here, and by that time this guy ought to be good and lost in the brush." Bubba patted the tiger's head. "And then the hunt will be afoot." He grinned.

"Are we—are we sure this is a good idea?" Tilly asked. "I mean, are we sure we're ready?" She was looking at Abner.

Abner opened his mouth to answer, but Bubba interrupted. "You bet your ass we're ready. That's what Einstein here said, right, Einstein?" Bubba clapped his hand on Abner's shoulder, jolting an unexpecting Abner a few inches forward.

Abner looked at the ground. "Yes sir," Abner said. His voice had lost its usual arrogant tone. "That is right."

"It better be right," Bubba said. Abner's mouth began to twitch, first into a smile, then a frown, then to the right. Then it opened and closed a few times, and it reminded Tilly of the mouth of a fish. Open. Close. Open. Close.

Bubba did not seem to notice Abner's tic. He slapped the tiger on the shoulders and said, "Let's fire this baby up."

Abner powered the animatron on. It animated, rising from its haunches to its feet.

"There we go," Bubba said. He grinned at the animatron like a proud grandfather. Tilly could almost see the dollar signs in his eyes.

Abner took a deep breath. He pressed a button on the tiger's remote control. The tiger began to walk forward, crunching through the dead winter grass.

"Looks fine to me," Bubba said.

"Just wait," Tilly said. Abner shot her a look.

"It *is* fine," Abner said. "He should work perfectly." His worried expression belied his confident tone.

The tiger plodded forward in the open pasture, walking straight toward the fence that guarded the tree line. The group followed it, with Abner in the lead and Ranger lagging behind at Tilly's heels.

Abner held the gate into the north pasture open for the tiger. It passed through the gate, and then the threshold of the tree line, and into the uncleared brush, without incident—it happened to be aimed at the empty space between two great oaks. Abner closed the gate behind it, and they all watched it walk deeper into the pasture.

The first thing directly in its path was a log, the carcass of a tree long-fallen. Tilly thought she heard Abner muttering something under his breath as the tiger approached the log. It was twelve feet away. Then ten. Eight. Six. When it was four feet away, the tiger gathered itself, spring-loading its weight on its hind legs. Then it leapt. It sailed through the air, clearing the fallen tree by several feet.

"Well, I'll be damned!" Bubba exclaimed when the thing took flight. The tiger landed soundly on the other side of the log.

Tilly recognized the catlike jump from the simulation she and Anna had produced while perfecting the mechanics of the leg. For a moment, she felt something close to *pride* at having contributed something to the whole operation.

The tiger began to walk forward again.

Abner exhaled a sigh of relief. "See?" he said, barely able to contain his excitement—or smugness. "Abraham works perfectly."

"Great work, Einstein." Bubba clapped Abner on the back. "That's good enough for me. Let me go pick up Fairbanks from the lodge."

The three—plus Ranger—turned away from the tiger to walk back to the workshop, leaving the animatron to bury itself deep in the wooded pasture for George Fairbanks to hunt down later. Just as they emerged from the shadow of the oaks at the tree line, they heard a gentle *thud* behind them. Then another. And again. In steady rhythm. *Thud. Thud. Thud.*

Tilly's shoulders tightened. She turned with the others to see the source of the noise—but they all knew what it was before they even laid eyes on it.

It was, of course, the tiger. The next obstacle in its path, after the log, was a pecan tree. It hadn't had as much luck with obstacle number two as it had with obstacle number one. Instead of stepping around the tree, as it should have, the animatron ran headlong into it. And when the path forward met it with resistance, it tried to step forward again, and again rammed its head into the trunk of the tree. *Thud.* And again. *Thud.*

"Abraham! No!" Abner shouted. He sprinted to the animatron. "Do not do that." He remembered the remote after a few more *thuds*, and pressed a button to power the animatron off. Abner knelt by the animatron, inspecting it—for what, Tilly didn't know.

"What the fuck was that?" Bubba asked. He looked between Abner and Tilly, accusingly.

"Just a little glitch," Abner said. He rose and dusted himself off. His mouth twitched.

"Who could have predicted?" Tilly said. Abner sighed in her direction.

"Well, if it's just a 'little glitch,' then let's fire it up again," Bubba said. "It shouldn't happen again, right? If it was a . . . 'glitch.'" He raised his eyebrows at Abner in a you-better-not-fuck-this-up stare.

"Right," Abner said. "It should not." He took a deep breath and positioned the front of the tiger toward a gap in the trees, so that it was facing in Tilly's direction.

"Let us try again," Abner said. Then, almost under his breath, he muttered, "Come on, Abraham." He pressed a button, and the tiger came alive again. It started to walk.

After a few paces, Tilly realized that she was directly in the tiger's path. She started to step out of its way. But as she did so, when the tiger was only a few yards from her, it picked up its pace, its eyes trained directly on her. Before Tilly could make sense of the situation or decide what to do, it was too late—she was in the tiger's sights. It began to charge. Tilly jumped to the side, out of the oncoming tiger's way. In the same instant, Ranger leapt into the space between Tilly and the tiger.

Ranger crouched low in the tiger's path, erupting in a fury of snarling and barking. He bared his teeth in a way that Tilly had never seen him do. With Tilly out of the tiger's sights and its vision—if you could call whatever sensor-based input the thing received "vision"—now occupied by the dog, the tiger stopped charging. It slowed again to its normal pace, still advancing straight toward growling Ranger. The dog's hair rose into a spiney plume on his back. The tiger drew closer.

"Ranger, come," Tilly called. He did not come. Stubborn. "Ranger!" she tried again. Still no response. Ranger only had eyes for the tiger. He barked ferociously, a big sound, disproportionate to the dog's size.

Tilly tried another tack. "Abner?" she called, her voice pitched high. Shouldn't he *do* something?

When the tiger had closed the gap to just a few feet, it stopped. It cocked its head. Ranger had his hackles up. Then he lunged at the tiger.

"Ranger, no!" Tilly shouted.

In an instant, the tiger swiped its large paw at the lunging dog. It made contact midair with a sickening *CRACK*. The tiger sent Ranger flying to the ground.

"Ranger!" Tilly shouted. She ran toward him. Before she reached him, he was up again. Ranger lunged again at the tiger, this time for its torso. He got a mouthful of the tiger's side, taking hold of its silicone skin and not letting go. Fake blood began to seep from the animatron's wound.

Abner was watching the events unfold with morbid fascination. "Abner, turn it *off*!" Tilly yelled at him.

Heart pounding, Tilly lunged to grab Ranger, in an effort to wrest him away from the tiger. But as she did so, the tiger curled its body around with surprising agility, putting itself between Tilly and her dog. When the tiger whipped around, so did Ranger—he wouldn't let go. Ranger shook his head viciously, ripping a chunk of pelt clean off the tiger's side. Separated now, the two creatures faced each other again, squaring up for another round.

"*Abner!*" Tilly yelled. As if waking from a dream, Abner seemed to come to, and he finally pressed the OFF button.

The tiger stilled. Ranger's sides heaved in and out with exerted breathing, and he held a chunk of silicone and fake fur in his mouth. His muzzle and chest were red with the tiger's blood—or at least, Tilly *hoped* it was the tiger's blood.

Tilly ran to Ranger and knelt by him. She ran her hands over him, checking for injuries. He yelped when she touched his rib cage.

"My poor baby," Tilly said softly to the dog. She pulled his head into her chest, embracing him, and he yelped again from the movement.

"Goddamn it, I'm so sorry." She carefully detached from him. He looked at her with big, mournful eyes. Tilly wanted to hold him and never let him go.

Bubba and Abner caught up to the scene. Bubba was winded from his attempt to rush over.

"Hot damn," Bubba said, through heaving breaths. "Wasn't that something?"

"That was amazing," said Abner, his eyes lit up.

Tilly turned to Abner, her eyes blazing. "*Amazing*?" she said. "*Amazing*?" She took a step toward him, and Abner dropped his smile. He took a step back, as if he thought she might hit him. Tilly thought she might hit him too. She didn't. "That thing could have *killed* Ranger! Or me, for that matter. Why didn't you turn it off when it was charging at me?"

"I wanted to see if it had learned."

"Learned *what*?" Tilly's anger made her feel ten feet tall.

"What to do when it sees a human," Abner said, as if reading from a textbook. Matter of fact.

Rage billowed around Tilly. Blooms of red fury crept across Tilly's chest and up her neck to her cheeks. "You *wanted* it to do that?"

Abner didn't respond, and he turned his attention to the tiger. He examined the bleeding spot on the tiger's side where Ranger had ripped away a chunk of silicon. The hole in its side exposed the animatron's metal innards.

Abner looked back up at Bubba and Tilly. His eyes shone with wonder. "It swiped at the dog." He breathed a little laugh that settled into a smile.

"I *know*," Tilly yelled. "What the *fuck*."

Abner turned to Bubba, explaining, "I did not reward that as a behavior in the artificial intelligence training. Abraham somehow picked that up on his own." He shook his head in disbelief. "Straight from the ether."

"That's good, then?" Bubba asked. His eyes were wide.

"It is *excellent*," Abner said.

"*Excellent*?" Tilly's rage had cooled to a smolder, and she was able to speak in a normal volume. Still, her voice shook. "It's *horrific*. You have to deprogram that, or make it unlearn or— or whatever."

"And ruin something so perfect?" Abner's voice had a filmy quality, like gossamer soaked right through with oil. "Why would I do that?"

Tilly looked hard in Abner's eyes, not sure what she was looking for, and not finding it. She felt a tentacle of unease wrap around her, then another, until she was bound tight in a chill of apprehension. Then she thought she saw something out of the corner of her eye. A man. Or a shadow. She turned. There was nothing there.

She took a deep breath and turned her focus to Ranger. Drained of the adrenaline that had quelled his initial pain, Ranger was now curled on the ground. Tilly pressed a hand to his side. He whimpered. He had at least one, maybe two broken ribs.

"I need to get him to my clinic," Tilly said. Neither man responded.

Instead, Bubba was absorbed by the sight of the tiger, taking stock of the hole in the animatron's side. "Guess the hunt is off for today."

"We can probably repair him in time," Abner said.

Bubba looked up at the sky, then at his watch. "No, I think we'll postpone. It's getting a little late," he said, though it was only late morning. Tilly thought she heard a ripple of unease in Bubba's voice. "We'll start fresh another day."

"I need to get him to the clinic," Tilly said again, louder this time. "Does anyone have something I can bind his torso with?"

"Yeah," Bubba said, shaking his head, as if pulling himself from reverie. "Yeah, sorry." He pulled an oversized handkerchief from his back pocket. Tilly gingerly bound the dog's torso as tightly as she could, to keep the broken ribs from shifting. Ranger let out a few halfhearted growls and a couple of soft whimpers as Tilly wrapped him up.

When she finished, she stood and stooped to lift Ranger up in her arms. He yelped. She made her way back to her truck so she could get Ranger to her clinic for X-rays. She took long strides, propelled by her anger and the icy unease that prickled at the nape of her neck, the darkness that nipped at her heels.

When she was almost to the truck, Abner called after her. "Wait, Tilly." Tilly turned to him, expecting an apology.

Instead, he said, "Do not bring it back unless you can train it not to attack the animals."

Chapter 16
Kangaroos

Tilly took Ranger to her clinic to x-ray him. As she suspected, he had two cracked ribs, but thankfully no wayward shards of bone to threaten his lungs. She prescribed him a few weeks of rest and left him under the watchful eye of her veterinary assistant at the clinic to sleep off the painkillers she gave him.

Still shaken and angry, Tilly resumed her workday. She had rounds to make to ranches around the county that required care for their larger, difficult-to-transport animals. Like kangaroos, for instance. When you're the only vet for fifty miles in every direction, you develop a varied client base. Her first stop would be Mr. Schmidt's ranch to vaccinate his kangaroo joeys.

Mr. Schmidt lived way out of town, in the far north of the county. Tilly rolled her windows down to let the chilly November air sweep into the cab of her truck, hoping it might soothe her anger away. She put in a Willie Nelson CD, too, for good measure. Neither kept her mind from going back, again and again, to the tiger attack. Seething anger boiled her blood into vapors.

Tilly turned up the volume on "Nothing I Can Do About It Now." She looked down the road ahead of her, and in the rearview mirror at the road behind her. It was open roads as far as she could see. She pressed on the accelerator. Her truck shifted gears.

The landscape began to pass her by more quickly, roadside fences blurring into solid lines of gray. The large oak trees that watched over the road came one after the other, faster and faster with less and less space between each, and then they were all one tree, an endless brush-stroke of brown and green. The air whipped into a frenzy through the open truck windows, a personal tempest. Tilly pressed her foot further down on the gas pedal. The truck's engine groaned.

Faster, faster, until the truck's speedometer needle wobbled at its rightmost point, the truck's engine unable to add any more might to its charge. The world around Tilly blurred into a tunnel of green and blue and asphalt-black. Her hair flung and swirled around her in the currents of air gusting through the cab as the truck sliced down the road. A curve in the road ahead, sharp and blind, raced toward her. She pressed the gas pedal to the floor.

Tilly held her breath. One second. Two seconds. Three seconds. She slammed on the brakes. The truck slowed just enough just in time as she went into the crook in the road, the weight of the truck shifting to the outside of the curve, but not enough to divorce the inside wheels from the ground. Spared by physics. Tilly exhaled.

She slowed further, down to a normal speed, and then slowed some more. Willie Nelson, who had been silenced by the noise of the air through the windows, started singing again. Tilly had arrived.

She turned into Mr. Schmidt's gate. She put the truck in park and looked at herself in the visor mirror. Her windswept hair formed a tangled cloud around her head. She tried running her fingers through the mess, but it was no use. She settled on piling the tangle of hair on top of her head into a messy bun. It looked passably not-crazy.

The gate was a modest entrance compared to the abject immodesty of the ranch, by far the largest property in the county. The gate was made from standard metal pipe, uncreative and unornamented, besides a humble scripted 'S.' Tilly let herself in.

She wound up the long drive to Mr. Schmidt's house and barns. She drove past the house, the gatekeeper to the ranching operations beyond. Mr. Schmidt waited for her between the house and the barns.

He sat on a stone bench, lorded over by an old and commensurately huge oak tree. He waved and grinned at her from beneath his well-worn, well-loved cowboy hat.

The bench was not alone beneath the oak tree. Two headstones rose from the ground under the tree's watchful limbs, standing sentry to the eternal homes of Mr. Schmidt's wife and only son. A wrought iron fence hugged the little plot tightly. Upon Tilly's approach, Mr. Schmidt rose from the bench, leaving a worn divot in the stone beneath him, testimony to how often he kept his wife and son company—his perpetual elegy to them, cast in stone.

Mr. Schmidt was a victim of life's cruelest of ironies. Fate often visits the prosperous with tragedy, to match the good fortune she has bestowed upon them—to balance her ledger. In Mr. Schmidt's case, the instrument of Fate's accounting was a plane crash. Mr. Schmidt was not on the flight. Someone left behind to feel the effects.

Mr. Schmidt had tried marriage again a time or two after the crash, but nothing stuck. He always came back to his ghosts.

Tilly parked and joined Mr. Schmidt by the private cemetery. She felt awkward, not knowing whether to acknowledge the somber setting or not. She never knew. Luckily, Mr. Schmidt spoke before she had to make up her mind.

"How do, Dr. Hutto?" He removed his hat in a gesture of chivalry and stuck out his hand in a gesture of camaraderie. "You're early."

Tilly shook his hand and noted, by comparison, that her own was still tense with adrenaline from her drive, and probably still some anger about the tiger. "I'm okay, Mr. Schmidt. It's a beautiful day."

"Some of God's finest work, if I do say," he agreed. A breeze swept past them and rustled the limbs of the oak tree. Mr. Schmidt glanced up into its limbs, and Tilly thought that she saw his brow furrow for a moment. Then he looked back at her, his friendly expression returned.

It was then that Tilly noticed for the first time that they were not alone by the cemetery. Mr. Schmidt wore a work belt, slung low on his hip. It sported several large pouches. One of them wiggled. A little black nose, and then a whole little head, emerged from the pouch to greet Tilly.

"And good afternoon to you," Tilly said to the kangaroo joey. It yawned.

"This one's Johnny," Mr. Schmidt said. "June's in the barn with their mama."

"Well, let's get to it," Tilly said. She retrieved her vet bag from the back seat of her truck.

The barn, large and red in the classic style, greeted Tilly with the familiar musty smell of old hay. The inside held quite the tableau. An adult kangaroo, the mother, lounged atop a stack of alfalfa hay bales. She watched as her other joey, June, hopped in quick, energetic circles around the barn. Oney, Mr. Schmidt's ranch manager, was in hot pursuit.

"Run, June, run!" Mr. Schmidt yelled. Oney gave him an exasperated look. Mr. Schmidt went from grinning to stitches.

The joyful chaos of the chase was a welcome diversion from the chaos of Tilly's morning, and she found herself rooting for the little kangaroo to evade capture. The joey hopped over hay bales and under the tractor, finally losing Oney when she squeezed under the John Deere grass shredder.

"Goddam it, you little shit!" Oney dropped to his belly and reached blindly under the shredder.

"Careful, she prolly got a friend under there," Mr. Schmidt said through bouts of chuckling. "Hissssss." He wagged his finger in the air like a rattlesnake's tail.

Oney ripped his arm out from beneath the implement. "Harold, I don't know what you want me to do. She don't wanna get her shots," Oney said.

"Well, why'd you tell her she was gettin' shots? You gotta be covert, Oney."

Oney sighed. Tilly took that as her cue. "Let me do Johnny first, then I'll see what I can do about June," she said.

"Sounds like a fine plan." Mr. Schmidt lifted the little joey from the pouch on his belt and presented him to Tilly. "Your patient," he announced. The joey—Johnny—was almost all legs, and the rest of him was ears.

"Here you go, big guy," Tilly said as she took him from Mr. Schmidt and placed him on her lap. He sat very still, docile in her hands.

"Good boy," Tilly soothed. She rummaged through her bag for the syringes she had pre-filled with the necessary vaccines. With one hand and her teeth, she pulled the cap off a syringe. In her other hand she held the joey. Without thinking, she started to hum.

She pinched the skin beneath the joey's forearm, stretching it out to give herself more canvas with which to work. Then, quickly, she stuck the little joey with the needle and injected its contents as fast as she could. He sat stock-still the entire time. Tilly kept a wary eye on the mother kangaroo throughout her ministrations, just in case she objected. She did not. She sat calmly, lazily, on the stack of alfalfa bales.

"There you go," Tilly said as she pulled out the needle. "Good little patient. I'd give you a lollipop if I had one." She patted the joey on the head.

"Now for the other kleine scheiße," said Mr. Schmidt. He took Johnny from Tilly's lap and placed him back into the pouch on his hip. The joey burrowed in. Mr. Schmidt gave the outside of the pouch a little pat.

Tilly walked over to the shredder, which was essentially a large mowing implement that could be attached to a tractor to mow a field. It was low to the ground—Tilly could not see underneath it even when she squatted down next to it.

"Hmm," she contemplated aloud. "How are we going to convince you to come out of there, June?" June did not answer.

Mr. Schmidt did. "Want me to go get my burnin' sage? We can smoke 'er out."

Tilly did not answer. Instead, she stood and looked around the room. Her eyes landed on the alfalfa bales, the mother kangaroo's throne. She plucked a handful of alfalfa from a bale.

"June," Tilly sang in a Snow-White voice. "Come out, June." She waved the handful of fragrant alfalfa under the shredder, hoping its sweet scent would lead the joey into the open. A gentle rustle in the joey-sized cavern under the shredder, then nothing.

"Looks like we're in a good ol' fashioned standoff," Mr. Schmidt said.

Tilly had an idea. "Hey, Mr. Schmidt, Oney, would y'all mind stepping outside for a minute?"

"Whatever the doctor orders," Mr. Schmidt said. He and Oney walked out, then closed the barn door behind them.

Tilly sat down on the ground by the shredder. She crossed her legs and let the silence build around her. The sweet smell of hay tickled her nose, and she could hear the mother kangaroo's soft breathing. Tilly closed her eyes and observed her own breathing, forcing it lower, slower. She felt the grit of the dirt beneath her, swirling her fingers in it, and she tried to become it, to disappear into it. She willed herself to invisibility with every low, slow breath. She imagined growing a shade more translucent with every inhalation, then, finally, achieving ecstatic transparency—nothingness—with a final exhalation that would carry her away on the wind.

She sat there in silence for several minutes, not doing anything besides being, and not really planning on anything else. It was the first moment that she felt fully at ease again after the tiger experience that morning—her shoulders relaxed and the tension at her temples eased. After a while, Tilly opened her eyes. To her disappointment, she remained a visible, solid form. After observing her own crossed legs and her own dirty hands, Tilly's eyes went to the dark space below the shredder. Two other eyes looked back.

June the joey crouched under the shelter of the shredder, just her head and its ears peeking out from beneath the shredder's awning. She watched Tilly, alert, transfixed.

"Hi, June," Tilly said softly, in not-quite-a-whisper—a whisper, in its sharp edges, is meant for another to hear. Tilly's words floated for a moment, barely registered by any ears, and certainly not comprehended, then they were gone.

The little joey continued to peer out at her, intently. Tilly was afraid to move, for fear that any movement would break the spell that held the joey still. After a few moments of communal stillness, Tilly heard a rustle behind her. She slowly turned to see the mother kangaroo hop down from her perch and amble over to observe the standoff. Tilly thought about moving out of her way, worried that she might have decided it was finally time to defend her joey from the human. But the mother stopped a few feet away, standing quietly at Tilly's shoulder.

Tilly was bolstered by the reinforcement. "See, June, we all want you to come out. I'm not gonna hurt you." *Not entirely true,* she thought to herself, as she thought about the syringe's needle.

Seeing her mother behind Tilly sparked some bravery in the joey, and she inched out from beneath the shredder. Tilly did not move a muscle, nor did she dare speak.

Little by little, the kangaroo joey came into the open. She held her mother in the lion's share of her gaze, but still kept a wary eye on Tilly. Tilly hardly breathed, thinking that maybe her invisibility experiment had succeeded after all.

A few more careful steps, then the joey was inches from Tilly. Gently, swiftly, Tilly swept June up into her arms. June started, kicking and struggling for freedom from Tilly's grasp. Tilly hugged her tightly to her chest, humming softly. Tilly half-expected to feel the mother kangaroo's claws on her neck at any moment, but she didn't. After a few moments of flailing, June stilled, her only movement the heave of each terrified little breath.

Tilly saw her opening and moved quickly. She drew the vaccine syringe from the breast pocket of her shirt and unsheathed it to administer the shot. In a second, it was over. Tilly gave June back her freedom. The joey scuddled to her mother.

"Not so bad, huh?" Tilly said, more to herself than the joey, who looked like she would disagree.

Tilly rose and opened the barn door to Mr. Schmidt and Oney. "All done," she said.

"Well, I guess your magic only works when we're not watching." Mr. Schmidt said, walking back into the barn.

"I can't give away all of my secrets," Tilly said, her eyes crinkling with a smile. "Job security."

Johnny jumped from the pouch on Mr. Schmidt's belt and hopped over to join June by their mother. The two joeys huddled at her flanks, and she curled protectively, instinctively over them. The pose—its balance and subtle drama—had the air of a Renaissance painting, exuding life in its stillness. The Madonna and Child(ren), rendered in dust and fur and dim barn light.

Tilly was not the only one to notice the gentle beauty of that moment—Mr. Schmidt and Oney were equally struck into silence. Then, Mr. Schmidt said, "I didn't think about it before, but we ought to do their baptisms while we're at it." He watched the little trio with the pride of a father.

Tilly laughed. The spell was broken. "Unfortunately, I don't carry holy water on me, Mr. Schmidt."

"That's too bad. I'll have to call up the preacher. 'Bout time for him to come 'round askin' for a tithing check anyway."

Mr. Schmidt noticed Tilly's mildly scandalized expression. "Only way I'm gettin' in," he said, pointing upward toward the heavens.

Tilly laughed again. "Add a little extra in this month for me, will ya?"

"You bet."

The soft crinkle of Mr. Schmidt's eyes reminded Tilly of something. "Seen any more coyotes lately?" she asked. "The bad-luck kind?"

Mr. Schmidt's face darkened slightly. "No. But I been seein' an owl in the oak tree," he said. He pointed to the big oak tree in the little graveyard. "Bad omen."

Tilly felt the old familiar sour feeling creep into her stomach. *Drip, drip, drip.* "I thought owls were good luck," she said.

"Not to me. Between the coyote and the owl, woah boy. It's gonna be a big one."

"Sounds like the animals are conspiring against you. They do that to me all the time," Tilly joked. She hated the dark tension that had taken hold of the conversation. "All the horses decide to colic on the same day, all the calves get pneumonia at the same time."

Mr. Schmidt smiled, but his eyes were still stormy. "Well, animals have always been a lot smarter than me," he said. "So I'm gonna listen to 'em."

"Let me know what else they say," Tilly said.

Tilly gathered her things, said goodbye to Mr. Schmidt and his kangaroos, and got in her truck. She was eager to get home to Ranger. As she started to drive away, windows down, Mr. Schmidt called after her, "Be careful, Tilly!" He stood in her rearview mirror with his hand raised in a wave.

In response, she waved a final farewell out the window. She drove back the way she came, slowly—carefully—this time.

* * *

That night. Sleep. Or something like it. Tossing—flailing—tangled in the covers. Standing. Something in her hand. A sharp pain.

Tilly woke up. She was in her kitchen with no recollection of how she got there. She stood over the kitchen counter. She held something in her right hand. Her left hand was in excruciating pain. She looked down.

Her right hand was poised, holding a kitchen knife, over a whole, uncooked chicken that was meant to be her lunch for the week. Her left hand held the raw, fridge-cold chicken down on the counter. Holding the knife like a scalpel, she had opened the chicken's chest cavity, its skin carefully cut away as if in surgery. Blood pooled in the chicken's open chest and dripped down its sides.

In a moment of confused, half-asleep horror, Tilly realized that it was her own blood. She had sliced into her left index finger during her operation on the chicken. She dropped the knife and ran to the sink, running water over her maimed finger. Her hands shook under the water. She tried to remember if you could get salmonella poisoning through contact with broken skin as she watched the blood run into the white sink, turning it pink. She looked at her finger, and she saw bone.

Chapter 17
The Ghost in the Machine

Tilly made her return to the workshop at the 999 soon after, this time to help Anna with some mechatronic adjustments. Tilly's left index finger was bandaged in thick white gauze, wrapped over stitches that she had done herself—she hated going to the doctor.

Nobody was waiting for Tilly outside of the lab this time. She let herself in and made her way to Anna's workshop. The building's air conditioner leeched the life out of the unseasonably warm outside air, leaving behind a cold and sterile atmosphere that seemed solid, palpable in its frigidity. The light that ricocheted through the mostly glass walls lit Tilly up like a spotlight, making her feel exposed, examined, vulnerable. She looked over her shoulder every few steps, every time surprised not to see Ranger trotting along behind her—she left him at home, partly because he was still recovering, and partly for his own safety. Tilly half expected to see something else, too—whatever the dark thing was that seemed to haunt the building just for her. *Drip, drip, drip.*

Anna had her back turned to Tilly at her computer. But another pair of eyes watched Tilly as she walked in. On the worktable in the center of the room, where Anna had her tools for tinkering with her creations, two human-looking eyes on a stand looked at Tilly from beneath plastic eyelids. They blinked.

"Ah!" Tilly reacted when they moved on their own. Anna turned to her.

"Good morning to you, too," she said.

"Sorry," Tilly said. "It's just—the eyes." She pointed at the pair of blue eyes looking back at her.

Anna looked confused for a moment, and then concerned when she saw what Tilly was looking at. Then, after a moment, her expression lightened. "Cool, right?"

"What are they?" Tilly asked. She took a step toward Anna. The eyes followed her.

"Another little art project," Anna said. "I get bored working on the same thing all of the time."

Tilly took another step forward. When the eyes continued to follow her, she took a few steps to the left to test them. They followed still. "Creepy," Tilly said.

"Thank you," said Anna. She glanced around the room. "Where's your buddy?"

"Ranger? I left him at home. I don't think he'll be coming out here with me anymore. I guess you heard what happened." Tilly sat down heavily in one of the chairs around the worktable. Tiger, Anna's cat, rubbed up against her leg.

"Yeah," Anna said, sitting down at the table with Tilly. "Abner said he attacked the animatron."

"Abner said Ranger attacked the tiger?" Tilly raised an eyebrow. Anna nodded.

"That's not quite what happened," Tilly said. She picked up Tiger—the housecat—and plopped him into her lap, stroking him. He purred.

"Either way, it's probably for the best," Anna said. "Safety first." She smiled warmly.

"Now," Anna said, clapping her hands together, her tone suddenly all business. "We have quite a bit of work to do. I'm sure you noticed that the tiger is a still a little . . . rickety, in motion."

Tilly nodded, confused by how Anna could move past the tiger attack so quickly.

"So we need to work on that," Anna continued. She grabbed a notepad from her desk and consulted her notes. "And Abner has requested more range of motion than the current model is capable of."

Tilly's brow furrowed. "How so?"

"It needs more lateral paw movement, apparently. Abner said something about it being able to realistically swipe its paw sideways."

"It can already do that," said Tilly. "That's how it injured Ranger."

Anna looked up from her notes. "It hurt Ranger?"

"Yeah. Broke two of his ribs. I am a little surprised that Abner didn't tell you that. Or Bubba, even."

Anna's brow furrowed. "No, no. Abner said it was a big success. That it went better than he could have hoped."

Tilly shook her head. "Not from Ranger's perspective."

"Is he going to be okay?"

"Yeah, he'll be fine. The breaks were clean, luckily. He just needs a lot of rest."

"That's good," Anna said. "Lucky thing he has a veterinarian for a mother. You know, the weird thing is that the current model isn't really designed to be able to do that. I guess it could get a little lateral movement in its front paws because I built in flexibility so it could walk over rough terrain. But to swipe its paw sideways . . . ." Anna trailed off into thought.

"It wasn't directly sideways," Tilly said. "It was more downward than to the side, I guess. Which is probably why things went as good as they did for Ranger."

"I guess that's why Abner wants improvements."

Tilly raised her eyebrows at Anna.

Anna laughed. "It's a joke, relax," she said.

Tilly scowled. She took a deep breath. She thought of her mother in the nursing home. And she thought of her bank account balance. "Alright," Tilly said. "Where do we start?"

They got to work, Tilly happy to end the conversation about the tiger injuring her dog, which she didn't want to think about more than she had to. Tilly had brought with her diagrams of the insides of a tiger, in its various layers of bone and muscle and tendon. In a verbal dissection of the animal, Tilly talked Anna through the parts and pieces of its anatomy, and what they did, and how. Anna jotted notes and sketched out blueprints for mechanical analogs to the natural designs.

Tilly marveled at the special genius that Anna possessed, which allowed her to make such quick work of translating flesh into machine. In a few strokes of a pencil, she could capture the machinations of complex sequences of joint and tendon in a blueprint of gears and rods. She was more of an artist than a machinist, really.

At one point, to explain how a tiger's toes could splay, Tilly picked up Tiger the housecat as a demonstrative. She gently spread his toes so that Anna could see how they functioned.

"Huh," Anna said, as she sketched out a model of a cat paw in machine parts. "It's been right here all along. I don't know why I didn't think to look to him as an example before." Anna scratched the cat beneath the chin.

"I'm glad you didn't," Tilly said wryly. "If you had, you guys wouldn't need me." *Though that may have been for the better*, Tilly thought.

When they had finished or, rather, when Tilly was no longer useful to Anna, Tilly departed in the usual way. As she wound her way out of the building, something caught her ear.

It was a sound so faint that it almost disappeared into the background. The sort of low sound one could think their way out of hearing, the sort of sound that a person could convince themself didn't exist at all. In bed, in a dark room, at night. A faint rustle. The sense of noise, more than the perception of it. *It's nothing.*

The sound grew from a trick of the ear into something more substantial as Tilly continued down the hallway to the exit, eventually taking shape into something unquestionably audible. Something inarticulable about it sent a chill down Tilly's spine. Tilly was approaching the room where she had seen the shadow man, the room where Ranger sensed something threatening. And so she thought the noise came from there.

She slowed her pace as a coldness sank into her stomach. Tilly wished that Ranger was there. Tilly wished that she herself wasn't there. She inched forward, wanting to leave—to escape—but not wanting to discover the source of the noise.

All at once, when Tilly got just near enough to the source, she recognized in the sound the cadence of human speech.

Tilly reached the source of the sound before she reached the door to the room with the shadow man. Another door off the hallway was cracked open. And from it came the noise.

The gap between the slightly ajar door and the doorframe sucked light from the hallway into a dark room. Tilly peered inside. On first look, she could hardly see anything besides a glowing light in the middle of the room. The room's outer wall, which Tilly assumed was made of glass like the rest of the building, was cloaked in a dark and heavy curtain.

Tilly's eyes refocused in the darkness. The glow, she realized, came from a cluster of several computer screens facing away from the doorway. At the end of its reach, the glow suspended a face in the darkness. Impossibly pale, the light from the computer monitors cast the face in grotesque shadows and angles. Tilly let out an involuntary gasp at the sight.

The face's mouth was moving. And it was making the noise. A whisper: *'I have given it to you on the altar to make atonement for your souls; for it is the blood by reason of the life that makes atonement.'*

The face looked up. It was Abner. Tilly's stomach flipped when he made eye contact with her.

Abner stilled his mouth through some effort. "Tilly," he said, his voice his own again.

"Abner," Tilly said.

The two stayed there for a moment, looking at each other. A tension built between them.

Abner broke the silence. "You look like you have seen a ghost."

"What was that—what were you saying? I think I have heard it before. Is it from the Bible?"

"I do not know what you are talking about," said Abner.

"Seriously? Just now—what were you saying?"

Abner shrugged. After another moment of confusion, Tilly shook her head. "Never mind, I guess." She paused, and then went on, "I'm sure you're wondering how Ranger is." She wasn't sure.

"Ranger?" Abner asked.

Heat rose in Tilly's chest. "My dog." She stopped herself from adding, *you jackass*.

"Ah, yes. It is fine, yes?"

"If two broken ribs is fine, then I guess so." Tilly's rising anger boiled over into her voice.

"Good, good." Abner broke into a grin. "Our own Laika the Soviet space dog. Ranger made a necessary sacrifice for science."

That did it. "What the fuck is *wrong* with you?"

"What?" Abner raised his eyebrows. "You should be glad. Your Ranger fared much better than poor Laika."

"What are you getting at here, Abner? This isn't the goddamn Soviet space program."

Abner shook his head, offended. "No, this is much more significant."

Tilly let out something like a laugh, involuntary and humorless. "More significant?"

Abner's eyes shone. "Don't you see what I'm doing here? This is not as simple as some Russians sending a few cosmonauts to space. I am *creating* the cosmonaut."

Tilly shook her head. "Look," she said, "you are here to line Bubba Skinner's pockets by making fake animals for some rich assholes to come to Verde to hunt. That's it. That's the goal. I don't know who you think you are or what you think you're doing, but this just isn't that big of a deal. You are not here to contribute to science. There's no reason for any of this to be actually dangerous."

Abner, who had patiently waited for Tilly to finish, said, "No. The goal has been the same the whole time. To create artificial intelligence that behaves like a real living thing. To make the mind, the *soul*, of a living being, in software form. I do not see what is so hard to understand about that."

"Create the *mind*? The *soul*?" Tilly said. "Do you hear yourself?"

"I understand that you may be confused. Though with your . . . science"—he had to force the word out—"background, I would have thought you would have understood."

"Understood *what*?"

"Where consciousness comes from. Call it the mind or the soul, et cetera. It is just a combination of chemical reactions and electric signals. These are all systems that we understand and can re-create through the proper algorithms."

"Okay first of all, that's nonsense. Second of all, that just isn't the point of any of this."

"It is *not* nonsense," Abner said, his voice rising. "I understand that throughout history, before humans overcame our ignorance, people have assigned some sort of special meaning to consciousness, have insisted that it must derive from some nonmaterial source. We have built our religions around this notion. But now we know, from a scientific perspective, that is just not true. We have eaten the apple, if you will."

"Eaten the apple," Tilly repeated. "You think that our *minds* are just chemical reactions?"

"And electrical signals. I do not think, I *know* this to be true. Science knows this to be true. *You* should know this to be true."

"How can you live in this world, and see all of the living things in it, and—and *be* a living thing, and think that you can reduce consciousness to—to *math*. *That's* ignorance. And arrogance."

Abner laughed. "*Everything* is math. And the brain is the computer that operates the body. Like a puppet.

"Just like the animatrons, *you* are a robot *too*. You are just made of meat and bone and skin. But you are *still* a robot, whether you like it or not. Descartes said, 'the body is nothing but a machine made of earth.' And time has proven him right. Just like our bodies are machines, our minds are simply the operating systems."

"This is unhinged, Abner. You sound fucking crazy. And it doesn't matter, anyway. Just do your fucking job—your only fucking job—and make toys to keep a bunch of rich guys entertained. That's it. It's not so . . ."—Tilly searched for the word—"so *existential*. Christ."

"And how am I supposed to do my job with a toy that cannot think? It is the only way to give these 'rich guys,' as you say, an authentic experience," Abner said. "And do you not realize the significance of what happened yesterday?"

"To Ranger?" Tilly asked.

"Well, as a collateral consequence, sure. But I am talking about what Abraham did."

"Injure my fucking dog?" Tilly was seething.

Abner smiled. "Swiping at the dog, yes. That was not a programmed behavior. It was *entirely* learned. Abraham did not just learn *when* to swipe, like he has learned when to leap. He learned *how* to swipe. On his *own*." Abner's face had an expression of horrendous wonder.

Tilly forgot about her anger for a second. She shook her head, confused. "How is that possible?"

Abner raised his hands in the air in an elaborate shrug. "I cannot know. The algorithmic neural network, at this point, is a living thing apart from me." Something in Abner's eyes made Tilly's stomach churn. *Daddy says he's not a nice man.*

He continued, "The significance of what happened yesterday, for science, is hard to quantify. What did Oppenheimer say when he made history? 'Now I am become Death, the destroyer of worlds.'"

His expression was as smug of one as Tilly had ever seen.

She laughed. She couldn't help it. "So, what? You think you're—you think you're *Oppenheimer* now? You think *you*, on a godforsaken fucking hunting ranch, in Verde, Texas, have done some equivalent of *splitting the atom?*"

Abner's eyes only shone brighter. "Oh no. It is much bigger than that." He took a breath, seeming to gather his thoughts. "What makes something alive, Tilly?"

"What makes something *alive?*"

"Yes. What is it? We all know a living thing when we see it—you can recognize a fish in a stream from a stick floating down it, for example. We recognize something in other living things that we have in ourselves, but what is that something?"

Tilly shook her head, unsure of why she was entertaining this.

"Well," Abner said, "it is as simple—and as ungraspably complex—as *mind*, is it not? The ability to *think*. To make a decision. To move the body to act on a decision. When something can think, it is alive. This is true, at least, of the animal variety of life, which you know well. Would you disagree?"

After a pause and feeling trapped by the question, Tilly said, "Well, no."

"So this—this achievement, what you saw yesterday—it is nothing short of the miracle of creation itself."

Tilly sighed. "You're not God, Abner."

"No, I am not. God spent billions of years evolving single-celled or-ganisms into thinking beings. I have done as much in mere months."

Tilly was done. "You are *such* an ass. The arrogance."

"Someday, you will understand the significance of this feat. Everyone will. And you will be glad you were a part of it."

"I understand that you're fucking insane," Tilly said.

Abner started laughing. "We will see about that," he said. And then he rose from his chair and walked toward Tilly, who was still standing in the doorway.

Surprised, Tilly took a step backward. She held Abner's gaze as he walked toward her. He stopped just in the doorway, one hand on the door and the other on the frame.

"Now," he said. "If you will excuse me. I have some work to do."

He closed the door. It came to its stopping place inches from Tilly's nose.

Chapter 18
Aviary

Thanksgiving snuck up on Tilly. It was her first without a father—and without a mother, she supposed. She had no plans other than an early turkey lunch at Resthaven with her mother. She was not looking forward to it, for the obvious reason that it was bound to be very depressing.

The day before Thanksgiving, Tilly ran into Royce at the 999. He was working in a shed near the deer pens, where Tilly had attended to a living, breathing animal patient. A newly dead deer—not Tilly's patient, thankfully—hung by its back legs from a hook in the ceiling. Royce was butchering it.

The buck had already been relieved of its head and skinned down to the shoulders so it could be taxidermied into a trophy mount. Now its headless and partially skinless body dripped blood onto the floor of the shed, which had a drain in the center of the room. The deer's organs had been removed. Tilly wrinkled her nose at the cavity of its rib cage, unnatural in its emptiness. She was mesmerized for a few moments by the *drip, drip, drip* of the blood onto the floor beneath the carcass.

Royce was examining the deer, a bowie knife in hand, when he looked up to see Tilly. "Hey, Til," he said.

Tilly tore her eyes from the deep red gore. "Hey," she said. "One of today's victims?"

"Sure enough," Royce said. "One of the hunters got 'im this morning." He palmed the deer's back, running his hand along its spine, as if feeling for something.

"What're you doing?" Tilly asked.

"Cutting out the backstrap." Royce found the spot he was looking for, then pierced the knife into the deer's back. Tilly thought of her sleep-walking chicken operation of a few nights ago.

"Just the backstrap?" she asked.

"It's all they want. It's the best cut of meat." Royce sliced along the deer's spine as he talked.

"I know it's the best cut, I—" Tilly took a breath. Of course she knew it was the best cut; she had grown up around hunting too, just like Royce. Heat was rising in her chest. She was mad, and it took her a second to realize that her anger wasn't for Royce. "It's just so wasteful." She exhaled. "A life gone for a few pounds of meat."

Royce shrugged, shaking his head. "It's the name of the game. These people that pay for hunts, they just want the horns." He removed one length of deep red muscle and placed it on some waiting butcher paper on a nearby table. "Makes 'em feel alive, killing something."

He looked up at Tilly, his expression hard. "If it makes you feel better, we freeze the carcasses and take them to the food bank on Fridays. It's almost a better use, if you think about it. People who really need food get to eat it. Instead of some rich bastard from Dallas."

"Yeah, I guess." Tilly watched a rivulet of blood trickle to the drain in the center of the floor. "Who was it?" she asked, looking at the deer, the soul gone from her voice. Royce looked puzzled at first, then followed her gaze.

"Oh." Royce blew a breath of air between his lips. "Um, ear tag number 48. A fourth-year buck."

"I think I treated him for pneumonia this year."

"You did," said Royce. Then his eyes met Tilly's. His expression softened. "Look, Til. It bothers me too. I hate it."

"I don't know how you do it." Tilly's voice was small.

"I try not to think too much about it. Compartmentalize. I mean, how do *you* do it?"

"How do I treat them, you mean?"

"Yeah. Only reason they need a vet to keep them healthy is so they can live long enough to be killed. It doesn't bother you?" Royce asked as he felt the deer's back for the second backstrap.

"Of course it does. But I—well, what's the alternative? I refuse to treat them on principle? That'd only compound their suffering. Maybe I am the only kindness they will get in this lifetime."

"A regular Saint Francis, you are," Royce said. He plunged the knife into the flesh of the deer, a regretful shadow darkening his brow. A silence grew, filled only by the squelch of tearing muscle.

After a beat or two, Tilly said, "Speaking of Francises"—she gestured generally at their surroundings of the 999—"do you get tomorrow off? Are you doing anything for Thanksgiving?" She tried not to sound like she was fishing for an invitation, though she supposed she was.

"Oh yeah, Dad's having a thing," he said. "It's obligatory, you know. I'd invite you, but I don't think you'd enjoy it—"

"No, no—I have plans," Tilly said. "I was just curious."

"Good, whatever they are, they are bound to be better than mine," Royce said with an apologetic smile.

Royce freed the second backstrap from the buck's spine and wrapped it up in butcher paper with the first one. He went to wipe his hands on his jeans, then thought better of it and washed them at a sink in the corner. Tilly left him spraying down the floor with a water hose, washing the blood down the drain.

* * *

The next day was Thanksgiving. Tilly went to Resthaven's Thanksgiving lunch to dine with her mother, who had absolutely no idea that it was Thanksgiving. They sat at tables that had been set up in the common area of the nursing home. Tilly and her mother happened to be seated at a table near the glass-sided cabinet that held the live birds. A favorite feature of her mother's, the old woman spent much of the meal watching the birds flit around on fake branches.

To Tilly, the whole experience felt like a fever dream. Rarely did Tilly see many of the nursing home residents out of their rooms—she generally only saw her mother when she visited. So the tableau of human suffering she now witnessed—set to the soundtrack of moaning and yelling and gibberish from the residents—was jarring.

One frail-looking, ghost-faced woman let forth an ear-splitting shriek when a younger woman—presumably her daughter—attempted to feed her a spoonful of mashed potatoes. The shriek got everyone's attention, even Tilly's mother's.

"That used to be Anna May Wetzel," Tilly's mother said, looking at the shrieking woman. It was the first thing she'd said the whole lunch.

"Used to be?" Tilly asked, humoring her. "Who is she now?"

Tilly's mother did not answer. She turned back to the birds.

As Tilly was trying to force down some of her lunch—everything on her plate, the turkey, potatoes, stuffing, green beans, had the exact same too-soft texture—she spotted a familiar face making its way to their table.

"Tilly! Ottalie!" said the face—well, the mouth. "How are my two favorite heathens—I mean, Methodists?"

It was Father Francisco, the town's Catholic priest. He winked at them. Then he sat down. Tilly pinched herself to make sure that she wasn't actually having a nightmare. She wasn't.

"Hello, Father," Tilly said.

He asked her how she was, and she lied and said fine, and they made a series of the expected exchanges common to all small talk. When the conversation (if you could call it that) lulled, Tilly hoped that he would leave to bother another table. He didn't.

Instead, he sat comfortably in a silence that wasn't silent at all, for the din of the other residents. Tilly sat uncomfortably in the quasi silence.

Ottalie appeared to endure the silence neutrally. They all watched the birds in the glass cage.

There were seven or eight of them, the birds. Two preened themselves in a little birdbath. Several others slept on branches. One pecked at seeds from a feeder. A little yellow one poked its head out of a birdhouse. The fluorescent lights of the common room reflected in rectangular strips on the glass of the cabinet, and Tilly wondered if, to the birds, the fluorescent light looked like a sun.

"I think that's a yellow warbler," Father Francisco said, looking at the bird in the house. "They're not native to this area."

"It's pretty," Tilly said. A few of the birds tweeted back and forth to each other. "Are you a bird guy?"

Father Francisco chuckled. "I have always liked them, yes. They get closer to heaven than any of us do in our time on Earth." He flapped his arms cartoonishly to underscore his point.

"Not these," Tilly said flatly, looking at the glass prison.

Father Francisco's brow creased. "No, not these."

"Do you think they were born in captivity?" Tilly wondered, softly—a thought to herself, escaped on a stolen breath. She didn't take her eyes off the yellow warbler.

"I like to think so," said Father Francisco. "It is certainly better than thinking they might know what they're missing." He looked to a window, which framed an oak tree in the parking lot.

"Maybe, even if they were born in the wild, they don't remember it. I wonder how long birds remember," Tilly mused.

"I don't know," he said.

"They remember," said Tilly's mother. Father Francisco and Tilly both jumped, startled to hear her break her silence.

"Isn't that right, Chester?" The old woman looked across to Father Francisco. Tilly didn't know if Father Francisco knew that "Chester" was Tilly's recently deceased father.

But an obvious professional at talking to the mentally addled, Father Francisco played along. "That's right, Ottalie. Of course, they remember."

"We remember what it was like before." The old woman nodded to reinforce her point. Then she closed her eyes.

Tilly felt her throat tightening and she had to look away from her mother and the birds, so she looked at Father Francisco. To Tilly's surprise, his eyes, too, shone with moisture. Tilly looked at her feet to keep the tears from coming; Father Francisco's acknowledgment of the simple tragedy of the circumstances made it even harder not to cry. He took her free hand in his and squeezed it.

"Father Francisco?" Tilly said, starting a question. Her voice wobbled just enough to give her pause.

"Yes, my dear?"

Tilly cringed at the cliche prompt from the priest. But, not really knowing what had gotten into herself, she pressed on. "What do you think makes us human?"

"What do you mean?"

"Like in your—in your . . . *professional* opinion, what makes us different from the animals?"

"Ah, I see. Well, the Bible would tell us it's the soul."

"But what *is* the soul—in your opinion?" Tilly felt like a child asking about Santa Claus, pulling the thread of thought that had been bothering her since her last talk with Abner.

Father Francisco took a deep breath. He shifted in his seat, and Tilly thought she saw something else about him shift as well. A shift into his ministerial role. "It's the breath of life breathed into us by the Lord—I like to think of it as the little spark of God in all of us."

"But you don't think animal have souls?" Tilly looked at the little yellow warbler. It was preening its feathers.

"My official answer on behalf of the Church is 'no.' But it is hard to look at that"—Father Francisco pointed to the warbler—"and not see a spark of God, isn't it?"

Tilly nodded. "I just—I just don't see the difference, I guess—between us and them." She kept staring straight ahead at the birds.

"Perhaps it's a matter of spirit, which is different from the soul," the priest paused, choosing his words. The woman who used-to-be-Anna-May-Wetzel shouted again as her daughter wheeled her out of the common room. When she stopped, Father Francisco continued, "The soul gives us consciousness and intelligence. The spirit is what connects us to God."

"So is the soul, like, the *mind*?" Tilly was getting to the root of what had bothered her since talking with Abner.

"I guess you could look at it that way—Catholics think the soul is what allows us to be intelligent, thinking beings. But, you must understand, it is not science, like you are used to in your profession. We have no real way of knowing the particulars—other than that we *know*, somehow, that we have something special making us alive, yes? That's where faith comes in. It is not something meant for us to know."

Tilly ignored the last, preachy bit of his explanation. She was more interested in picking the priest's philosophical mind. "Do you think, then, that we can re-create it? That people could, like, replicate that intelligence—that ability to be a . . . *thinking* being?"

"Replicate the spark of God?" Father Francisco laughed. "I think you know what my answer to that one is, Tilly."

Tilly nodded. Her mother sat silently beside her. The old woman's eyes, watery, stared straight ahead but no longer watched the birds; they were instead fixed on nothing.

Tilly took a deep breath. Then she asked, "So, Father, if the soul is the mind, what—what does it mean when your mind has gone away?" She was looking at her mother.

Father Francisco, too, looked at the old woman next to Tilly, her eyes vacant. His lips pursed into a thin line. And he took a moment before saying, "I am afraid, contrary to what some may think, I just don't have all of the answers, Tilly."

He broke into an unexpected grin. "I suppose the soul is, as they say, like pornography—hard to define, but you know it when you see it."

Blood rushed to Tilly's cheeks at the mention of pornography from the priest. Then she started to giggle. And Father Francisco did too. So did Tilly's mother, though Tilly suspected she didn't know why. Soon they were all in stitches, the tears that had been waiting in Tilly's eyes while they watch the birds leaked out, redirected in laughter.

Chapter 19
The Quickening

Tilly awoke the next day to a text message from Abner. It was the first she had heard from him since he closed his office door in her face.

He is ready. Come to the lab first thing this morning, the message read. It had been sent at 5:12 a.m. Tilly resented the authoritative tone of the message. She also resented that her morning was free enough, workwise, that she did not have a good excuse to say no. She kept Friday mornings open for surgeries, and there were none scheduled this week.

"Jesus, why couldn't a horse have needed colic surgery this week?" Tilly mumbled to Ranger as she pulled the covers over her head to try to keep the day away for a few more minutes. Ranger didn't know.

Tilly rose and dressed and thought of her mother and the nursing home and money as she tended to Ranger and made sure he'd be comfortable, his torso bound tightly in a bandage to hold everything where it was supposed to be. She wrapped her sliced finger in much the same way. Then in an act of subtle defiance, she stopped at the diner for coffee before going to the 999.

The MISSING flier of Rachael Gonzales greeted Tilly when she walked in. It was right next to a new LOST DOG poster for someone's Great Pyrenees livestock guard dog. Other fliers and business cards advertising local services—lawn care, housekeeping, fence mending—dotted the diner's bulletin board.

Tilly sat down with Mr. Schmidt's group of old men.

"Good morning Dr. Hutto," Mr. Schmidt said as he raised his coffee cup in a sort of toast to her. The other men joined in with a chorus of *Mornin', Tilly* and *How ya doin', Dr. Hutto.*

"Mr. Schmidt, Mr. DeLeon, Mr. Garza, Mr. Nunley," Tilly listed off her greetings in turn.

"Johnny and June said to say 'hello,'" Mr. Schmidt said.

"Tell them hi back," Tilly said. The waitress put a cup of coffee down in front of her, and Tilly stirred cream into it.

"What's the word around town, fellas?" Tilly asked. "Any good gossip?"

"We've just been talkin' about the missing goats," said Alfonzo De-Leon. Tilly was pretty sure he was the youngest man at the table. She knew that he was roughly her father's age—she was pretty sure they had been in the same grade in school, if she remembered some of her father's stories correctly—so that would put him in his mid-seventies.

"Missing goats?" Tilly asked.

Mr. Schmidt picked up the conversation. "Oh yeah. Missing goats all over the county."

"What do you mean?"

"Well, people been having goats go missing," Tad Nunley chimed in. He had silver hair and skin so tan and wrinkled from years of working in the sun that it did a passable impersonation of leather. "They just up an' disappear overnight."

"Well isn't that just a trend lately," Tilly said, looking at the poster of Rachael and now the dog, near the door. "Whose goats?" she asked. This was the first she had heard of this.

Richard Garza piped up. "Oh, several of us. I had two go missing two nights ago. I heard that the Barrow Ranch had some go missing that night too. And word is that Augie Wilson had a few go missing last night."

"See, I told y'all trouble was comin'," Mr. Schmidt said. "First the coyote, then the owl. It was inevitable—the animals don't lie."

"You heard anything about this, Tilly? Any other animals going missing or turning up injured?" Mr. DeLeon took a long sip of coffee.

"No, I haven't. What do y'all think it is? Has anyone seen a mountain lion around?" Mountain lions weren't a regular feature in Verde, but one would pass through from time to time.

"See, that was my first thought," said Mr. Schmidt. "I thought we had ourselves a mountain lion come into the area."

"But you don't think it's a mountain lion?"

"No, I do not. Exhibit A: You ever heard of a mountain lion killing at least six goats over the span of just two days?"

"No, I haven't." Tilly sipped her coffee. The pleasant din of restaurant noises and pleasing smells of breakfast foods made for a cozy atmosphere, which helped Tilly shake a bit of the chill that had clung to her since she woke.

"And Exhibit B," Mr. Nunley said. "No tracks. Nobody has seen any mountain lion tracks around their goat pens. Ain't that right, Richard?"

"That's right. I didn't find a single paw print. Ever known a mountain lion to cover its tracks?" The question was directed at Tilly. She sensed they had already run through this conversation among themselves a couple of times this morning. They seemed excited to share the well-rehearsed performance with Tilly.

"No, I haven't ever seen that one before." Tilly smiled at the absurdity of the conversation, but the men all had serious expressions. Losing livestock was serious business.

"Exhibit C," Mr. DeLeon boomed. He sounded like a courtroom lawyer. "Nobody's found any remains, that I know of. No skeletons, no buzzards circling over the rest of the carcass in the pasture. Nothing."

"What about blood? Did you find any blood in your goat pens, Mr. Garza?"

"I did not. I even called the sheriff out, because with two goats missing I thought it looked more like a theft than anything. Hard for a predator to get two goats from the same herd in the same night, see. The rest of the herd usually wises up after the first one gets got."

"Right."

"And for good measure, the sheriff brought his hound out. And nothing. The hound didn't find any blood neither."

"So, you're probably right," Tilly said. "It's not a predator."

"Nope, no way it's a predator," Mr. Garza agreed.

"Prolly Satanists," Mr. DeLeon said, raising a meaningful eyebrow. "Like with that calf on the Wells ranch a few weeks ago."

"It's probably city kids coming out here to steal 'em for something untoward," said Mr. Nunley.

"I think this one could be the aliens," Mr. Schmidt said. "No blood, no tracks—like something picked them up from above. Poof," he made an accompanying hand gesture. "Whatever it is, I told y'all, I knew somethin' bad was gon' happen. I just knew it." He looked down at the Formica tabletop.

"So it's a mystery," Mr. Garza said. The table sat in silence for a few moments, pondering. Tilly looked down at her fingernails, thinking.

Then Mr. DeLeon broke the silence. "Reminds me of a time me and your daddy went on a mountain lion hunt, Tilly."

Tilly looked up from her fingernails. "Oh, yeah?"

"Yeah. We were in high school, and we heard that there was a mountain lion around Verde. People had seen tracks and such. I think someone said they'd seen it down by the old bridge.

"Anyway," he went on, "we decided we was gonna hunt it. We thought if we killed it, we'd get in the paper. We'd be heroes, you know, for saving the sheep and goats and calves and housecats of the county." The old man laughed, his eyes twinkling.

"So we set out one night with your daddy's dog, Willie. Willie was trained to hunt rabbits, and I guess your daddy thought that was close enough to be useful." That brought a laugh up from the table.

"So we're out by the old bridge, trespassin' all over creation lookin' for the mountain lion. Willie was useless, of course. And we had no idea what we were doin' either."

"So, no luck, I'm guessing? No Verde fame or fortune?"

"No luck. We didn't find a single mountain lion track, even. Though, your daddy insisted that he heard it yowl. They sound like a lady screamin', y'know. I didn't hear anything." He shook his head, his eyes shining with fond memories.

"Lucky for Willie he was so bad at mountain lion huntin'. He wouldn't've stood a chance if y'all found one," Mr. Schmidt said. Everyone laughed again.

Just then, Tilly's phone rang. It was Abner. She didn't answer, but she knew what he was calling about.

"I have to go, fellas," Tilly said. "Vet work awaits."

"Go save some animals," Mr. Schmidt said.

Tilly laughed at the irony. "I'll do my best," she said. Then she left for the 999.

Tilly found Abner in his usual place at the workshop, in the lab at the rear of the building. He was not quite waiting for her but was clearly ready for her arrival. He stopped what he was doing immediately when she entered the room and turned to her.

"Good morning," he said.

"Hi." Tilly didn't quite know how to act around him. She was still mad, of course, about what had happened to Ranger at the hands of Abner's creation. But his tone, his expression—they were fresh, clean-slated, like nothing had happened. Tilly hadn't had enough coffee this morning to initiate a confrontation. So, she decided to join Abner in pretending like everything was fine and normal.

"I am glad you are here," he said, with a not-so-discreet glance at his watch. It was 9:00 in the morning. "It's time for Abraham's field test. I want your input."

"Okay," Tilly said, drawing out the word. For perhaps the hundredth time, she wondered what she had gotten herself into.

She soon found herself following Abner outside, back the way she had just come. The warm outside air was a welcome embrace. Tilly had not realized how tense she had been until she felt the comfort of the outdoors again. She was so relieved to be rid of the icy vise of the lab that she almost came to tears before she could consciously stop them. Her emotions had been strung tight since the nursing home the day before. She was relieved to get ahold of herself by the time she saw the tiger.

The robot tiger was contained in a small enclosure, essentially a cage, on the edge of the larger pasture to the north. It paced back and forth across the length of the cage, switching its tail with every step. It had a new air about it this time, a dynamic energy that ran through its not-muscles as it paced with purpose. *It looks so real*, Tilly thought, unnerved that the animatronic apparently had to be contained in a cage as if it were a living, breathing wild animal. Tilly couldn't put her finger on what was different about it. It looked essentially the same, but somehow the sum of its parts made a whole that was more natural, more alive, than it had been before. When the tiger saw Tilly and Abner, it raised a lip to bare its teeth.

"Abraham!" Abner chastised the thing. "Do not worry, it is just us." Abner sounded downright joyful.

The tiger obviously did not speak English, and it continued to worry despite Abner's assurance. It responded to Abner with a low growl that sent Tilly back to that first time, when she met the first tiger. Before she knew it was a robot or what machine learning was. The turning point in her life between country veterinarian and not-just-country-veterinarian.

"We have been working on the program all week, right, Abraham?" Abner said. The tiger crouched down, its tail flicking. Tilly noticed its claws, sharp little daggers shown off by the splayed toes of its paws.

"So, what's the plan?" Tilly asked. The words came out in a compulsive rush, a subconscious quest to anchor herself in this reality, to break free of the dreamland that she felt trapped in by the pacing not-tiger. It didn't work. She felt a knot in her stomach as she watched the tiger.

"In a few moments, I will set him loose in the pasture. Then we will see."

"See what?"

"How real he has become."

Tilly looked at Abner, to see if he was serious. He was. They stood right outside of the cage now. The tiger's growl grew louder and more aggressive. It climaxed into a piercing feline scream as the tiger launched itself toward them. It was impeded by the fence, of course, but Tilly still jumped backward a few feet. The tiger's roar poured salt on her raw nerves.

"Easy, tiger," Abner said. He looked over to Tilly, beaming at what he must have thought was a joke, clearly expecting a reaction. Tilly gave him a weak smile that felt, from inside her head, more like a grimace. But Abner seemed satisfied. He turned back to business.

The shared fence between the small enclosure and the larger north pasture, where they would set the tiger free, had a gate that could be opened by pulling a lever. Abner gripped the lever.

"Ready?" he asked. His tone was excited, and Tilly's mind nonsensically flashed to a nonspecific Christmas morning of childhood. That was the feeling she heard in his voice.

"Not really. Does it matter?" Tilly asked, just as, at the same time, Abner pulled the lever without waiting to hear her answer. *I guess not*, she thought.

The gate opened with a slower creak than the drama of the moment called for. Tilly winced a little all the same, watching the scene through half-closed eyes.

Tilly's mind was prepared for immediate excitement when Abner pulled the lever, like the opening of the starting gates at the Kentucky Derby. *And they're off!* But nothing happened right away. The tiger kept its eyes—cameras? sensors? Tilly didn't really know how it perceived the world, she realized—on her and Abner. It didn't seem to notice that it had been gifted an opportunity for escape.

"Shoo," Abner said. "Shoo!" He waved his arms in the air at the tiger. The tiger backed away from the fence a few paces. Abner's mouth curled into a genuine smile, distinctly purposeful compared to his usual mouth tics.

"Get out of here!" Abner yelled. He kicked the fence, making it rattle. He kicked it again. The tiger backed as far away as it could, then when it reached the boundary fence between the enclosure and the pasture, it looked behind itself. That is when it saw the opening. In a second, less than a second, it spun around and flew through the open gate. Tilly followed it with her eyes for its first few long strides, but it quickly dissolved into the brush.

"Wonderful, just terrific," Abner said. "Was that not amazing?"

"I guess," Tilly said, her chest tight. She looked at Abner. "How did you get it to act like that? I mean, its reaction—to us. It was . . ."—she paused, looking for the word—"authentic."

Abner tapped his forehead, a twinkle creeping into his eye. "Learning," he said definitively, as if that was all the answer Tilly needed. It was all she got. "How far we have come." He beamed with pride.

Tilly shook her head. "Learning *how*?"

"YouTube," Abner said.

The answer was so unexpected that Tilly laughed. "You're saying the robot learned from *YouTube*? You just—what? Do you, like, just make the computer watch videos of tigers to figure out how to act?"

Abner laughed, decidedly *at* Tilly, not with her. "In the most rudimentary sense, yes."

"And that works, just like that?"

"Apparently," Abner said, and he swept his arm toward the pasture in the direction of the tiger and smiled. "Come on, let us find him."

They got in an ATV and started into the pasture. Tilly had no idea how they would ever find the tiger in the thick brush.

"How are we going to find it?" Tilly shouted over the rattle of the ATV's engine.

"It has a tracker!" Abner yelled back. He pulled a little electronic box with a screen out of his pocket. A green dot moved across the screen.

Abner steered the ATV through the trees, over small hills, and around blind corners. Tilly was impressed with how far of a head start the tiger must have gotten; it was taking a substantial while for them to catch up. The air kissed Tilly's cheeks as the ATV rushed through it, and the smells of nature—the smell of cedar, mostly—enveloped them. Here and there, a deer or a rabbit darted across the road in front of them, scared into action by their aggressive shattering of the peace.

Everything about the pasture around them was as it should be, as it always had been, consistent in its sights and smells—the same today as they had been in Tilly's childhood, and before she was born, and so long before that that she couldn't wrap her mind around such a great span of time. Things were right and orderly. Tilly felt a homey sense of comfort in the familiarity of the Texas countryside. Her tight jaw loosened.

"We are close," Abner said. He slowed the ATV to a crawl, the noise of its engine roaring louder now in Tilly's ears because it no longer had to compete with the sound of the wind whipping past them as they drove. Abner held the steering wheel in one hand and the tracking device in the other.

Tilly scanned the brush for the tiger. She searched for the color orange and for movement. Her eyes swept back and forth, back and forth. Nothing. She found herself relieved not to find anything.

"Do you see it?" Tilly asked Abner.

"No. It should be right here." His voice had the slightest tinge of worry.

Tilly kept looking. Abner had slowed the ATV down so much that they were barely moving. Dense brush surrounded them—they were far off the cleared driving paths. Prickly pear bushes, their paddles densely packed in tight masses, jeered at Tilly as her eyes tried to penetrate through their walls of green in search of the tiger. The stands of cedar trees on either side of the ATV seemed purposeful in their obfuscation; Tilly almost thought she could see them draw their branches closer together to hide the tiger, wherever it was.

"Anything?" Tilly asked.

"No," Abner said. Then, without warning, he shouted, "Abraham! Come out!" Tilly jumped at his suddenly raised voice.

"Did you show the algorithm videos on how to speak English, too?" she asked.

Abner threw her a sidelong glare. But his eyes revealed his worry.

"We'll find him," Tilly reassured him. She hated herself for being so nice. The instinct to comfort lived loudly within her, often asserting itself of its own volition.

Abner brought the Mule to a complete stop in a stand of oak trees. He killed the engine. The silence of the pasture, now confident in the absence of the engine noise, was loud. Nothing made a sound, not even the birds. Tilly looked all around them: forward, to the sides, and behind. Nothing. She realized her hands were balled into tight fists. She unclenched them.

"It should be here," Abner said. "Maybe the tracker is broken." He hit his palm on the little display several times, in a very unscientific manner.

"That fix it?" Tilly gibed. She couldn't help her urge to relieve the tension. Abner didn't answer. His breaths started to condense themselves into short staccato bursts as he stared at the stationary green dot on the tracking device screen.

Tilly felt a twinge of pity for him. "Well, let's just go old-school. Keep driving and we can look for it. I brought my binoculars." Tilly raised the binoculars as evidence.

"Fine," Abner said. He revved the engine and put the ATV back into drive. They inched slowly forward. Tilly kept her eyes peeled for the tiger and marveled at its talent for going missing. Her eyes probed every gap in the brush, every small clearing through the trees. She suspected every cactus of hiding the tiger from them. They continued through the oak stand at speeds of about 100 feet per hour.

Then, suddenly, like a bolt of lightning sent from the heavens, an almighty *THUD* crashed down on the roof of the ATV. At the same time, a familiar feline scream pierced through the peaceful pasture, ripping its silence to shreds. Tilly's scream joined it.

She looked up. The plastic roof of the ATV sagged beneath the tiger's weight. The sickening sound of claws-on-plastic grated her ears. The tiger scrambled on the slippery surface, apparently trying to regain its footing. A large orange paw peeked over the side of the roof in the bustle, then disappeared again. Mere seconds had passed since the initial pounce. Adrenaline erupted through Tilly's system, pulsing through her nerves like a white-hot knife. Pure, unadulterated fear seized her heart and squeezed.

"Abner! Do something!" Tilly looked over at him. He was frozen and ghost-pale, the only movement his nervous, somersaulting mouth. "Abner!"

Abner broke from his terrified reverie and hit the gas. The ATV lurched forward, and the sound of the tiger's claws scraping on the ATV's surface intensified, then stopped. Tilly heard a thud behind them as they sped into the pasture. She looked back to see the tiger, on the ground but rising to its feet.

"Go, go!" she yelled.

"The—the remote!" Abner said.

"What?" Tilly shouted.

"Pocket!"

Tilly found the breast pocket of Abner's shirt. There was something there. She reached in and emerged with the little remote that could turn the tiger off. Tilly stared at the buttons, not sure what to do. The ATV flew through the trees.

"Which—" Tilly was cut off mid-sentence as she was ripped, suddenly and violently, from the ATV. She and Abner flew forward, out of the ATV and onto the ground. Tilly lay there for a moment, immersed in the sudden quiet and stillness, dazed. It was a few seconds before she realized that they had crashed into a tree. Another moment before she remembered that a tiger was chasing them, and a second more for her to remember the remote. She looked down at it in her hand, seeing it for the first time, it seemed.

"Abner—" She was interrupted by the rhythmic sound of paws striking ground. The tiger was still behind them and getting closer. "Abner!" she yelled, unable to form a question, unable to ask what button to press. He lay on the ground, not moving.

Tilly sat up and looked around. They had crashed in thick brush, and Tilly couldn't see any further than a few yards in any direction. The rushing sound of the pursuing tiger grew louder as it crashed through brush nearer and nearer to them, snapping brittle autumn branches of the pasture shrubbery.

Tilly stared at the remote, helpless. The buttons all looked the same and none were labeled. Tilly briefly wondered what kind of psychopath would make an unlabeled remote, but then she finally saw the orange movement through the trees that she had been looking for for the past hour. The tiger.

She started pressing. She pressed every button on the remote, running her fingers down the length of it, pressing down each one with more force than it needed or deserved. The tiger bound another stride, and then another, toward her. By the time she hit the last button, she could see the shine of its eyes. The final button caused it to collapse to the ground, a few feet from her.

Tilly collapsed too, overwhelmed with pure relief, adrenaline still coursing through her veins. She lay back and looked up at the light filtering between the trees, the blue sky between the branches. A tear leaked from her eye and made its way down her cheek, looking for the ground.

Abner stirred beside her. Tilly didn't bother to look at him or check that he was alright. Instead, she stared at the light above. She felt, strangely, very peaceful. On some level, she registered the feeling as being at odds with her quick breathing. Abner made more noises of movement—a grunt, a rustle.

"Amazing," he breathed. The word brought the world back into clarity. Tilly wanted to hit him. And that was when Tilly felt the pain in her shoulder.

"Jesus *Christ*."

Chapter 20
Characters with Long Ears

Tilly left Abner and the tiger in the pasture by the wrecked ATV. Without a word to Abner, she walked back to the workshop. She got into her truck and slammed the door hard. The vibrations sent stabs of pain through her throbbing right shoulder. Tilly revved her truck engine to life and sped away from the lab, her left hand on the steering wheel and her right arm held close to her body, bent across her stomach, the way that it hurt the least.

Tilly flew through the pasture to the back gate of the ranch, then flew down the county road to the main entrance of the 999. She skidded her truck to a halt in front of the main office. She went inside.

Rosanne, the receptionist, looked up in surprise when Tilly yanked the office door open. "Hi there, Tilly, what can I . . ." She trailed off as Tilly stormed right past her desk.

"He's on the phone," Rosanne called down the hallway to Tilly as she marched to the door at the end.

Tilly barged through the door at the end of the hall. Bubba sat behind his desk, tethered to it by the cord of his desk phone, receiver pressed to his ear. He looked up in surprise when Tilly walked in. Tilly stopped in front of his desk.

Bubba smiled, politely enough, and held up a finger—*One minute,* he mouthed—then gestured for her to have a seat in one of the chairs in front of his desk. If he noticed her angry expression—her lips pressed paper-thin, her eyebrows reaching for the bridge of her nose—he didn't show it.

Tilly reached across Bubba's desk and yanked the phone from his hand.

"Hey, what—"

Tilly interrupted him by slamming the phone into its cradle.

"Goddamn it, Tilly, that was important. What's got your panties in a wad?" Bubba glared at her, hard. "And why are ya bloody?"

Bloody? Tilly didn't know what Bubba was talking about. She looked down at herself. She didn't see any blood on her clothes.

"Your forehead," Bubba said. His tone was slightly softer. Tilly reached a hand to her forehead. Sure enough, she could feel dried blood, enshrined in crusty rivulets, streaking from her temple. The dried blood had crystalized her eyebrow into a scabby mass. A couple of ambitious streams of blood had crept almost all the way to her chin.

"Oh," Tilly said. The steam of anger that had carried her into Bubba's office lost some of its pressure. "I—I—" She sat down in Bubba's chair. "Abner."

"What about him?"

"He's a problem."

"Whadya mean?"

Tilly reached to her forehead again with the hand of her good arm. She kept the painful one gingerly bent across her stomach, as if held in an invisible sling. She absentmindedly fingered the dried blood on her forehead.

"He's dangerous. And crazy, I think." Tilly's words came out a lot less authoritatively than the angry thoughts that had marched through her head just moments before. Her voice sounded smaller than she would have liked.

"Did—did he do that to you?" Bubba asked, nodding to her forehead. His expression shifted from angry to concerned.

"No, no." Tilly's hand dropped from her forehead. "Well, in a sense, I guess, kinda he did, yeah."

"Alright, just tell me what happened," Bubba said, frustration creeping into his voice. The stuffed giraffe head behind his desk leered down at Tilly over Bubba's shoulder.

"The tiger," Tilly started. Then she took a deep breath. "Today we tested the tiger. Abner has been working on the AI programming since the hunting incident."

"Uh-huh." Bubba nodded for her to go on. Tilly took another deep breath.

"So, he got it to a good place and thought we should test it. So, we did. Today. Just now. We turned it out into the pasture, to see if it would act like a tiger, and not run into trees, et cetera."

"And I am guessing it didn't go so good." Bubba nodded toward her bloodied forehead.

"No. Well, it depends on what you think 'good' is, I guess. Abner thinks 'good.' I think 'terrible.'"

"Spit it out," Bubba said, impatient. "What happened?"

"It attacked us. The tiger—it climbed a tree and waited for us, then when we drove underneath the tree, it dropped down on top of us. Well, on top of the ATV. Just like a—like a *real* tiger would do." Tilly deflated with the anticlimax of the story.

"Just like a real tiger," Bubba repeated. "Well, that is sorta, ya know, the idea."

"I know, it's just—I mean—" Tilly took another deep breath. Her shoulder ached and her head was starting to too, now that she knew about the blood.

"It was violent, Bubba. It chased us. Abner wrecked the ATV, he was so panicked. And we flew out and it almost attacked us. If I hadn't hit the kill switch just in time . . ." Tilly paused. "Well, I guess I don't know what would have happened. I think it would have been bad."

"Abner wrecked the ATV?" Bubba's eyebrow shot up.

"Bubba, that's not—"

"I know, I know," he interrupted. "Look here, I'm sorry that dipshit wrecked the ATV and that you got hurt. But you hit the kill switch and the tiger stopped, so I don't see what the big deal is about the tiger. Nothin' happened. The kill switch worked. Sounds like a successful experiment."

"Bubba, Abner was so pleased with how it acted. He seemed, I don't know, *excited* that it attacked us. Like it was doing what it was supposed to be doing." Tilly felt the various taxidermied animals around Bubba's office staring at her with their glassy eyes. They were unimpressed.

"Well, it was, wasn't it? Actin' like a tiger," Bubba said, his tone imminently reasonable. "Tigers attack," he added.

Tilly sighed, completely exasperated. "But this is *not* a real tiger, Bubba. It's a robot. It could easily be programmed *not* to attack. It could act like a tiger in every other way, but I don't see the need, for our purposes—"

"Tilly, look. Abner's a little off. I get it. He's weird. But he's doin' a good job at what I'm payin' him for. You are too. You oughtta be pleased with your work."

Tilly didn't know what else she could say to get through to him. "Bubba, I think it's more serious—"

"Tilly, you're in shock from the wreck. Go home, get some rest."

Heat flared to Tilly's cheeks. "If I'm in shock, it's because I narrowly avoided being attacked by a robot tiger that has no business doing any attacking!" Tilly's raised voice took Bubba aback.

"Tilly," he said, his voice saccharine, artificially nice. "Y'all ain't gotta do any more tests. It worked. It's okay."

"But the hunters—"

"The hunters have guns," Bubba said. "And bows and arrows, and knives, and you name what else. They'll be fine. They want excitement—they're payin' for excitement. And see, look at you—all excited! This is what they want!"

Tilly wanted to scream. "Bubba, if you don't talk to Abner about this, if you don't tell him to tone it down, I'm gonna quit."

Bubba raised his hands in mock surrender. "Okay, okay. I'll talk to him."

"Good," Tilly said. She rose, suddenly exhausted. She wanted to run out of the room, but she restrained herself to walking.

She almost ran into Abner in the doorway. "Talk to me about what?" Abner looked past Tilly, at Bubba. Abner looked about as banged up as Tilly, but he was smiling despite the fact that one of his arms hung limp at his side.

Tilly had to take a deep breath at the sight of him. "What do you think, you jackass? Your reckless fucking science experiment."

Abner beamed. "That's exactly why I am here. Have you told Mr. Skinner?"

"I damn sure did." Tilly scowled, holding herself back from a sudden urge to lunge at him.

Abner turned to Bubba himself. "It is truly magnificent," he said. His face had the awed expression of someone who had witnessed a miracle.

"That's what it sounds like to me," Bubba said, beaming too.

"*What?*" Tilly wanted to scream. "Bubba, it's so *dangerous*. Don't let him do this."

"Now, Tilly," Bubba said. "You're the veterinarian consultant, not a safety officer."

"This is a scientific breakthrough," Abner said. "We cannot stop now. Abraham has learned behaviors that I had no role in teaching him. He is moving fluidly and appropriately, he has reflexes, he is reacting to external stimuli—in other words, dare I say . . ." Abner took a deep breath, his excitement visible. He delivered the punch line with grandiosity, "Sentience."

A pause as Bubba seemed to wait for further explanation. Then he said, "Well, I don't know what that means. But it sounds like money to me." Bubba rose from his desk. He reached across the desk to shake Abner's hand, switching his offered hand when he realized he was reaching for the limp one.

Abner took Bubba's hand. "Great job, son," Bubba said. Abner's smile widened.

Tilly turned without a word and left. She didn't say goodbye, for dramatic purposes, mostly, and because she suddenly felt like she might cry and she was afraid that if she opened her mouth to say another word, she would provide an escape route for a sob.

"Well, bye," Bubba said to her departing back. "See ya Saturday."

Tilly stopped in the doorway. "Saturday?" No sob, thank God.

"The first tiger hunt, take two."

Tilly was stunned into silence, seized suddenly by the sour feeling of dread she had come to know well in the past weeks. She didn't know what to say. After a few moments, she landed on, "Okay."

Without another word, she left the office. Rosanne didn't try to talk to Tilly on her way out.

Chapter 21
Tigerstripe Bull

Tilly got in her truck and rolled the windows down. Her hands were shaking, and her shoulder throbbed. She felt *so* tired. Instead of reaching to turn the keys in the ignition, she leaned her head back on the headrest and closed her eyes.

She sat like that for several minutes, listening to the ranch sounds around her. The birds chirped and the soft breeze brushed past her. She thought, after a while, that she might be asleep, and she stayed peacefully that way for a bit longer. Then she dreamed that someone called her name. She ignored them, because it was her dream, and she could do what she wanted. But they called her name again.

"Tilly?" the person called, this time louder, the sound coming from a closer place. "Tilly, are you okay?" The dream dissolved away. It was a real person, really there, asking.

Tilly opened her eyes to a squint. The sunlight felt aggressive, white-hot on her eyes. Royce stood next to her truck, looking at her through the window. "Hi," she whispered.

"Hi," he echoed. "What're you—is that blood?"

Tilly reached her good-armed hand to her forehead. The crust of blood was still there. "Yes," she answered.

"What happened? Are you okay?"

"Tiger attack," Tilly said, still so sleepy. The words felt like chiffon in her mouth.

"What?" Royce's expression took a concerned turn. Whether the concern was because he thought she got attacked by a tiger or because he thought she sounded crazy, Tilly couldn't tell.

Then it hit her. *Oh fuck*. She forgot she wasn't supposed to tell him—or anyone—about the robots. She marshalled her sluggish thoughts, trying to figure out a way to correct the misstep.

"Tigerstripe bull," she said. The creative effort felt herculean. "At the Fischer Ranch this morning. Their bull—a tigerstripe—butted me into a fence."

"Okay," Royce said. He drew out the word into a long thought. Then gently, "Til, you don't look so good, I think you need to go to a doctor."

"No, no," Tilly said. "I'm fine. I just need to get cleaned up."

Royce looked dubious. "Really, I'm fine," Tilly insisted.

"Okay, I guess you'd know. But I'm not letting you drive like this. Wait here. I'll get my truck and drive you home."

Tilly didn't protest. Royce started to walk off but then turned back. He reached into the window of the truck and across Tilly. He pulled the keys from the ignition. "Just in case," he said.

Tilly waited in a gauzy dream for Royce to return. The birds sang in blues and pinks and the clouds swirled in a waltz in the sky above. The wind tickled Tilly's hair across her face in the key of E♭. Tilly closed her eyes. Just when she decided, again, that she must be asleep, or might be dead, she heard the rumble of Royce's diesel truck pull up beside hers. Truck door open, truck door close.

Truck door open. Tilly suddenly felt empty space beside her. She opened her eyes and there was Royce, standing in the open truck door next to her.

"Come on, let's get you home," he said. He held out a hand to help her down.

Tilly took it and stepped out of the truck. A wave of nauseous dizziness hit her, and her first step was more of a stumble. She swayed.

"Woah, easy there," Royce said. He wrapped a steadying arm around her shoulders. His gentle touch felt like a stab.

"Ah!" Tilly cried out. "Shoulder."

"Woah, sorry," He dropped his hand to her waist. They walked like that, bound together, the few paces to Royce's truck. He got Tilly situated and buckled her in, then got in the truck himself.

"You hurt your shoulder?" Royce asked. He started the drive to Tilly's house.

"Yeah, I think it's dislocated," Tilly said. Her eyes were closed, and she leaned her head against the truck window. The glass was cool on her skin.

"You probably know better than I do, but I can take a look when we get to your house if you want. I saw my share of dislocated shoulders in college." Tilly didn't answer, and Royce must have taken her silence as confusion. "Football," he explained. Still, Tilly didn't say anything. Her eyes had drifted closed again, and it felt so nice to keep them that way.

Royce must have seen this. "Hey, Til, do me a favor and keep your eyes open for me," he said.

"Why?" Tilly groaned. But her eyes fluttered open despite her protest.

"Just in case you have a concussion. Gotta keep you awake. Looks like you hit your head pretty good."

"Okay," Tilly said. At that moment, it was the only word she could think of.

A few moments of silence filled the truck. Then Royce said, "I thought the Fischer Ranch raised Brangus cattle?"

"Huh?"

"You said you got pinned by a tigerstripe bull. I just thought they raised Brangus, is all. You know I'm always tryin' to keep up with the latest cattle trends." Royce threw her a smile, which Tilly tried her best to reciprocate.

"Oh, it's new," she ad-libbed, kicking herself for her earlier slip of the tongue as the cover-up grew. "Just a trial run, I think. I wouldn't be surprised if they got rid of him after today." The lies flowed more easily when she didn't think about them too much.

"Yeah, I bet he's a hamburger by Monday," Royce said. Tilly smiled.

Royce kept up the chatting the whole rest of the drive. He kept a wary eye on Tilly to make sure she didn't close her eyes or doze off. When they arrived at Tilly's house, Royce helped her inside in the same manner he had helped her into the truck. He sat her down on the couch.

"Okay, wait here," he said. He went into the bathroom. Tilly's shoulder throbbed anew with the movement from the truck to the couch. Ranger ambled over to say hello, his own movement hindered by the tight bandage around his torso. He lay at Tilly's feet. "Aren't we a pair," Tilly said. Royce came back with a wet washcloth.

"Let's get your face cleaned up," he said. He gently wiped the dried blood from Tilly's chin, cheek, and forehead. With his face so close to hers, Tilly really looked at him, and as she peered out through the filmy haze that cloaked her mind, she felt like she was seeing him for the first time. Blue eyes. Sharp jaw. Five-o'clock shadow. It was a nice face. Tilly winced when Royce's washcloth brushed over the cut at her hairline, the fountainhead of the rivulets of blood that had dried down her face.

"Sorry," he said.

"It's okay," Tilly said softly. Royce, whose eyes had been focused on Tilly's bloody forehead, dropped his eyes down to hers and saw that she was staring at him. Color rose in his cheeks, and he tried to hide his blushing behind an easygoing smile.

Royce handed Tilly the washcloth. "Here, you better do the rest. I don't wanna hurt you."

Tilly took the washcloth. It was streaked with an alarming amount of red. Royce took a couple of steps back.

"Um, do you want me to look at your shoulder? Or I could drive you to the emergency room, if you want," he said.

Tilly had almost forgotten about her shoulder. The reminder sent a sharp pain shooting through it. "Oh—yeah," she said. She unbuttoned the top few buttons of her shirt so she could pull the right side down beneath her shoulder.

Royce kept his eyes on her shoulder. Tilly looked too. She didn't like what she saw. A grotesque out-of-place bump protruded from the side of her upper arm.

"Well, it's definitely dislocated," Royce said.

"You don't say," Tilly said. She sighed. "I don't wanna go to the doctor. I hate the doctor."

"Now you know how the animals feel when they see you coming," Royce said. His face was beginning to fade back to its natural color. "I can try to pop it back in if you want me to."

Tilly's stomach churned at the thought. She wasn't squeamish, normally—her job would be impossible if she was. But something about the thought of her own joints scraping together . . . She shuddered. But it was better than the doctor—probably.

"Okay, yeah, let's do it," she said. "What do I do?"

"Stand up."

Tilly stood. Royce spun her around to face away from him. "Ready?" Royce asked.

"I guess so." Tilly closed her eyes and braced herself.

Royce must have seen her tense up. "It'll hurt less if you're relaxed," he said.

"Kinda hard to relax under the circumstances, Royce," Tilly said through gritted teeth.

"Okay, I have an idea. Hold on." Royce walked to the corner of the living room, where Tilly's mother and father's old record player stood. He pulled a record off the rack and put it on the turntable. He carefully placed the needle in the small gap between two tracks. He turned the player on.

Johnny Cash joined them in the living room, crooning about autumn leaves and missing someone. Royce turned back to Tilly, looking pleased with himself.

"What are you doing?" Tilly asked. She wasn't sure she had the patience for any shenanigans, in her state.

Royce walked to her and stood in front of her. He placed his hand on her waist and held his other out to his side, miming dancing position, without the benefit of a partner that could move her arm to join her hand in his. Tilly's right arm, with the bad shoulder, remained bent across her torso.

"*We* are dancing," he said.

"Royce, I don't have time for this. Just do my shoulder. Let's get it over with." She was coming out of the hazy feeling and into a pain-induced short temper.

Royce didn't answer; instead, he started guiding her in a two-step with his hand on her waist. She didn't have much choice but to follow along. Soon, she eased into the rhythm of the music and her feet fell into the old familiar steps.

"See, not so bad," Royce said. They swayed around the living room, Royce taking the lead to steer them around the coffee table and the couch.

"This is ridiculous," Tilly said. But, despite her best efforts, her mouth curled up a little at the corner. The record clicked over to the next track—"Understand Your Man."

After a few more turns around the living room, Tilly almost forgot about her shoulder. It didn't feel as awkward anymore, either, to dance with her right arm crossed over her stomach herself instead of raised up and out with Royce's. The sensation that Tilly noticed the most, that predominated over her other senses, was the feeling of Royce's hand on her waist, guiding her steps.

"Ready to spin?" Royce asked.

"What? No, I can't—" Royce grabbed Tilly's right hand and raised it up above their heads. Pain shot through Tilly's shoulder and radiated out through the rest of her body in searing ripples.

"Ah!" Tilly cried. Royce spun himself behind Tilly like a top on a spindle. He grabbed her around the waist with one arm and held her right arm high above their heads with the other. Then, in a quick motion, he bent her right arm down behind her head at a forty-five-degree angle, bringing her right wrist to her left shoulder. Before Tilly knew what was happening, he gave her right arm a yank, pulling hard and down.

Tilly screamed. *Pop.* She felt her humerus slip back into the proper relationship with her scapula. "Sonofabitch!" Tears of pain and relief sprung from her eyes. Royce spun her around to face him.

"Better?" he asked. Then he saw that she was crying. "Oh, no—did I make it worse? Oh god, I'm so sorry."

Tears streaked down Tilly's face. The initial pain of the adjustment was terrible, but her shoulder did feel better now, back in its proper place. Still, she was alarmed to find that she couldn't stop the tears. "Not worse," she sobbed. The tears ran hot down her face.

"Okay, but is it better? If not, we're going to the ER. I'm so sorry." Royce's brows were knitted, and the corners of his mouth tugged down into a frown.

Tilly's tears were uncontrollable now. It wasn't the pain in her shoulder; it was the tiger, and the bloody scalpel, and Abner, and Ranger, and her mother, and the dark feeling that had followed her out of the lab on the first day and never left. It was all the times she had wanted to cry over those things and stopped herself. She gulped in air in a crescendo of gasping breaths.

"It's better—it is." She managed to push the words out between sobs, but they barely squeaked through. They came out high-pitched and broken. Her eyes continued to shed more tears than she thought possible. Her chest felt like it was going to cave in. The record clicked off of the last track, and the dulcet tones of Johnny Cash were replaced by the gray sound of the needle dragging across smooth vinyl.

"What is it then?" Royce looked stricken.

Tilly answered only with another heaving breath. Royce searched her face, trying to divine the answer on his own. Tilly wasn't sure what he found there, but whatever it was made him wrap his arms around her and pull her into a tight hug. Tilly first felt the remnants of ache in her shoulder, but then the warmth took over. The comfort. Something about it made Tilly cry even harder.

"Hey, it's going to be okay. It is okay," Royce said into her ear. "You're okay."

Tilly's tears eased a little, enough for her to eke out the word, "Concussion." A rational enough explanation for her torrential crying. But Tilly knew her tone was not convincing.

"I know," Royce said. "I know." And he just held her there, standing in the middle of the living room.

After a while, Tilly's sobbing ebbed, and her tears slowed to a trickle and started to dry in salty streaks on her cheeks. Her breathing took up a regular rhythm again. "I'm sorry," she whispered.

Royce pulled back and held her at arm's length. His eyes, for the first time that day, let in their usual twinkle. "Why, what'd you do?"

Tilly didn't have an answer. She sunk down on the couch. Royce sat next to her, and they stayed that way for a while. Ranger nudged his head up beneath Royce's hands to be petted. Royce obliged.

Royce broke the silence. "Are you gonna be okay, Til?" The question was so broad, Tilly didn't know how to answer. She landed on answering as to her physical injuries.

"Yeah," she said. "I'm gonna be okay."

Chapter 22
The Heifer Becomes a Cow

The next morning, as promised, Tilly did feel better. Royce had stayed with her until long after dark to make sure she wasn't going to—as he said—"lapse into a coma or die." He tried to convince Tilly to go to the doctor, to get checked out just in case, but she wouldn't. So instead they just sat together.

Tilly's survey of her appearance in the mirror made her want to get back in bed. The cut on her head—she still wasn't sure exactly how she got it, hitting a rock when she flew from the ATV, maybe?—had scabbed over as it was supposed to, but it had raised the tissue around it into a swollen mass. Her eyes were puffy from crying—even her upper eyelids were heavy and bulbous. And they were red, shot through with angry veins. She did her best with makeup and Visine and a bandage over the goriest of it.

After satisfying herself that her appearance was as good as it was going to get, she went to let Ranger in from his morning potty break in the backyard, which abutted a wooded area behind her house.

"Ranger," she called. He came trotting up from near the tree line at the back of the yard. He had something in his mouth. A relatively large something. He dropped it at her feet.

To Tilly's immense horror, the something was a dead tabby cat.

"Ranger! What did you do? Oh, god." She shooed him away from the cat and into the house. Tilly took a closer look at the dead cat.

It was definitely dead, and it looked freshly so; it did not yet have the smell of death. "Ranger," Tilly chastised the dog in her you're-in-trouble tone. "Why would you do this?" Ranger answered by dropping his head.

He slunk past her into the house. Tilly had known Ranger to give in to his predator instincts before—he had caught the occasional rabbit or squirrel in the backyard—but a *cat*? And in his injured state?

Tilly turned the poor cat over with her boot. It was stiff—*too* stiff if it was Ranger that had caused its demise, because he had not been outside for long. This was the rigor mortis of an animal dead several times longer than that. When the cat was turned over, Tilly finally saw the full scope of the damage.

Its skull had been cleaved open—just like the calf at the Wills ranch weeks ago. A familiar incision ran down its back. And just like the calf, the cat's brain and spinal cord were missing.

Tilly's stomach dropped. This clearly wasn't the work of her dog. "Ranger?" Tilly called into the house. "Where did you find this?" He didn't answer. And something horrible crept into Tilly's mind. A sinister suspicion.

Tilly tried to remember if she had any dreams last night, after Royce had left, after she had gone to sleep. She tried to remember if she ever woke—or didn't wake—and got up from bed. She tried to remember if she came outside. She tried to remember if she had a knife. Or a scalpel. But she couldn't remember. She couldn't. It was all sleep and blackness and probably concussion. Should she call the sheriff?

Before she could decide, her phone rang. It was just a little too early in the morning for any normal business or social call. She knew before she answered that it was bound to be some sort of emergency. It was. A rancher asked her to hurry out to tend to a calving emergency. She did. She was glad for the distraction.

* * *

Doing her best to forget the cat, Tilly drove to the Rowe Ranch, winding down county road after county road. It was a twenty-minute drive and time was not on her side, so she drove quickly. Hank Williams sang from the radio, which was tuned to the sole Verde station, the slogan of which was *This ain't your daddy's country, this here's your grandaddy's country.* Tilly turned up Hank William's "Jambalaya" and let it take her back to a time before she knew about robotic tigers, or her scalpels in places they shouldn't be, or the subtle pain of watching a loved one be slowly stolen by dementia. For the first time in a while, she felt the tension unwind itself from her shoulders and things felt right and orderly, even as she rushed to address a real-animal emergency—maybe because of that.

She let herself onto the property and drove to the cow pens, her truck stirring up billowing clouds of dust from the dry December ground. She had been here once as a vet since returning to Verde, but she knew the property from childhood; one of her best childhood friends was a Rowe, and so Tilly had been a frequent guest. She found Mr. Rowe waiting by the cow pens, but did not see a laboring cow in the squeeze chute, as would have been ideal. Mr. Rowe jumped in the passenger seat of her truck.

"She's in the west pasture," he said without greeting. Tilly sped in that direction.

Then, when he looked at her, he asked, "What happened to your head there?"

"Oh," Tilly said, her free hand going to the knot on her forehead. "Um, a bull pinned me."

"Goddamn," Mr. Rowe said.

Tilly changed the topic back to the task at hand. "Is she down?"

"Yeah, she was already down when we found her. We didn't have time to get her to the chute. I think the calf is turned."

"Okay. Is she a heifer?"

"Yep, it's her first calf. Been in labor at least two hours already."

"And nothing yet?"

"Nothing." Mr. Rowe directed Tilly through the pasture roads. She tore through brush, sometimes through spaces so tight that shrubbery scraped both sides of her truck in grating screeches. She never hit the brakes.

They came to a clearing, where a ranch hand and a younger Rowe boy stood around the heifer. She was a white-gray Brahman heifer, adorned with a bulbous hump between her shoulders and long, elegant ears. Tilly and Mr. Rowe got out of the truck.

"We cain't get close to her. She either kicks at us or tries to get up an' run. Mean bitch," the younger Rowe said.

Tilly looked sideways at him. Brahman cattle were notoriously human-averse. "I don't blame her," Tilly said. "I'm not sure I could be nice to you either."

Tilly walked around the heifer. She was not quite fully grown, only about two years old. She lay on her side, one silky long ear in the dust, the moistness of her nose and eye creating her own personal mud where head met dirt. She was breathing heavily, and every now and then her whole body rippled with a fruitless contraction.

"Poor thing," Tilly said, squatting down to look at the heifer's back end. "She's dilated, but I don't see any hooves yet." Tilly sighed. "I bet you're right that the calf is backwards." Like all mammals, calves were meant to come into this world headfirst. To do otherwise was danger-ous—usually deadly without intervention—to both mother and baby. A belabored labor often signaled an ill-positioned calf.

The heifer kicked backward at Tilly with a grunt of exertion. Tilly jumped up when she saw the initial movement—years around animals had given her an almost preternatural ability to predict aggression. The heifer's substantial hoof plowed through the air where Tilly had been.

"See? She don't like you neither," said the young Rowe. He spat a wad of tobacco juice into the dirt.

"I'm going to sedate her, if that's okay with you," Tilly said, looking at the elder Mr. Rowe. He gave her the go-ahead. She went to her truck to retrieve the necessary things: her vial of ketamine, the tranquilizer; a syringe; arm-length latex gloves.

She found the gloves and the syringe where they should be. But not the ketamine. She rifled through the large satchel of medical supplies she kept in her truck for ranch calls, looking for the bottle. Several glass vials of medicine shook around in the bag, and she scrutinized the label of each, but none of them were what she was looking for. She looked on the floor of the truck, in the door compartment, and in the center console. She felt under the seats for a small glass bottle. Nothing.

"You coming?" Mr. Rowe called to her.

"Hold on," Tilly said. Her shoulders were tightening as she dug again through her bag. The heifer moaned behind her. Tilly sighed, disappointed in her less-than-optimal organization. She abandoned her search for the sedative and grabbed several lengths of rope from her truck's toolbox instead. She went back to the group.

"Bad news," Tilly said. "My ketamine isn't in my bag. I'm sorry. We'll just have to manage without it."

She tied a loop at the end of one length of rope and handed it to the younger Rowe. "Loop this around her back leg—the one that's in the air. So she can't kick at me."

"Y'mam," he said, and he took the rope. *Little shit*, Tilly thought.

"Wait for me to say when, though." Tilly fashioned the other rope into a double-looped figure eight. She gave it to the ranch hand. "We're going to use this as a halter; we need to get this on her head so we can keep her from trying to stand while I'm working." The ranch hand nodded.

"Okay, we're all going to need to move at the same time. Mr. Rowe, I need you to kneel on her shoulder while we halter her. That's when you'll rope her back leg," she directed the younger man. Tilly put her palpation gloves on, pulling them up over the sleeves of her button-down shirt. She positioned herself near the heifer's tail. The animal was panting.

"Okay, one." Tilly looked at around to make sure everyone was in position. "Two." She took a deep breath.

"Three."

In concert, the elder Mr. Rowe—by far the heftiest of the group—knelt one knee onto the heifer's shoulder. She bellowed and tossed her head up and down in the dirt. Mr. Rowe held her head while the ranch hand tightened the makeshift halter over the heifer's poll and around her nose. At the same time, impressively on his first attempt, the young man looped his rope around the heifer's kicking back leg, pulling it tight around her fetlock joint.

"Okay, you pull your rope back toward me," Tilly directed the ranch hand. He pulled the rope to the heifer's tail, parallel to her body. Her head tucked to her chest, which would prevent any attempt to stand.

"And you"—she looked at the younger Rowe—"you keep that leg as far away from me as you can."

The heifer bellowed angrily. "Alright, lady," Tilly said to the animal. "Let's do this."

Tilly knelt where she did before. She hoped to see a calf, emerging front-hooves-first, coming into the world. But there was no sign of an emerging calf.

"Alright, pretty lady, this will be over before you know it," she said in her most calming voice. Tilly started to hum.

Mr. Rowe looked at her. "Are you humming?"

"Mmm-hmm," Tilly hummed. "It's calming." She did not clarify that it was calming to herself; she had gotten in the habit of humming while pulling calves in vet school to distract herself.

What started as an amorphous tune turned into "La Vie en Rose." By the chorus, the heifer had stilled, either in calm or paralyzed panic. Either worked for Tilly as she reached into the birth canal, searching for tiny hooves. She found them, but to her expectation and disappointment, she also felt a tail.

"Sure enough," Tilly said in a singsong voice, so as not to break the tune of her hum. "It's backwards."

"Goddamn it," Mr. Rowe said. He was still kneeling on the heifer's shoulder.

"It's okay. I'm gonna get him out," Tilly said, breaking her tune. She did not feel as confident as she hoped she sounded. She resumed humming, this time to the tune of "As Time Goes By."

She grabbed the little calf's legs above the fetlock joint and began to pull when the heifer pushed. After several heaves, the calf's back hooves saw the light of day. Tilly felt up to the calf's rump. She turned the calf so that the widest point of its pelvis matched the widest point of the heifer's pelvis. Even if she delivered the calf alive, the second biggest risk was crushing its pelvis or rib cage.

Satisfied with the alignment and keeping in mind the necessity of speed, Tilly resumed pulling. When she felt the calf's pelvis emerge from the heifer's, she gave an almighty yank and brought forth a miracle of tail, torso, shoulders, head, front feet—a new life. Tilly fell backward with the absence of resistance; the calf plopped in a wet gray mass to the dirt near her feet. Tilly stopped humming.

"There you go, mama," Tilly said to the cow. "Good work." The calf was curled on the ground, legs—too long for its body—akimbo. It was wet, naturally, and the moisture escaped the heat of the calf's body as wispy steam rising into the December air. Tilly wiped placenta from its eyes. It blinked up at her, its little body a wonderment of blood and cells and energy, bound together in a biological process, the logistics of which Tilly could recite in her sleep, but could never dream of truly under-standing. *You know it when you see it.*

Though Tilly had witnessed and facilitated perhaps hundreds of births, the continuation of life from mother to child was a miracle every time. Tilly removed her gloves and placed her hand on the calf's fore-head—warm and wet.

"It's alive," Tilly announced. She ran her hand over its rib cage and back end. "And I don't think anything's broken," she said, relieved.

"Alright!" Mr. Rowe said in triumph. "Good work, Tilly."

The crew remained in their positions. The heifer—now a cow—was still breathing heavily but lay still in exhaustion. "When we get up, we're all going to need to get pretty far away from her pretty quickly," Tilly said.

"Don't have to tell me twice," said Mr. Rowe.

Tilly stood, then took a knee on the cow's pelvis, opposite Mr. Rowe on her shoulder. "Alright, fellas, get the ropes off of her—quickly." They did as instructed and slowly backed away from the cow to their truck.

"Mr. Rowe, you and I will need to get off of her at the same time. Ready?"

"You bet."

"Okay—one, two, three." At the same time, the two sprang up, Mr. Rowe slower than Tilly, but still surprisingly spry. The cow sprang up almost immediately after them.

"Truck!" Tilly yelled, as she was already turning to run. Mr. Rowe hadn't waited for her instruction—he was already a few paces ahead of her. The cow snorted behind them, warning them away from her baby. Tilly and Mr. Rowe sprinted, the cow's heavy hoofbeats rumbling behind them in pursuit. Mr. Rowe ran around the truck to the safety of the passenger side and fumbled his way into the cab at the same time Tilly used the back tire to launch herself into the bed of the truck. She turned, breathless, in time to see the angry cow fill the space Tilly had occupied a half second earlier. Snot dripped in strings from her snorting nostrils. She pawed the ground with a front hoof, throwing great plumes of dust into the air with every curl of her leg, the loose skin of her dewlap jiggling beneath her neck with every kick. After a few moments, seemingly satisfied that the human danger had passed, the cow turned with a final huff to tend to her new baby.

"What a good mama," Tilly called after her. "Protective."

"You coming?" Mr. Rowe called from inside the truck.

"I want to make sure the calf gets up okay. Hold on."

Tilly watched the cow go to her calf and begin licking its eyes and nose to clean it of the remnants of birth. The ritual continued from the calf's head to the rest of its body as the cow ran her tongue from its ears to its tail. After ten minutes or so, when the calf had started to dry from gray to white, it started to try to get its legs under it. Called by hunger, it struggled to get its legs to cooperate enough for it to rise. After a few minutes of wobbling, it got all four legs on the same page and was able to stand. With the same instinctual knowing that had compelled the cow to lick her first baby clean, the calf made its way to the cow's udder and began to suckle.

"Looks okay to me," Mr. Rowe called from the truck.

Tilly watched a moment longer, absorbing the beauty of the moment. She felt tears tugging at the corners of her eyes and blinked them away. She didn't know when she had become such a crier, but lately the tears came easily, shepherded to the surface by almost any emotion. She turned away from the cow and calf, and the imprint of the image of them in her mind recalled the print of the Angus cow and calf that she had hung up in her mother's nursing home room. She blinked harder.

Tilly joined Mr. Rowe in the truck.

"Thank you, Tilly. I couldn't afford to lose any more of this year's calf crop. I've had a helluva time with calves dying of pneumonia this year, as you know."

In the beauty of the moment, Tilly had almost forgotten that the calf was born with a death sentence—a commodity destined for slaughter. By safely delivering it, she had merely delayed its demise. A death deferred. It was part of her practice as a ranch vet, of course, but like so many things lately, she tried not to think about it.

"Yeah, I know," she said. She turned the truck's heater up against the chill of the winter air. They rode away in silence, and in the rearview mirror, Tilly saw two buzzards swoop down from the heavens to feast on the cow's afterbirth. The mama cow chased them away.

Chapter 23
Buzzards

Tilly awoke the next morning to her phone ringing. It was Royce. He sounded worried when he said hello.

"What's wrong?" Tilly asked.

"I need you to come out to the Triple Nine and look at something."

"What is it? An animal?" Tilly pictured one of the 999's deer in distress.

"No, well—just come, please. It's not something that I can describe without sounding . . ." Royce trailed off. "You just need to see it, okay?"

"Yeah, okay, sure," Tilly said. She tried to sound calm, to assuage whatever Royce's worry was, but his worry was more contagious, and it got to her before she could impart any calmness onto him. It sounded like *drip, drip, drip*.

"Okay good. I'll meet you at the entrance to the east pasture."

As Tilly neared the ranch, she saw a dark, spiraling column in the sky ahead, a swirling mass of black particles reaching hundreds of feet into the heavens. Buzzards. Hundreds of them. A beacon in the sky to mark the final resting place of something dead. And whatever was dead had to be large, to have enough meat for the pickings of so many scavengers.

Tilly found Royce where he said he would be, right by the gate to the east pasture. He smiled when he saw her, as he always did, but his smile didn't radiate its usual warmth, and instead to Tilly it looked a little garish, an awkward stretch of mouth across face, teeth glinting.

"Your face looks better," he said in greeting. Tilly knew that was a lie because the bruise on her forehead had only acquired more colors since Royce had seen it when it was newly formed. But her face had also been covered in blood when Royce last saw it, so perhaps that was what he meant.

"What's going on?" Tilly asked. She had a clue in the spiraling column of circling buzzards that, now that she was closer, Tilly could tell did indeed rise from the east pasture of the 999.

"Come with me," Royce said. They left Tilly's truck at the gate and drove out into the pasture in an ATV, guided by the buzzards like a north star. Tilly expected a nasty surprise at every turn in the road, perhaps a waiting man made of shadows, but nothing jumped out to get them as they made their way to the to the base of the buzzard spiral, to find whatever it was that had attracted the birds.

When they neared the spot on the ground that seemed to project the beam of buzzards into the sky, they had to leave the ATV and walk on foot into trees and brush too dense for the ATV to pass. A few hundred feet and they came to a clearing, and in it was what they were looking for.

Tilly recognized the stench of death—the acrid rotting smell that registered on a fundamental, primal level—before she realized what she was looking at. The few buzzards that hadn't flown away as Tilly and Royce crunched through the trees toward the clearing—brave in their hunger—finally flapped into the sky when the people came into view. They joined their friends circling in the sky above, advertising the meal to others, far and wide.

"What the—" Tilly started, then she was silenced by her own concentration, as she tried to figure out what it was that she was seeing.

All around the clearing, small piles of rocks, most of them three or four feet across, rose up in jagged mounds, like so many pustules pockmarking the land. On closer inspection, a few of the piles had crumbled, the rocks falling away to reveal what they attempted to conceal. Tilly's eyes finally caught up with her nose.

The rocks were stacked atop the dead things that had attracted the buzzards. Tilly walked to a faulty pile, one that had fallen away to give up its secret. What lay beneath was not readily identifiable, other than that it was organic and had once been alive, but was now quite dead. Tilly kicked some rocks away to get a better look. The carcass of whatever it was had been contorted into an agonizingly unnatural twist. The thing appeared to be something that once had four legs, but Tilly counted only three. The legs had delicate cloven hooves, and so, at first, Tilly thought it was a deer, but she wasn't sure. Its muscles and hide had been torn away from their natural places, ripped apart into ribbons. Tilly felt suddenly very cold. *Drip, drip, drip.*

"What do you think this is?" Royce asked.

"The animal or the . . ."—Tilly gestured around her, not sure how to describe the scene—"the graves?"

"Pretty sure the animal's a goat." Royce kicked the remaining rocks away from the creature's head. From its mangled face stared back an unharmed eye, open, its pupil tellingly rectangular.

"Goat," Tilly affirmed. She thought back to her conversation with the men in the diner. She looked around the clearing to do a quick survey. There were eleven piles of rocks. A rush of chills swept up Tilly's spine and down her arms, unleashing a shudder. "There've been missing goats," she said quietly.

"I know. My Uncle Augie . . ." Royce trailed off. "I'm more curious about what did this," he said, eyes darting from rock pile to rock pile.

"Why do you think it's a 'what'?"

Royce blanched. "Well—well, I just thought that maybe it was, you know, a predator. Like a mountain lion."

"A mountain lion burying its kills?"

"I thought they did that."

"I mean, they'll hide them under leaves sometimes. I don't think a mountain lion is capable of doing this." Tilly gestured to the piles of rocks.

"So you think, what? It's a predator of the two-legged variety?"

"I think you need to call the sheriff."

Royce agreed. He called the sheriff, who said he'd be there in twenty minutes. So Tilly and Royce were left waiting in the goat graveyard.

"Weird that they're not more eaten, if it was an animal," Royce said.

"They don't look very eaten at all," said Tilly. "I don't think it was an animal."

Royce was looking down at his boots. He dug the toe of the left boot into the dirt. Then he said, "You don't think it was, you know, a cult or anything like that?"

"I don't know. It does look . . . ritualistic?" The word sat heavily on Tilly's tongue. "But there's no blood on the ground. They weren't killed here."

"What the fuck is happening in this town," Royce said. He looked at his boots. He kicked a pebble around with his toe.

Tilly looked around again at the scene. All of the little piles were approximately uniform, stacks of limestone gathered from the rocky pasture, neatly piled except for the few that had been disturbed by the buzzards. Tilly looked to the sky, where the great mass of buzzards still circled, waiting for the humans to leave. Or, Tilly supposed, waiting for the humans to die, too, because buzzards knew that all living things would be food eventually—that was the whole life of a buzzard, waiting on the other lives to expire, earthly bodies finally useful in death. Tilly shook her head to dispel the thought, but another one, worse, took its place. As she thought of dead things and the odd happenings around town, the image of the missing girl, Rachael Gonzales, from the poster in the diner swam into her mind.

"Hey, Royce?" she said.

"Yeah?" He was pacing back and forth between an agarita bush and a prickly pear cactus.

"Are you sure all the graves are goats?"

Royce stopped pacing and looked at her. "No, I—why?"

"Well, just the sort of person that would do this . . ." Tilly left the thought for him to complete. Another second of almost calm, then Royce's eyes widened in realization.

As if taking up the steps to a choreographed dance, at the same time the two went to the undisturbed pile of rocks nearest to them and toppled it. They went around the clearing, kicking rocks away from the graves, Tilly worried that with every rock she removed she would see a nose, or an ear, or a lock of human hair. And with every pile she kicked over, she felt more watched, like every destruction let something evil and dark take a step closer to her, and then she looked to the sky again and there were the buzzards, circling and waiting and watching, and the clearing felt somehow smaller, the trees and cacti closing ranks to trap their prey and swallow it up.

"All goats here," Royce said, and it was nice to hear a reminder that she wasn't alone in the woods.

Tilly kicked the last of her piles down. "Same here," she said. Relief. A buzzard cawed.

Royce looked as relieved as Tilly felt, and she wondered if he felt the watching too. Then a rustling in the brush. They both jumped and turned to watch the approaching sway of bushes as a ripple of movement came toward them. Tilly felt an energy well up around them as the movement inched closer, like the steady build of pressure that forces a loosened champagne cork toward release. And then the thing sprang out from the bushes. *Pop*. Tilly and Royce jumped again.

It was the sheriff. Tilly heaved a sigh. When he spotted them, Sheriff Valdez waved.

"How do, Royce, Tilly," the sheriff said.

"Hi, Mr. Valdez," Tilly said at the same time that Royce said, "Howdy, Sheriff."

"Good lord, Tilly," the sheriff said. He was looking at her forehead and her colorfully bruised eye. "There somebody I need to arrest?"

Tilly's cheeks reddened at the attention. "I don't think you have jurisdiction over bulls, unfortunately."

"Sure don't," Valdez said. He looked around the clearing. "Now, what do we have going on here?

Tilly and Royce made way for the sheriff to get to the goats in the clearing. Neither tried to explain to the lawman what he was looking at.

"Well, I'll be a sonofabitch," Sheriff Valdez said when he saw the sight. "Weird shit just keeps happening." He walked around the toppled rock piles, inspecting the mangled goats.

"We think it's gotta be a person, Sheriff," Royce said. "Or *people*, could be more than one, I guess. You know some folks around town have had their goats stolen recently."

"Oh yeah, I'm aware." The sheriff studied the rocks that were now scattered around the clearing where Royce and Tilly had kicked them away. "And you said rocks were piled on top of 'em?"

"Yeah," Tilly said. She surveyed the clearing, and she saw that it now just looked like a clearing with a bunch of dead goats, instead of a clearing with a bunch of goat graves. Here and there a rock remained atop a leg or what was left of a mauled torso, but most of the rocks had resumed their roles as natural parts of the landscape, perhaps more numerous in this clearing than in other areas, but not suspicious in themselves.

"We were worried there might be something . . . else underneath," Tilly explained. "You know, with—with that girl missing, and all."

"So you moved all the rocks to check for yourselves?" the sheriff asked.

Tilly felt blood rising in her cheeks. "Yes," she said.

"Royce, I see we already forgot what I told you about touching the evidence, huh?" he said. He was referring to the found scalpel, which seemed now, to Tilly, like a thing from long ago.

"Well, we didn't know it was *evidence*, per se," Royce explained. "I didn't even think of that, to be honest. We were thinking this might be some kind of cult thing. Like with animal sacrifice and, maybe, I don't know, torture." He looked around at the goats, resting most unpeacefully.

"I'm thinkin' animal. See? Looks like bite marks," the sheriff said. He tapped one of the goat's wounds with the toe of his boot. "Somethin' big."

Tilly and Royce squatted down near the goat that held the sheriff's attention. This one was less mangled than the others, with identifiable stretches of coat remaining—gray and coarse, free of blood. Sure enough, twin arcs of puncture wounds dotted the goat's torso. The uneasy feeling that had taken up residence on the periphery of Tilly's mind ever since that first day in the workshop moved closer to front and center. She thought immediately of the tiger, but then she remembered its silicone teeth—it couldn't have done this.

"Mountain lion, likely," the sheriff said.

"Not with the way the rocks were piled," Tilly said. "They were so neat. Mountain lions can't—they can't do that." Tilly wished that they had left just one of the graves intact, so he could see.

The sheriff didn't answer and continued his tour around the carcasses, stopping at one to nudge something away from it with his boot. It was a mass of flesh, separated from the body, but buried with it all the same. Once Tilly saw that one, she noticed that several other goats were in the same way, lying there next to disembodied muscle and fur that had rested with them beneath the rocks.

"Why'd an animal leave all that without eating it?" Royce asked.

"Dunno. I think I have heard that some big cats kill for sport, like lions—you know, the African kind. Tilly, that true?"

"Uh, yeah," she said. "But this doesn't quite fit that bill."

"How'd it get into the pasture though?" Royce asked. "We've got ten-foot game-proof fence around the whole thing."

"Maybe you need to check for holes in your fence."

"Shouldn't you look for tracks or something? We'd find the cat tracks if it was a cat, rule out humans."

"Royce, you and Tilly, and now me, have been walking all over this place. Of course there's gonna be human tracks. And I don't have the time to hang around and scour for cat tracks just to confirm that I'm right."

"You don't think it has something to do with the mutilated calf?" Tilly asked. "And the blood in the pasture with the scalpel?" Her voice hung on the last word. She almost mentioned the cat that Ranger had found near her house the day before, but something stopped her.

The sheriff shook his head. "Maybe," he said. He sighed. "I don't know what's related anymore."

The sheriff took a deep breath. "Tell you what. I'll send some of the boys out to investigate, take photos and look for prints. See what we see. Sound good?"

They both said that it did. And they left the goats and made their way out of the pasture, the plume of buzzards descending onto the clearing once again, their patient vigil rewarded.

Chapter 24
The Goats, Redux

Nighttime. The moon hung low in the sky. It was cold. The clearing where the goats were found in the east pasture of the 999 was quiet.

Tilly awoke. She looked down at herself. She was in her pajamas and very much not in her bed. She stood in the middle of the clearing. She looked around, disoriented. A bird cawed from a tree nearby. The disturbed piles of rocks around the clearing lay mostly as Tilly and Royce had left them that morning. The goat carcasses had been picked nearly clean by the buzzards. Tilly's heart raced, her blood pressure pushing her heartbeat audibly into her ears. The thud of her heartbeat told her that she was, in fact, awake.

Her breathing grew shallow, panicked. *How did I get here?*

Tilly realized that she held something in her hands. Something furry. She looked down. It was the decapitated head of one of the goats. Its eyes had been pecked out by buzzards. Looking into the empty eyes of the goat skull, Tilly screamed. She screamed louder than she ever had in her life. She dropped the goat head.

Tilly ran from the clearing. The cedar and agarita branches scraped her arms, her legs. She tripped over a rock and stumbled but did not fall. She kept running. From the corner of her eye, she thought she saw a man made of shadows. Was he chasing her? She ran.

She ran until she arrived at the familiar pasture gate. By some bewildering miracle, her truck was there. Her cell phone was inside. She called Royce.

A few rings, then "Hello?" He sounded groggy. It was 3:00 a.m.

"Royce you have to come get me I'm at the Triple Nine I don't know how I got here I think I drove but I don't remember and I think I might have been asleep and I just woke up—"

"Tilly—Tilly," Royce interrupted. "Where on the Triple Nine?"

She told him. "I'll be right there. Stay put."

She did. She sat in her truck and sobbed, and wished sleepwalking-Tilly had thought to bring Ranger along so that she could hug him close to her. She caught her breath and watched the darkness outside, afraid of what she might see. But all she saw was wilderness and her own reflection in the truck window.

Royce arrived about twenty minutes later, less time than it should have taken to arrive at the 999 from his house. Tilly jumped when Royce tapped on her window, convinced that the shadow man she had been looking for in the trees had come for her at last. But it was only Royce.

Tilly collapsed into him when he opened the door. He caught her.

"Woah, now," Royce said. "What's going on?"

He gently nudged Tilly to the passenger seat and slid into the driver's side himself.

"I don't know," Tilly said, sobbing. "I went to bed and then—and then the next thing I knew—" Her voice broke, and she couldn't go on. She gestured generally to the pasture around them.

"You woke up here?" Royce asked.

Tilly nodded.

"And no one else is here?"

Tilly shook her head.

"So you drove," Royce said, drawing the only logical conclusion as they both sat in Tilly's truck.

Tilly nodded again. "I guess." Her voice cracked. She wiped the tears from her face, which had gone splotchy from crying. "I think I sleepwalked. Or sleep-drove, I guess. Jesus Christ, Royce." Tilly collapsed into her hands.

"Have you sleptwalked before?" Royce looked concerned.

Tilly nodded. "In high school. It stopped when I moved away for college."

"No, I mean, like, recently."

"Oh," Tilly said. "Yeah, actually. I woke up writing checks at my kitchen table one night." She thought of the dissected chicken. And the scalpels in the window boxes. The cat.

She said, "And I think there's a chance I sleepwalked one other time, but—I don't know. If I did, I guess I must have gotten back into bed without ever waking up."

And finally she articulated the fear that had plagued her since she found the scalpels. "That's what scares me, Royce." Her voice sounded so small, even to her. Like a stranger's. "What else have I done when I've been asleep?" Saying the thought aloud was like releasing a pressure valve in her mind—and horrible, horrible thoughts flooded in. But so did relief.

She caught Royce's eyes for a moment, and he shook his head, brow furrowed. "I don't know, Til," Royce said. He sounded far away. He started the truck and began driving Tilly home, leaving his own truck behind.

"I mean, what if I've—what if I've *done* something?" Tilly felt the memory of the goat head in her hands.

"Like what?" Royce asked.

"Like—like something *bad*."

"Like sleep-driving?"

"Or something worse," Tilly said. Royce didn't press her any further.

"I think I'm going crazy, Royce," she whispered. He didn't respond, and she wasn't sure he had heard her. They rode the rest of the way in silence.

Back at home, Tilly didn't go back to sleep. She sat at her kitchen table until the sun rose.

Chapter 25
The Life of the Flesh Is in the Blood

At an acceptable hour, Tilly made herself a cup of coffee. It was the day of the next attempt at a tiger hunt. Sitting at the kitchen table with her coffee, she thumbed through yesterday's edition of the *Verde Echo*. She barely got past the headlines on the front page—"Christmas Festival next week;" "Verde girl, 15, still missing;" "School board approves plans for new agriculture barn"—before she got up and relocated to a chair outside. A few more minutes of trying to read, and then she gave up entirely. She took Ranger on a walk around the block. She showered and got ready. It was only 7:00 a.m. She went to the diner.

Before she knew it, Tilly was sitting down with Mr. Schmidt and a couple of the other men at the diner.

"What in God's name happened to your forehead?" Mr. Schmidt asked when he saw her.

Tilly had almost forgotten about the purple knot at her temple. "Had a run-in with a bull," she said as she sat down.

"Did you win?"

Tilly forced a laugh, still not in much of a laughing mood after the night's activities. "Yeah, obviously. You should see the other guy—he's gonna need a good veterinarian."

The men chuckled. Then one of them said, "We hear you and Royce Wilson found something unusual at the Triple Nine yesterday." *Of course the word of the goats was already around town.* After some prodding, Tilly told them about the goats, but only her first encounter—she left out the part about returning to them in her sleep.

"And they was under piles of rocks?" Mr. Nunley asked.

"Yeah, neat little piles," Tilly said. She mimed the shape of a rock pile with her hands, then found a loose thread on her jacket and started to pull at it.

Mr. Garza piped in. "Was one of them my missing nanny goat? Kind of brownish black with white marks on her face?"

Tilly shook her head, her mouth pulled down in a frown. "I'm not sure."

"So what do you think, is it a mountain lion?" Mr. Schmidt said.

"Could be, I guess," she said. "I'm really not sure."

"It don't make sense to me," Mr. Schmidt said. "I never heard of a mountain lion stacking rocks." He buttered a piece of toast on his plate.

"It has to be people," another man said. Several men around the table nodded in agreement.

"But why would anyone *do* something like that?" another said.

"I don't know," Tilly said softly, looking at the table. Thinking of her late-night misadventure to the 999's east pasture.

"I still think it's gots to be Satanists," Mr. DeLeon said. "Something with the occult."

"Y'all don't reckon it has anything to do with that missing Gonzales girl, do ya?" Mr. Schmidt asked between bits of toast. Tilly looked over to the bulletin board by the diner door with the MISSING flier for Rachael Gonzales.

The group sat in silence for a moment. "Anyone heard anything about that?"

"The paper yesterday said there weren't any developments," Mr. Nunley said, staring into the blackness of his coffee cup.

Lynette, the waitress, brought over a fresh pot of coffee to top off their cups. "Y'all hear about Evelyn Krane?" she asked. Tilly was glad for the topic to change. A combination of *No*-saying and headshaking gave Lynette her answer. She raised her eyebrow in a dramatic way, then announced, "She's *engaged*."

"No!"

"You're kiddin'!"

Tilly was ashamed that she gasped at the news.

"And her husband not two-months dead," Mr. Nunley said.

"What ever happened to waiting year, at least? I thought that was the rule." Mr. DeLeon cradled his cup of coffee in his hands. "I mean, at least be discreet for more than two months!"

"Now, everyone grieves in their own way," Mr. Schmidt said. He was leaned back in his chair. No one said anything else. The authority on grieving, Mr. Schmidt had the last word on the subject. The conversation turned to who had killed the biggest whitetail buck so far in the season, and Tilly took that as her cue.

Tilly rose to leave, but just then a man burst through the door. Tilly knew him as a local farmer. He was sweating, and his eyes were like saucers. The din of the restaurant quieted, knives and forks and coffee cups clanking down on the table, and all eyes turned to the man in the doorway. Tilly sat back down.

"Have y'all heard?" the man shouted, the ambient silence shining a spotlight on his words.

The diner-goers returned blank stares, some looking confused, and others amused.

"They found her! They found the Gonzales girl!" the man cried.

A moment of silence. Then the diner erupted into a chorus of whispers and murmurs, and people pulled out their phones to spread the news.

"Where?" someone shouted.

"She alive?" someone else asked.

But without answering, the man turned and was out the door, on to spread the news at the next establishment. Tilly shared bewildered looks with a few of the men at her table. Then she rose again, and this time left. In a sort of haze, she set out to the 999 for the tiger hunt. She thought of the girl and wondered at her fate, and didn't know whether to feel relieved or horrified at the discovery.

Tilly turned her mind to the scenery as she drove. It was a bright, clear December day, so fully enveloped by light that it seemed impossible for the sun to be its only source; it had to come from everywhere else, too—light from the ground, from the trees, from the buildings in town. Every detail of the world seemed so newly vivid in the brightness that it occurred to Tilly that up to that point in her life, she must have been viewing the world through a veil. And today the fog had lifted to show her every little green-leaf, blue-sky detail.

A few miles out of town, the perfectness of the day was shattered. Two police cars blocked the highway, their lights strobing in reds and blues. Just beyond the cars was a bridge across the dry bed of the Verde Creek. Sheriff's deputies were pulling yellow tape across the path down to the creek bed. Another deputy waved Tilly to a stop before she reached the police car blockade. He motioned for her to roll her window down. She did.

"Ma'am, you need to turn around," he said.

"What's going on?" Tilly asked. The scene at the diner was at the forefront of her mind. "Is it Rachael Gonzales?"

The deputy narrowed his eyes, and said only, again, "You need to turn around. Go another way."

"There's not another way to where I'm going. I'm going to the Triple Nine Ranch. This is the only way."

The deputy sighed. "What's your business out there?"

Unable to think of anything other than the tiger hunt, Tilly simply said, "I'm a veterinarian."

She then saw Sheriff Valdez among the melee in the creek bed. She shouted to him, "Sheriff Valdez!"

"Ma'am!" the deputy scolded her. Tilly was unabashed.

"Sheriff Valdez!" she yelled again. The sheriff turned to her. He waved when he saw who it was. He trudged up the bank of the creek to the road above.

"Sheriff, can y'all let me through so I can get to the Triple Nine? I've got veterinary business out there. It's a little time-sensitive, as you can imagine."

"Yeah, yeah, let her go, fellas," he said to the gathering deputies.

"Y'all find Rachael Gonzales here?" Tilly asked. Her curiosity overwhelmed her good manners.

Sheriff Valdez glanced around at the deputies, then leaned toward the open window of Tilly's truck and said in a low voice, "Sure 'nuff. Under the bridge. Needle in her arm."

"Yikes," Tilly said. She peered under the bridge, then back at Sheriff Valdez. She whispered, "Dead?"

Sheriff Valdez looked at the ground. "Yep, looks like she hasn't been dead for very long."

"Shit," Tilly said.

"Yeah, shit," the sheriff echoed. He dug the toe of his boot into the ground.

"Sorry, Sheriff," Tilly said softly. He just nodded. Then without saying anything else, he stepped back from Tilly's truck and waved her around the blockade of cars.

When Tilly looked back at him in her rearview mirror, the sheriff was watching her drive away. She couldn't be sure at the distance, but she thought his eyes caught just a little too much of the day's brilliant sunlight. Tilly was glad she couldn't see beneath the bridge as she continued on to the 999.

* * *

At the ranch, Abner was waiting by the small pen that served as the gateway to the larger pasture where the hunt would take place. The tiger paced back and forth inside, once again looking very much more alive than it should. Tilly's most recent memory of it charging toward her made her want to kick it, or run away, or scream.

But instead, she simply said, "Good morning, Abner." She had decided she would try to be nice to him, for the sake of her own mood and sanity. Even though, of course, the tiger-attack-ATV-crash debacle was fresh.

Her anger at Abner was soothed a little by the fact that his left arm was in a brace. The visual manifestation of Karma pleased Tilly, and she almost felt guilty in her smugness. But then she remembered that the same incident that had given Abner the brace had given *her* a concussion. Her eyes narrowed.

Abner said "good morning" back, without taking his eyes off the tiger pacing back and forth in the pen.

"Is it broken?" Tilly asked.

"No, he was not very damaged, actually. I had to make some small repairs, but now he is good as new." Abner's gaze stayed trained on the pacing machine.

"I meant your arm."

"Oh. Just a fracture," Abner said. He turned to look at her. That was when Tilly saw that the right side of his face was covered in angry red scrapes and bruises. He had a bandage over his temple to match Tilly's own. His right eye was swollen—almost to the point of being swollen shut—and ringed by a nauseatingly purple bruise.

"Good thing your face broke your fall, I'd say," Tilly said. It was hard being nice to him.

"We match," Abner said. He tapped his index finger to the bandage on his forehead and looked at the one at Tilly's hairline. He was smug.

"Thanks to you," Tilly said, sincere anger pushing her insincere manners out of her mind.

Before Abner could respond, the tiger did for him. The thing emitted a low growl as it paced past where Tilly and Abner stood outside of its pen. Its nose twitched like it was sniffing the air, searching for her scent. Tilly was nearly certain that the animatron did not have an olfactory function, so the nose twitching was only theater. But it served its purpose—the tiger was all the more believable for it.

"Howdy!" a voice from behind them yelled. Tilly jumped. Abner did not. It was Bubba, who'd arrived with the day's hunter.

The hunter was tall, a refinement of dark hair and the kind of too-perfect teeth that advertise wealth. Abner and Tilly greeted him, but he didn't bother greeting back. He had eyes only for the tiger. He watched it as it watched them, pacing back and forth in its enclosure.

The second thing Tilly noticed about the hunter, after the fact that he didn't say hello, was that he had—no, was *adorned*—with an armory of weapons. A rifle slung across his back; a pistol in a leather chest holster; two hunting knives sheathed in his belt. If it weren't for the modernity of the weapons, he would have looked like a safarist in Colonial Africa. *Daddy says he's not a nice man.*

"Team, this is George Fairbanks. He's hunting today." Fairbanks kept his back to them as he watched the tiger.

Bubba cleared his throat. "Um, George—this is my team. We have Abner Ubel, he's the brains of the operation." Tilly rolled her eyes. The hunter—George, apparently—finally acknowledged them, and turned from the tiger to shake Abner's hand.

"And this here is Tilly Hutto, our consulting veterinarian," Bubba said as he presented Tilly to the man. Tilly was impressed with Bubba for not prefacing her profession with her gender.

"'Tilly'? That's cute. Is that short for something?" George asked. Tilly bristled. Fairbanks very noticeably—to Tilly, at least—did not initiate a handshake with her, as he had done with Abner.

"'Matilda,'" Tilly responded coolly, as she stuck out her hand toward him. "It's a family name."

Fairbanks took her hand. Bubba had mentioned previously that their first hunter was some sort of investment banker from Dallas, and his handshake felt like it. Confident, assertive, arrogant.

"Tilly and Abner are along today as observers. We are always working on product improvements," Bubba explained.

"Fine," Fairbanks said, as if Bubba had asked a question. "As long as they stay"—he looked Tilly up and down—"out of the way."

"Oh, don't you worry about that," Bubba said. "They will. Right?"

He looked at Tilly and Abner. "Right," they said in unison. Tilly gave Bubba and the hunter a tight-lipped, narrow-eyed smile. Abner looked at the ground.

"Abner," Bubba said sharply. Abner started and looked up. "Care to continue the introductions? George wanted to meet our friend, here, before we turn him loose for the hunt." Bubba swept his arm toward the tiger enclosure.

"Right," Abner said. "Yes, meet Abraham." He walked to the fence separating the people from the machine.

"Abraham," George repeated. "'*And I will make of thee a great nation.*'"

Tilly remembered something amorphously religious from her youth. The others ignored the verse.

"Abraham is an animatron whose actions are powered by artificial intelligence. Almost everything you will see him do today, he has *learned.*"

As Abner continued to prattle on about the miracles of artificial intelligence—the miracle that was Abraham (and the miracle that was Abner)—George Fairbanks watched the tiger. He put his hand on the fence. Leaned in close.

The tiger, which had paced unceasingly to that point, stopped. It crouched down on its haunches, then took two slow, spring-loaded steps toward Fairbanks on the other side of the fence. All at once, it launched itself toward him, huge paws swiping into the metal posts of the fence. Tilly jumped back, a reaction no doubt informed by being twice attacked by the robot. The force of the impact was enough to send a shock wave through the towering fence, making it sway.

Fairbanks did not flinch. After a beat of a silence filled only by the noise of the reverberating fence, Fairbanks broke into laughter, as if he hadn't just been saved from certain mauling by a few inches of metal. The tiger resumed its pacing.

"Wonderful," the hunter said. "It looks so real." Abner beamed at what he took as a personal compliment.

Tilly's hands were shaking, her sunny-day mood darkening with every pass of the pacing tiger.

"Well, let's get to it, we're burnin' daylight," Bubba said.

"Shall I set him free?" Abner asked.

"Go ahead."

The group gathered around Abner, who stood at the lever that opened the gate from the enclosure into the pasture. Tilly could feel the excitement of the men in their stances, the electrified way they held themselves, like sprinters waiting for the starting pistol to fire.

Then Abner pulled the lever. The tiger bolted through the gate immediately. Tilly recalled the last time—the first time—she and Abner had released the tiger into the pasture, when it took some time to realize it should run through the gate. With its quick reaction this time, it must have remembered—must have learned.

The group watched it run off into the pasture, following the orangeness until it was swallowed up by the green and brown and gray.

"Yee, saddle up, boys!" Bubba said. "And Tilly," he added.

And then he led the way into the pasture, breaking the surface tension of the group's bubble, so that the others had no choice but to flow after him.

Chapter 26
Wild Asses (Swift Animals)

Tilly had never been on a tiger hunt before. She tried to remind herself that she wasn't on one now; she was on a robot hunt. But it felt real enough as she and the group trudged through the pasture. Buck Owens's "I've Got a Tiger by the Tail" looped through her mind as the group trekked through the cedar and oak trees, adding a layer of internal absurdity to an already absurd situation.

The strategy, Tilly gathered, was to search for the tiger on foot. Their four-person group of hunters could never successfully stalk a tiger in the wild—four people make too much noise. But Bubba wasn't one to let reality get in the way of a good time. And the hunting posse had the advantage of confinement in the fenced forty-acre pasture. They had to run across the tiger eventually.

Despite the ample noise of their footsteps and the rustle and crackle of limbs and branches as they swept them out of their path, the group remained ceremoniously silent, reverent in the ritual of the hunt.

Tilly didn't realize the degree to which she didn't want to be involved in any of this until it was too late. She had been swept into the pasture with the group, driven by their excitement into a march after the tiger, before she even really thought about how she didn't want to be in the pasture with the tiger again, especially not on foot. By the time she decided that she wished she had stayed behind, she was in too deep. She didn't think she could get away with turning back now, and moreover she didn't want to walk back to the safety of the other side of the fence on her own—and weaponless. So, she continued.

The group had naturally fallen into a roughly single-file line, the better to navigate through narrow gaps between trees and shrubs. Bubba led the way, the natural hunting guide as the person who best knew the ins and outs of this pasture. George was next, of course. Then Abner, who scampered after Bubba and George like a rabid fan to a boy band. Tilly followed Abner.

And so they proceeded through the pasture. As best as Tilly could tell, they were making their way through the pasture in a zigzag pattern, so as not to pass the tiger by to their left or to their right. Besides the tiger itself, Tilly wasn't sure what she was supposed to be looking for—tracks in the dirt? a newly cleared path through dense brush?—but she decided that it wasn't her job, and resolved not to worry about it. She did wonder what her job *was* in this context—she didn't really see the need for her presence. But she was being paid. So, here she was.

The group trudged through a stand of cedar trees, evergreen even in the winter. The densely packed cedar needles on the densely packed cedar branches blocked the sunlight, cocooning the hunting party in a room of green shadows as they pressed through the foliage. Tilly found herself looking for the silhouette of a man in the darkness. She didn't see one.

In fact, Tilly realized that she hadn't seen any sign of life since they began their trek. None of the expected animals—no deer, no jackrabbits, no armadillos. Not even a squirrel. And other than their footsteps, the pasture was quiet. No birds, no anonymous animal rustling in the brush. Just walking. And breathing. And thoughts rattling about in Tilly's brain.

Tilly thought that they had been walking for about a half hour and that they were about halfway to the pasture's back fence. Still, there was no sign of the tiger. The men in front of Tilly looked noticeably less excited now, their initial enthusiasm worn down by an uneventful, sweaty hike. Bubba picked up the pace.

"See anything?" Abner whispered to no one in particular.

"No," returned Tilly and Bubba, at the same time that Fairbanks responded with an angry *Shhhhh*.

Abner said, "I don't think his microphones are sensitive enough to—"

"Quiet!" Fairbanks said.

The whole group obeyed, falling back into silence. Bubba was under no obligation, obviously, to heed Fairbanks's commands—but weapons, especially when worn openly, have a way of lending authority to their bearers. The group marched on in a slog that felt, to Tilly, far from the recreation it was meant to be.

A few minutes more of weaving through the oak trees, pushing aside the whitebrush and agarita bushes, and stepping around prickly pear, then Bubba stopped cold and without warning. Fairbanks didn't see him in time to stop, his attention elsewhere, searching for the tiger in the brush, and so he ran right into Bubba's back. Abner, just a step behind, continued the domino dog pile, and soon all three men were wobbling to keep their footing. Tilly had enough warning to stop before she added herself to the pileup.

"What—" Abner began.

"Shhhh." Now it was Bubba's turn to shut him up. Bubba batted the air down with his hand, signing to them: *Quiet*. He kept his eyes straight ahead, trained on whatever had stopped him in his tracks.

The other three people fanned out to either side of Bubba to see what he was looking at, moving with as quiet of footsteps as they could manage. Ahead was a clearing, and they had to squeeze tightly together for everyone to see into it. Tilly had to stand on her tiptoes to see over Abner's shoulder.

The sight in the clearing sent a chill up Tilly's spine. The group drew in and held a collective breath. In the middle of the clearing was the tiger, jarringly orange against the black-dirt, brown-grass ground. It lay on its stomach, perpendicular to the group, and it did not look at them.

Instead, the robot tiger's attention was focused on the thing it held pinned to the ground in its paws: the mangled carcass of a yearling whitetail doe. The poor animal was almost as much red and pink as tawny brown. Tilly's stomach churned. As they watched, the tiger ripped a chunk of flesh from the deer's flank in a mouthful of sharp teeth. It liberated the deer of its flesh with violent, head-shaking tears. Once it had freed a chunk of meat, it chewed enough to throw the bite to the back of its mouth, then made a swallowing movement in its throat, the artificial muscles in its neck rippling. But with nowhere for the food to go, no esophagus to take the flesh to a digestive destination, after the show the tiger opened its jaw to drop the mouthful of deer to the ground. Then it went in for another bite. And that was when Tilly realized.

Bubba spoke first. "What the—"

CRACK. In a flash, Fairbanks had drawn the pistol from the holster on his chest and fired.

The tiger recoiled, throwing its head back for a moment before going completely limp, falling to its side. Tilly watched it closely, looking for the spring of blood from the bullet wound, but there was no blood besides the deer's, smeared through the tiger's fur around its mouth and paws. (*What's black and orange and red all over?*) Tilly thought that the artificial circulatory system must have malfunctioned.

Bubba noticed too. "Where's the blood, Abner?" Bubba asked.

"I think he hit him in the head."

"I did," Fairbanks said. He still held the pistol in his right hand. It pointed toward the ground, an extension of his arm.

"The heads do not bleed." Abner shifted back and forth on his feet. "Because they are detachable. It is not possible to connect the circulatory system."

"Heads don't bleed," Bubba repeated. His voice sounded far away, like he was talking through a dream.

Without a word, Fairbanks shoved his way past Bubba and walked to the tiger in the clearing. He drew the knives from his belt without missing a step. Then he knelt beside the tiger. A flash of silver above his head. A cracking thud. The tiger's circulatory system was not broken.

Chapter 27
The Mountain Lion

Two things clicked into place in Tilly's mind in the next moments. First, she was sure that the tiger had killed the goats. The way it had ripped the deer apart, the way that it took mouthfuls of flesh and mimed eating, just to spit them back out again—Tilly had seen the result of that form of maiming in the goats. It was the same. This realization brought her a minor sense of relief.

Second, Tilly knew that someone had to give the goats to the tiger. And she knew who it was.

Anger welled in her chest, so intense that it could not be contained on the ethereal plane where emotions live in the body, and it manifested in the physical, sending flames of heat up Tilly's neck to her face, boiling her cheeks to a blood-red. Tilly took a step forward and shoved Abner from behind. Her hand connected with his shoulder—hard—and sent him stumbling forward.

"Hey, what—" Abner started, righting himself.

"The goats, you jackass. You killed those goats!"

"No." He shook his head. "The tiger kil—"

"You stole those goats and gave them to the tiger. And you changed its teeth." Tilly stepped toward Abner, her anger a whipping tempest, her body the teapot. The anger, the indignation, escaped beneath the lid in gusts, sending her arms out toward Abner in a force of nature outside of Tilly's control. Abner started backing away.

Bubba caught Tilly around the waist before she could get to Abner again. "Now Tilly," he said as she tried to pull his arms away from her. "We don't need one of your hissy fits today."

Tilly struggled against him. "Let. Me. Go." He did. Tilly spun to glare at him, her anger uncontainable—unrecognizable.

Bubba took a step back from her and raised his hands in surrender. Tilly took a deep breath to still herself—contain herself. The boiling sphere of pure rage in her chest shrunk in size, but not mass—it condensed, distilled, but did not evaporate.

"Now," Bubba said. "What is this all about?"

"Did you know?" Tilly asked Bubba.

"Know *what*? Tilly, I don't even know what's happening right *now*." As Bubba spoke, George Fairbanks rejoined the group, a knife dripping from his belt.

"Don't you see?" Tilly's voice shook. "The tiger killed those goats. The ones in the east pasture. It wasn't a mountain lion, or a person." *Or me,* Tilly almost added.

"And someone had to *steal* the goats and give them to the tiger. And then dump the goats in the pasture. Someone with *access* to the Triple Nine." She turned now and looked at Abner. The others turned too, all eyes on Abner now.

"Care to weigh in, Abner?" Bubba asked, an eyebrow raised.

Abner was looking at the ground. As he looked up to meet everyone's eyes, a smile spread across his face. The smile could have been charming, if Tilly didn't know Abner or the context.

Abner, too, raised his hands in the air. "Caught me," he said. "I had to do it. I had to test Abraham."

"You had to . . . test him?" Bubba clarified, his eyes narrowing.

"Right. I have been teaching the AI that is Abraham's mind with videos of real tigers. There's one video in particular where a tiger kills and eats a goat. So, to see if he was learning, I had to put him to the test."

"So you *stole* peoples' goats? They make their living off their livestock, you know," Tilly said. Then, under her breath, "fucking city slicker."

"Abner," Bubba said. "If you had to do that, why not just go buy goats at the Tuesdee livestock auction?"

Abner shrugged. "I didn't know anything about a livestock auction." The final two words sounded unfamiliar in his mouth. *Of course he didn't*, Tilly thought.

Tilly looked at the bloody tiger and the mangled, bloody deer, and her anger cooled to sadness, the tempest refined to cold, dense grief. She wanted to gather up the doe, her disparate pieces and parts, and sew it all back together. To fix her.

She thought of Royce and saying a prayer, and she began a silent prayer in her mind: *Dear God—*

But she stopped when she realized that she didn't know what should come after that—certainly not the prayer of thanks ministered by Royce. So instead, she mentally concluded with *I'm so sorry.*

Calmer now, Tilly asked, "*Why* did you do this, Abner? None of this is necessary."

"But it is," Abner said. "I—*we*—are attempting to imitate reality. We *are* imitating reality. Maybe even making something—something . . . *better.*"

Bubba cleared his throat. "Now, there's no need to be stealin' from folks around town," he said. "And we don't really need to be so realistic. It's for sport, nothing else, Abner."

Abner let out an audible huff. "The *else* is the point, Francis," Abner said. "I mean, *Bubba.* For me, anyway. And that matters, does it not? That *I* am pleased with the work?"

"Well—" Bubba started.

Abner interrupted him. "I should be more clear. I create the AI that I want to create." Abner gestured to the bloodied tiger. "Or I leave. And good luck finding another qualified person to come out here and work in the middle of nowhere. Almost no one can do what I do. And those that can would never agree to this."

"Hey," Bubba said, an anger rising. "I was your last option, if I do recall, you little fucking twerp. Good luck to *you* getting another job anywhere else."

Abner took a deep breath to respond, but he was interrupted by George Fairbanks silently turning to leave. He seemed to have grown bored of them.

As they watched him walk away, Abner turned to Bubba. He was calm again. "I *will* leave, Francis. If I lose my creative freedom." And then he started back toward his workshop.

Tilly wanted to leave too, and she looked again at the now-lifeless machine that had seemed so alive just ten minutes ago. It was too stabbed to bring back to life, too broken to walk itself back to the lab. They would have to get it back down some other way, and Tilly thought again about how that wasn't her job.

So she said to Bubba, "I need to go. I just got a text about a colicking horse." She hoped that he didn't notice that she hadn't looked at her cell phone.

Then Tilly left. And when she drove away, when she got out to the county road that would take her back into town, back home, when she was safely nestled in the emptiness of the miles of uninhabited pasture all around, Tilly rolled down her windows and screamed into the evening sky until she couldn't breathe and the scream no longer belonged to her, but to the quiet world around her.

Chapter 28
Pianists

Tilly woke the next morning to a sore throat—the dull, aching, scratchy sore of raw emotion reduced into physical pain. She couldn't stop envisioning the goats in her mind, or the mangled deer. She stepped into the shower and turned the water to its hottest setting. She took a deep breath, inflating her lungs with steam, hoping that when she exhaled, the steam would carry the bad out with it.

Tilly wanted to call Royce to tell him about the goat revelation, but she didn't, of course. She also thought of calling Sheriff Valdez—surely there was a "crime" exception to her NDA. But Tilly's better angels—or maybe the worse ones—called to mind the thought of her mother in the nursing home, and she decided that justice for the goats perhaps wasn't worth a pay cut.

So she went about her day with a cloud over her head, trying everything she could to keep her mind off of the feeling that she had done something wrong. Somehow a whole day passed relatively normally, as if there wasn't a goat-maiming animatron within a twenty-mile radius.

Tilly went to her clinic Monday morning. Monday mornings were reserved for her small animal patients, the sort that could actually be transported into the clinic for an appointment. Tilly spent the better part of her morning plucking quills out of Pam Johnson's golden retriever—he had lost a tussle with a porcupine. Tanya Ulbrek brought in a new litter of barn kittens for their vaccines. Tilly gave Tim Parson's corgi a clean bill of health after an alarming digestive anomaly (turns out, he just ate a blue crayon). Tilly started to feel normal again.

Until an unexpected appointment arrived. Tilly was typing up notes from a puppy checkup at the computer in her examination room. There was a knock at the door.

"One minute," Tilly called.

The door swung open anyway. Tilly spun around, expecting to see her next patient and its owner.

"You're not Duchess," Tilly said to the pet-less man in the door.

"Astute observation," said Sheriff Valdez. "You must've been top of your vet school class, Tilly." He winked.

"I was, actually," Tilly said. She leaned back against the counter that held the computer.

Tilly gestured to one of the room's chairs, inviting him to sit. He waved a hand in a gesture of refusal.

"What can I do for you?" she asked him.

"Well, I am hoping you can help me out, Dr. Hutto," he said.

"I'll do my best," Tilly said. "Hit me—what this time? Another mutilation?"

"Not quite," Sheriff Valdez said. He placed his hands on the examination table in the center of the room. Tapped his fingers. Took a deep breath. Leaned forward on his palms.

Tilly didn't like the building silence. Or the thoughts that could sneak into her mind in the quiet. *Scalpels. Goats. Sleepwalking.* "What's going on?"

Sheriff Valdez took another deep breath. He looked Tilly in the eyes. His eyes were bloodshot and puffy. "Tilly, do you ever use ketamine in your practice?"

Tilly's stomach dropped. But her brain took a bit longer than her body to identify why the question sent her reeling.

"Yes," she said. Her brow furrowed. "It's used as a sedative in animal medicine."

"I thought maybe so," the sheriff said. He sighed. "How do you keep inventory?"

"What do you mean?" Tilly's mind raced. So did her heart.

"How do you keep track of your supply of the drug?"

Another pang of stress twisted Tilly's stomach. "I don't have a formal system. I just keep a few bottles on hand, you know, and then order more when I see I'm running low." Things were beginning to click into place. "Why?" Tilly demanded.

"I probably shouldn't tell you this," Valdez said, but he went on anyway. "You know that Gonzales girl?"

"Yeah, of course," Tilly said. And Tilly's mind superimposed over the sheriff's face his tearful eyes of Saturday morning, when she had seen him near the bridge. And then a horrible thought muscled in. *Oh no.*

"Well we just got her toxicology results back," Valdez said. "And turns out she overdosed on ketamine."

The blood drained from Tilly's face.

The sheriff's voice swam in her ears as he kept talking. "—and we figured we'd ask around with you and the doctor in town, ask the folks at the pharmacy, just trying to figure out where she might have gotten it. It isn't a typical drug we see . . ."

The ringing in Tilly's ears started to drown out his voice. "—'course it might be . . ." His voice started to cut in and out. "—out of town."

The ringing became all Tilly could hear. It filled up her mind, pushing out every thought. It even overbore the subconscious ones that told Tilly's lungs to breathe and her heart to beat. She held her breath. The sheriff's mouth was still moving. Her heart seemed to stop, and her brain was underwater—in the ocean, in the waves. In the Mariana Trench. *Ringing, ringing, ringing, ringing.*

Then an external input. A hand on her shoulder. The world rushed back in. "Tilly?" Sheriff Valdez said. "Tilly, you still with me? You alright?" His face radiated concern.

Tilly gulped in a breath, as if finally surfacing from water. "It went missing. I noticed about a week ago." The words tumbled over each other out of Tilly's mouth.

"What went missing?"

"The vial of ketamine in my vet bag. I went out to the Rowe ranch to pull a calf and I was gonna sedate the heifer and I looked in my bag for my ketamine, where it always is, and it wasn't there and I just thought I had lost it or it fell out of my bag and rolled out of my truck or—"

"Woah, woah, woah," the sheriff said. "Slow down." He pulled a small spiral notepad out of his shirtwaist pocket.

"Now, tell me, what was the last time you remember seeing that bottle of ketamine in your bag?" He was already writing something down.

Tilly did her best to answer his questions. She told him who was at the Rowe ranch with her. When she went. Who she had seen before. She wasn't sure the last time she saw the ketamine in the bag, but she could check her records for the last time before then that she had administered some.

"It's interesting that this is the second time your veterinary supplies have turned up in recent investigations," the sheriff said. "First the scalpel, now . . ." He raised an eyebrow and let her fill in the blanks.

The implication took Tilly aback. They couldn't have both been hers, and even if they were—well, that was just a coincidence. *Right?* "We don't know they're mine," Tilly said, defensive, trying to convince herself as much as the sheriff of the fact.

"Right," the sheriff said. "Except your fingerprints *were* on the scalpel."

There was a knock at the door. "Just a minute," Tilly said. She looked at the sheriff. Her breath still wavered in her chest. *I think I'm going crazy, Royce.*

"We're just about done," the sheriff said. He closed his notebook and put it back in his pocket. "Thank you for your help."

"Of course," Tilly said. "I just—if it *was* my ketamine, I mean, Christ—"

The sheriff gave her a sympathetic look. "Cain't do anything about it now, darlin'." He clapped her on the shoulder, then turned to walk away.

If his words were meant to comfort Tilly, they didn't. He added over his shoulder, "Keep your shit locked up from now on, word to the wise."

The sheriff made his way out of the examination room. He stopped at the door. "Oh, and Tilly," he said as he grabbed the doorknob. He turned back to her. "I almost forgot to tell you. I think we solved our little goat mystery."

If it was possible, Tilly's heart both dropped into her stomach and rose into her throat at the same time. She was thinking of the tiger. And how he must know of the tiger. And did that mean she, Tilly, was in on the crime? *Was* there a crime? Tilly's whole body was a heartbeat, shiny and wet and red and in a glass box. *Thump-thump, thump-thump.*

"Someone heard what sounded like a lady screaming out by the Triple Nine a couple nights ago. You know what that means."

Heat rushed to Tilly's cheeks. Two evenings ago, when she left the 999 after the tiger hunt—the scream of frustration she let loose on her drive home echoed in her mind.

The sheriff went on. "It was a mountain lion after all—you know that sound they make. Sounds just like a screamin' woman. Case closed, I guess." The sheriff smiled.

"Mystery solved," agreed Tilly, her voice hollow.

"Now if only I could solve a mystery that matters." The sheriff patted the little notebook in his chest pocket.

"Good luck," Tilly said.

"Thanks," the sheriff said. He opened the door. "Shall I send in your next patient?" he asked, eyeing someone in the hallway.

"Please," Tilly said. Her mind was miles away from her clinic.

The next thing Tilly knew, a Great Dane was plodding into the room, pulling its owner behind it on a red leash.

Tilly took a deep breath, trying to bring her mind back to herself. She put on a smile. "Hello, Duchess," she greeted the dog.

* * *

Later, Tilly went to check on her mother. Her hands trembled as she gripped the steering wheel of her truck. She tried to watch the scenery of the drive to take her mind off its wonderings of whether she was a manslaughterer. Prickly pear bush. Leafless oak tree. Dead Johnsongrass. Buzzards eating an animal carcass. Black trash bag in the ditch, poked through by the unidentified rib cage of something rotting. *Guilt.*

At the nursing home, Tilly's mother was in her room. Her eyes were closed.

"Hi, mama," Tilly said. Her voice wobbled.

The old woman opened one eye and glared at Tilly from it. "Who the hell are you?" she asked.

Tilly's throat tightened. "I don't know," she said. And then a laugh escaped from her chest, either in a recognition of the absurdity of it all, or in hysteria. Likely the latter, Tilly imagined.

Tilly told her mother about the ketamine, and the dead girl, and her guilt. The old woman listened, a dutiful confidant. And at the end of the tale, Tilly's mother said nothing, and the silence consumed them. They sat there like that for a while.

After some time, Rosa, the nurse, came into the room to greet them and check on Ottalie. She sat on the bed next to Tilly.

"We missed having a Hutto at the church picnic this year," Rosa said. "It was yesterday. You know, your mama was basically in charge of the picnic up until last year."

"Yeah," Tilly said, her voice stretched tight. "Hard to imagine she could have done that just a year ago."

Tilly and Rosa observed the old woman, now incapable of feeding herself, much less arranging the feeding of others. Her decline had been rapid after Tilly's father died.

"Maybe next year, you can help out in her place," Rosa said. "We'd love to have you."

"Yeah," Tilly said. "Yeah, we'll see." But her chest loosened a little at the invitation. In a room with a mother who didn't know who she was, where Tilly had so much love to give to someone who thought her a stranger, Rosa's warmth filled a cold void.

"And how are you today Ottalie?" Rosa asked Tilly's mother.

"Good, good." The old woman still had her eyes closed, as was her custom more and more lately. "Chester is just out hunting, and then he's coming to get me."

Tilly started at the mention of her dead father. Even though her mother had been this way for months now, Tilly was still startled sometimes to be reminded that her mother lived in a different world.

"Well, you let us know if Mr. Hutto gets a big one, okay?" Rose said amiably.

Tilly's mother didn't answer. "She's been living in the past a lot more lately," Tilly said quietly to Rosa. "I don't remember the last time she recognized me."

Rosa rubbed a hand back and forth across Tilly's shoulders. "It's hard, mija, I'm sorry. The worst part about Alzheimer's is that you lose them twice—once when their mind leaves and again when their body does."

Tilly's throat started to ache, and she looked at the ceiling to try to hold back tears. They came anyway.

"Oh, Tilly, it's going to be okay. You are so *strong*." Rosa pulled Tilly in for a hug. She held her there for several moments, and Tilly heaved several sobs into Rosa's shoulder.

Tilly pulled away. "I'm sorry, Rosa, I don't know what's gotten into me lately."

"Never apologize for grieving," Rosa said. She patted Tilly's hand. "Is everything else okay? Are you getting out of the house and seeing people?"

"Yeah," Tilly said absently. "I'm getting out of the house plenty. Maybe even too much lately." Tilly thought of the trouble she could have avoided recently by just staying home.

"That's good then," Rosa said. She rose to leave. "You're going to be okay, Tilly. You're a tough cookie." Tilly didn't respond. Rosa left.

"Tilly," Tilly's mother said. Tilly's heart jumped hearing her name on her mother's lips. "What a pretty name," the old woman mused.

Tilly deflated. "Thanks," she deadpanned.

"Chester's coming to get me when he's done hunting."

"That's nice, Mom." Tilly leaned back on her mother's bed and played along.

"I should pack," the old woman said.

"Where are you going?"

"We're taking a train ride."

Tilly leaned in. "Okay. I'll get your suitcase."

"We better hurry. He's coming soon."

"What should I pack for you?" Tilly didn't move from her seat. Her mother's eyes were still closed.

"That red dress I wore to Jet's wedding. And my hat."

Tilly smiled. "You got it. I'm packing those."

They sat there for a while longer, the old woman listing clothing items she wanted Tilly to pack for her, some of which Tilly remembered her wearing in Tilly's childhood, and Tilly assuring her she'd pack them. When her figurative closet was exhausted, the old woman fell silent again. Tilly took her leave.

Chapter 29
The Guard Dog

Most veterinary clinics facilitate cremation services for pets that have passed on. Tilly's clinic was not an exception. The services were most commonly invoked after an animal had to be euthanized at the clinic, in old age or due to grave injury. Sometimes, though, pet owners brought pets that had passed at home into the clinic for the service. This was the case for the dog Tilly received for cremation the following day at the clinic. Sort of.

Tom and Pam Miller, a married couple in their sixties who had lived in Verde their whole lives, arrived at the clinic midmorning. Mrs. Miller was in tears. Mr. Miller, for his part, also had red-rimmed eyes. They had asked to see Tilly at the front desk. She came out to them between scheduled appointments and immediately noticed something conspicuous about the Millers in the vet clinic waiting room: They did not have a pet with them.

Tilly flipped through her mental rolodex of townspeople's pets, trying to figure out who belonged to the Millers and was missing from the equation. They had several horses, a house cat, a small goat herd, and a goat guard dog. Tilly soon found out which animal prompted their call.

"It's Dolly," Mrs. Miller sniffed. *Dolly. The guard dog.*

"What's happened?" Tilly asked.

"She's been missing for about a week," Mr. Miller explained. His arm was around Mrs. Miller's shoulders. Mrs. Miller held a tissue to her mouth and looked at the floor.

"I'm sorry," Tilly said. "Do you have posters? We can put one on the bulletin board here in the waiting area. Maybe someone's seen her." Then she thought of the poster of the missing Great Pyrenees at the diner, and it clicked that they were one and the same—they had already put up posters. Tilly's mouth pressed into a thin line at the grim realization.

"No," Mr. Miller said. "We found her."

Mrs. Miller's streaming tears told Tilly that they hadn't found her in good condition.

"Injured?" Tilly asked, hoping for the best.

"Yes," Mr. Miller said, his voice cracking. He looked down. "Fatally."

"I'm so sorry," Tilly said.

"But there's something—there's something else," Mr. Miller said.

"What?" Tilly prompted when he didn't continue.

The Millers looked at each other. Tom raised his eyebrows at Pam. She nodded. Tom took a deep breath.

"It's probably nothing," he said. A dark feeling took hold of Tilly. Mr. Miller paused.

"Well, let's hear it," Tilly said, a note of impatience creeping into her voice. She wanted to get the bad news over with.

"Actually, maybe it's better if you see for yourself. She's outside." Mr. Miller started for the door before Tilly could agree or decline to follow. She followed.

"We found her under the bridge on old Highway 173," Tom said over his shoulder. "Well, a friend did, and he called us."

Mr. Miller opened the bed of his truck. Mrs. Miller stood back from the scene, on the side of the truck by the driver-side door. She couldn't see into the truck bed that way.

Tilly, of course, could see into the truck bed. There was a tarp covering a lump of something. Mr. Miller pulled it back.

"Sorry about the smell," he said. The odor of rotting flesh assaulted Tilly's nose as the tarp revealed what it held beneath. She thought of the goats. She pulled the top of her shirt over her nose.

"You see, she's been dead for a while," Mr. Miller said.

Tilly did see. The tarp revealed a decomposing Great Pyrenees. Once majestic in her sheer size and white coat, now poor Dolly had withered to a husk. Her skin had shriveled and crisped, ripping away to reveal sun-dried muscle and bone in places. Her white coat was dry and lifeless. Her eyes were missing.

"It looks like she's been dead for at least a week," Tilly said.

"About as long as she's been missing," Mr. Miller agreed.

"So—so what is the thing that's probably nothing?" Tilly asked.

"Look at her mouth," Mr. Miller said.

Tilly did. The skin around the poor dog's mouth had shrunken and stretched away, pulling her lips into something like a smile. And the smile revealed—nothing.

"Her teeth," Tilly said.

"Exactly," Mr. Miller said. "They're gone."

The dead dog had rows of fleshy holes where her teeth had once been. A chill ran up Tilly's spine, but she couldn't immediately put her finger on why.

Mrs. Miller walked around from the side of the truck, shielding the side of her face with her hand so that she didn't have to see Dolly's remains. Mr. Miller covered Dolly back up with the tarp.

"We just want some closure, if you know how this could have happened," Mrs. Miller said. "I mean, is there some animal that would have done this? We heard there's a mountain lion in Verde County."

Tilly was tired of answering that question. "No, I don't think an animal would have done this. In fact, I think we need to call the sheriff. This looks like human work—I don't think this could have been done without tools. Or opposable thumbs." Tilly was also tired of giving that answer.

Mrs. Miller's face scrunched into a painful sob, and she covered it with her hands. Mr. Miller gave Tilly a scolding look, and wrapped his wife in a hug.

Tilly pursed her lips at her own words. She had always had a way with them—and it wasn't a good one.

"Sorry to be so blunt," Tilly continued. "But this isn't the first animal mutilation I have seen in the past few months. I think there's something going on here."

"Mutilation?" Mrs. Miller cried between sobs.

"Yes—I'm sorry," Tilly said. She closed her eyes took a deep breath of the chilly December air. "Look—how did you say Dolly went missing?"

"She just vanished," Mr. Miller said. "She stays out in the goat pens, y'know, to protect them. And we woke up one morning and—no Dolly."

The missing-in-the-night refrain was a familiar one. "Do you mind taking her into the sheriff's office? I think they need to see this."

Mrs. Miller was wracked with another sob. Mr. Miller pulled her in closer to him.

"Yeah, okay, if you think it will help," he said. Then, looking at his wife, he said to her, "No harm in them takin' a look before we have her cremated." She nodded, dabbing tears from her eyes.

They gathered themselves and left. Tilly waved as they drove away in the direction of the sheriff's office.

* * *

That night, Tilly dreamed she was a sheep in a field. Her god was a big white dog. And the devil—an approaching wolf.

Chapter 30
Snake in the Garden

Tilly went to the workshop at the 999 the next morning to quell a feeling she couldn't shake. It was not a day she had been scheduled to work there, and so she was unexpected. She didn't see anyone as she rushed inside, past Abner's office and workshop. She did not stop until she got to Anna's workroom, propelled by a growing suspicion.

She burst in without knocking. Anna had her back to the doorway.

"Why did y'all decide to change the teeth?" Tilly asked as she strode toward Anna's desk. The question practically exploded from her mouth.

Anna jumped and turned. "Jesus, Tilly," she said with her hand to her chest. "You scared the shit out of me. I didn't know you were coming in today."

"I wasn't," Tilly said, impatient to get answers. "The teeth—the tiger's teeth. They used to be silicone. The other day, on the hunt, with the deer, they weren't. Why change them?" Tilly had come to an uneasy stop standing over Anna, where she sat at a worktable.

Anna's brow scrunched. She put her pencil down. "Tilly—what deer? Is everything alright?"

Tilly was tired of everyone asking her that. *Of course everything wasn't alright.* "The deer that the tiger killed the other day, and the goats—Christ, am I speaking Greek? What's going *on*?" Tilly was vibrating with frustration. She felt *so close* to figuring out what had been going on in Verde lately.

"I don't know what you're talking about." Anna shook her head. "Truly." At first, anger took hold of Tilly. But a look at Anna's face told her that Anna was sincere.

"You don't know about—about the goats?"

Anna shook her head, a look of concern in her eyes. Tilly was suddenly very aware of how unhinged she must sound. She took a deep breath and a step back from Anna's workstation.

"Please, sit," Anna said, pulling a chair up for her. Tilly sat. "Now, tell me what this is about."

Tilly recounted the discovery of the goats and the short-lived mystery of how they had ended up that way, which was solved when she saw the tiger ripping apart a doe in the same manner. Anna looked even more confused at the end of Tilly's tale.

"But that's not possible, Tilly," Anna said. "You've seen. The tiger's teeth are made of soft silicone."

Tilly sighed. "*I know*. That's my point. They *were* made of silicone. But now they obviously aren't. And my question is: Why?" Tilly was boiling with exasperation. Her temples were tightening with every passing second.

"But—but they are still silicone. I haven't changed them."

"Well, *someone* did." Tilly looked meaningfully at Anna.

Silence overcame them. After on the other side of it, Anna asked, "You mean, *Abner*?"

Tilly slowly nodded. "Almost had to be. Don't you think?"

"But how? He doesn't know how to use the 3-D printer, or the software, or how to do anything that I do, really."

Tilly closed her eyes. A thought was forming—a theory. But before it was fully realized, someone knocked on the doorframe.

Abner cleared his throat. "Tilly, you are not supposed to be here today."

Tilly turned to him. "And yet, here I am," she said.

Abner ignored her and looked at Anna. "Francis is ready for us," he said.

Anna narrowed her eyes at Abner. Then she said, "Sorry, Tilly. Duty calls." Anna rose and walked out of the door. Tilly followed her.

"Not you," Abner said, raising a hand to her chest to stop her.

"Don't fucking touch me," Tilly said.

Anna turned to Abner, suddenly a co-conspirator. "Tilly has to come. I need her help."

Abner took a deep breath and let out a very controlled exhalation. "Fine," he said. And so the three made their way to the main workshop, where Bubba was waiting.

"Tilly?" Bubba greeted her. "What are you doing here?"

"'Hello' to you, too," said Tilly.

"I think I could use Tilly's input on some of the muscular machinations," Anna chimed in by way of explanation.

"Alright, fine, I guess," Bubba said.

The four stood uncomfortably for a moment. It was then, for the first time, that Tilly wondered what this was all about.

Behind Abner, in the center of the room, was a lumpy something covered in a sheet. She had been seeing a lot of those lately. Tilly guessed this one was the object of the meeting. It was smaller than a tiger, but other than not-the-tiger, Tilly didn't have any idea what it could be. She had visions of the tarp-covered thing of yesterday: Dolly the guard dog. Tilly's insides churned. She had the sinking suspicion that whatever this was, it was worse than a dead dog.

Finally, Bubba said, "Well, let's get going, we're burnin' daylight."

Abner took his position by the cloaked object. He looked at Tilly, then at Bubba. "Are you sure?" he asked Bubba, nodding toward Tilly.

After a second, Bubba nodded to Abner. "Alright," Abner said. "Fine." He took a deep breath. "I present to you," he said, turning his full attention to Bubba, "the seventh prototype of our *Most Dangerous Game* animatron."

Abner pulled the cover off the lumpy thing.

Tilly jumped backward at the sight of what was beneath: the torso, head, and shoulders of a man.

The man's eyes were closed, and his mouth hung slack. His bare torso, cleaved at the hip and holding itself upright of its own volition, was motionless. It took a second of panicked observation for Tilly to realize that the man she was looking at was not alive, nor had he ever been. The realization hollowed out a place in Tilly's heaving chest and stayed there. *The shadow man.*

"Well, I'll be damned," Bubba said. His eyes were sparkling. "Would you look at that."

"What the hell is this?" Tilly asked. "You're doing *people* now?" She looked at Abner and her anger about the goats and the deer and everything else bubbled up into her throat and made her voice hot and sharp.

"I call him 'Adam,'" Abner said. He was beaming.

"Naturally," Tilly said. "I'm surprised you didn't call him 'Abner.'"

Abner—of the human variety—smirked.

"Boy, if you didn't have me fooled for a second there. He looks like the real deal, don't he?" Bubba said.

"I don't think I fully understand. This is for *hunting*?" Tilly waved her arm at the torso. "You're going to sell, what, *murders* now?" The word "murders" weighed heavily in her mouth; it reminded her of the ketamine and the dead girl.

"Well, now, it ain't murder. It ain't real people, see," Bubba said. "It's more like a video game." *Daddy says he's not a nice man.*

Abner chimed in. "It is just like a video game. The *most dangerous* game." Abner smiled at his own joke.

Tilly rolled her eyes. Anna was silent during all of this.

Tilly's mind was spinning. She took a step closer to the torso of the man. The skin looked almost real, but maybe dewier than real skin, and besides realistic ripples of veins down the forearm, it was entirely unblemished. The shading of the skin was perhaps too uniform in color throughout, instead of darker or lighter depending on where the sun would most touch. Tilly reached out to touch the torso, running a hand down the animatron's abdomen. It felt slick and springy.

"It's a silicone polymer," Anna finally spoke up.

Tilly nodded and continued to study the robot. She regarded its face now, and shuddered at what regarded her back.

The whole thing was so *close* to looking real—but not quite. The skin was too smooth, stretched unnaturally into flat planes, sloping over the angles of cheekbone and jaw. Skin absent of the imperfections that convey humanity. The proportions and positions of mouth, nose, eyes, and ears were too perfect. The size, shape, and distancing of the features had clearly been calculated to mathematical precision, but the effect was a face so symmetrical—so *perfectly* human—that it looked unearthly. The animatron's eyes were closed, and they made Tilly think of a doll she had as a child. She wondered, if she tilted the animatron the right way, if its eyes would open, if it would wake up.

"What do you think?" Anna asked.

"Looks like some goddamn money to me," Bubba said. He slapped Abner on the shoulder. Abner grinned.

"It's creepy," Tilly said. She couldn't muster any niceties.

Anna nodded. "We're still working on that. We're trying to find our way out of the Uncanny Valley."

"The what, now?" Bubba asked.

"The Uncanny Valley. That's what we call the psychological effect of looking at something that is close to looking like a realistic human, but not quite. The robot's close enough in appearance to flip a mental switch that you are looking at a human, but when you look closer, something falls a little short. The appearance tends to make people feel . . . uncomfortable."

"Can confirm," Tilly said. The thing made her skin crawl.

"This is the seventh prototype, if you believe it," said Anna. "You should have seen the earlier ones. Yikes." She performed a theatrical mock-shudder and smiled.

Tilly's mind flashed again to the silhouette of the man in the storage room—the shadow man that had haunted her for so long—and wondered what iteration he had been.

"And you," Tilly said, turning to Abner. "It's the same thing with the programming? The algorithms and the thinking and all?"

"Yes, this animatron will also have artificial intelligence," Abner said. "Except this time, of course, it will be more . . . *human* than animal."

"How's that coming along?" Bubba asked.

"Very good, Mr. Skinner. Here, look," Abner said as he walked over to a computer against the wall. The computer's glow cast his face in sharp angles. The others in the room fell silent, watching him clack on the keyboard.

Then suddenly, presumably in response to some combination of Abner's keystrokes, the animatron awoke. Its eyes opened and its arms shot out to its sides to form a T-shape.

The sudden movement made Tilly gasp. Bubba, too, was startled and took a step back in surprise. The animatron, seemingly at Abner's direction, began to move its arms about—straight in front, bent at the elbows, above its head. The torso twisted at the truncated hip, and the natural movement of the upper body emphasized the absence of a lower half. When it turned, Tilly could see the back of its head, which had a panel of its artificial "skull" missing. Its brain was wires and circuits. The moving half-man made Tilly's stomach churn.

Then the eyes—it was really the eyes that did it. Glass marbles—blue—that looked, for every possible description, exactly how one imagines human eyes to look. But something was missing, and Tilly identified that the *something* was the spark of light in all living eyes that comes not from the biological structures of the carbon body, but from a source both unknown, and unknowable.

"Amazing, yes?" Abner called over his shoulder. Tilly tore her gaze away from the dead eyes of the animatron, forfeiting an unwinnable staring contest. She looked at Abner, his expression eager, then to Anna, who looked down, then to Bubba, in whose face she briefly recognized something that she felt in her own stomach—disgust.

Bubba collected himself. "Well," he said. "Let's see it do something. You know—think for itself."

Abner nodded, taking a deep breath. He came back to the group, and the animatron. From his pocket, he took a remote that looked identical to the one used to operate the tiger. He pointed it at the animatron. He clicked.

In a moment, the robot ascended to the next level of life. From its relative stasis, the robot took up the basic movements of humanity. Its chest rose and fell in simulated breathing. It turned its head from side to side, in realistic-looking glances around the room. It raised its eyebrows at the sight of the real people there.

Abner's face relaxed into a relieved smile.

"Alright, alright," Bubba said. "Look who's joined us."

At the sound of Bubba's voice, the animatron's eyes widened, in an impersonation of fear. But despite well-choreographed efforts, its facial movements were stiff, and, to Tilly, unconvincing.

"Uh-oh, did I scare you, fella?" Bubba took a step toward the animatron. In response, it turned as far away from him as it could with stationary hips and started to pump its arms backward and forward, as if attempting to run away. This was, naturally, impossible to do without legs. Still, the animatron's chest heaved more deeply in its feigned exertion, and it even emitted a sound like panting. It periodically looked over its shoulder for effect. It chilled Tilly to think of why *this* was the response to humans that the robot had learned.

"Impressive," Bubba said. "But let's see if it can do the important stuff."

With that, Bubba pulled his pocketknife from his back pocket and flipped it open. He walked to the stationary, fleeing animatron. It stopped miming running and spun back to him, eyes wide. Bubba raised the pocketknife above his head. Then he plunged it downward toward its chest. Tilly closed her eyes.

A moment later, the room erupted with laughter. Tilly peeked between her fingers at Anna, who was not laughing. She looked at Abner, who also wasn't laughing, but instead looked horror-struck. Finally she looked to Bubba and the animatron. Bubba was not laughing.

The cackling, instead, came from a speaker somewhere in the animatron. It was a recording of human laughter that didn't fit the animatron's physical appearance—the animatron's mouth was somehow open too wide, agape in a garish smile that did not match the pitch or tone of the inhuman sound. Nor did the attempted joviality reach the animatron's dead-looking eyes. Perhaps most unsettlingly, the animatron had no reason to be laughing.

As the robot cackled, artificial blood poured from the place Bubba's knife had plunged into the animatron's shoulder. More jarringly, the blood was pouring all over Bubba, because the animatron's reaction to being stabbed, for some reason, was to grab his attacker and pull him in for something like a hug. The robot held Bubba against his chest, even as Bubba fought to push away. All the while, it laughed.

"What the fuck?" Bubba said. "Get this goddamn thing off of me!" He struggled against the vise of the animatron's robotic, silicone-covered arms.

Abner fumbled with the remote. He pressed a button. Nothing happened. He pressed it again. Still, nothing. Tilly and Anna watched on in horror as the animatron seemed to ignore Abner's electronic commands completely.

"What is going on, Abner? Turn it off!" Bubba yelled. The thing appeared to be squeezing him ever tighter.

"It is—it must be the batteries." Abner slapped the remote in his hand a few times, then tried it again.

The animatron stopped laughing, and for a moment, Tilly thought the remote must have worked, and that it had been turned off. But still it held Bubba tightly in its embrace. And it blinked its dead blue eyes. It turned its head to look straight at Abner. And then it spoke. "Not the batteries," it said in a terrible digital voice. "Not the batteries," it repeated in monotone. "Not the batteries. Not the batteries."

It repeated the phrase over and over again, all the while squeezing Bubba in its arms. He struggled against them; Tilly saw genuine fear in his eyes. Bubba's face was turning even redder than usual.

Abner continued to wrestle with the remote. Anna marched to the animatron and stuck her hand into the open panel of skull in the back of its head.

"No. No. No," the animatron repeated in measured beats as Anna did this. It turned to Tilly, and Tilly caught its gaze uneasily. And she couldn't look away. Then it said, as Anna rummaged in its skull and Tilly stared into its fake blue eyes, which were somehow horrible now: "Help."

The word shot through Tilly like a revelation.

"Help," it said again. And for a second, she had an impulse to help the thing, to wrest Anna's hand out of its skull and to pull the knife from its shoulder and to *do something*. It spoke again: "Tilly, help."

Tilly's mind spun. Had it just said *her name*? Did she imagine it?

Then Anna found what she was looking for in the machinery of the skull and maneuvered something inside the animatron's head. It went limp. Anna looked at Tilly, the horror on her face matching Tilly's own.

Released, Bubba staggered backward from the thing.

"I do not know why he did that," Abner said. Bubba's face was aflame with anger, blood rushing to it so intensely that his face rivaled his blood-ied shirt in hue.

"What was that, Abner? Did it—did it ignore the remote signal?" Anna asked. "Did it *decide* not to be turned off?"

Abner didn't answer. Tilly wondered, too, if the animatron's artificial mind had overpowered its hardwired commands, and it was somehow able to ignore the remote-control inputs. Tilly supposed that would be the ultimate end of an instinct for self-preservation.

"Did it say my name?" she asked. "Did y'all hear that?" Nobody an-swered her. Anna, eyes wide, looked from the animatron to Abner, and back to the animatron.

"I thought," Bubba said, turning to Abner, his tone disconcertingly calm, "that you said it was ready."

"I did," Abner said. "I did say it was ready. It is ready."

"You call *that*"—Bubba practically threw an accusatory finger at the bloody torso of the fake man—"You call that *ready*?"

"I—" Abner began.

Bubba interrupted. "I have three goddamn hunts scheduled for this week. Deposits paid. What are you going to do?"

"Do not worry, like I said, we will be—"

Before Abner could finish, Bubba turned on his heel and left, shaking his head on the way out. He left a trail of fake blood droplets in his wake. Abner scrambled after him, his mouth twisting, jerking, and gaping in silence. Tilly wondered what his mouth had to say for itself.

Tilly looked at Anna. "Three hunts this *week*?" Tilly didn't know if she was more concerned about the apparent unfinished state of the project with such a short deadline looming, or if she was more horrified that three people, at least, would pay money to simulate committing murder.

"There's absolutely no way." Anna shook her head. "I had no idea— they cannot be ready by then."

"Abner seems to think so."

"Well, let's ignore that Abner's algorithm just did . . . that," Anna said. "It's not looking very intelligent at the moment—artificial or otherwise. But the bigger problem is on my end. It can't walk yet."

"What do you mean?"

"I haven't been able to get the animatron ambulatory. That's why we just demoed the torso today. It's the only part that works right now. Turns out bipedal physics are a bit more difficult than quadrupedal physics." Anna huffed. "Who knew?"

"Does Abner know that?"

"Of course he does. He just doesn't care. It's my problem, I guess."

Tilly took in the bloody animatron torso. The fake blood that had been pressed and smeared all over its front by its embrace with Bubba was drying in the cold air of the air-conditioned building. It was an unnaturally bright color when dried.

"This is all so fucked up so begin with," Tilly said. "No offense." And not for the first time, she wished that she didn't know anything about this operation, and that she never agreed to work on any animatrons, and that her only contact with the 999 was working on its living, breathing whitetail deer.

"Yeah," Anna said hollowly. "Yeah. It is."

"I mean, it asked me for *help*," Tilly said. "Christ."

Anna just nodded, staring vacantly at the floor.

A moment of silence passed between them. And Tilly suddenly remembered why she had come to the workshop that day. "What about the teeth?" she asked.

"The teeth," Anna repeated in a daze. Then the focus came back into her eyes, and she remembered. "Yes, the teeth. Like I said—I didn't switch them."

"Well, somebody did," Tilly said.

"We can check easily enough. Here, follow me."

Tilly followed Anna to a different storage room than the one she'd peeked into before, where she saw the shadow man. This one was smaller, and the flick of a light switch revealed that it was devoted entirely to the tiger animatron. There were rows of shelves with spare tiger parts—extra legs, extra skulls, stacks of pelts. An egg carton–type storage container filled with rows of tigers' eyes. In the center was the beast itself.

It was standing upright and staring dead ahead, eyes wide. For a moment, Tilly forgot where she was, and she could have been in any natural history museum observing a well-taxidermied tiger specimen. She came back to reality when Anna unhinged the tiger's jaw with the press of a button at the mandible joint. It fell open in an unnatural and silent scream.

Tilly moved closer to inspect the teeth. Anna grabbed one and tried to bend it. And, just like the first time Tilly had seen the tiger in the workshop, the tooth bent.

"Still silicone," Anna said. "See?"

She stepped back to make way for Tilly to inspect the teeth. Tilly went around the tiger's mouth, bending the teeth one by one, every time expecting resistance. She was never met with any.

"I don't understand," Tilly said. She pictured the goat victims of a few days ago, how they had been ripped to shreds. And the deer. "It doesn't make any sense. These teeth can't rip an animal apart."

"No, they can't," Anna said. "I don't know what to tell you."

"Maybe I'm going crazy," Tilly said. Had she imagined those things? Dreamed them?

"Maybe so," Anna said good-naturedly.

Then suddenly Tilly had to be out of there. Before Anna could ask any clarifying questions, Tilly was out the door to the storage room and striding down the hall. The atmosphere of the building felt as chilly as always, as haunted as the first day Tilly set foot in it. But now she knew what haunted it.

Chapter 31
Deliverance

Tilly confided the ordeal to her mother at the nursing home. She told her of the robotic man and how it had held Bubba and drenched him in blood. She told her of the goats and the deer and her sleepwalking. She told her about the missing ketamine and the dead dog with the missing teeth.

The old woman nodded through the tale. At the conclusion, she said, "Must be the Russians." This made Tilly laugh, and she agreed.

"Yeah," she said. "It's the Russians."

"I'd quit that job, if I was you," Ottalie said. "It's bad news."

Tilly was startled at her mother's seeming sudden coherence. The mood of the room took a solemn shift. Tilly nodded. "Yeah," she agreed once more. She felt an unexpected sense of liberation.

Ottalie went on, "That skunk lady's gonna die, you know."

Tilly laughed again; her mother's coherence—or what had seemed like it—had been short-lived. "No, I didn't know that," Tilly responded. "That's a shame."

"Yes indeedy, sure is." The old woman closed her eyes and rocked back in her chair, her energy for conversation exhausted. Tilly sat with her a while more.

* * *

Tilly called Bubba on her way home from visiting her mother. The evening was cold and pitch dark. Her drive was illuminated only by the orange glow of streetlamps and the Christmas lights that adorned the houses on either side of the road.

Bubba answered the phone with a grunt. "Yeah?"

"I quit," Tilly told him.

"You beat me to it," he said. "I'm no longer in need of your services on the special project. We've moved past the animal phase."

This statement struck Tilly as audacious, given that she had already quit. It angered her for a reason that she couldn't quite pinpoint. "Right," Tilly said.

"Pick up your last check at my office," Bubba said. "An' remember your nondisclosure agreement."

Tilly hung up without saying goodbye. Her mind spun on its axis, a steam-driven thing powered by the simmering anger she just couldn't shake, her thoughts jumping and reaching—but for what, she did not know. All of the oddities of the past few months started to run together, and formed themselves into a large lumbering thing that was missing its spinal cord and had dead, dead eyes.

Chapter 32
The Reckoning

The defining aspect of the next few weeks of Tilly's life was her complete inability to sleep. Every night she lay awake for hours, unsure if she was fighting harder to fall asleep or to stay awake. Unresolved thoughts about calves and robots and dog teeth swirled in her mind every night, and the fear of sleepwalking was stronger than her biological need for sleep.

Several weeks after Tilly had ended her work on the animatron project, she lay in bed on one of these sleepless nights, trying to muster slumber. She counted sheep. She counted goats. She counted vials of ketamine in her inventory.

Then her counting was interrupted by a sudden flood of bright white light. It illuminated her whole room. It made Ranger look like a big white dog. Where were his teeth? Tilly looked out her window for the source of the light. She expected to see a flying saucer, or little green men, or maybe they wouldn't be green after all. Maybe they would be red instead, covered in blood from mutilating a calf.

But the light that flooded Tilly's room didn't come from a spaceship in her yard; it was the brief illumination of the headlights of a passing truck. The lights passed and the room darkened. And Tilly wondered, then, who *had* mutilated the calf? Maybe it was whoever was in the truck. *Maybe it was me.*

Ranger, curled up at the foot of her bed, snored. Tilly looked at him. He wasn't white anymore. He wasn't Dolly anymore; he was Ranger again.

Tilly thought of Dolly, the Great Pyrenees, and wondered if the Millers had indeed taken the dog to the sheriff's station, and if so, what Sheriff Valdez had thought. And before Tilly knew it, she was out of bed and in her truck—she was awake this time—and driving in the direction of the sheriff's home. It was late; he wouldn't be at the station.

In the time between knocking on the sheriff's door and his opening of the same, it occurred to Tilly that she wasn't exactly sure what it was that she meant to say. The door swung open.

"Tilly?" Sheriff Valdez said. He was not in his uniform, and instead wore shorts and a T-shirt. He was barefoot. Tilly found his dressed-down appearance unsettling. She wasn't sure what she had expected.

"Hi," Tilly said. She shifted from foot to foot, feeling suddenly very silly. "Did the Millers bring you a dead dog with missing teeth? Their Great Pyrenees?"

"What's that now?" Valdez rubbed his eyes.

"You know. Dolly. Dolly the sheepdog. With missing teeth."

The sheriff shook his head. "Tilly, I'm not sure what you're talking about. I haven't seen any dead dogs lately. I'd think I'd remember one with missing teeth."

"Goddamn it," Tilly said. Anger steadily rose in her voice. "They were supposed to bring her to you. It's another animal mutilation—like the calf. Have you found out anything about that?" The last question was shrill and wavering and, even to Tilly's subjective ear, sounded unstable.

"No, I—" Sheriff Valdez paused and took a deep breath and looked over his shoulder into his house. Apparently finding what he was looking for there, he said, "Tilly, why don't you come inside."

Tilly did. Tilly and the sheriff sat at the kitchen table. He poured them both a glass of some kind of brown liquor. Tilly took a sip. Bourbon.

"Tilly," Sheriff Valdez said. "How are you doing? You have a lot on your plate with taking care of your mama, and this whole thing with the ketamine cain't be easy on you. You look tired."

Tilly was caught off guard. She didn't come here to talk about herself. "Yeah, I—I'm fine," she lied.

"Okay because, you know, if you need someone to talk to . . ."

Sheriff Valdez let Tilly fill in the blanks. And she did. She realized exactly what was happening here.

"Sheriff. This—this isn't about—this isn't about *that*. Something is going on here. Something *bad* is happening in Verde. We need to get to the bottom of it."

As soon as she said it out loud, Tilly realized that there *was* at least one bad thing happening in Verde that she could positively identify. "Do you know about what Bubba Skinner is doing at the Triple Nine? I am starting to think it might all be related, but I don't know how."

"What do you mean, 'what Bubba Skinner is doing at the Triple Nine'? You mean the prostitutes?"

"No, not—the what?" Tilly paused, thinking she hadn't heard him correctly. "Did you say 'prostitutes'?"

She thought of the woman she had seen smoking outside of Bubba's poker game, what felt like forever ago. The realization struck Tilly like the glow of a cigarette illuminating a white streak of hair—*flash*. It made sense, of course, that Bubba would hire sex workers for his hunting guests, given his dubious relationship with the law and penchant for making money by, it seemed, any means necessary.

The sheriff cleared his throat. "Never mind that—what are *you* talking about?"

Tilly took a deep breath and made a mental note to ask Royce about the working girls at the 999 later. NDA be damned, she said, "The robots—the hunting robots?" The statement rose into a question.

The sheriff's brow furrowed. After a pause, he said, "Tilly are you sure you're doing okay? Should—should I call someone for you? Royce Wilson maybe?"

Tilly exhaled an angry breath. "What—what do you think, I'm just making this up? Going crazy?" Tilly couldn't blame him if he did think that. But she didn't want him to.

"No, no, I—" Sheriff Valdez took a deep breath.

A moment stretched between them, during which Valdez seemed to contemplate something. Then, seeming to make up his mind, he sighed and said, "Okay, tell me. What is this about—*robots*, did you say?"

And with this validation—this *permission*—it all came rushing out. "Bubba Skinner is making robots for hunting at the Triple Nine and they started making people now and I think they stole the dog's teeth to use on the tiger and maybe have something to do with the other animal mutilations but I just don't know what."

Sheriff Valdez took a long drink of his bourbon. "Can you give me a little more detail, Tilly? I'm afraid I'm a little slow on the uptake." His voice was gentle. Perhaps too gentle—like he was speaking to a child.

Still, Tilly took his request seriously. She started from the very beginning. She explained the animatronic hunting enterprise and how she came to be involved in it. She explained artificial intelligence and neural networks the best that she could. She explained the early failings of the tiger project and then its alarming success. She told the sheriff of the automaton that looked almost like a man and what they planned to do with it.

"So—you say Bubba Skinner has this whole *other* outpost on the ranch, and it's a laboratory where they been building robots to—to hunt."

"Yes," Tilly said. "It started with tigers and now they're doing people."

"They?"

"Well there's the guy that does the artificial intelligence programming—Abner. I know for a fact that he's responsible for those missing goats. And another woman that works there who does all of the mechanical stuff, but I don't think she knew about the goats. That's—that's why I am telling you all of this. Technically, I'm not supposed to because I signed an NDA, but—but I think something bad is going on. Like, criminal. It's all related. It has to be."

Sheriff Valdez took a deep breath. He looked down at his hands, which were clasped on the table. Then he looked up at Tilly. "Tilly, even if what you say is true—and I'm not saying it's not"—he raised his hands in a gesture of innocence—"I am not sure there's anything I can do. I can't just go in and search this place because you have a bad feeling about all of this. I would need some kind of reason to go in. And as far as I know, hunting—well, shooting robots or whatever—isn't a crime."

"But—but what kind of reason do you need?"

"Well, some kind of proof, I guess."

"Proof," Tilly repeated. "What kind of proof?"

"Well—that's just it," Sheriff Valdez said. And in his voice Tilly finally identified the tone that gentled his timbre—it was the same tone that her own voice fell into when she would play along with her mother's imaginings in the nursing home. Tilly's heart sank.

The sheriff continued, "I don't know what kind of proof you'll need, without knowing what they're doing that's illegal. If anything."

Tilly took a deep, resigned breath. "Okay. I'm going to get proof."

Then the sheriff's phone rang. He looked at the caller ID, and his face paled. "Excuse me, Tilly. It's sheriff's business." He stepped away to take the call.

When Tilly realized Sheriff Valdez didn't believe her, she drifted into a fog of her mind's making, a vaporous, swirling cloud of thoughts and ideas of how to prove herself—no, not herself, the robots and all the rest—to the sheriff.

Tilly overheard Sheriff Valdez talking on the phone in the hall. "Another one?" He heaved a sigh. "You thinkin' ketamine again?"

Ketamine again. Tilly's stomach dropped when she heard. Aloud, she mumbled to herself, "Proof. Okay. Proof." Her voice sounded far away, like it didn't come from her own mouth, her own thoughts.

And while the sheriff kept talking on the phone—*'Where?' 'I'll be right there'*—Tilly floated away on the fog, out of the sheriff's house and into her truck and down the driveway. And she heard him calling after her, "Tilly, be careful! Take care of yourself."

And she meant to. She really did.

Chapter 33
Lamentations

Tilly asked Anna to meet her at the diner the next morning. Tilly arrived first and slid into a corner booth facing the doorway. She ordered two cups of coffee. She tried to avoid eye contact with the other diners, most of whom she knew. She was in no mood for chatting.

Tilly kept an eye on the door. It swung open for person after person, none of whom were Anna. Tilly finished her cup of coffee and called Lynette over for a refill. Anna's cup was no longer steaming.

About halfway through Tilly's second cup of coffee—long after her caffeine craving subsided, she continued to take sips out of pure habit and to have something to do—Anna walked through the door. She sat down across from Tilly. Her eyes were puffy and red.

"Jesus, Anna," Tilly said. "Are you alright?"

Anna sniffed. "Yeah," she said. "Well—kind of, I guess."

Tilly didn't say anything, giving Anna room to elaborate.

She did. "One of my . . . friends, I guess, from my support group"—she patted the crook of her arm, where her track mark scars were—"fell off the wagon yesterday. He OD'd." Anna drew in a shaking breath.

"I'm so sorry," Tilly said. She recalled the phone call that Sheriff Valdez had gotten the previous evening. *Ketamine again?*

She knew it was rude, but she couldn't stop herself. "Heroin?" Her tone was impolitely hopeful.

"I guess," Anna said. Tilly felt relief, and then felt bad for feeling relief. One death that she wasn't responsible for, at least. "It's weird though," Anna continued, "because they found him with the needle in his arm."

Tilly nodded receptively before realizing that she didn't understand what Anna meant. "As opposed to . . . ?"

"Well, most addicts will inject somewhere else as long as they can before doing the arms. You know—between the toes and the like."

"Oh," Tilly said. She did not know.

"Yeah, it's less noticeable that way," Anna said. She sniffled again.

"Like Rachael Gonzales," Tilly said.

"What about her?"

"They also found her with the needle in her arm."

"Is that what happened? I didn't know that. Also odd for her, I would think, since she was so young. Unless she was a known addict; it's weird for a newbie."

"Huh," Tilly said in contemplation. She didn't know what else to say.

"So," Anna said in a new tone for a new subject, "what's the occasion?" She gestured between herself and Tilly.

"Oh," Tilly said. "Right. How are things at the Triple Nine?"

"I wouldn't know," Anna said. "I was fired a couple of weeks ago. About the same time you were." Anna stirred several packets of sugar into her coffee.

"*Fired?* How?" Tilly asked.

"Bubba told me I was done after we tried the first animatron hunt— you know, with the human-looking one. Of course, it didn't work. It wasn't ready, and I told him that. But he didn't listen, and it failed just like I said it would." She raised a resigned eyebrow at Tilly.

"But who is doing your job now?" Tilly asked.

"I don't know. He said they already had a replacement lined up." Anna took a sip of her coffee. Lynette set an order down at the next table over—pancakes, bacon.

Tilly took a deep breath. "Well, this is bad timing," she exhaled.

"You're telling me," Anna said. She looked down into her cup of coffee. "Wait—why is it bad timing for *you*?"

Tilly leaned across the table toward Anna, lowering her voice. "I was going to see if you could sneak me back into the workshop."

Anna exhale a singular, joyless laugh. "Why on *earth* would you want to do that?"

And so Tilly started to fill in the blanks. "Remember the thing with the tiger's teeth and the dog?"

"Yeah." Anna nodded.

Tilly told Anna her theory that the dog's teeth and the tiger's non-silicone teeth were one and the same. And she relayed her general suspicion that all of this had something to do with the animal mutilations, but that she wasn't sure how, but at the same time wasn't sure how it had taken her this long to correlate things. And how now she needed proof to take to the sheriff so that he would investigate.

"Woah," Anna said when Tilly was finished.

"Yeah," Tilly agreed. "What do you think?

"Well, it's insane," Anna said. Tilly's heart sank. "But I've heard crazier things that turned out to be true."

Tilly brightened. Anna started rummaging through her purse. "They took my key, of course, when they fired me."

Heart sinking.

"But—" Heart rising. "I lost the key at one point, and so they gave me a copy. The copy is what I gave back to them."

She continued to rummage through her things. "Aha," she said. She held up a silver key. "And then I found the original key. Sometimes it pays to be unorganized." She slid the key across the table to Tilly. "Here, be my guest."

"Thank you," Tilly said. She pocketed the key. "Tell Lynette I'll get her next time for the coffee."

"Yeah, sure," Anna said.

Tilly rose to leave.

"Good luck, I guess," Anna called after her.

Tilly was out of the door before she could say thank you.

Chapter 34
Babylon

Tilly drove straight to the 999. It was Sunday, so she didn't expect anyone to be at the workshop, but despite the expected vacancy, she decided to park her truck on the county road that bordered the back of the property instead of driving all of the way in. She didn't want to give herself up before she had even begun; she would walk to the workshop.

She climbed the fence into the workshop pasture and began to make her way toward it. Every step through the winter-dead grass was a crunch; every pull of a branch out of her path was a rattle. These things sounded loud to Tilly in the silence of the pasture.

As she walked through the brush, it occurred to Tilly that there may be people who did in fact go to the workshop on Sundays—janitorial staff, or maintenance men, or delivery guys. And so the closer Tilly got to the workshop in the pasture, the more she tried to disappear. She began to tiptoe and willed the grass beneath her to accept her steps without noisy protest. She shallowed her breathing. She wished herself into an invisible vapor. None of these things made her go away.

As Tilly got closer to the workshop, she heard a noise that stopped her in her tracks. *Voices.* They were too far away for Tilly to make out what they were saying. She stood stock-still and listened, trying to at least figure out which direction they came from. *Dead ahead.*

Tilly knew at that moment that she should turn around. The logical thing to do would be to go back the way she came, get in her truck, and go home to Ranger. But her curiosity fought logic and won. She crept forward toward the tree line on the edge of the clearing where the workshop was. When Tilly got to the edge of the clearing, she crouched behind a guajillo shrub. She watched. She found the voices.

The voices were standing near the small enclosure on the edge of the north pasture where the hunts took place—the pen where the subject of the hunt was staged first before release into the pasture. One of the voices belonged to Bubba. He was talking animatedly to another man beside him. The other man wore cartoonishly exaggerated hunting clothes, which by the looks of them had only just been separated from their price tags. He had a semiautomatic rifle slung over his shoulder, the kind used by the military, or mass shooters, or game hunters with bad aim and an inferiority complex.

Tilly looked past Bubba and the hunter to the enclosure. She expected to see the tiger pacing back and forth, waiting to be released into the pasture for the hunt. But the tiger wasn't there. Instead, to Tilly's horror, in the enclosure was a person. Or, at least, something doing a very fair impersonation of a person.

It was the human-looking animatron. Since the last time Tilly had seen it—legless in the lab—the animatronic man had crossed the threshold from mechanics to biology. In the shine of its eyes, in the warmth of its cheeks, in the delicate blemishes on its skin, there was the inarticulable essence that all biological creatures can recognize, though scarcely define, in one another—life. Sometime since Tilly's last day at the workshop, the vital force of humanity had been distilled and breathed into the animatron. The spirit had come to the bones. Tilly stared in awe at the creation, which seemed to her so far beyond a miracle of engineering that it reached into the realm of magic. *Is the magic fairly ruined for you?*

Tilly's momentary awe dissolved into disgust as the animatron moved about the enclosure. It paced back and forth, and it grabbed the fence separating it from Bubba and the hunter, and it looked *so* real. And *so* wrong.

Then it spoke. "Please—please, I'm begging you," the animatron pleaded with its captors as it rattled the fence. Its voice, too, sounded less robotic. Tilly thought of when she had first met the animatronic man in Abner's workshop, and its plaintive plea: '*Help.*' The pleading of the iteration of the animatron now before her in the pasture was much more realistic and much, much worse to listen to. Tilly's stomach turned in disgust at the whole operation.

"Convincing, ain't it?" Bubba asked his hunter. His eyes shone with pride.

"It really is," the hunter said. Then he reached out to touch the animatron's hand, which was wrapped around a fence post. The animatron jerked its hand away from the fence before the hunter could touch it.

The hunter chuckled. "Feisty. This is going to be fun."

Tilly couldn't watch any longer. She followed the brush line around the clearing to the other side of the workshop, away from and out of sight of the terrible spectacle. She heard the lever pull that opened the gate from the small enclosure to the hunting pasture. She heard Bubba say, "You better run!" and then something large—human-sized—moving through the brush.

After a few minutes, when she knew that the hunter and Bubba would be far enough into the pasture for her to get away with it, Tilly stole away from the cover of the trees and made her way toward the entrance to the workshop. She felt exposed in the open. It occurred to her for the first time that there might be cameras, that the area may be monitored. She looked for cameras and didn't see any, though this brought her little comfort.

The door to the building was not locked. Tilly let herself inside. Her steps echoed through the empty building. They were the only sound besides Tilly's breathing. She wasn't sure what she was looking for, and she had no real plan for how to proceed. She took in her surroundings—hallways and closed doors. She decided the best course was to start opening them.

The first door led to an empty office. The second to a closet with cleaning supplies. The third to an empty storage room. Behind the fourth was Abner's office. Tilly tried the handle, expecting it to be locked. But it wasn't.

Tilly went inside. It was as she remembered it when she had last spoken with Abner in the office; things were usual. There were computer monitors and their usual trappings on the desk. It was tidy. Tilly opened the drawers and found nothing but office supplies. There was a whiteboard on one wall with some equations scribbled on it. *Cliche*, thought Tilly.

Suddenly aware of the passage of time, Tilly decided to call Abner's office a wash and move on. She was nearly out the door when something on the wall near the door caught her eye. A framed newspaper clipping.

On the page, Abner beamed from a black-and-white photo in what appeared to be a professional headshot. It accompanied an article. Tilly's heart dropped at the headline:

UC Berkeley Professor Fired for Stealing Human Brains

Tilly's heart accelerated as she continued to read the article.

(Berkeley, California) A professor at UC Berkeley was fired yesterday from the school's computer sciences department after being caught with human brains that he had stolen from cadavers in the medical school. The organs were in various states of dissection when a student assistant found former professor Abner Ubel studying slides containing brain matter under a microscope. The student assistant immediately reported the troubling scene to school authorities. Ubel was fired Thursday after an emergency meeting of the Berkeley Board of Trustees.

Ubel worked in UC Berkeley's computer sciences department, where his scholarship focused on artificial intelligence. Ubel says that the brain heist was in advancement of his work, claiming that he sought to better understand human neural networks in an attempt to mimic the organic networks with his algorithmic programs aimed at achieving general artificial intelligence.

The head of the Berkley computer sciences department assured that the field is far from achieving generalized artificial intelligence, which she described as a state of artificial consciousness in which a computer can independently think and reason. She added that studying the physical human brain could not logically advance this goal. "It's nonsense," she said. "Mr. Ubel went off the rails."

A spokesperson for UC Berkeley says the school will continue to investigate the incident.

Tilly's temples tightened and she felt her pulse racing up her neck. Her mind flew from question to question. The *implications*. She stared at Abner's photo accompanying the article. He smiled back at her.

Tilly was brought from the confines of her mind back into the real world by a sharp *CRACK* from somewhere outside of the building. It was the familiar sound of gunfire. A moment or two passed and the first *CRACK* was followed by five more in quick succession. Tilly winced at each one. In her mind's eye, she could see the animatron torn apart by the bullets, lying in a pool of fake blood on the ground.

Tilly knew that she needed to leave the workshop now, and fast—Bubba and the hunter would return at any minute—but she couldn't not keep searching for evidence while she had the opportunity. She left Abner's office and continued down the hall.

The next room was the familiar storage room where Tilly had first seen the shadow man that turned out to be an early iteration of the animatron. She tried the door. It was locked. She almost moved on before remembering that she had Anna's key. She tried it. To Tilly's mild surprise, it opened.

The room was cluttered, as ever. Tilly wandered between aisles of storage shelves, taking in their contents. It was mostly boxes of spare parts for the animatrons. There were a few instances of lab equipment that appeared to be broken, or dated, or redundant to other machines Tilly knew to be in use.

The torso that had haunted Tilly from the back of the room that first time—the shadow man—was no longer there. Tilly figured that it had been called up from the reserves for spare parts or target practice. She probed the corner where it had been.

And that's when she saw them. Lining the back of a shelf, in shadows, were several liquid-filled glass jars. Tilly knelt down to inspect them more closely, and she gagged. It wasn't the liquid that was jarring—it was what was suspended in the liquid.

The jars contained what looked like lumpy gray flesh—it took Tilly a moment to realize that the jars contained various iterations of *brains*. There were a few small ones—Tilly surmised that they were about deer- or goat-sized brains—and one that looked like a small bovine brain. She shuddered. One jar contained a brain that looked terrifyingly human. A couple of jars contained various species of eyeballs with their optical nerves attached. Several of the organs had bits sliced out of them or were not-so-neatly mangled.

Tilly's horror erupted. She barely contained a scream. It was Abner. It was *all Abner*. Tilly's mind spiraled. Then she heard a noise from outside. And she remembered where she was, and that her time was limited, and that she shouldn't have decided to come in here in the first place.

Tilly pulled out her phone and snapped photos. Then, worrying that Abner would have time to destroy the evidence if he discovered that Tilly had found him out, she grabbed one of the smaller jars with one of the smaller brains—maybe a cat's?—and tucked it under her arm. She fled the storage room, listening carefully at the door for any noises in the hall. None.

She crept out of the room and down the hall toward the exit. She cradled the stolen brain in her arms as she snuck down the hall, waiting for a noise or an appearance that would ruin her heist.

Tilly made it to the exit. She looked outside through the windows and didn't see anyone or anything that would impede her flight. She was about thirty yards from the safety of the tree line. She just had to make it to the tree line. She opened the door a crack and peered out. The pleasant, fresh air that hit her face felt out of place in the terror of her situation. She looked for signs of Bubba and the hunter, or even Abner—any source, really, of the outside noise. She didn't see anyone. She slid through the door and gently closed it behind her. She looked around her once more before running for the tree line. That was her mistake.

Because from this wider angle, she saw a truck that had just been out of her line of sight from inside. It was backed up to a gate into the north pasture, where Tilly had witnessed the hunter chase the human-looking robot into the brush not so long ago. Tilly froze. And despite every fiber of logic in her being, she watched. She couldn't look away.

A man was dragging a bloodied animatron feetfirst into the bed of the truck. It was limp and flopped heavily over the edge of the tailgate. This one looked like a woman. Its head knocked on the tailgate's edge. And when it did, the head was knocked to the side. And that's when Tilly spotted a white streak of hair through its otherwise dark tresses. And it was familiar. And the white streak of hair was attached to a piece of skull that flapped open, revealing beneath not circuitry, not a computer, but a very human, very biological, very maimed brain.

And at the revelation of what was really happening in the back pasture of the 999, Tilly could no longer contain it. She screamed. Loudly. And instead of turning to run, which of course she should have done, she couldn't tear her eyes away from the man or his truck. Because she knew both of them.

The man looked up from his macabre task when Tilly screamed. They locked eyes. He dropped the dead woman's feet into the bed of the truck with a *clang*.

"Tilly?" he asked.

"Royce," Tilly said. It was an accusation. It was a resignation. Her head shook back and forth on a pivot, out of her control. She began taking steps backward, toward the tree line, where she always should have been going. "No, Royce, no. No—no, no, no, no. No!" Tears leaked down her face. Tilly didn't notice them. "How—how could you *do* this?"

"Wait—wait, Tilly—Tilly, stop." Royce climbed down from the bed of the truck. His hands and pants and shirt were covered in blood, just like when Tilly had seen him butchering that deer before Thanksgiving, what seemed like forever ago. "Tilly, stop." He put up a bloody palm in a "stop" gesture.

And for some reason outside of reason, Tilly did. She stopped there in the clearing as her bloody friend walked toward her.

"How?" she asked. Her voice was small. She barely heard herself.

"I can explain—just, just wait. I can explain." Royce advanced toward her. She knew she should turn, should run, but she couldn't. It was *Royce*.

"You—you *killed* a *person*." Tilly's voice trembled just like her hands, her legs, her whole body.

"No, no—I didn't. I did not kill her. I'm just cleaning up." He was almost to Tilly now.

"Just *cleaning up*? That's—that's not a deer, Royce. She's a real person. A *real person*." Breath came to Tilly only in shakes.

"Tilly—you don't understand. It's my job," Royce said. "I have to do my job." He was feet away from Tilly now. He stopped.

"No, you don't." Tilly shook her head, her tone incredulous. "You don't have to do this job. *What?*"

Royce stopped in front of her. "Tilly, she's—she was a druggie. A hooker. One less in the world—why does that matter?" His expression was pleading.

Tilly exhaled in disbelief. "She was a *person*, Royce! Like me! Like *you*, for fuck's sake!" Tilly bridged the distance between them with a backhand slap to Royce's chest. It wasn't a hard slap, but still Royce winced. "How do you think this is okay?"

Before Royce could explain himself any further, another person came out of the brush of the north pasture. "What's going on out here, Royce—I heard screamin.'"

It was Bubba. He stopped in his tracks when he saw Tilly standing there, tears streaking down her face, jarred brain in her hand. He looked at the bloody mess in the back of Royce's truck, then back at Tilly, his expression stricken. "Tilly," he said. "Fuck."

"You *sorry* sonofabitch," Tilly said. Her horror, her *fear,* was eclipsed by rank anger. "You greedy piece of fucking trash," she hurled at Bubba. "Is it the money? People are *paying* to hunt people? The money's that good?"

Bubba didn't answer. He looked at Royce, knowingly. "You're gonna need to take care of this, son. You know what you need to do."

"But—no, no," Royce said, shaking his head. "I can't—"

"C'mon, we got another hunt in an hour, we're burnin' daylight. Do it," Bubba spat.

"But Dad—"

"Do it, boy," Bubba said, his voice sharp. "Do it, or I'll whoop your sorry ass. *Do it.*"

Royce looked at Tilly, and to Tilly he looked suddenly very small. "I'm so sorry, Til," he said. Royce grabbed Tilly's arm. Firmly but not violently.

Tilly looked down at his hand on her arm. Her brow furrowed. She looked Royce in the eyes. "Royce, no—"

"I'm so sorry." His grip on her arm tightened.

And Tilly realized it was too late to run. And this was how it was going to be. And she braced for a blow to the head, or something similar. But instead, Royce pulled a syringe from his pocket. He uncapped it and went for her neck. And in that moment Tilly was every animal she had ever treated.

The needle plunged into her neck. In seconds the world dimmed, and her mind floated away. The last thing she observed was the brain in a jar that she had held in her arms shattering to the ground as she went limp, and Royce catching her in his arms, repeating over and over, *I'm so, so sorry.*

Chapter 35
Sloth

Royce
Several Months Earlier

"Royce, come see me in the office when you finish up," Bubba said. Royce was stacking fifty-pound sacks of feed into the grain shed on the 999.

"Yeah, sure," he said. It had been a long day and he just wanted to go home. Have a beer. "You got it." He threw another sack on the pile. It landed with a dull smash. His shoulders hurt.

Royce did what he was told. His dad was waiting in his office when Royce got there. The new hire—the scientist, Abner—was there as well. Royce sat down in an overstuffed leather chair.

"Royce, we got a new project for you," Bubba said.

"Alright." Royce's gaze was fixed on the taxidermied giraffe hanging behind his father's desk.

Bubba looked at Abner. Abner nodded. Bubba said, "You know our new venture, Abner's project?"

Royce nodded, looking at Abner. Abner smiled at him. *Smug little fucker*, Royce thought.

"Abner needs your help with something."

"Yeah?" Royce locked eyes with Abner and raised his eyebrows. Abner looked down at his lap.

Bubba said, "Yeah. Tell him what you need, Abner."

Abner looked up and cleared his throat. "Right," he said. "I need a young brain."

"A young brain? Not mine, I hope," Royce said. He smiled at his joke and looked to Bubba for commiseration. Bubba didn't smile back. Royce's mouth fell back in line.

"No, no, yours would not be useful," Abner said. Bubba laughed at that.

"What I need is a developing brain. Any mammal brain will work, really, but a larger brain would be the most helpful."

Royce thought he must be misunderstanding. "Wait. You mean, like, a physical brain?" he asked. "Why?"

"Huh," Bubba huffed. "What is this, peer review? You a scientist now, boy?"

Royce looked at the floor and he was suddenly nine years old again. "No sir."

"You damn right, you ain't. You don't mind what it's for and just do what you're told. Yeah?"

"Yeah, okay," Royce said. His shoulders were curved over his torso in a melt of a man.

"It is okay," Abner said. "I do not mind explaining." The gleam in his eyes told Royce not only that Abner didn't *mind* explaining, but also that he rather enjoyed it.

"I need a brain that is still in the development stage so that I can observe the neural synapses in their nascence, as they form," Abner explained.

Royce nodded, even though he didn't really understand. "So, what then, you want me to get you a deer brain or something? How does this involve me?"

"A deer?" Bubba said. "You want him to use a brain from one of our deer? Now don't that sound like a colossal waste of money to you, son, or are you that fucking stupid? You want him dissecting a ten-thousand-dol-lar brain?"

Abner interjected, looking almost sympathetic, which Royce imme-diately resented. He hated being pitied. "Well, the problem with that, too, is that I think this year's batch of fawns is too old now for their brains to be useful to me. They are all born in the summer, right?"

Royce nodded. His gaze was focused on a brass ashtray on his father's desk. He sucked his cheek into his mouth, between his teeth. He bit down, softly. Then harder.

"Instead," Abner continued, "I was thinking, perhaps, a calf? You should be able to find a baby calf still in October, right?"

Royce nodded, then looked from the ashtray to Bubba. "Where am I supposed to get a calf brain?"

"Royce, son, when you're drivin' around, do you ever notice those big animals with four legs standing out in all of the pastures? In herds? Black, brown, white, spotted, a lot of times they're eating grass. Now, those are called—"

"Alright, I get it," Royce said. "Ha ha." He shook his head. "So what, you want me to just—to just take a calf out of someone's field?"

"There it is," Bubba said. "Now you're catching on."

"Why not buy one at the livestock auction or something?" Royce offered.

"And leave a record of sale? I don't think so."

Royce took a deep breath that turned into a sigh. "Okay. Fine. When do you need it by?" he asked Abner.

"Tomorrow would be great," Abner said.

Royce nodded again, his eyes emptying of light.

"And while we are at it, bring the eyes too. And the spinal cord."

"Yeah," Royce said. "Sure."

And that was that. Royce left his father's office.

* * *

The night came quickly. Royce had been dreading the darkness since leaving Bubba's office with his nighttime mission, but when it came, he found comfort in it, in the concealment it brought. Royce sat in his truck on a dark county road—the most remote one he could think of. His headlights and engine were off. He took a swig of bourbon from the bottle he had brought with him. There was a handgun with a silencer on the barrel next to him on the passenger seat. He sat like this for some time.

Finally, the resolve came to him around 1:00 a.m. He took another pull from his bottle of bourbon. He stepped out of the truck.

Royce knew Mr. Wills always rotated his cattle into the west pasture of his ranch in the fall. And he knew his way around the property. Royce knew these things because one of Tom Wills's sons was in the same grade as him in school. Now the younger Wills was a tractor mechanic at the ag equipment shop in town, but back then, he and Royce and some of the other Verde boys spent hours roaming through the pastures of the Wills ranch on various adventures. And now that knowledge was useful.

The old trails of the pasture came back to Royce as he made his way from the fence line, through a brushy area, to the stock tank where he suspected the cattle would be bedded down for the evening, because that is where the Wills cattle had always bedded down for the evenings when they were in the west pasture in the fall.

Soon Royce came upon them where he thought they'd be. They were mostly lying down, white blobs of living thing dotted in clusters around the stock tank. The Willses raised Charolais cattle, one of the gentler breeds—a breed more likely to tolerate a person in their midst.

A few of the cows rose to their feet as Royce approached. One of them lowed—a friendly sound. Royce stopped when he reached the herd and surveyed his options. There were several very small calves among the herd. Royce weighed what Abner had said—a young brain, but large. Hoping to achieve that balance, Royce picked out a calf that looked like it was about two months old. At about 150 pounds, it would still be manageable to him.

After making up his mind, Royce became paralyzed. He stood on the outskirts of the herd, and the cows watched him, placidly chewing their cuds. There wasn't a bull among them, which was good. Bulls, of course, could be aggressive. One cow bravely walked toward Royce as he stood there, unmoving. He knew that he should be scared—or at least wary—of her. But her demeanor was gentle. Royce was disappointed; it would have been better if she was angry, mean, chased him away. Instead, she came to him. Royce instinctively stuck out his hand. She pressed her nose into it and wrapped her sandpaper tongue around his fingers. She was looking for food.

"Sorry," Royce said to her. "I don't have anything for you."

The handgun in his waistband was cold against his abdomen. "Sorry," he said again. The cow blinked her big soft eyes. Her breath was warm against his skin.

Royce shook his head and looked away. Then he took a deep breath and walked past the friendly cow. She lowered her head to graze.

The other cattle watched Royce as he walked toward the chosen calf. The moonlight lent a golden hue to its cream-colored hide. It turned its head toward Royce as he approached. One cow moved toward him as he got close—likely the calf's mother. Her head was lowered defensively, ready to fight off the perceived threat to her baby. Royce raised his arms out and above his head to make himself look big. "Yaah!" he shouted. She stopped her advance.

But then, too, the calf rose to its feet and started to trot toward its mother. Royce had to act fast, and he did. He pulled the pistol from his waistband. He cocked it and fired. There was a sharp *crack* sound, quieter for the silencer, but still jarring. The calf made a horrible, strangled noise and dropped to the ground. Blood started to spread across the white expanse of its shoulder. For all of his apprehension about the task, or maybe because of it, Royce now felt strangely empty.

The rest of the herd, startled by sound of the gunshot, immediately bolted—except for one. The mother of the felled calf remained, and she moved between the calf and Royce. She bellowed. He raised his arms again to shoo her. She took a step back. Then she looked at her baby.

The throes of death had already passed; the calf was still. A knowing seemed to dawn upon the cow, and she turned to hurry after the others, away from the man with the gun and the empty body that was once her baby.

Like a scavenger, Royce descended upon the calf—still warm with the heat of life—and set about his messy work.

Chapter 36
Avarice

A short time later, Royce pulled into the driveway of his house in town. It was late—or early, depending on perspective—and the full moon hung low on the horizon.

Royce had been instructed to put the calf's organs on ice to slow the breakdown of the tissue, and he had done so. He had put them in an ice chest—one he usually used to ice down beer. It was in the back of his truck. Like Royce's clothes and arms and hands, the white ice chest was smeared with blood.

Royce's street was quiet. But it wouldn't be too long until the earliest risers greeted the day. He knew he needed to make quick work of getting the bloodied ice chest—and his bloodied self—inside the house.

He let the tailgate of his truck down gently, quietly. He slid the ice chest to the edge of the truck bed. It left a trail of blood in its wake; this, for some reason, was the sight that churned Royce's stomach. He wanted to immediately get the garden hose, or a washcloth, or anything, and scrub. Scrub.

He shook his head to clear it. He heaved the ice chest into his arms. It wasn't as heavy as it should have been, Royce thought, for what was inside.

Royce took the ice chest and closed the tailgate, and all that was left to do was walk inside. The red glow of the truck's taillights backlit Royce's silhouette like a fiery halo, and the soft light of the moon made shadows of the angles of his face. And for a moment he was an otherworldly vision—an apparition—and in that liminal moment someone from the sidewalk said, "Mr. Wilson?"

Royce turned, horrified to face the speaker. He was even more horrified to recognize her. It was a neighbor of his from a few houses down. A high school girl—Rachael, maybe?

Her face reflected his own horror back at him. And in her gaze he felt, for the first time, his own immense guilt. And then more guilt for the fact that he only felt guilty now that he had been caught.

Royce tried to force an amiable expression. "Hey there—what are you doing out this late?"

The girl didn't answer. She only stared at his bloodied shirt, his bloody hands.

"Don't you worry," he said. "Just a little hunting." He tried on a smile.

In the silence that followed, Royce's mind started to run through the implications of the girl on the sidewalk looking at his bloodied self. Surely the mutilated calf would be the talk of the town tomorrow—and someone seeing him covered in blood in the night? The inference was obvious. She'd call the authorities immediately. They would be knocking on his door by the sunrise. The *crimes*—animal cruelty? Theft? Cattle rustling? He'd have to face Mr. Wills, the father of an old friend, and try to explain himself. And he couldn't.

And the worst would be his father—having to tell him. Or would it be worse if he found out on his own? Would his father be in trouble too? For what—just the calf, or whatever the project was that he needed it for? And the rest—Royce knew his dad wasn't exactly clean. Royce could think of several technical crimes, mostly financial, that would be revealed with only a little poking around the 999. And then what? The ranch, the deer, the money. *Then what?*

Royce watched an empire collapse in the eyes of the girl that stared at him from the street. He couldn't face him. He couldn't do it. It couldn't all be his fault. Not this time.

This collapse of thought happened in seconds. And at the dark bottom of this spiral of mind, there was a void. And in the void, there was no thought. Only action.

Royce set the ice chest with the organs on the ground. He walked toward the girl. She didn't run. She didn't scream. She only stared.

"I have to," Royce said to her. "It's okay."

When he reached her, and she still just stood there, Royce grabbed her upper arm. He looked at a point beyond her head as he drew his arm back. And he closed his eyes when he swung. He caught her when she fell.

He dragged her into his house. Then he retrieved the ice chest. Then he sat next to the unconscious girl, his clothes still bloodied, on the couch. He waited until the clock struck six o'clock to call his father.

Chapter 37
Pride

"And this was your best idea?" Bubba asked Royce. He was standing with Royce in his living room. The girl was still on the couch. She was awake, now, but it did her little good—Royce had zip-tied her hands and duct-taped her mouth. Her eyes were wide and darting between her two captors.

"What else was I supposed to do?" Royce asked. "She caught me."

"I don't know Royce, you ever heard of *bribery*?" Bubba grabbed Royce by the shirt. "Or hell, just *denying* you did anything?" He gave Royce a shake. Royce's eyes widened to match the girl's.

"You butcher animals as part of your living, dumbass. There's very few people who can come home covered in blood and not be suspicious, and you're one of 'em." Bubba released Royce with a shove, and Royce stumbled backward.

"I—I thought we didn't want other people to know," Royce stammered. "You know, no loose ends."

"So this is the alternative?" Bubba gestured forcefully at the girl, and she winced. "*Kidnapping*? *Assault*? This a big fucking loose end, son. I cain't believe even you'd be this stupid."

"What about a bribe now? We put her back and pay her and her family or whoever."

The girl started nodding her head violently. She said something, repeatedly. It was hard to make out with the duct tape on her mouth, but it might have been '*Please*.'

"Put her *back*? It's too late for that, son. You've committed a felony. Felon*ies*. It's too late. Even I couldn't get you out of this one—you'd go to jail." Bubba's face was inflamed with anger.

At that the girl screamed. It was muffled by the tape, but still loud enough. "Stop it," Royce said. "Stop!"

The girl didn't stop. She screamed at the top of her lungs. "Shut up!" Royce yelled at her. "Shut up, shut up!"

Then he struck her, hard, across the face. She stopped screaming.

"Jesus, Royce," Bubba said. He looked at his son in disbelief.

Royce started to sob.

Bubba shook his head and strode to the window of the living room, which had its shades drawn. He peered out. "Goddamn it, Royce," he said.

"What?" Royce asked. He heaved in a breath and quelled his sobbing. He left the girl on the couch with a cautious glance and joined his father at the window. A police car had just pulled up to a house down the street from Royce's. It was the girl's house. She must have been discovered missing.

Royce's heart skipped a beat. "Fuck," he said.

Bubba stepped away from the window and took stock of his son. Royce's clothing and hands were caked with dried calf's blood—it was dark in its dryness, almost black, and gathered in horrible stripes where his skin creased. His face, too, had blood smeared on it where he had wiped either sweat or tears away at some point in the night. The blood on his cheeks was streaked through with a geometry of tear tracks; his face was a lurid, bloody clown mask.

Bubba shook his head. "You need to shower," he said.

Royce was surprised at the comment, then looked down at himself. "Yeah, I guess I do. Wasn't at the top of my concerns."

"Well, it should be. You look like a criminal," Bubba said.

Royce looked at his hands. He had tried to wipe them clean after liberating the calf of its nervous organs, but the unmistakable hue of blood remained. *Red-handed*, Royce thought. *Red-handed, red-handed, red-handed.*

"Alright, here's what we're gonna do," Bubba said. "You're gonna go shower. And I am gonna figure out what to do with her."

Royce did as he was told. When he got out of the shower, Bubba was gone. The girl was still on the couch, petrified and silent.

"Dad?" Royce called. Nothing.

The girl looked toward the front door. Following her gaze, Royce peered out of his front window. His father's truck was gone.

He called him. Bubba answered.

"Where did you go?" Royce asked, panic in his voice.

"I'm going to work, Royce. I would hope you wouldn't be far behind me."

"But—but what about—what am I supposed to *do*?" A sob welled in Royce's throat again.

"You're gonna handle this one on your own. Clean up your own damn mess for once."

"But—but how?"

"You'll figure something out. Just don't make a mess."

"What do you—"

Click. Silence filled the other end of the line. Bubba had hung up.

Royce paced the living room. He looked out the window down the street. The police were still there. Royce sat on the couch next to the girl and sobbed.

Chapter 38
Envy

By some miracle, Royce made it to work on time. He performed his daily inspection of the deer that were in the pens. He found the prize sire buck, Remington, with a limp. As if his day could get any worse.

He called Tilly Hutto, the veterinarian who had just moved back to town. He tried to calm his frazzled nerves while he waited for her. She arrived.

"Morning, Tilly," Royce greeted her.

"Good morning," Tilly said back. "Where's my patient?"

Royce said, "Follow me."

Royce couldn't stand the silence as they walked. To fill it, he asked, "Any interesting adventures in medicine lately?"

"As a matter of fact, yes," Tilly said. "First thing this morning I got called out to the Wills Ranch. Someone killed a calf and then took its brain and spinal cord. It was horrible."

Royce's blood pressure rose. *So they had already found it.* He knew this moment was coming in some form or another, but he didn't expect it so soon. And not from Tilly. He wouldn't have guessed that they'd call a veterinarian; he had left the calf in such a state that it was obviously very dead, unsalvageable. He tried to think of something to say. "Shit, that's not something you see every day."

"And not something I ever want to see again," Tilly said.

Me neither, Royce thought, shuddering internally at the memory.

He wondered what the state of the investigation was. "So what's the diagnosis?" he prodded. "Aliens? Some kind of animal sacrifice?"

"Beats me," Tilly said. "Maybe Sheriff Valdez will come up with something."

Royce's heart caught in his throat. His vocal cords froze; he couldn't say anything in response. So they continued in silence, with Royce drowning in thoughts of arrest and interrogations and trial and jail.

These thoughts continued even when they reached the deer pen, even when Royce shook the bucket of corn to lure Remington over to them. There were two Royces in that moment—Mind Royce, who could only think, and was only thoughts, and couldn't escape them, and Body Royce, who carried on without mental direction.

Body Royce threw a handful of dry corn out for the buck. Mind Royce did not register when Tilly opened the gate to the deer pen and went inside.

After a few seconds of Tilly kneeling beside the buck, unprotected, Royce registered the scene. He came back together, mind and body. He said the things he knew he should.

"Careful, Til," Royce said. "Do you want me to get the dart gun? He almost gored one of the hands last week."

"No, it's okay, let him eat a minute. Poor guy." Tilly told Royce she needed to x-ray the Buck's leg. Royce offered again to get the tranquilizer gun to dart the deer.

"Hold on. I've got a syringe of ketamine in my bag there." She pointed to the medical bag she had left outside of the pen. "In the outside pocket. Hand it here."

"You sure?"

"Yeah. Give it to me."

"I don't think that's a good idea, Til."

"Royce, he's in pain. Just hand me the syringe." Tilly was stern.

Royce acquiesced. He fetched the syringe from the pocket of Tilly's medical bag. And as he did so, a thought snuck into his mind. The nascence of an idea.

He handed Tilly the syringe. "Thank you," Tilly said.

No, Royce thought. *Thank you.*

As Tilly turned her attention back to the buck, Royce turned his attention back to Tilly's medical bag. He opened the main compartment. He kept one eye on Tilly and the buck as he visually sorted through the bag's contents. There were several glass vials of liquid medicine in pockets lining the bag's middle section. Royce took a leap of faith and quickly grabbed one. He was lucky.

Ketamine, the label read. He tucked the vial into his jacket pocket. He noticed something glinting in the medical bag when he bent back down to close it. A scalpel. Without thinking, and without knowing why, he grabbed that too. He closed the bag and looked back up at Tilly. She was still absorbed in her task of x-raying the buck.

Chapter 39
Wrath

Royce
A Month or So Later

Things calmed down for Royce after he got rid of the girl. Or, perhaps, everything else he did in the following weeks seemed benign compared to murder. Or maybe he was just numb. Tilly's ketamine, it turned out, was the perfect way to deal with his Rachael Gonzales problem. When he got home, after lucking into the vial of tranquilizer, he simply gave the girl a shot. It felt, almost, *humane*.

At his father's request, Royce harvested more animal organs for Abner's project from various beasts, wild and domestic. Folks around Verde organized search parties for the missing girl. Royce participated, all the while knowing that her body was in the walk-in freezer of the 999, where they kept deer carcasses awaiting butchering for the ranch hunters. It was locked, and only Royce had access. It was perfect. For a time.

When the search party passed through his Uncle Augie's ranch, Royce had a close call. He had harvested the organs of several wild whitetail deer he killed on the ranch, and one of the searchers came upon the dried pool of blood of his latest victim (the carcass was in Royce's home freezer, not to go to waste).

Royce hadn't realized at the time, but he had left behind the scalpel that he had stolen from Tilly, which he'd been using for his organ extractions. When he heard a searcher had found the scalpel, he, luckily, got there before the law did. Royce picked up the scalpel to cover his tracks and make sure there was a plausible reason for his fingerprints to be on it. And the plan seemed to work. No one suspected him, of either mutilation or murder.

When he had found the anomaly of the goats in the pasture—which were not his doing, and at the time, unknown to him to be Abner's doing—he saw an opportunity to confuse the animal mutilation investigation even more. He called Tilly and called the sheriff, hoping they would be thrown even further off his scent.

And Royce decided to take advantage of the confusion, and—having decided that the girl couldn't stay in the freezer forever—decided to arrange for her to be found. He took her out of the freezer and let her thaw, then placed her under the bridge of Highway 2676 in the night, completing the scene with a syringe of ketamine stabbed into the crook of her arm.

When they found the girl, things went just as he had planned—the authorities assumed an overdose, and when the toxicology report returned a positive test for ketamine, that was that. No one seemed to suspect him. He was free to go on with his life. As the days went on, he felt more justified in his actions, more confident that he had made the right decision. The ship was righted. Smooth sailing ahead.

Bubba had him help with the special animatron project now and then. He was a trusted source of manual labor when Abner or Anna needed extra muscles to move or construct something. He carefully avoided Tilly at the animatron workshop—partly because Bubba had told him to, and partly because he knew that if he saw Tilly there, and Tilly saw him, somehow the whole thing would unravel.

It was in this capacity that Royce came to be present at the first hunt of the human-looking animatron. He arrived at the workshop early in the morning on to help Abner get the thing situated to begin the hunt.

Royce hadn't yet seen the thing fully formed. It stood in the middle of the workshop, supported by a metal stand of identical height to the robot, like one that would hold a new doll, still in the box. The animatron was about Royce's height.

Its legs were disproportionately long. And, though Royce could tell much effort had been put into making the skin look authentic, it was deficient. It did not necessarily look fake, but it somehow looked *cold*. Unreal. He thought of the very cold girl that he had recently liberated from his freezer. She wasn't real either. Not now, not to Royce. Perhaps she never had been. Royce steered his thoughts away from her.

"What do you think?" Abner asked, clearly excited to share his latest creation and looking for positive feedback.

"Are you gonna put clothes on it?" Royce asked. The animatron was naked.

"Oh," Abner said, his face falling. "I had not thought of that."

"I think I got some extras in my truck, if you want. It should have clothes, I think."

Abner did want, and Royce fetched a change of clothes for the animatron. He came back and dressed it in a pair of jeans with mud crusted around the hems and a plaid button-down shirt with flecks of blood—likely from a deer, but who knew, now—scattered up one sleeve.

Abner took in the sight of the now-dressed robot. He looked at Royce, who was also wearing jeans and a plaid shirt. "Twins," he said, gesturing between them with a grin. Royce just nodded, and secretly he felt sick.

Wearing clothing, the animatron did a fair impersonation of a human. Though at certain angles, when the light caught the animatron's skin just so . . . The whole thing seemed ungodly, but Royce wasn't particularly religious, so he hadn't anything to do about it.

"So, what now?" Royce asked. "Can it walk itself outside?"

Abner shook his head. "No," he said. "I am not sure—I would not want something to happen to him before we get outside."

"Alright," Royce said, confused about what could possibly happen to the animatron in the short walk from the workshop to the pasture. "Okay."

"Luckily for us," Abner said, "it has wheels." He tilted the animatron in its stand with a flourish to demonstrate the mobility of the be-wheeled mannequin stand. When the thing tipped beyond a certain angle and more of its weight rested in Abner's arms than the floor, Abner wavered, clearly struggling under the weight. Royce reached forward to steady the animatron. Even with the two men now shouldering the weight, the thing was heavy.

"How much this thing weigh?" Royce asked.

"About four hundred pounds," Abner said. The strain of the weight rippled through his voice.

Royce helped Abner right the robot so that it was once again supporting its own weight. Then they wheeled it outside.

Bubba and Anna waited for them by the smaller pen that led into the larger hunting pasture. A stranger was there, too—Royce presumed him to be the hunter.

Anna looked angry. As the men wheeled the animatron into the waiting pen, she muttered to herself, "there's no way." It was just loud enough for Bubba to hear. He shot her a look. She rolled her eyes.

Bubba explained to the hunter how the hunt would work, as Royce and Abner eased the robot out of its stand. Its feet on the ground, it wobbled under its own weight. The men steadied it.

They exited the pen, leaving it alone in there.

"Alright," Bubba said. "Abner, fire 'im up."

Abner looked surprised to be addressed, as if he had forgotten what they were there in the pasture to do and his role in it. "Right," he said. He took a small, familiar remote from his coat pocket. He pressed a button.

The animatron's eyes shot open. It started to breathe. It looked around, taking in the scenery with its countless sensors and unseeing eyes.

"There we go," Bubba said, looking proud. For a moment, green jealousy billowed in Royce's chest. Then he felt embarrassed for feeling jealous of a robot.

Abner manipulated the remote control again, releasing the animatron from its resting state.

This was where things took a turn. Given its full freedom of movement, the animatron sprang to life. It looked down at itself, taking itself in. Then it began to grasp at its shirt. It ripped at the buttons, more and more frantically.

"What's it doing?" Bubba asked. He looked nervously at the hunter, who watched the spectacle, transfixed.

"I guess he does not like his outfit," Abner joked. Nobody laughed, and Bubba glared at him.

The thing tore its shirt—Royce's shirt—ripping pieces of it away.

"Hey!" Royce yelled at it. "Stop that!" He wasn't sure if he truly thought that he'd get his loaned shirt back, but it was hard to watch the robot tear it up right in front of him.

Bubba hit him in the side to shut him up.

The animatron appeared to be panicking, now. It mimed hyperventilation in a show that was almost sympathetic.

Bubba picked up a rock from the ground. "That's enough," he said. He hurled the rock at the robot. The rock struck it in the shoulder.

The thing stopped tearing at its clothes and looked up at the people who watched it. An expression that looked almost like fear seized its face. It turned to run.

But it didn't. It attempted one step, then toppled to the ground. On the ground, its arms continued to pump in time with its flailing, ineffective legs. It flailed in this way until Bubba said, "Enough, damn it."

He took the remote from Abner's hand and turned the robot off. It stilled.

A moment of silence as the real humans all watched the fake one wither on the ground; Anna broke it. "I fucking told you," she said. She turned away from them, and left.

"Yeah, well, you're fired!" Bubba called after her.

She flipped the bird over her shoulder and kept walking.

Chapter 40
The Nightmare

Tilly
The Present

Tilly was having a nightmare. She lay alone in a wide-open field. Every-thing around her—the ground, the grass, the night sky, the moon—was a swirling mass of vapor, so black in color that it was somehow more than *dark*; it was the complete absence of light. It was nothing. The landscape was various shades of nothingness, with one thing distin-guishable from the next thing not by sight, but by some combination of feeling, and temperature, and knowing.

And in this way Tilly knew that she lay on her back in a field of swirling grass. She felt the weight of the *nothingness* of the place on her chest; it was surprisingly heavy. As soon as Tilly registered her situation, the vapors began to move around her. Long blades of nothing-grass around Tilly wove themselves together, then, of their own accord, the braided strands of grass started to grab and grope her. They pulled themselves up and wrapped around her where they could—the wrists, the legs, the neck. Tilly struggled against the clutches of the grass, to no avail. It wound tighter and tighter, binding Tilly to the twilight land. Tilly gave up the struggle. She relaxed.

It wasn't painful, really. Tilly was squeezed, and she condensed, and was pulled apart into her various particles. And Tilly got smaller and smaller as the grass vapors pulled her down and down and inward unto herself. And then she was a Tilly-vapor, and then just a vapor, and then she was completely indistinguishable from the swirling fabric of the dreamscape. Nothing.

* * *

What seemed like a lifetime later, Tilly awoke. She didn't know where she was; wherever it was, it was dark. The darkness of her nightmare seemed to stay with her still, pervading her wakefulness—so much so that she wondered, for a spell, if she was still dreaming after all.

But a noise near her told her she was awake. And that she wasn't alone.

Feet away from Tilly in the darkness was the unmistakable sound of another person stirring. Clothes gently rustled together. The rubber sole of a shoe scraped across a concrete floor.

"Hello?" Tilly said into the blackness. There was no response.

The space where she was seemed small. A sliver of light stole in beneath a door. As her eyes adjusted in the darkness, she saw that she was in a closet of some sort. There were shelves, and cleaning supplies, and an unidentified man that sat across from her on the floor. He was slumped atop himself.

"Hey," Tilly said to him. He responded with a sleep-veiled groan.

Tilly tried to kick his foot to wake him. But then she realized that her own feet were bound together. She tried to bend forward to untie them. But her brain seemed disconnected from her body. She couldn't move. Her paralysis was due in part to her feet being tied and, she realized, her hands, too—but even her *attempts* to move were delayed from her thoughts about moving, and overall belabored. She felt drugged.

And then she remembered. She *had* been drugged. And it had been Royce who'd done it. It all came rushing back.

Chapter 41
Lazarus

Tilly remained tied in the closet—she presumed somewhere within the animatron workshop—for hours. The man there didn't wake. Tilly guessed that he had been drugged, too.

Tilly's cell phone had been taken. She worked at the cord that bound her wrists, trying to loosen it, to no avail. The knots wouldn't budge, and the only good she did was rubbing the skin on her wrists raw from the friction.

Finally, Tilly heard footsteps approaching from outside. A shadow disrupted the sliver of light that spilled beneath the door. Keys jangled. A lock clicked open. The doorknob rattled. And then turned.

The door swung open. The figure in the doorway was, for a moment before Tilly's eyes adjusted, a dark angel, ringed by fire—features indistinguishable, the mere suggestion of a person—a black, glowing monolith. And it had brought the light of heaven—or hell—with it. And then Tilly's eyes adjusted again to the light, and her drug-clogged mind caught up to the vision in the doorway. And it wasn't an angel, of course. The person's features came into focus.

"Abner," Tilly said. The word came out slurred.

"Hello, Tilly," Abner greeted her. He looked briefly at the other man, who was still passed out on the ground. So did Tilly. The man looked worse for wear—clothes and hair dirty, unshaven. He didn't stir.

"What the fuck are you *doing* here, Abner?" Tilly asked. Her voice sounded far away.

"I am here to get you. Come on, get up."

Tilly looked between Abner and her feet. "My feet are tied," she deadpanned. "And you know that's not what I meant."

"Here." Abner bent to Tilly's feet and loosened the cord that bound them. They were still tied but had a greater length of rope between them than before. "You can walk," Abner declared.

Tilly just glared at him.

"Well, come on," Abner said. "Get up. We are wasting time."

"Whose time?" Tilly asked. She was scared—she felt a black knot of fear in her stomach—but also angry, combative. She felt, in her core, *betrayed*. "What's going on here?"

"Just come *on*," Abner said, clearly frustrated. He grabbed Tilly beneath her arms and hoisted her to her feet. He was surprisingly strong.

Tilly tenderly put weight on her feet. They felt like they hadn't been used in ages. Her legs wobbled.

"Come on," Abner repeated. He waved a hand impatiently to prompt Tilly to move.

Tilly didn't move. "Untie me, jackass," Tilly said. "Let me go."

Abner smirked. He pulled something from his lab coat—a small handgun.

This annoyed Tilly more than anything. "You've got to be fucking kidding me," Tilly said. "Do you even know how to use that?"

"Only one way to find out," he said. He cocked the hammer of the gun.

And suddenly the reality hit Tilly that a gun was pointing vaguely in her direction, and the fear in her stomach gripped her insides even tighter. She decided that Abner was serious. "Alright, easy does it," she said.

"Walk," Abner directed. Tilly did.

He steered her out of the closet by her shoulder, the barrel of the pistol pressed into her back. She staggered in front of him like a hobbled horse, hoping she wouldn't fall and bring Abner down with her—he was bound to misfire the pistol in a tumble.

Tilly's initial suspicions had been correct—she was indeed at the animatron workshop. The closet where she had been stowed with the other captive was off the main hall. Tilly and Abner passed the familiar sights of the workshop—Anna's office, the main animatron laboratory, the storage room where the shadow man lived.

"Where are we going, Abner?" Tilly asked.

"You will see," he said. He did not elaborate.

Abner ushered her outside. Tilly was bewildered to see that it was nighttime. It hit her that she really didn't know how much time had passed since she had arrived at the 999 for her investigation. She had no idea how long she had been passed out in the closet in a drug-induced stupor. Was it even still the same day?

Outside, in the comfort of the wide-open spaces, Tilly surveyed her surroundings, looking for an escape. Royce's truck was gone, and left behind where it had been was a dark splotch of something liquid on the ground. Tilly saw the woman with the white streak of hair in her mind's eye. Holding a cigarette. Blowing smoke. Bleeding out in the pasture. Losing pieces of her skull.

Tilly and Abner trudged forward. There was no one else around. And suddenly she knew with a sinking feeling where he was leading her—the small pen that led to the larger hunting pasture, where the prey was staged before release for the hunt. Tilly's heart rate increased with every step closer to the hunting pasture.

Tilly frantically looked left and right into the open pasture to the east and west—looking for help, for an escape, anything. "Don't even think about it," Abner told her. He squeezed her shoulder from behind and guided her firmly forward.

Tilly scanned the small staging pen ahead of them. She looked for the tiger, or the animatronic man, or even another living person, like she now realized she had seen before. She had a terrible *hope* that she would see something—someone—else in the pen. But she didn't. It was empty. Ready for the arrival of the prey.

Abner opened the gate to the staging pen. "In you go," he said to Tilly. She didn't move. She couldn't.

"Go," Abner said with force.

"No," Tilly said. She wanted to turn to him, to look her former colleague in the eye, but she didn't dare move with the pistol pressed into her back. Instead, she pleaded over her shoulder, "No—Abner, you don't have to do this. I don't know what Bubba has on you, but you don't have to do this for him. It's not worth the money."

"The money?" Abner made a sound that was almost, but not quite, a laugh. He pressed the barrel of the pistol more firmly into Tilly's back. "Just go inside."

Still, Tilly couldn't move. "Go!" Abner shouted. Before Tilly could process what was happening, the handgun was gone from her back, and there was a loud *CRACK* of gunfire. Tilly jumped. A plume of dirt billowed from the ground near Tilly's right foot.

"Go in," Abner said. He shoved her shoulder. "I will not miss next time."

Tilly did as she was told. She walked into the holding pen. The gate slammed behind her with a rattle.

Tilly finally turned to face her captor. She met Abner's eyes through the tall fence posts, which looked more like prison bars to her now, from this vantage point. Abner looked back. Tilly wondered what she looked like to him—were her eyes yellow like a cat's, was her skin striped orange-and-black?

"Abner," she pleaded. "Please. You don't have to do this."

"Do what?" Abner said. "I am not going to be doing anything." He smiled. "You know, this was your friend Royce's idea."

Tilly winced at the sound of his name. She felt betrayed anew. Royce was—or *had been*—her best friend in Verde, besides Ranger. Maybe even something more than that. She wondered if this other Royce, this horrible, unfeeling Royce, had lurked inside her friend the whole time. The fact that the man who had so caringly adjusted her dislocated shoulder, had gently wiped blood from her forehead, was the same man who had plunged a syringe of ketamine into her neck was unfathomable to Tilly. She found Abner's suggestion that any of this was Royce's idea almost impossible to believe. And yet here she was, drugged and restrained, living proof of Royce's duplicity.

Abner continued, "We had a terrible time with the human animatron. The mind was perfect, but Anna could not get its legs to work. And so we had to move on to something else."

"Something else?" Tilly said, appalled at Abner's flippant tone. "You mean murdering *real* people?"

"'Real'? What does 'real' mean?" Abner scoffed. "Something that can *think*? Something that *bleeds*? Something with a *mind*?"

"Someone with a soul," Tilly said.

Abner laughed. "How very scientific. And what does that mean—a 'soul'?"

Tilly didn't answer; she was tired of trying to follow his line of thinking, tired of entertaining it seriously.

Abner went on, "You cannot say, can you? Of course, you cannot. Because there is no such thing as a 'soul.' What we perceive to be our—our *essence* is just a fiction created by our minds. What you think of as 'yourself' is just a chemical reaction in the electrified piece of meat that is your brain."

"If it's that simple, it's a wonder you failed so horribly at re-creating it," Tilly said. "You couldn't imitate humanity, so you've had to steal it."

Abner frowned. "Adam's mind was perfect—an exact replica of a human mind. Maybe better. It was his body that failed."

"Sure," Tilly said. She was tired of him.

"Plus, we have mostly gotten degenerates off the streets for our specimens. Like your friend in the closet back there. No big loss to society. And then if we have messed up, like if Royce gives them too much ketamine when he first gets them, we can just put them on the street with a needle in their arm. And no one thinks anything of it."

Tilly thought of Anna's friend that had been found dead the day before and wondered if he had been one of the kidnappings-gone-wrong. *Ketamine again?*

"You're a terrible person," Tilly said. "You all are."

"What does that mean, a 'person'?" Abner asked, a twinkle in his eye. Tilly didn't answer. He was plainly enjoying toying with her, and she resented it.

Abner looked at his watch. "It should not be much longer now."

An owl hooted in a tree not far away. A lone cricket, anomalous for the season, chirped a lonely ballad in the brush. The moon was just a sliver, clinging close to the oak trees of the pasture. A light suddenly and briefly broke through the brush. It disappeared, then reappeared again. *Headlights*. A truck was approaching through the pasture.

Abner noticed too. "Ah, here we go," he said. "Right on time."

The truck pulled into the clearing by the staging pen. Its headlights illuminated Tilly and Abner in the night, spotlighting a horrible scene on a nightmare stage. The truck was green. It was Royce's. Tilly tried to peer inside the truck's cab, but she couldn't, for the brightness of the headlights.

Bubba got out of the passenger side, and a stranger removed himself from the back seat. The stranger had a gun—he was the familiar, camouflage-clad, amorphous hunter that Tilly had grown accustomed to seeing here. Tilly didn't need to know his name—she knew exactly who he was. They were all the same. Whoever drove the truck did not get out of it. Tilly knew who that was, too. *Coward.*

Bubba led the hunter to the staging pen and introduced him to Abner, like he usually did. Bubba took a habitual glance at Tilly, and she thought for a moment that he would introduce her, too. But he didn't, of course.

"Hi, Bubba," she said. He jumped. So did the hunter. Tilly took satisfaction this small exertion of power—it was all she had.

After a moment, Bubba looked at the hunter and then turned back to Tilly. "Howdy, bitch," he said.

He turned to the hunter. "Abner's a magician. I don't know how he does it," Bubba said. "Don't be surprised if it knows your name, too." The hunter nodded appreciatively.

Tilly didn't know what to do. The reality of it all suddenly hit her. She was a trapped animal. She ran at the fence and shook it, pounding her fists against the wire. She screamed.

The hunter took a step back.

"She's lively," he said. "I wasn't expecting it to be so . . . lifelike." A hopeless agony overtook Tilly, and she burst into tears. They burned hot on her very real cheeks. "I'm not sure how I feel about it," the hunter said to Bubba as he watched Tilly wipe her tears away.

"That's something a lot of our hunters encounter," Bubba said. "It can be a bit . . . disconcerting at first. But you'll get used to how real it looks. The important thing is—it's not."

"Yes, I am!" Tilly screamed at them. She slammed her hands on the fence, rattling it. She locked in on the hunter. "Don't do this," she said to him. "You are about to hunt and kill a *real* person."

He just stared at her. "I'm Tilly Hutto. I'm a vet in Verde," she blurted out. "I have known Bubba Skinner all of my life—I treat the deer on his ranch. I'm friends—I know his son, Royce. I know that you paid to come hunt an animatron that looks like a person, but that's not what this is! They're lying to you. I am a *real* person, goddamn it!"

The hunter continued to stare. Then he brought his hands together in a slow clap. "Bravo," he said to Bubba and Abner. "I'm impressed."

Bubba beamed. "Much obliged. We've worked hard on this little project."

"Even I am surprised at how profound they can be sometimes," Abner added.

Bubba asked the hunter, "Are you ready to get started?"

"Please, no—" Tilly said. Adrenaline shot through her, and her heart pounded so hard that she thought it might escape her chest. She didn't know what to do.

The hunter said he was ready.

"Alright, like I explained, we'll give it a bit of a head start," Bubba said.

Tilly's words had left her. She couldn't say anything else to convince them not to do this. She sobbed.

Bubba continued. "This here opens the gate that will let her—it out into the pasture." He showed the hunter the lever mechanism on the outside of the fence. "You pull it when you're ready."

The hunter took a deep breath. "You ready?" he asked Tilly, eyes gleaming.

He didn't wait for an answer. He put his full weight on the lever. The gate to the hunting pasture sprung open.

Tilly stood there for a moment, knowing what was expected of her but unsure what to do. Then from somewhere near Royce's parked truck, a familiar voice yelled: "Tilly, run!"

At the same moment, a *CRACK* of gunfire ripped through the air. Tilly didn't wait around to see where the bullet went.

Chapter 42
Revelations

Rosa

It was Sunday evening, and Rosa was making her rounds at the nursing home, checking room to room to make sure the residents were safely in bed. In the last room on the hall, Ottalie Hutto was sitting up in her bed.

"Rosa," Ottalie called to her. Rosa was startled. Though they'd known each other in the community for as long as Rosa could remember, Ottalie hadn't recognized her since she'd moved into Resthaven.

"Yes, dear?" Rosa went to her side.

"Tilly's in trouble," the old woman said.

Rosa laughed. "Uh-oh, did she get arrested again, mija?" Rosa sat at the foot of Ottalie's bed.

"That Royce Wilson has her in trouble," Ottalie said. "Daddy says he's not a nice man."

"Oh, Ottalie, I don't know—Royce isn't so bad."

"He's got that Skinner blood in him, you know," Ottalie went on. "He can change his name to his mama's, but he cain't change who he really is."

Rosa smiled. "What did Royce get Tilly into? Did they rob a bank together, like Bonnie and Clyde?"

"She's going to get hurt, Rosa. You have to check on her." Ottalie's voice was stern and serious.

Something in the old woman's tone made Rosa's joking banter falter. Ottalie's eyes were clear and pleading. And it occurred to Rosa that she hadn't seen Tilly that day, which was unusual for a Sunday. In fact,

Rosa was sure that Tilly hadn't missed a Sunday visit since her mother had been at Resthaven.

"I will, Miss Ottalie," Rosa told her. "I'll check on her." The old woman looked relieved. She lay back on her pillow. Rosa tucked her in.

"Goodnight, Ottalie," she said. She turned out the light as she left.

Rosa finished her rounds and sat at her desk. She started sifting through the usual paperwork. But her mind wasn't on it. It kept returning to Tilly.

She picked up the phone and called Tilly's cell. After two rings, the phone went to voicemail. Puzzled, Rosa tried again. The same. Genuine concern crept up on her.

She decided to call Royce Wilson for good measure. His phone just rang and rang.

As she set the phone back into its cradle, an ear-splitting scream erupted at the end of the hall. It was from Ottalie's room.

Rosa sprinted down the hall to Ottalie. The old woman sat bolt upright in bed again. Her eyes were wide in horror, more whites than irises, and her mouth was agape in a never-ending shriek. Rosa looked around the room for the culprit. But no one was there. Ottalie's eyes were fixed on nothing as she continued to scream.

Another nurse arrived to assist. Rosa left her there, attempting to calm the old woman, and ran back to her desk. She picked up the phone again and made one final call.

"Hello?"

"Sheriff Valdez," Rosa said. "I'm not sure where or how, but I think Tilly Hutto is in trouble."

"Did Royce Wilson call you, too?" the sheriff asked. The background of the call was filled with the sound of road noise—he was driving. "I'm on my way out there now."

"No—" Rosa started.

"Look, I gotta go," Valdez said. Rosa heard the siren on his truck briefly erupt before he hung up on her.

Chapter 43
The Doe

Tilly

Branches and shrubs clawed at Tilly as she sprinted through the pasture. She didn't know how long she had until the hunter came after her. And she had no plan. She just ran into the pasture, into the night. Ran and ran.

When her lungs felt like they might explode, and she couldn't run any longer, Tilly slowed. She could hardly see anything—clouds had crept in front of the moon. Tilly felt her way behind a cedar tree and squeezed herself between its brushy branches. She willed herself smaller. She willed herself invisible. She willed herself somewhere else. None of these things worked.

She listened. There were the usual night sounds of the pasture—the calls of the nighttime birds, branches rustling in the breeze, the snap of a twig. Was it beneath an animal's foot, or a person's? The pasture teemed with shadows and unseen ghouls and the things that go *bump* in the night.

Then suddenly the quiet of the night was disrupted by yelling in the distance, from the direction of the workshop. There were at least two voices, but Tilly couldn't make out any words. To her relief, they sounded far away—for now. And after a few moments the voices quieted. Shouts of joy at the start of the hunt, perhaps?

Tilly stayed where she was. With the hunter possibly anywhere in the pasture by now—and, in that way, everywhere—Tilly didn't know if there was any safe direction to run. Still, she plotted. She knew that she had to get to the outer boundary of the pasture and from there figure out her way over the ten-foot-high deer-proof fence. Once out of the hunting pasture, she could find her way off of the 999 and out to the county road, where she had parked her truck. Then she would be home free. An escape would be difficult, but not altogether impossible.

But the first step to any escape would be leaving her hiding spot—and she couldn't. Anytime Tilly even thought about moving, her feet seemed to grow roots that bore deeper into the ground with every additional thought of running.

So she waited and wondered what would happen when she was found. Would it be quick? Perhaps he would shoot her from afar without her ever seeing him coming. Perhaps it would be painless. Perhaps his rifle was aimed at her right now. But what if the hunter's weapon of choice required a closer range? Would she be expected to fight back if he came upon her with a knife? Could she?

And then there was someone near her. Approaching. She heard steps crunch through the dry grass. They were delicate and creeping. She looked for a man, but only saw the dark pasture around her— branches and shrubs and cacti, in shades of greens and gray and black. Still the rustling grew closer. Tilly strained her ears to gain some sense of the direction or distance of the approaching sound. She focused on the area of the pasture where she thought the noise came from, waiting for the shadow man to show himself. The rustling continued.

And then—it stopped. And Tilly became acutely aware of the feeling of eyes on her. She was being watched. Goose bumps ran up her arms. She looked for the watcher, but she couldn't find it—couldn't watch it back. Another rustle. And another. Slow, crunching steps toward her. She stared at the spot where the maker of the noise should be, but there was nothing.

Tilly scanned the agarita shrubs and whitebrush and persimmon trees—still nothing. Until all at once the brush itself seemed to come alive, and the abstract lines and shapes of the shrubbery came together suddenly into a figure. Tilly's heart stopped. And then started again. It was a deer—a whitetail doe. The doe took another step toward Tilly.

Tilly and the doe stared at each other for several moments. The doe was small—delicate. Her ears flicked back and forth as she listened to the noises of the pasture. Tilly had a new sympathy for her plight as prey—always waiting for a predator.

The doe suddenly perked up, alerting to something in Tilly's direction. And then she broke away from Tilly's gaze and fled in a streak of tawny brown and white tail and hooves.

A moment later, Tilly realized why the doe had fled. She heard it first. A heavy crunch behind her. Then the sweeping aside of branches. Then an arm around her chest. A blade to her throat. Cold. Sharp.

"Gotcha," said the hunter, his mouth inches from Tilly's ear.

Chapter 44
The Swan

Tilly instinctively grabbed the hunter's wrist, trying to pull his hand away from her neck. He forcefully spun her around to face him, holding her tightly by her upper arms.

"Well, well," he said. "That was easier than I hoped it would be. They should've programmed you to run more."

Tilly went rigid. Her mind raced, searching for a way out.

"What, no fight? I thought you were supposed to be feisty." The hunter gave Tilly a shake.

The shake brought Tilly back to herself. She spat at the hunter, a glob of saliva hitting him beneath the eye. This took him by surprise. He wiped the saliva from his cheek and looked curiously at his palm.

"It looks so real," he said softly.

"It *is*," Tilly said, her anger at the whole situation boiling over. The hunter looked up at her, bewildered. She thought for a moment that the truth was dawning on him—that she was a real person, really being harmed.

She took advantage of his confusion. In one swift movement, she kneed him in the groin. He doubled over in surprise and pain, releasing Tilly in the process. Tilly took that as her opportunity to run.

She sprinted back toward the workshop, the pasture a blur around her. Her heart beat in time with her frantic footfalls. Pounding, pounding, *pounding*. She seemed to move straight through bushes and branches, as if they weren't there.

"Get back here, you bitch!" the hunter shouted from behind her. The sounds of his pursuit nipped at her heels.

Then another shout from ahead of her. "Tilly!"

The voice was familiar. "Tilly! Where are you?" It was Royce. His voice hit her chest with a pang of sadness. He must be trying to recapture her. Tilly continued running.

Tilly cut a diagonal path across the pasture, running still from the hunter and trying to avoid Royce now, too.

She stumbled on a rock, falling briefly to the ground and scraping her hand. She rose quickly and continued, her hand and knees burning. And soon she was back at the staging pen. And she heard multiple sets of footsteps not far behind her.

Tilly was stopped by the fence that divided the hunting pasture from the staging area. She surveyed her surroundings. There was a gate to the side of the pen that led straight to the outside. This was where the hunter entered the hunting pasture—where Tilly herself had entered the hunting pasture before, for the tiger tests and tiger hunt.

Tilly assumed it would have been locked behind the hunter after he entered the pasture in his pursuit of her. But she tried the latch anyway. And it opened.

Tilly stared at the open gate for a moment. The world on the other side of the gate looked serene and alien. She stepped into it.

She closed the gate behind her and wondered why no one had thought to lock it. She supposed the animatrons weren't taught to open gates. *A perfect mind*, Abner's words echoed in her head.

Tilly stood there, catching her breath and wondering what to do next. She knew that she wasn't quite home free yet.

"Tilly!" came a shout from behind her, in the hunting pasture. Then footsteps. She spun around, expecting to see a gun pointed at her through the fence. But there wasn't one. There was just Royce. He slowed when he came to her. He stopped on the other side of the tall gate. He didn't open it.

"Tilly," he said again, breathing heavily. He put his hand on the gate, almost as if reaching for her.

And then everything caught up to Tilly all at once. Her eyes brimmed and her face crumbled and broke apart into a sob. She tried her best to hold herself together, but tears escaped from her, and she found herself reaching for Royce's hand through the fence, despite everything horrible she knew now. He clasped it.

"What have y'all done?" she asked him between sobs. "What have y'all *done*?"

He shook his head. His blue eyes shone, and they held Tilly in their gaze, and they looked, for every possible description, exactly how one imagines human eyes to look. But something was missing—extinguished. "I'm so sorry," he said. "I don't know—I don't know how—"

He was interrupted by a *CRACK*. A single gunshot rang through the night. At the very same time, Royce's face exploded outward in a bloody eruption of skin and bone and goo. It rained upon Tilly. She screamed.

"Gotcha, bitch!" the hunter cried from the brush behind Royce— behind what had been Royce—from some distance away. Royce's body fell against the fence and was supported for a moment by it. At just above her eye level, Tilly could see straight through Royce's head to the pasture behind him. Tilly released his hand in horror—her own was covered in blood. His blood. She collapsed to the ground in a pile of sobs.

The hunter came grinning from the bushes, triumphant in his success. And then he saw. Royce on the ground with a shell of a skull. Tilly on the ground covered in blood—not her own—and sobbing.

"Oh, shit," he said. "Oh goddamn it." The hunter knelt down next to Royce, as if to check his vitals, even though there was very clearly nothing to be done.

The blood had drained from the hunter's face. "I—I didn't mean—I thought—" he stuttered. He looked at with disbelieving eyes. Then suddenly the ghost-white canvas of his face lit up in flashing red and blue.

Tilly looked behind her. The sheriff sped into the clearing in his truck, his police lights flashing. He bleeped his siren when he saw Tilly on the ground. Two more squad cars pulled up behind him.

"Nobody move!" Sheriff Valdez hit the ground running before his truck could even come to a complete stop.

And before Tilly knew it, they were surrounded, and the hunter was handcuffed, and Tilly was stumbling through the story of what had happened, and Royce was covered in a sheet, like a ghost.

Chapter 45
Finale

At some point, someone ushered Tilly into the back of a squad car. More law enforcement arrived, and they swarmed around the workshop like so many ants. Tilly gave them directions on where to find the hostage man in the closet and where to find the brains in jars. They went inside.

After some time, Sheriff Valdez emerged from the workshop, looking grim. He asked her to follow him inside, "for identification purposes," he told her. Still in a haze, Tilly didn't know what he meant and didn't think too hard about it. She went with him.

They walked through the workshop to Abner's lab. Sheriff Valdez spoke as they walked, but his words didn't register with Tilly. She was in a dream again, a nightmare. Swirling black nothing.

The door to Abner's lab was open but had been taped across with yellow crime scene tape. Sheriff Valdez, his expression apologetic, lifted the tape for Tilly to duck underneath, and gestured for her to walk through. She did.

The room was in chaos. Computers and lab equipment had been knocked over, including at least a whole shelving unit that had previously stood floor-to-ceiling against one wall. What appeared to be blood spatter adorned the floor and several other surfaces. In the corner of the room was a lump covered in a sheet. Tilly recalled the first time she had been confronted with something lumpy covered with a sheet in this room—it had been the tiger. This time it was not.

Sheriff Valdez stood over the lumpy thing on the floor. "Now, like I said, I'm really sorry I have to ask you to do this," he said. His voice came from a fog—it was delayed in reaching Tilly. Tilly eventually nodded, still not sure what she was being asked to do.

Sheriff Valdez pulled the sheet partially away from the lump. "Is this Abner Ubel?" he asked Tilly.

She took in the mangled, corporeal face, which had three terrible, parallel gashes running from one temple to the opposite jaw. The eyes were closed, but one top eyelid was slashed open so that the green iris beneath shown through. The nose barely held on to the rest of the face. The mouth hung open several degrees past the natural angle of its hinge, and a few teeth were displaced. The sight was horrific. Tilly couldn't look away.

She nodded. "Yes," she said. "That's Abner."

Sheriff Valdez pulled the sheet back over Abner's face, forcibly breaking Tilly's stare at Abner's maimed visage. She looked around the room instead. Among the chaos, Tilly spotted something familiar—a mass of orange and black and machine piled in a corner of the room. The tiger's claws were bloody.

Sheriff Valdez followed her gaze. "That thing was locked in here when we busted the door in," he said. "It was still on top of him. It turned on us, but we were ready. *Bang.*" He fired a finger gun at the tiger on the ground. Tilly just nodded again—it was all she could do.

She walked up to the tiger. It had a single, neat bullet hole through its forehead. She touched the hole, expecting it to be warm and wet. It was neither. *Heads don't bleed.* But, still, the tiger did a fair impression of a recently living thing. Like Abner.

Tilly lifted its lip. Beneath the unnatural pelt was a row of shiny teeth. Not silicone. Tilly felt one and it was hard, and it was discolored in all the right places, as if it had been in a living, eating animal for some time. Tilly wiggled the tooth, and it gave in one direction. She was able to twist it out of the tiger's jaw.

She held it up to the light. And it was exactly what she thought it'd be: a large dog tooth. Abner had haphazardly shimmed it onto a screw post so that it could be screwed in and out of the tiger's jaw.

The sheriff cleared his throat behind her. "There's a note," Sheriff Valdez said. He held up a piece of paper. "Looks like he did it on purpose." He gestured at Abner lying dead on the floor.

The sheriff began to read. "'What consumed me in life has now consumed me in death. With regrets, I deprive Science of my mind—'"

"Enough," Tilly said. Sheriff Valdez looked up at her from the note. "That's enough," she repeated. She was tired. So tired.

The sheriff stopped reading.

Sheriff Valdez got busy with something else, and Tilly wandered back outside. The sun was rising over the pasture of the 999, bathing the tree-tops in a bright, clear glow.

Tilly walked away from the melee to the tree line of the pasture. She expected one of the police officers swarming the ranch to stop her, but no one did. She found a large oak tree, and she knelt at its trunk.

She dug a shallow hole in the dirt with her fingers. When it was deep enough, she took Dolly the Great Pyrenees's tooth from her pocket. The rest would be evidence, but this one was hers.

She placed the tooth in the hole in the ground, and swept dirt on top of it. She said a little prayer.

Epilogue

Bubba Skinner tried to run from the law for a nearly a week before his attorneys convinced him to turn himself in on the Verde County Sheriff's warrant for his arrest. He pleaded not guilty at his arraignment on second-degree murder charges. He was released on bond.

* * *

The remains of Royce Wilson were cremated almost immediately after they were released from the authorities. There was no funeral service.

* * *

Ottalie Hutto passed peacefully not long after the ordeal at the 999. Tilly held her hand as she passed through the veil one final time. Tilly thought she heard a train whistle on the wind at the moment of her mother's departure.

The funeral was a few days later. It was at the Methodist church, but Tilly insisted that Father Francisco, a Catholic priest, say a few words at the graveside memorial. He spoke as her mother's casket was lowered into its final resting place. *May Christ, who called you, take you to himself; may Angels lead you to Abraham's side.*

Tilly found herself searching for someone at the service, and after a while she realized that she was looking for Royce among the other familiar faces. The thought sent tears rolling down her cheeks even faster than they had been flowing before.

After many hugs and condolences at the conclusion of the service, and one last look at her mother's casket, Tilly walked alone back to her truck. As she walked, movement in a nearby tree caught her eye—a flash of yellow. She stopped and searched the tree's branches for the source of the movement. Her eyes found it: a yellow warbler, preening on a branch.

Afterword and Acknowledgements

Can you believe nobody wanted to publish this book? Ha!

Carnival of the Animals borrows its title from Camille Saint-Saëns's 1886 musical suite of the same name. The chapter titles also mirror the suite's animal-themed movements. Give it a listen.

I have many people to thank. First, those who have encouraged me throughout this process: Amanda, Austin, Emily, Hallie, Jordan, Kolten, Laura, Lily, Rebecca, Ryan. The list could be much longer if I included everyone who has offered a kind word after enduring (usually) alcohol-induced ramblings about "my book." Thanks to you guys, too.

My heartfelt thanks to Matthew Revert for his brilliant cover design, and for whipping this manuscript into shape for publication. Thanks also to the team at Kevin Anderson & Associates for their capable editing services. Sorry about all the commas (especially the ones I kept after you told me to get rid of them).

Of course, I must thank my family for basically everything that has led to this point. And I would be remiss if I did not acknowledge the special little town I grew up in, which I won't name in order to preserve anonymity, but without which Verde would not exist.

And if you are still reading this: Thank *you*. I, quite frankly, don't expect many people to read this self-published novel. So if you are here, I am *so* grateful that you took the chance to read something outside of the traditional publishing sphere. I hope you enjoyed it.